Praise for the Author Who "Enchants Readers" (Romantic Times) LINDA LAEL MILLER

Yankee Wife

"Sweeping and complex . . . *Yankee Wife* is a beautiful and meaningful romance—one of Ms. Miller's best and destined for 'bestsellerdom.'" —*Romantic Times*

"You'll have the time of your life keeping up with this quartet! Read this highly entertaining tale. . . ." —*Rendezvous*

Daniel's Bride

"Linda Lael Miller is in top form as she brings readers into this warm, tender and exciting love story with touches of humor, poignancy and great compassion. *Daniel's Bride* is a delectable tid-bit." —*Romantic Times*

"Linda Lael Miller is the greatest! *Daniel's Bride* sizzles with humor, danger and romance, encompassing every emotion and leaving you breathless." —*Affaire de Coeur*

Caroline and the Raider

"Funny, exciting and heartwarming, *Caroline and the Raider* is a delight—another romance that's as wonderful and hot as you'd expect from Linda Lael Miller!" —*Romantic Times*

Books by Linda Lael Miller

Taming Charlotte
Yankee Wife
Daniel's Bride
Caroline and the Raider
Emma and the Outlaw
Lily and the Major
My Darling Melissa
Angelfire
Moonfire
Wanton Angel
Lauralee
Memory's Embrace
Corbin's Fancy
Willow
Banner O'Brien
Desire and Destiny
Fletcher's Woman

Published by POCKET BOOKS

LINDA LAEL MILLER

TAMING CHARLOTTE

POCKET **STAR** BOOKS

New York   London   Toronto   Sydney   Tokyo   Singapore

An *Original* Publication of POCKET BOOKS

A Pocket Star Book published by
POCKET BOOKS, a division of Simon & Schuster Inc.
1230 Avenue of the Americas, New York, NY 10020

ISBN: 978-1-4516-1110-6

First Pocket Books printing November 1993

10 9 8 7 6 5 4 3 2 1

POCKET STAR BOOKS and colophon are registered
trademarks of Simon & Schuster Inc.

Cover art by Yuan Lee

Printed in the U.S.A.

For those who came to celebrate:

Debbie Macomber, Robyn Carr, Nancy Higginbotham, Jill Marie Landis, Janet Carroll, Kim Bush, Patty Knoll, and Ginny Hillard, with big-time love and much gratitude (and honorable mention to the guy Irene hired to sing "New York, New York").

My dear sister,

I hope this letter finds you well and happy. Of course, I have no reason to doubt that it will, since you have always been healthy as Papa's best oxen. As for your joy in your forthcoming marriage to the young pastor, well, there could be no questioning that, even from so great a distance. Do you realize that every word you've written to me in the past year, Millicent Quade, has been but a single note in an ongoing serenade to the wonders of love in general and Lucas Bradley in particular? Even Lydia cannot praise the man enough, though fortunately for me, our beloved stepmother at least takes the trouble to tell me that Papa and the boys are well and that Uncle Devon and Aunt Polly and their brood are thriving as usual. If I had to depend upon you for a complete understanding of events in Quade's Harbor, I would know a great deal about your intended and absolutely nothing about our family and friends!

No, darling, of course I'm not scolding you. If anything, I'm a little jealous of your Grand Passion. (I confess to wondering precisely how *grand* passion is allowed to be, with a minister of the gospel. I'll ask you

1

about it when I return home, and know the answer by your blush.) In any case, you needn't run straight to Papa and tell him I'm hankering to get myself married off, because I'm not.

Millicent, if you were here beside me, you would hear me sigh quite sadly at this juncture. I'm twenty-three now, as you know, and I've long since completed my education here in Europe. Needless to say, I am now officially an old maid, at least by standards in Washington Territory. And I am quite aware that I cannot delay coming home much longer; soon enough, I'll sail into that familiar harbor and Papa will have a row of prospective husbands lined up on the dock. I've resigned myself to becoming a wife, and bearing children, and I'm certain that I will be happy enough, once I've mourned the death of my dreams. I mustn't forget, too, that I will still have my painting for solace, when and if I am spared the time.

Oh, Millie, do forgive me for being so dreary about the whole thing. I don't object to the idea of being a wife and mother, truly I don't, but I wanted so to have one splendid, *glorious* adventure first, before settling down. It would seem, though, that I shall have to content myself with a brief journey to the shore in southern Spain, and a possible side trip to the island of Riz, with the Richardsons, those friends of Papa's and Lydia's who are traveling in Europe now. As you already know, I will be making the trip home to Seattle in their company. You remember their daughter, Bettina, I'm sure—she is still as timid as a deer, and will probably want to sit in a corner and crochet edgings for pillowcases rather than do any exploring.

How I wish you were here instead!

I find myself sighing again, Millicent, and continue writing only after gazing dreamily off into the distance for an interval. Is it truly too much to ask that, before I become a matron, subject to vapors and washday and plumpness, I could experience just one magnificent exploit? Something so undeniably fabulous that I could draw on it forever, in those times when my spirit will surely be in famine?

I fear it is indeed too much to expect, and I grieve for my lost hope, though I put on the bravest front at all times and shall certainly continue to do so.

I will see you soon, darling, and watch proudly as Papa escorts you down the aisle to join your bridegroom at the altar. Please, set aside a little time for me, after the honeymoon. We have so very much to tell each other!

Do give my everlasting love to Papa and Lydia, our tribe of rambunctious little brothers, and to Uncle Devon, Aunt Polly, and all our many cousins. Don't forget to greet Dr. Joe and Etta and their little ones, too. And kiss your handsome reverend once for me, if that's proper—oh, *never mind* if it's proper. Do it anyway!

I cherish you.

As ever,
Your Charlotte

1

EVEN AT THAT MIDMORNING HOUR, THE AIR OF THE MARKET-place, or *souk,* shimmered and undulated with heat. Chick-ens squawked, vendors shouted and argued, monkeys wear-ing little vests and fezzes shrieked for attention, and strange, incessant music curled among the stalls in place of a breeze. The smells of spices and unwashed flesh competed with pungent smoke from cooking fires, and the bright silken folds of Charlotte's borrowed robe and veils clung to the moistness of her skin.

She was enthralled.

Her companion, Bettina Richardson, who was a few years younger than Charlotte and clad in a similar disguise, did not share this enthusiasm.

"Papa will *murder* us if he finds out we've come to this dreadful place!" she hissed, the veil covering her pretty face swelling with the rush of her breath. "Why, we could end up being carried off to the desert by some sheikh!"

Charlotte sighed. "We won't, more's the pity," she said, just to annoy Bettina.

"Charlotte!" Bettina cried, shocked.

Charlotte smiled behind her veils. The Richardsons had sailed to the island kingdom of Riz, which lay between Spain and the coast of Morocco, to visit old friends, wealthy merchants they had originally known in Boston. Bettina had wanted to stay in Paris until it was time to sail for London and then the United States, but Charlotte had campaigned against the idea. She wasn't about to miss a chance to visit such an exotic place as Riz, since there was at least *some* potential for adventure.

That, of course, was exactly what vexed Bettina so much. She'd had to be coerced into borrowing the robes and veils from their hostess's wardrobe, sneaking out by way of a side gate, and venturing through the narrow, dusty streets, following the odors and the cacophony of sounds to the *souk.*

Standing in front of one of the market stalls, Charlotte touched a crudely made basket tentatively. She would remember this day all her life, and out of desperate boredom, she would no doubt embellish it at some point. She might add a grand sheikh mounted on a fine Arabian stallion, riding to the marketplace to buy slaves, or perhaps even a band of marauding pirates, scattering chickens and merchants in every direction with their swords . . .

A stir at the end of the row of tawdry little booths and crevices in the ancient walls interrupted her colorful musings. Bettina grabbed Charlotte's forearm with surprising strength and whispered, "Let's go back to the Vincents' house, Charlotte, *please!*"

Charlotte stood staring at the tall man striding through the crowd, barely able to believe her eyes. For a few breathless moments, she was thirteen again and back in Seattle. She'd climbed up into the rigging of a sailing ship, the *Enchantress,* and high off the deck her courage had fled. She'd clung to the ropes, too terrified to climb down on her own.

Patrick Trevarren had come up to fetch her.

Bettina gave her a little shake. "Charlotte!" she pleaded balefully. "I don't like the looks of that man! He's probably a brigand!"

Charlotte couldn't move, and she was especially grateful

6

for her veils because she knew the fluttery smile trembling on her mouth would be an idiotic one. Patrick hadn't changed a great deal in ten years, though he was broader through the chest and shoulders, and the angles of his face were sharper; he still wore his dark hair a little too long, caught back at his nape with a thin black ribbon, and his indigo gaze was as incisive as before. He walked with an arrogant assurance that infuriated Charlotte, and yet her heart was hammering in her throat and it was all she could do not to run to him and inquire if he remembered her.

He wouldn't, of course, and even if he did, she had been only a girl when they'd met last. She had dreamed about him all these ten years, weaving fantasy after fantasy around the young seaman, but he'd probably never given her so much as a second thought.

He drew nearer, and even though there was a smile on his darkly tanned, aristocratic face, his eyes were cold. He plucked a ripe orange from a fruit stand, using the point of a dagger drawn from his belt, and flipped a coin to the crouching vendor.

Charlotte neither moved nor made a sound, except to breathe, but something about her must have given him pause. He came and towered over her and the trembling Bettina, staring down into Charlotte's amber eyes with an expression of bemusement.

Say something, Charlotte ordered herself frantically, but she couldn't. Her throat was shut tight.

Patrick pondered her for another moment, ran his gaze over the clinging robes she wore, and then proceeded around her with a shrug. He peeled the orange as he went, tossing the parings to one of the chattering monkeys.

"That's it," Bettina said firmly. "We're leaving, Charlotte Quade, *this very minute.* That was a pirate if I've ever seen one!"

Charlotte watched as Patrick stopped to look up at a veiled and shapely creature dancing on a board stretched between two large barrels, and felt a jealousy so intense that her throat opened and her lungs started drawing air again. "And we all know you've seen your share of pirates," she retorted, with unusual sarcasm. Instantly she felt a twinge of

7

remorse for her sharpness. For all that Bettina and she were not perfectly matched as friends, Bettina was a decent sort and quite fragile, undeserving of such treatment.

Tears had already welled in Bettina's green eyes. She was an only child, gently raised, and it had not been easy for her to disobey her parents by sneaking out of the Vincents' home to explore a foreign marketplace.

"I'm sorry," Charlotte said gently, feeling broken as she watched a smiling Patrick lift the dancer down from her improvised stage and toss a coin to a robed man slumping nearby. "We'll—we'll go now."

Determined not to look back again, Charlotte squared her shoulders and started off in the direction of the Vincent compound. Her senses were in a riot of shock at seeing Patrick Trevarren so unexpectedly, and she couldn't bear even to consider where he might be taking the dancer.

She was distracted, and conscious of Bettina's rising anxiety, and finding the path they'd blazed only an hour earlier proved difficult, without the noise and flurry of the marketplace to guide her. All the impossibly narrow streets looked the same, and any one of a dozen might have led to the quiet residential area she had left so boldly.

Bettina was sniffling, and she dried her eyes with her veil. "I knew it," she fretted, "we're lost!"

"Hush," Charlotte snapped, impatient. "We'll just go back to the marketplace and ask directions."

"We don't speak the language," Bettina reminded her, with maddening accuracy.

"Then we'll simply start out again, trying every route until we find the right one," Charlotte answered. She sounded a great deal more confident than she felt.

Bettina mewled in alarm. "I shouldn't have listened to you," she cried angrily. "I *knew* something terrible would happen if we disobeyed Papa, and I was right!"

Charlotte bit her lower lip to keep from telling Bettina to shut up. "We will get back safely," she said, in a purposefully gentle voice, when she had her impatience in check. "I promise we will. But you must be calm, Bettina."

The younger girl drew a deep, tremulous breath and

looked around at the empty street. It was eerie, how quiet the place was, after the clamor and excitement of the *souk*.

"I shall have to drink poison if we are taken captive and forced to live in a harem," Bettina warned, quite matter-of-factly, when she'd recovered a little of her composure.

Charlotte might have laughed, under less trying circumstances. The fact was, they probably *were* in grave danger, wandering unprotected in a city where the culture was so profoundly different from their own.

There was nothing to do now but return to the marketplace, try to find Mr. Trevarren, and prevail upon him to rescue her a second time. It would be an exquisite humiliation, especially since he was bound to be occupied in a most scandalous fashion with the dancer, if he was around at all, but Charlotte could see no alternative. She and Patrick had not parted on particularly cordial terms that long-ago day in Seattle, but he was probably the only person in the *souk* who spoke English.

She linked her arm with Bettina's. "Come along. We'll be back where we belong, sipping tea and eating chocolates, before your mother and father even miss us."

The marketplace, crowded before, was swelling with people and donkeys now. Charlotte stood on tiptoe, searching for Mr. Trevarren's bare head among the covered ones of the merchants and customers, but there was no sign of him.

Bettina let out a strangled whimper, and Charlotte controlled her irritation.

It was then that the crush of men pressed around them. A dirty cloth, pungent with some chemical, was placed over Charlotte's mouth and nose, and her arms were crushed to her sides. She heard Bettina screaming hysterically, and then the world receded to a pinpoint, disappeared. There was nothing except for an endless, throbbing void.

Patrick Trevarren laid his hands to the sides of the dancer's trim waist and hoisted her back up onto the board. Feeling especially generous, he favored her with a grin and a surreptitious coin, and in that moment a shrill female scream punctured the thick atmosphere of the *souk*.

In Riz, as well as the rest of the Arab world, women were a commodity, but Patrick had grown up in Boston and studied in England. As a result, he was cursed with a strain of chivalry, and even though he sensed that responding to the damsel's noisy distress would be a mistake, he could not stop trying to find her.

He made his way through the crowd and found one of the two foreign women he'd encountered earlier. Her veil had slipped, and by the nasal quality of her continuous, snuffling wails, Patrick identified her as an American.

Exasperated, he took her shoulders in his hands and gave her a shake. "Stop that sniveling and tell me what's the matter!"

The curious Arabs retreated a little.

"My f-friend!" the girl sobbed. "M-My friend has been k-kidnapped by pirates!"

Patrick clamped his jaw down tight as he remembered looking into the other woman's wide amber eyes earlier. There had been something disturbingly familiar about her. "Where did this happen?" he asked, struggling for patience. "How many men were there? Did you see which direction they went?"

The girl made another loud lament. "There were at least a *hundred* of them," she eventually managed to choke out. Her green eyes were red-rimmed and puffy, and the end of her nose already looked raw. "And how should I know which way they went? I can't even find my way back to the Vincents' compound!"

Patrick picked a familiar face from the crowd, an earnest little boy who sometimes ran errands for him, and gave him a few pieces of silver. He knew the Vincents and had visited them on several occasions.

In quick Arabic, he instructed the boy to take the lady home—she would obviously be no help at all in finding her friend. Then he began questioning bystanders.

Despite Patrick's easy command of the local language and the fact that he was well-known in the kingdom and received in homes on all levels of the social scale, he was still an outsider. The men frequenting the marketplace would sympathize with the kidnappers, not the girl. To them, the selling of innocent young women into virtual slavery was honest commerce.

Still, Patrick searched the alleyways that snaked away from the *souk* in every direction, a feeling of panic rising in him as he struggled to accept the hopelessness of his pursuit. The girl was lost; there would be no saving her from the fate that awaited her.

In the late afternoon, when the sun glared mercilessly down on the ancient, dusty city, Patrick returned to the harbor, where his ship, the *Enchantress,* was at anchor.

She was in a dark, cramped hole, a place that smelled of rats, mildew, and spoilage. Her head ached as though she'd been felled with a club, and nausea roiled in her stomach. Patches of tenderness all over her body told her she was black and blue, and where there wasn't a bruise, her skin stung with abrasions.

Charlotte wanted to throw up, but she was gagged, and when she moved to uncover her mouth, she discovered that her hands were bound as well. Tears of frustration and fear burned her eyes.

You wanted an adventure, she scolded herself. *Here it is.*

Hysteria threatened, but Charlotte would not surrender. She knew it was crucial not to panic; she had to think calmly and come up with a plan of escape.

Instead of strategy, however, she thought of Bettina. Had the kidnappers taken her, too? Charlotte shuddered to think how terrified the girl would be if that was true, and guilt lanced through her spirit. If Bettina came to harm, it would be Charlotte's own fault and no one else's. She had literally browbeaten her companion into visiting the *souk,* and the result might well be tragic.

Another rush of bile seared Charlotte's throat, and she swallowed. If she kept her wits about her, she might be able to find Bettina, and the two of them could flee their captors together. On the other hand, she might never see her friend again.

Colorful and patently horrifying pictures filled Charlotte's mind. She'd often pretended, in the privacy of her mind, to be a harem girl, with Patrick Trevarren as her sultan. It had been an innocent game, heating her loins and bringing a frustrated blush to her cheeks, but the reality of facing a life of white slavery was no schoolgirl fantasy. Of course, she wouldn't be sold to the man she'd dreamed about all these years—oh, no. She would surely become the property of some whoremaster, or a concubine to some sweaty, slobbering wretch who valued her no more than he would a dog or a horse.

Charlotte thought of her home in Quade's Harbor, on the green shores of Puget Sound, where her father owned and operated one of the largest timber operations in Washington Territory. Brigham Quade was a man of very firm opinions, with no inclination at all toward nonsense, but Charlotte had never doubted his love for a moment. She and her sister, Millie, had always known he would give up his own life before letting anything happen to either one of them, and because of this certainty, they'd grown up to be confident and secure.

Lydia, their stepmother, had taught them to be strong women, unafraid to take risks and let their intelligence show, and for the most part, these traits had stood Charlotte in good stead. Until that morning—if indeed it had been that morning—when she'd awakened with the brilliant idea of putting on robes and veils and exploring the forbidden *souk.*

Charlotte pictured Millie, her beautiful, spirited sister, all dressed up in her lacy white wedding dress, eyes sparkling with love and excitement. She imagined each of her five younger brothers in turn, and grieved for them, one by one. Their names swelled in her heart; Devon, Seth, Gideon, Jacob, Matthew.

There was a very good chance she would never see any member of her family again. Even worse, her loved ones would surely suffer over her disappearance and obvious fate, and Bettina's parents would be devastated. Their daughter was all they had, and because of Charlotte's impulsive actions, they had lost their child.

Despair would almost certainly have overtaken Charlotte in that moment if she hadn't been given something more immediate to think about.

12

Door hinges creaked, and a slash of light appeared in the darkness. Then a small man entered the chamber. He wore Arab garb, but that was all Charlotte could make out in the gloom.

Her heart pounded with fear and helpless rage as he approached her, wrenching her roughly up off the floor and then pulling off her gag. He produced a cup of tepid water and pressed it impatiently to her mouth.

Charlotte bit back all the inflammatory things she wanted to say, all the frantic questions she yearned to ask, and drank greedily. The heat was intense, and she realized she was wet with perspiration.

"Who are you?" she asked hoarsely, when she'd satisfied her thirst.

The man mumbled something in Arabic, and while Charlotte missed the meaning of the words, she caught the attitude. Her captor was not contemptuous, or even hostile; he was indifferent.

"What is this place?" she burst out, more in an effort to discourage the Arab from gagging her again than from any hope of getting a reply she could understand. "Why are you keeping me here?"

Charlotte's visitor shouted something at her; like his earlier conversation, the remark needed no translation. He wanted her to keep quiet.

To demonstrate this, he put the gag back in place and tied it a little tighter than before, so that the filthy cloth chafed at the corners of her mouth. Then he shoved Charlotte, hard, sending her toppling to the floor.

For the first time, a slow, almost imperceptible sensation of rocking penetrated the fog of fear and anger surrounding her, and she realized she was in the hold of a ship. It gave her comfort that she'd identified her prison, but she also had to face the forlorn reality that escape would be even more difficult.

As Charlotte watched the guard leave her makeshift cell, she was actually glad to be wearing the gag. The scrap kept in the flow of scathing and very colorful invective she'd learned in her father's logging camps. Even though he didn't speak English, the Arab would have known he was being roundly insulted, and his already thin patience would probably have snapped.

Charlotte forced herself to draw in deep breaths through her nose and let them out slowly through the cloth. Whatever happened, she must stay calm, taking every care not to lose her temper or show fear.

The heat in the dark hold was dense, and now that Charlotte knew the place *was* a hold, she picked out the sound of rats scampering overhead in the beams and foraging in the supplies stored around her. She shuddered and offered up a silent prayer for a miracle to happen.

Soon.

Patrick sighed and turned away from the rail of the *Enchantress.* Usually he enjoyed watching the last fierce light of day shatter into glimmering liquid on the water, but that evening he was troubled.

His friend and first mate, Tom Cochran, was standing behind him. "Do we set sail with the evening tide, then, Captain?" he asked. He was a solidly built man, of medium height, and a gray-white stubble of beard covered the lower half of his face. "I imagine that Khalif fellow will be looking for us to put in sometime tonight."

Patrick gave a distracted nod. He had gone to school with the sultan in England, and Khalif was a good friend, but that night the prospect of visiting his luxurious palace lacked its usual appeal. "Yes," he said, somewhat hoarsely. "Give the order to set sail."

With that, Patrick descended to the lower deck and entered his private quarters, a relatively small chamber holding a bed, a wardrobe, a desk and chair, and several bookshelves. He made no move to light a lamp but instead collapsed into a chair with another long sigh.

He heard the shouts of the crew members above, on the deck and in the rigging, but his mind was stuck on the girl kidnapped in the *souk* that day. What was it about her that troubled him so? Unfortunate though it was, unwary young women were often snatched from marketplaces, ships, and street corners in this part of the world, and most were never seen again.

14

The nape of Patrick's neck clenched tightly, then began to throb. He cursed and sent a small book clattering against the wall.

A knock sounded at his door.

"Come in," Patrick called grudgingly, knowing that if he didn't speak, the cook's boy would just keep knocking.

That night, however, it was Cochran who brought the captain's dinner tray.

"For mercy's sake, man," the old sailor said, "light a lamp. It's as dark as the devil's root cellar in here."

Patrick reached up for the lamp suspended over his desk, removed the chimney, and struck a match to the wick. He knew his expression made it obvious he wasn't pleased at the interruption.

"What's chewing on you?" Cochran demanded, setting the tray down on the desk with a thump. "Didn't you find that little dancer in the *souk*, the one you've had your eye on ever since we dropped anchor?"

A surge of unexpected shame swept through Patrick, though he couldn't imagine why. He was an unmarried man, after all, and he'd betrayed no one by following the girl into her tent and enjoying her feminine attributes.

"I found her," he admitted, dropping his eyes to the tray. Lamb stew, brown bread, and weak tea—again.

Cochran chuckled and made himself at home by folding his arms and leaning back against the closed door, though he hadn't been invited to stay. "Don't tell me she wouldn't have you."

Patrick refused to dignify that idea with an answer. He just glared at Cochran for a long moment and then tore a piece of brown bread between his teeth and began to eat.

"I guess I lost my head." Cochran grinned. "Forgot for a moment that no lady has ever refused Patrick Trevarren. If it isn't the dancing girl, what is it that's troubling you so much?"

Patrick shoved away the tray, tossed the bread down beside his bowl. "This is a merciless world," he said gravely.

The first mate pretended profound shock. "Now, there's an insight for you," he replied mockingly. "And here I thought it was all rose petals and angels' wings." Cochran, unlike most of the *Enchantress*'s crew, was an educated man. In fact, Patrick knew he'd once been a tutor in a boys' school in New York, though his friend didn't talk much about the days before he'd gone to sea.

Massaging the knotted muscles at his nape with one hand, Patrick told Cochran about the kidnapping. He didn't mention how the maple-colored eyes haunted him, though.

"You can't save them all, Patrick," Cochran said, when the woeful tale was through. "Besides, some of those girls end up living like queens, you know that. The pretty ones get servants of their own, and fine clothes, and all the fancy food they can tuck away."

Patrick bit the inside of his lip to keep the floodtide of furious despair coursing through him from coming out as a bellow.

Cochran laid a hand on the captain's shoulder. "Was she pretty?" he asked quietly.

"Yes." Patrick's admission was gruff.

"Then she'll be all right," the seaman told him. With that, Cochran opened the door and went out.

Patrick propped his feet on the desk, just to one side of the tray, and tilted his head back with a groan. His headache was getting steadily worse, and even with his own lids stubbornly closed, he could still see those golden eyes looking up at him in the marketplace.

In the next instant, Patrick remembered. He and his uncle had docked the *Enchantress* in faraway Seattle, back in '66 or '67, and stayed a few days to enjoy the local hospitality and unload some of the goods they'd brought from both California and the Orient.

He'd returned to the ship one afternoon, after spending the morning with a local merchant, and looked up to find a scrap of a girl swinging in the rigging.

He'd yelled to her to come down, and she'd called back, in a reasonable enough tone, that she couldn't move. He'd climbed up to retrieve her, of course, and they'd exchanged words.

Patrick didn't remember her name, but those amber eyes were engraved in his consciousness. Impossible as it seemed, that adventurous young woman and the one he'd encoun-

16

tered in the marketplace, just prior to her abduction, were one and the same.

He knotted one fist and slammed it down on the desktop with such force that the silverware rattled on his tray.

Charlotte lost track of time after three days. She was given very little to eat or drink and allowed to relieve herself only once every twenty-four hours or so. Her veil had long since disappeared, and her borrowed gown was twisted around her, torn and dirty. Her skin burned with fever, and the bruises and cuts hurt more with the passing of time, instead of less.

No one had come to ravish her; that was some consolation. She could endure hunger, thirst, general discomfort, and a bladder that was about to explode, but the prospect of rape terrified her.

When her irascible guard came to collect her one night, jerking her to her feet with his usual lack of ceremony, she thought her luck had finally dried up and blown away like so much fine sawdust. She fought desperately, though she knew all the while there was no chance of winning, and the Arab finally backhanded her across the face. The blow was so hard that she fainted.

She awakened—whether it was minutes or hours later, she had no way of guessing—to find herself squashed inside what felt like a burlap bag. She could see light through its loose weave, then make out the shadowy forms of several men.

They were laughing as they engaged in some game of cards, and Charlotte was practically convulsed with fury. She started to scream that they were all beasts and found that she was still gagged. A second later, her eyes widened as the realization came to her that she was naked inside that scratchy burlap sack.

The gambling went on, and Charlotte dozed, opened her eyes, dozed again. Finally she felt the bag that enclosed her being slung over some man's shoulder like a bag of chicken feed. She struggled, but that only made whoever was carrying her laugh out loud.

"She's a spirited one, all right," a voice said, in un-

17

adorned American English. "Raheem won't be happy when he finds out you lost her at poker, but she might improve the captain's mood some. He's been growling for the better part of four days."

An American, Charlotte thought, nearly faint with relief. Now she could explain what had happened, book passage home to the United States, live a blessedly ordinary life . . .

After a lot of jostling, Charlotte heard a loud knock. Again she felt the rhythm of a ship beneath her.

"Yes?" someone called, in none too friendly a tone.

"I brung you somethin', Captain," answered the man who carried her. "Me and the rest of the crew, well, we've been lookin' for a way to cheer you up a mite."

Door hinges creaked, and Charlotte felt a peculiar combination of excitement and fear. After all, she'd been stripped of every stitch, and she was in desperate need of a bath and shampoo. When the bag was opened, she was going to make for a very unnerving sight.

The sack landed on the floor with a thump; she felt pulling as the rope or twine at the top was untied. The burlap fell around her in a rough pool, and she snatched it back up far enough to cover herself.

When she finally found the courage to look up, she found herself staring into the astonished ink blue eyes of Patrick Trevarren.

N AKED THOUGH CHARLOTTE WAS, HER SKIN SCRATCHED AND itchy from the burlap bag, her muscles cramped, she felt real hope as she looked up into Mr. Trevarren's handsome face. A lamp swung from a low beam in the small quarters, and there was a comfortable clutter of books and charts on the sturdy-looking desk. She smiled, even though her ordeal had robbed her of all but the dregs of her courage.

"I can explain everything," she said.

Mr. Trevarren nodded brusquely to the sailor, dismissing him, and after the door closed, her host went to his bed and wrenched off a woolly white blanket. "I sincerely hope so," he replied at length, offering her the covering.

Charlotte accepted gratefully, but she was too weak and achy to rise from her humble position on the floor. "I was taken captive while my friend Bettina and I were trying to find our way home from the *souk* . . ."

Bless him, Patrick had poured wine into a wooden cup, and he extended this to Charlotte, then sank into his desk chair to regard her in attentive silence.

Charlotte was not accustomed to strong drink, but she

clutched the cup in shaking hands, raised it to her mouth, and drained every drop before rushing on.

"It's been quite a devastating experience, I can assure you, Mr. Trevarren . . ."

He frowned, took the cup, filled it again from an elegant carafe. "How do you know my name?"

Charlotte blushed and then gulped down the second cupful of wine. She was both relieved and injured that he did not seem to recall their encounter a decade before, in the high rigging of the *Enchantress*. "We met once," she said, and then hiccuped. "May I have more wine, please?"

"Certainly not," he said, with decided disapproval, settling back in his creaky chair with all the assurance of a man who received gifts of naked women every day of the week. "You're already getting drunk. What you need is some food and, from the looks of you, a bath."

In all her fantasies about Patrick Trevarren over the years, Charlotte had never once envisioned being received so casually. "Don't you even want to know my name?" she asked, in a small voice, when her formidable Quade pride was looking the other way.

Mr. Trevarren sighed. Now he'd gone from nonchalance to an attitude of distracted bother, as though he found her arrival tiresome. "All right, then," he conceded, gesturing. "Who are you?"

Charlotte was stricken by his lack of friendliness, but she wouldn't have let him see that even for a ticket home to America. She straightened, inside the swirl of soft wool cloaking her, and glared at him. "I don't intend to tell you," she said. "There. How does it feel to be treated rudely?"

He rubbed the back of his neck with one hand, the way Charlotte had seen her father do when he was exasperated with her stepmother, Lydia. After that, Patrick rose abruptly from his chair, took hold of her blanket-covered shoulders, and raised her to her feet.

"This is no time for schoolgirl games," he snapped, glowering down at her.

The moment he relaxed his grasp, Charlotte's knees folded, and to her abject humiliation, she started to sink back to the floor.

20

Patrick cursed under his breath, caught her, and swept her up into his arms. He carried her, blanket and all, to the bed, and dropped her ungracefully onto the mattress. The feathery softness all but swallowed her.

Charlotte's eyes went wide. She had imagined this event innumerable times, but finding herself faced with the reality was another matter entirely. Her throat clenched shut with fear.

Patrick's manner softened a little, though his size and masculinity still overwhelmed her. He leaned over Charlotte, his hands pushing deep into the mattress on either side of her, and smiled. "I'm not going to hurt you," he said. His voice was low, mesmerizing. "Now, tell me your name."

The wine had spread into every tiny tributary of Charlotte's veins, every cell and pore. Her fear was receding behind a rising wall of darkness, and she yawned. "Aphrodite," she said. "Daughter of Zeus."

Picturing her father in a toga, standing atop his personal Mount Olympus on Puget Sound and glaring imperiously down on mere humanity, she giggled.

"Beware the thunderbolts of Zeus," she warned Patrick, turning sage in the space of a moment. "If my father finds out about this, he'll be absolutely outraged."

Patrick sighed and thrust himself away from Charlotte and the mattress. "There's no point in talking to you now," he said. "Go ahead and sleep, little goddess."

She pulled the blanket up under her nose and peered at him over the plain edge. "Don't you dare ravish me," she said.

He smiled, and Charlotte was quite dazzled by the flash. "Rest assured, my dear—my taste doesn't run toward pampered rich girls."

"Pampered—?!" Charlotte tried to sit up, wanting to offer a vehement protest, but she simply had no strength left to do that. She collapsed against the pillows, closed her eyes, and slept.

Patrick sent a passing sailor for Cochran, who appeared momentarily, bearing a basin of warm water, some liniment, and a stack of clean washing rags. The first mate looked at the girl for a long moment, then made a *tsk-tsk* sound.

"Poor little thing. She's been poorly used these past few days, I'm afraid."

Patrick glanced at her smudged, pale face. Her matted hair was the color of maple syrup, and it would glow in the lantern light once it had been washed and brushed properly.

"What do you mean, 'used'?" he demanded. He knew he was scowling at Cochran as though the man had done the using personally, but he couldn't help it.

Cochran smiled, set the things he carried on the stand bolted to the floor beside Patrick's bed. "I wasn't speaking of her virtue," he said. "The kidnappers wouldn't have lowered her value by enjoying her favors, though God knows they must have been tempted."

Patrick swallowed hard. He was relieved, but at the same time, for some unfathomable reason, he wanted to grasp his friend's shirtfront and send him flying backwards against the closest wall. With effort, he managed to control both his temper and, he hoped, the expression on his face.

"She won't tell me her name."

"Probably thinks you're no better than those wasters who nabbed her in the marketplace," Cochran said with a shrug. "It's no great wonder if she's been a little fractious, now is it?"

"I guess not," Patrick conceded, though somewhat ungenerously.

The vixen stirred in her sleep, turned onto her side, and whimpered softly at the pain the motion caused.

An angry flush surged over Patrick's jawline.

"They bruised her pretty badly," Cochran commented in a quiet voice, looking down at the trail of black and blue marks on her bare arm and shoulder. "Maybe we'd better get Ness in here to check her over and bind up any wounds."

"I'll tend to her myself," Patrick said. Once he'd finished speaking, he was embarrassed, because he'd spat the words at his friend like pieces of red-hot lead. He made a forcible effort to calm his renegade emotions. "We'll find out who she is soon enough—I know she's from Seattle or thereabouts—and send her home."

22

"Yes," Cochran agreed, somewhat heavily. There was no conviction in his voice. "Just remember that some folks are of a mighty strange turn of mind when it comes to situations like this one."

"What the hell do you mean by that?"

Cochran had reached the door of the cabin and he paused there, one hand on the latch. "Whether the young lady has been . . . er . . . deflowered or not, a lot of papas and mamas would see her as used merchandise, a shame to the family. Not a few would refuse to take her back."

Looking down at the nameless waif, Patrick saw the child he'd rescued from the rigging so long ago, not the woman she'd become. He felt a twisting sorrow just to imagine her being spurned by the very people who were supposed to love and protect her. "Go now," he said, in a tone of defeat, and he heard the door close behind Cochran.

With a gentleness he hadn't had occasion to use since the year he was ten, when his dog had been run down by a carriage and he'd carried the spaniel out of the street, Patrick turned back the blanket. First he washed the lady's dusty, swollen skin, and then he treated the worst of her scratches with dabs of good brandy. She flinched a few times, but didn't awaken, not even when he lifted her up and maneuvered her into one of his shirts.

Clearly she was exhausted, and Patrick felt no small amount of tenderness toward her as he stood for a time, watching her sleep. After a while, he turned the lamp down until there was barely any wick to burn, then went up on deck to make sure all was well with the ship.

When he returned, his lovely guest was sleeping on her side. She'd kicked free of the covers, and her long, shapely legs, as white and translucent as the finest porcelain, lay as if she'd been running.

Patrick sat down on the end of the bed, kicked off his boots, then rose to unfasten the buttons of his breeches. He favored the wide-sleeved, open-throated kind of shirt that made him look like a swashbuckler in a three-penny opera, and this he pulled over his head and tossed across the back of his desk chair.

He crawled into bed, next to the wall, settled in with his

customary strenuous stretch and loud, sighing yawn, then turned his back on the waif.

She made a sound in her sleep, shifted, and laid one hand full on Patrick's right buttock.

He tensed, from his scalp to the soles of his feet, and his member was suddenly as erect as the main mast. Patrick murmured a swear word and reluctantly moved out of her reach, but up on deck, the watches changed and then changed again before he was able to sleep.

When Charlotte awakened, fierce sunshine was pouring in through an open porthole and she was alone in the captain's quarters. At least, she *assumed* Mr. Trevarren was the captain, since he had such fancy accommodations all to himself and seemed accustomed to ordering people about.

She wriggled up onto the pillows, which were wadded against the plain wall that served as a headboard, and stretched. That was when she realized she was wearing one of Patrick's shirts, that he must have unwrapped her from the blanket and put the garment on her while she was sleeping.

The idea mortified Charlotte, but she wasn't about to let it take too much of her energy. Her first thought, upon being delivered to Patrick like a bagful of walnuts plump for the cracking, had been that she was safe now, in the hands of one of her own countrymen. Now, however, as she mulled over the fact that the pillows next to her own still bore the imprint of a head, she wondered.

Horror made Charlotte's heart lurch. She'd had wine the night before, and she'd been rendered almost witless by the things that had been happening to her. Had she been besmirched?

She spread her legs beneath the blankets and felt herself tentatively with the fingers of one hand, but there was no soreness, no change. There was, however, just the slightest twinge of pleasure at the scandalous thought of Patrick touching her so intimately.

Charlotte slapped both hands down on top of the covers and pulled her legs together with such force that her knees knocked.

24

A rap sounded at the door, and before Charlotte could call out that she preferred to be alone, the hinges creaked and Patrick strode in, grinning.

Charlotte glowered at him. "It is not proper for you to be in here," she pointed out.

He laughed. "Wrong. It's not proper for *you* to be here, goddess. These are, after all, my quarters."

She pulled the covers up to her cheekbones. "You slept in this bed," she accused, her voice muffled by the blankets.

"I often do," Patrick conceded blithely. "Feeling better this morning?"

Charlotte remembered the disturbing excitement she'd felt a few minutes before, and her cheeks grew hot again. "I'm fine. Now, if you'll just send me home—"

"Gladly." There was a tray on the desktop, Charlotte noticed, and Patrick was engaged in pouring fragrant Turkish coffee into a cup. "All you have to do is tell me your name."

It still rankled that he didn't remember, but she supposed she couldn't hold that against him forever. "Charlotte," she said. Instinct stopped her from adding her surname. The Quade name meant wealth and power in Washington Territory, and it was possible that Patrick was not merely the dashing captain of a clipper ship, but a slave trader and kidnapper in the bargain.

If he realized what a high ransom she would command, it might be just the start of her troubles instead of the finish.

He brought the steaming cup to the bedside and offered it, and Charlotte reached out to clasp the handle, being careful to keep the blanket in place at the same time.

"Charlotte," Patrick said, musing over the name, as though it were some ancient riddle he was anxious to solve. "Charlotte what?"

"Just Charlotte," she responded, after taking a cautious sip of the strong, hot brew he'd given her.

He narrowed his indigo eyes at her for a moment, and she thought he meant to argue, but then he must have changed his mind. He treated her to another of his bright smiles.

"You're making this very difficult," he said pleasantly. "I

have half a mind to sell you when we dock, or hand you over to my friend, Khalif, for his harem."

Charlotte nearly dropped her coffee. "It is reprehensible of you to make jokes about such things! Don't you think I've been through enough as it is?"

Patrick rolled his eyes. "Not only are you a saucy little wench, and all too friendly of a night, when a man's trying his best to sleep—"

The cup rattled against the bedside table as Charlotte set it down. "I beg your pardon?"

He laughed and folded his gracefully muscular arms. "I thought that would catch your attention. You and I slept together last night, darling Charlotte, and damned if you didn't reach out and grab a round place on my anatomy."

For the first time in her life and, she sincerely hoped, for the last, Charlotte blushed so hard that her face hurt. "I would never do such a thing!" she hissed.

Patrick smiled. "Yes, you would. You did. You're just lucky I'm such a gentleman, that's all."

Charlotte could not believe his audacity; it evidently had no limits. Mr. Patrick Trevarren was decidedly *not* the man she'd spun so many lovely dreams around for ten long years. Her logging camp vocabulary came back to her in a rush.

"Don't you dare call yourself a gentleman in my presence, you bloody bushwhacker—you sorry son of the devil's donkey—"

Patrick gave another startling burst of laughter and bowed low. "Why, you're very welcome, Miss Charlotte No-name. No need to regale me with your thanks!"

"Get out!" Charlotte screamed.

"This is my cabin," Patrick replied, unruffled. "If anybody gets out, goddess, it's going to be you."

"Gladly! Just give me some clothes and I'll be gone so fast, you'll think you imagined me!"

Her fury seemed to amuse Patrick, which only made her angrier.

Whistling, he opened a chest in a corner of the compact room and took out a pair of black breeches and a wide leather belt. He flung the items to her, and they landed askew on the bed.

26

"Trousers?" she questioned.

Patrick smiled. "I'm sorry if they won't do, darling Charlotte. Since I don't wear dresses, I've never seen reason to carry them about in my sea chest."

Charlotte closed her eyes and took ten deep breaths before she was calm enough to speak to the captain in a civil tone. "If you'll just grant me a few minutes' privacy."

"Certainly," he conceded graciously, but he didn't leave the quarters, he only turned his broad, imperious back.

Using the covers for a tent, Charlotte scrambled into the breeches, which were too large for her at the waist and tight across her bottom, tucked in the tail of the shirt she'd slept in, and cinched the belt around her middle. She needed to use a chamber pot in the worst way, but she wasn't about to do *that* with Mr. Trevarren in the room.

"Where are we?" she asked instead, moving to the port-hole and looking out. She saw turquoise water, beaches so white that they dazzled her, a spacious palace flanked by a desert of snowy sand. "Is there an American embassy here?"

Patrick answered her questions in reverse order. "I'm afraid not, goddess. As for our location, we're just a short swim from the palace of the sultan of Riz." She felt his gaze touch her, rather than saw it. "I wouldn't recommend jumping into the drink and splashing for shore, though, since there are probably at least a hundred sharks circling the ship, waiting for galley scraps."

Charlotte shuddered, but her aplomb was the only defense she had left, and she wasn't about to abandon it. "I don't splash when I swim, Mr. Trevarren," she said. "I have an excellent stroke."

He stood beside her at the porthole, gave her a sidelong glance and an irritating grin. "All the more fun for the sharks. They probably like it when their breakfast puts up a fight."

Charlotte's stomach growled right then, at that very inauspicious moment. She couldn't help it; she needed a big meal in the morning, the sooner after she woke up, the better.

"I want to go home," she said, and suddenly her eyes were brimming with tears.

To her surprise, Patrick behaved like his fantasy self and touched her cheek lightly with the fingers of his right hand. "You will," he said hoarsely. "I promise you, Charlotte—no one is going to hurt you."

She wanted to believe him—oh, she wanted it desperately—but Charlotte was no fool, and she knew the rules governing her life had changed significantly since the kidnapping.

"Your family," Patrick began seriously. "Would they want you back?"

"Why wouldn't they, for heaven's sake?" Charlotte rested her hands on her hips. Although she wouldn't have admitted the fact, she liked wearing breeches and wondered why women hadn't adopted the fashion.

He studied her face solemnly with those dark, dark blue eyes. "Even considering that the kidnapping wasn't your fault—beyond the unquestionable idiocy of wandering without a male chaperon in the marketplace, of course—your reputation is not what it probably was before. There are people who wouldn't receive you in their parlors, Charlotte, or acknowledge you on the street."

Patrick's words were not only patently unfair, but true, and Charlotte's fury was partly despair. "The ones who matter, my papa and my stepmother, my sister and brothers, my aunt and uncle and cousins and my friends, would not only accept me, they'd welcome me home!"

He took her gently in his arms, pressed her to his chest, and she heard and felt his heart beating against her cheek. "Of course they will," he agreed. "Of course. Now, let me get you something to eat."

Charlotte went to the porthole the moment Patrick had left the cabin and searched the dazzling horizon for some means of escape, but all she saw was sand, sea, the palace, and the merciless, sugar white desert beyond.

Immediately she propped the desk chair under the door latch and made a quick search for a chamber pot. Finding no such article, she finally squatted over a spittoon, eyes clenched shut in embarrassment at the necessity and the telltale noise.

She had just finished, hidden the spittoon to be emptied

later, and removed the chair from in front of the door when Patrick returned. She washed her hands.

He put a tray containing porridge, bread with butter and jam, and coffee on the desk, and Charlotte fell to eating with no hesitation at all.

"I'd like to go out walking on the deck," she said. If she was going to be on board a ship, against her will or otherwise, she reasoned, she might as well make an event of it and see what was there to be seen.

"Some other time," Patrick answered, busy rifling through a logbook he'd taken from the storage chest. "We're expected at the palace, goddess, and my friend the sultan is not a man to behave graciously in the face of disappointment."

Charlotte's hearty appetite immediately fled. Patrick had been relatively kind to her, except for a little teasing, and she'd shoved the possibility of his villainy to the back of her mind. Now it sprang out at her like a weasel stuffed behind the door of a flimsy cupboard.

"Disappointment?" she asked, her voice thin as thread.

Patrick looked up from his logbook, frowned pensively, and returned his gaze to the pages before him. He was holding the volume in the curve of one arm. "Khalif's a sociable man," he said.

Charlotte swallowed the bile that rushed into the back of her throat and shoved away her half-finished breakfast. She looked down at her ungainly breeches and shirt and had a desperate inspiration. "I haven't the proper clothes to go calling—especially not when the host is royalty."

Patrick closed the logbook, tucked it into a tight space on one of the few shelves. "Don't worry," he said, his mind clearly fixed on some other matter. "There are lots of women at the palace. They'll be able to outfit you with something appropriate."

With that, he started toward the door.

"Wait!" Charlotte barked.

He turned slightly, looked back at her over one shoulder. "Yes?"

"I don't want to belong to some man's harem, sultan or not!"

Enlightenment shone in Patrick's eyes; a sudden smile lit his face. "Oh. You thought I was going to sell you to Khalif, or present you as a gift. Well, goddess, you were wrong—I was only teasing before. This is merely a visit, and it would be a shame if you missed out on the exotic food and music."

The adventuress in Charlotte was stirring again, but she was still suspicious. After all, her situation was most precarious. "How do I know you're telling the truth?"

He raised one of those damnably magnificent shoulders in a shrug. "I guess you don't." With that, he went out and closed the door. Charlotte was already moving toward it when she heard a key turn in the lock.

Having no other choice, and knowing she'd need her strength, Charlotte went back to her tray and began to eat again.

Barely an hour later, a man came for her and she was escorted onto the familiar deck of the *Enchantress*. She'd dreamed of the ship so often, drawn so many sketches of its graceful masts and wind-billowed sails, that she almost felt at home aboard the vessel.

Patrick was waiting for her at the rail, where a rope ladder had been tossed over the side. He grinned, surely thinking of the time fear had held her stuck in the very rigging swaying above their heads.

"Shall I carry you down?" he asked, with politeness so elaborate, it could only be mockery.

Charlotte was incensed. She and Millie had climbed many a tree, and she was no coward. She tossed Patrick a look full of acid and swung over the railing to find the first rung of rope with her bare feet.

She was careful not to recognize the dark shapes moving with deadly grace under the surface of the clear, blue-green water, or to calculate the distance between the rail and that tiny dinghy down there, bobbing on the waves.

Charlotte made the rest of the descent with her eyes firmly closed, and was relieved when she felt a man's hands take her by the waist and set her in the boat. She watched Patrick's deft climb with an expression of obdurate defiance.

The line anchoring the smaller craft to the ship was disengaged and pulled up over the railing, and Patrick and

30

the other man took up oars and began rowing. Charlotte watched the colorful fish navigating the bright coral reef beneath the surface of the water, wonder-struck. She'd wanted an adventure and she'd gotten one, which only went to prove Lydia's old adage that a person had to watch what she wished for because she just might get it.

The palace soon drew her gaze, and she studied its arched doorways and windows, its pillars and porticoes. Two people awaited them on the shore, wearing colorful robes and turbans.

Charlotte moved a little closer to Patrick, since he had his back to her and wouldn't see, and hoped she could trust him to keep his word and take her with him when he left the palace.

"Just let them take care of you, and whatever you do, don't talk back," Patrick warned her when they reached the beach and the men in turbans came to pull the boat up onto the sand. "When it's time to leave, I'll come for you."

Patrick was greeted with great goodwill and ceremony, but when the taller of the two men took in Charlotte's rolled-up trousers and sagging shirt, his dark face was pinched with disapproval. He clapped his hands together and shouted something, and two women swaddled in silk, with only their hands and eyes visible, rushed out to collect her like so much debris washed up on the beach.

They shuffled Charlotte across a cobbled courtyard, surrounded by high walls and boasting a beautiful pink marble fountain at its center, and into the palace. Their dark eyes held wondering consternation as they hurried her along a hallway and under a great arch decorated with gold-painted carvings.

One of them clapped her hands together, as officiously as the man on the beach had done, and all over the huge room, women rose from couches and mats to surround Charlotte. They stared at her trousers and bare feet and touched her tangled, dirty hair cautiously, as though expecting something to come scurrying out.

Charlotte couldn't remember a time when she'd been so insulted *or* so intrigued. She was scared, and with good reason by her reckoning, but she was also the only young

31

woman in her circle of acquaintances to set foot inside a sultan's palace. "Do any of you speak English?" she asked, with all the dignity she could manage.

The response was another burst of indecipherable chatter. Charlotte was taken in hand again, and firmly led to the edge of a large pool of water lined with painted tiles. In the next instant, she felt her borrowed clothes being removed, and though she had an impulse to fight, she knew it would be no use, for there were a dozen or more women surrounding her, and they were strong.

3

T HE WATER IN THE LARGE, TILE-LINED POOL WAS DELICIOUSLY warm, and aromas of musk, cinnamon, rose, and gardenia scented the steamy air. Because Patrick had promised Charlotte she would be safe in the palace, she submitted quietly to the forced but not ungentle ablutions.

Every inch of her skin, with the exception of her face, was scrubbed with pumice. Her hair was washed with egg yolk, rinsed, and washed again, and then Charlotte was half led and half carried from the pool, in a state of such intense relaxation that she nearly fell asleep on her feet.

She was dried with soft towels, laid facedown on a low couch upholstered in cloud-soft red velvet. While someone carefully combed the snarls from her hair, another person began massaging fragrant oil into her skin. She sighed as the last tautness was kneaded from the muscles in her shoulders and back.

Charlotte was as intoxicated as if she'd been given ardent spirits, and she uttered a soft sigh when she was covered with a blanket as light as an angel's wing and left to sleep. After that, she drifted, hearing the tinkly music of strange

33

instruments, the chatter of women, the splashing of the water in the pool.

She dreamed she was back on board the *Enchantress* with Patrick, lying naked and perfumed on his bed. And he was touching her . . .

"So pretty," a speculative voice said. Someone smoothed Charlotte's damp hair back from her forehead, as though she had fever. "So pretty and so far from home."

The fact that the words had been spoken in English finally penetrated Charlotte's daze, and she slowly lifted her eyelids. A blue-eyed, blond woman, probably in her early thirties, smiled down at her.

The woman's hands were stained orange with henna, a custom Charlotte had read about. Her robes were of the finest blue silk, and a border of tiny birds and flowers trimmed the sleeves, bodice, and hem, each minute figure worked in silver thread. Her hair tumbled down her back, wavy and soft and just the color of a palomino's mane.

"I am Alev," she told Charlotte. "I am a favorite of the sultan, and I will soon be a *kadin.*"

Charlotte knew her eyes had gone wide, but she couldn't help it. She and her friends at school in Paris had read every naughty harem novel they could get, and she knew that Alev aspired to be a wife.

"You will be a favorite too, I think," Alev went on, assessing Charlotte with troubled eyes. "Perhaps tonight you will dance for Khalif, and if you catch his fancy, you may also share his couch."

Charlotte sat bolt upright, forcing the other woman to draw back. She saw then that Alev was heavily pregnant.

"I'm not sharing anybody's couch," Charlotte said fiercely. "I'm a friend of Captain Trevarren's and I'll be leaving with him when he sails."

Alev looked Charlotte over again, this time with a pitying expression. "You are very naive," she said, "but you will learn the ways of men and of harems in time."

Charlotte blinked, covering herself as best she could with the blanket. It was made of some gossamer fabric, white and loosely woven, smooth against the skin. "I'm not staying," she insisted.

34

Alev patted her hair, which had curled in the humid air. "Whatever you say," she agreed, with an indulgent sigh. "It's very nice here, you know. We have every luxury, and Khalif is not a bad master."

"Who are you?" Charlotte asked, unable to believe she was in such a place, having such a conversation. She frowned at Alev's fair hair. "You can't have been born here, in Riz."

The other woman sighed and sat on a nearby couch, smoothing her skirts with elaborate care. "Once, I was called Olive. I was sailing from England to France as a girl, to attend a special boarding school, and our ship was overtaken by pirates."

Charlotte's throat constricted with horrified sympathy. "How old were you?"

"I was sixteen," Alev answered, in a detached tone, as though such things happened every day. And maybe in that part of the world, Charlotte reasoned, they did.

"You must have been terrified!" Charlotte couldn't help taking one of Alev's hennaed hands in her own. "Why didn't the government do something?"

Alev smiled contentedly. "Governments are not as eager to save individual citizens as we would hope. And yes, I was frightened, but I have since learned to enjoy my luxuries. I'm pampered here—I have a slave and apartments of my own. Khalif sees that I am given all the sweetmeats and chocolates I want, and he is . . ." She paused, blushing, and averted her eyes. "He is very handsome, and he knows how to make a woman happy."

Charlotte blushed, too. She knew about intimate relations between men and women, of course, because she'd grown up in the American West and attended school in Paris. Still, she'd never had what she and all her friends called the Experience, and there were definite mysteries attached. "Happy?" she squeaked, curious even though she knew it was rude to pry.

"You will see," Alev said, with a look of wicked mischief in her eyes. "When you lie with Khalif, he will show you what a glorious thing it is to be a woman."

Charlotte was hardly comforted by these words; no matter how appealing Khalif might be, she had no desire to "lie" with him. She'd never thought of any man in those terms, except, of course, for Patrick. She clenched her fingers tightly to her palms. Had the captain been untruthful in promising to take Charlotte with him when he sailed away from Riz?

"You are hungry," Alev observed, quite rightly. "Things will not seem so hopeless when your stomach has been filled." At this, she clapped her hands together smartly, and a young, dark-eyed girl appeared.

Alev spoke to the woman-child in rapid Arabic, and she scuttled off to obey the command. Like Alev and the other women Charlotte had seen, the servant wore simple, airy robes.

"Pakize will bring refreshment," said the future *kadin*. "Now, tell me—how did you come to be taken captive?"

Charlotte swallowed a rush of protests at Alev's choice of words; after all, she *had* been abducted in the marketplace that ill-fated day when she had so arrogantly chosen to ignore the warnings of her elders. Briefly, and with searing guilt, she thought of Bettina, and wondered how the poor creature was faring.

Folding her hands on top of the blanket that still cosseted her otherwise naked person, Charlotte explained that she'd been on her way home from Paris, in the company of family friends, and that the Richardsons had decided on a side trip to Riz at the last moment. Shame-faced, she admitted that she'd all but dragged poor Bettina to the *souk* one morning, and there the two of them had been seized. Later—and just the memory of this was such an affront to Charlotte's pride that it brought bile rushing into her throat—she'd either been sold or given to Patrick Trevarren like a cigar or a glass of wine.

Alev barely reacted to the story; no doubt she had heard similar ones many times before. Her own history, after all, was no less dramatic. "You were an American, then," she said. "I thought so, by your speech."

"I *am* an American," Charlotte corrected. "I'm going back there, and when I get off the mail boat at Quade's

Harbor, I swear I'll kiss the ground and never think of the place as boring and provincial again."

Alev simply patted Charlotte's hand, as if to say it was a nice fantasy that would soon be discarded in favor of reality.

The servant girl returned, carrying a brass tray loaded with sliced fruit, melons and bananas and a few things Charlotte didn't recognize, along with an assortment of cheeses, a small bowl of olives, and a dish of sherbet made from some purple berry. Setting the food on a small table near Charlotte's couch, Pakize took an ornately decorated cup from the tray and extended it.

"That is *boza*," Alev explained. "It's made from barley, and it's very sour—deliciously so."

Reluctantly Charlotte accepted the chalice, nodded her thanks. The drink was cool enough that a mist had formed on the cup, and she smelled cinnamon as she lifted it to her lips. She took a cautious sip and found the tartness of the *boza* very refreshing.

After her thirst had been satisfied—Pakize immediately refilled the chalice from a matching carafe—Charlotte consumed sherbet, fruit, and cheese with exuberance. Alev had been right; she was hungry. Once the nourishment began to reach her bloodstream, she was again certain that everything would turn out all right in the end. Patrick would not leave without her; indeed, he would see that she got home to Washington Territory.

Once Charlotte had finished eating, a golden robe of the same delicate fabric the others wore was brought to her, along with wooden sandals Alev called clogs.

Charlotte donned the robe gratefully, but she looked at the clogs with concern. The soles were four inches thick.

"I'll fall and break my neck if I wear these," she said bluntly.

Alev shrugged and sent Pakize away with the sandals. "Come then," she said, clapping her hands at Charlotte now, though not in quite such an authoritative way as she had with the servant. "I will show you the seraglio."

Charlotte was still anxious, but she was interested, too. How many Americans—female or otherwise—got a firsthand look at the inside of a harem, after all? Why, she could write a book about her experiences when she reached home, perhaps even go on the lecture circuit, like those women who had been taken captive by Indians and later released. She would be a person of notoriety and renown, inciting controversy everywhere she went.

"These are the baths, of course," Alev was saying, pointing out other pools, all sizable and all lined with richly painted tiles. There were couches everywhere, and thick cushions dotted the splendid marble floor, so cool and smooth under Charlotte's bare feet. At least a dozen other women watched their passing with open curiosity.

"Unlike many Europeans and Americans," Alev continued, "we bathe every day, sometimes more than once. It is a very pleasant ritual, often taking hours."

Charlotte thought of her own bath and shivered with residual pleasure. She'd never had a more sensually soothing experience.

They walked under another great archway, ornately decorated, and entered a huge room.

"This is the *hamam,* where we gather to socialize, sew, play games, watch various entertainments that are arranged for us—things of that nature."

The walls of the *hamam* were high, like those of a great room in an English castle, and beautiful weavings hung between towering, arched windows. Here, too, women lounged on beautiful couches, or talked and laughed softly in little clusters, but there was a new element.

A handsome black man stood on a dais, arms folded, watching the goings-on with a placid expression.

Charlotte tugged at Alev's sleeve. "A eunuch?" she asked, recalling the stories she'd read.

Alev smiled. "Yes."

God knew, she'd never have laid eyes on a real, live eunuch in Quade's Harbor—wait until she told Millie about this! "Is he a servant, like Pakize?"

Alev laughed and shook her head. "No. Except for Khalif himself, and the *sultana valide,* his mother, no one has more authority in the harem. Rashad keeps order among us mainly, and arbitrates disputes, so that Khalif and the sultana needn't be bothered."

After the *hamam*, Alev led the way to a spacious courtyard, where palm and date trees offered blessed shade, along with a single stately elm. Here, still more women sat on benches, embroidering or simply keeping quietly to themselves.

"Why does one man need so many wives?" Charlotte whispered. She was looking at the elm tree as she spoke. It was close to the stone wall, and might lend an avenue of escape, should the need arise.

After all her cordiality, Alev was impatient with the question. "They are not wives," she said tersely, reining in Charlotte's attention by her tone alone. "Some of them will never be called to Khalif's apartments. Others will be sold or traded or given as gifts. Only the special ones become *odalisques,* let alone favorites or *kadins."*

The words "sold or traded or given as gifts" stuck in Charlotte's mind like stinging nettles. "You are slaves," she said. "All of you, no matter how much favor you might enjoy!"

Alev returned Charlotte's gaze with coolness. "If we are slaves, so are you," she said, in an even tone. "No matter what your captain may have told you."

A chill spiraled down Charlotte's spine, but she refused to give in to her fears or sacrifice her principles to circumstance. "You should revolt, all of you," she whispered. "You should stand together, all the women of the harem, and—"

Alev interrupted with a roll of her eyes and an impatient sigh. "You Americans are such rabble-rousers. You have no concept of tradition. Well, let me tell you something: If I could snap my fingers and be back in England in the next instant, I wouldn't do it." She took Charlotte's sleeve and tugged her away into a quiet corner of the courtyard. "You mustn't ever speak of rebellion again," she warned, in deadly earnest. "If the sultana hears of it, she will have you punished. Here, we do as we are told."

"If you do as you're told," Charlotte countered, "why do you need a eunuch to keep the peace?"

39

Alev's nose was within inches of Charlotte's, and her breath smelled of sweet spices. "Those who do not behave themselves are soon sorry for it," she said, and then she turned in a whirl of robes and walked away.

Charlotte stared after her for a few moments, feeling a confusing mixture of liking for the other woman and anger, and then turned her gaze back to the tall elm tree next to the wall.

Patrick sat cross-legged on a thick cushion in Khalif's quarters, his second cup of *boza* in one hand. The tangy, slightly fermented drink was one of the many things Patrick enjoyed about visiting the palace.

"So she was originally to be sold to Raheem," Khalif said, frowning. He wore ordinary clothes, much like Patrick's, instead of the robes and turban a stranger might expect, and his dark hair was cropped. His black eyes showed concern.

Patrick nodded, then smiled. It seemed he smiled whenever he thought of Charlotte, provided she wasn't there to see. "One of my men won her, gambling, and presented her to me as a gift."

Khalif sighed and came to sit facing Patrick on another colorful, fringed cushion. "Do you know of Raheem, my friend?"

"I've never met him," Patrick responded, with a shrug. He knew Raheem was a pirate and a no-good in general, but in this part of the world, those traits were common.

Khalif still looked worried, distracted. "He is a very brutal and vengeful man," he reflected, apparently saddened by the pirate's shortcomings. "If his men took your Charlotte from the *souk,* it was probably because Raheem had ordered them to bring him a light-skinned woman. No doubt he is furious that his desires have been thwarted."

Patrick frowned and set aside his cup. It wasn't like Khalif to be troubled about such matters; he had a kingdom to rule and he took his responsibilities seriously. Although the sultan was by no means a cruel man, he simply didn't have the time or energy to concern himself with every kidnapping that took place in his domain.

"Are you afraid of this man?" Patrick asked, and he

40

smiled when, in the next instant, he saw rage kindle and then blaze in Khalif's eyes.

Khalif muttered an Arabic curse, one of the many he had taught Patrick when they were rooming together at Westhaven School for Boys just outside of London. "I fear no one," he glowered, "and least of all an ignorant pirate such as Raheem. But I can see that you care about this girl you speak of, and I must warn you as a friend. Raheem will stop at nothing to avenge what he surely sees as an injustice. He would not be above slitting the woman's throat and having her remains delivered to you in a basket."

Like Khalif, Patrick feared no other man—not, at least, for himself. Charlotte had added a disturbing new dimension by her appearance in his life, however; she had endeared herself to him just enough to become a liability. "I'll protect her," he said angrily, all his masculine instincts roused. He even laid his hand on the hilt of the knife he carried in a leather scabbard attached to his belt.

Khalif raised his eyebrows. "Yes, if you are with her when Raheem strikes. But you are often busy with your trading, Patrick—can you drag a woman with you wherever you go and watch over her constantly?"

Patrick found the idea of having Charlotte at his side oddly appealing, considering that she was one of the most irritating females he'd ever had occasion to deal with. "No," he said. "What are you suggesting?"

"That she stay here in the palace," Khalif replied, reaching for the gold-inlaid carafe to refill both Patrick's glass and his own. "Just until you've completed your business in Spain."

The idea made Patrick's throat constrict with fury, and jealousy stabbed his middle, sharp as a dagger, but then he reminded himself that Khalif was one of his oldest and most trusted friends. Still, he had to ask, "Just exactly what role would Charlotte play in your harem?"

Khalif chuckled and lifted his cup in a salute. "You are flushed with angry emotion," he pointed out, "like a boy challenged in the schoolyard. I will not summon your little friend to my couch, Patrick. My honor is more important to me than my life; you know that."

Patrick looked away for a moment, ashamed of his primitive response to his friend's kindly suggestion and annoyed at Charlotte for turning him into a fool. "If I had a sister," he said truthfully, "I wouldn't be afraid to entrust her to you."

The other man stretched out a hand to slap Patrick's shoulder affectionately. "It is understood, then. You will leave the girl here for the time being."

Patrick considered the promise he'd made to Charlotte, that she would sail with him when the *Enchantress* raised anchor, and weighed that against the fact that she would be in danger the moment she stepped outside the palace. It was true enough that he had some important trading to do before setting out for the other side of the world, and he simply would not be able to supervise Charlotte every moment.

"Yes," he finally replied, his voice gruff with reluctance. "Charlotte will stay until I've seen to my business on the Continent."

Khalif nodded and made an innately Arabic sound meant to convey approval. "I will have her sent to your apartments tonight, so that you may tell her good-bye," he said.

Patrick felt an overwhelming sadness at the thought of turning his back on Charlotte, and he knew she would see his decision as a betrayal. "I want one promise from you," he went on, setting his glass aside and standing, along with his host. "Charlotte is not to be punished at the whim of some eunuch—or of your mother."

The sultan sighed with a sort of ancient wisdom, an affectation that made him sound much older than his thirty-four years. He'd been doing that since he and Patrick had met, when they were both twelve. "She must follow the rules of the harem, like the others, but I will see that Charlotte is disciplined by no one other than myself."

Patrick had to agree; he knew Khalif was being generous. While the women of this particular harem were pampered and even cherished by their sultan, strict order was kept, and rebellions, minor or major, were dealt with by every means from a severe tongue-lashing to beheading. The culture was ancient, and so were its traditions; he could not

42

rightly expect ingrained customs to be overturned for the sake of one saucy American wench.

Khalif slapped Patrick's shoulder again and laughed. "Do not worry, old friend. I will not separate the young lady from her head, or have her stripped and beaten at the gate, I give you my vow."

Patrick sighed and summoned up a sheepish grin. "I wouldn't speak so rashly if I were you—you don't know Charlotte."

Charlotte sat down on the stone bench underneath the elm tree and leaned back against it, looking up through the leafy branches at an aquamarine sky. She would not be so foolish as to attempt an escape now, but she needed to make a plan. If Alev was right, and Patrick had lied about his intentions, drastic measures would have to be taken.

One by one the other women who had been enjoying the shady courtyard went back into the palace, each casting a curious look in Charlotte's direction. When she was finally alone, she hiked the skirts of her robe and shinnied up the trunk of the elm.

It had been years since Charlotte had climbed a tree—before she left Quade's Harbor to be educated in Paris, in fact—but it all came back to her. In two minutes, and with only a few scrapes on her knees and the insides of her thighs, she had gained a high branch.

Clinging to the gnarled old trunk with one arm, she turned to look out over the wall, and the startlingly beautiful spectacle of a turquoise sea met her gaze. A few hundred yards from shore, the *Enchantress* rocked gracefully at anchor. There was nothing to be seen in three directions except for more ocean, so Charlotte eased her way around to look to the south.

Desert, for as far as the eye could see.

Charlotte sighed with discouragement and, in the next moment, nearly fell from the tree when a female voice screeched at her from below.

She did not understand the language, but the tone was plain enough. She was to climb down, immediately.

Flushed with indignation at being treated so summarily,

Charlotte nonetheless complied with the dictum. When she reached the ground, she found herself face-to-face with a small, robed woman with a huge beak of a nose.

The crone shook a henna-stained finger under Charlotte's nose and carried on her shrill diatribe.

Charlotte's patience, already taxed by events of recent days, suddenly snapped. "Now, just a minute! Whoever you are, you *will not* speak to me this way—"

Just then, Alev came to Charlotte's side and silenced her by putting an arm around her and squeezing hard enough to compress her shoulder blades into one crackling mass of bone. She spoke rapidly, and from her tone Charlotte knew Alev was trying to placate the old woman.

Finally Alev turned to Charlotte and said sternly, "If you would not be beaten with a strap, you will stop being so—so *stubborn*. This is the *sultana valide*, Khalif's mother, and she has great power here!"

Charlotte's natural impulse was to rebel, for she had never in her life been beaten by anyone. The very idea rankled, and yet some sense warned her to listen to Alev and keep her opinions of this backward society to herself.

"Make a curtsy and tell her you're sorry," Alev instructed, giving Charlotte a subtle but bruising pinch in the upper arm to emphasize her earnestness.

After swallowing a throatful of scathing invective, Charlotte managed the slightest of curtsies and muttered an apology.

Alev began to chatter again, elaborating, no doubt, making Charlotte's words seem much more abjectly remorseful than they had been. Finally the sultan's mother narrowed her eyes at Charlotte in eloquent warning, then turned and tottered away on her ridiculously high sandals.

"You actually want that dreadful woman for a mother-in-law?" Charlotte marveled, shading her eyes to watch as the little crow disappeared into the palace.

Alev made a sound of pure exasperation. "No," she answered, rather sharply, "but I must win her approval if I would have Khalif for a husband. What were you thinking of, climbing that tree?"

Charlotte gave Alev a look meant to let her know she

considered the question a silly one. "I was trying to see over the wall, obviously. It seems to me it would be easier to escape Devil's Island than this place."

The other woman took Charlotte's arm and hustled her toward the high, arched doorway the *sultana valide* had just passed through. "Holy Mary, Mother of God!" Alev exclaimed, apparently having forgotten, for the moment, her conversion to the Islamic beliefs of Khalif's people. "Are you insane? First you speak of rebellion, then of escape! Do you *want* to be punished?"

Charlotte tried to pull free of Alev's grasp, but the pregnant woman was stronger than she looked and she wouldn't let go.

"Of course I don't want to be punished!" Charlotte hissed. "But you insist on overlooking the fact—like that cranky old biddy just did—that I'm a *guest* here. I don't belong to the sultan, or to any man, and I won't be ordered about and bullied as if I did!"

For the second time in their brief acquaintance, Alev rolled her eyes. "It is true what they say about Americans— they are hardheaded and impossible to reason with, if you are any example." They were inside again, in the cool, spice-scented *hamam*. "No more arguments now; you have been summoned to the sultan's quarters. We must see to your appearance."

Charlotte stopped, digging in her heels. "What?"

"Khalif has sent for you. You must not go to him with your hair all tangled and full of leaves and your robe torn and dirty."

Charlotte drew a deep breath, let it out slowly. She clearly had little choice in the matter; therefore, she would go to the sultan with dignity. Surely Patrick would be there, too, and offer his protection.

It was Khalif, Charlotte reflected as she walked beside Alev, who needed protecting. As soon as she saw him, she meant to tell him exactly what she thought of his barbaric behavior.

Half an hour later, dressed in a clean, canary yellow gown, her hair brushed and braided and woven through with pearls and ribbon, her body perfumed, her wide eyes

45

accented with kohl, Charlotte followed the eunuch, Rashad, through a complicated series of hallways. After many twists and turns, which collectively convinced Charlotte that it would be simpler to find her way out of a maze, they walked beneath a doorway as high as some she'd seen in European cathedrals.

The colors in the room were wondrously bright, the walls were covered with spectacular tapestries and weavings. A man wearing a red silk robe and a jeweled turban stood on a dais edged with hundreds of tiny mirrors, his arms folded.

Charlotte gulped. The sultan was handsome, just as Alev had said. He was also more intimidating than Charlotte could ever have imagined.

"Come forward," he said.

Charlotte looked around desperately for Patrick, but saw no sign of him, and her heart sank to the pit of her stomach. In that moment, it seemed a certainty that Alev had indeed been right: Patrick had abandoned her to an unthinkable fate.

4

CHARLOTTE TOOK A FEW WARY STEPS FORWARD, IN OBEDIENCE to the sultan's command, but she did not lower her head or avert her gaze. Scared as she was, she would not assume a submissive attitude.

"Your name?" the sultan asked. Khalif was breathtakingly handsome, with his ebony hair and shining, dark eyes, and she could see why Alev found him so attractive.

The captive raised her chin. "Charlotte," she replied in a clear voice.

Khalif smiled indulgently. "Charlotte," he repeated, as though tasting the name. "Charlotte Brown? Charlotte Clark? Charlotte Smith, perhaps?"

"Just Charlotte," she said. She had not revealed the Quade name to Patrick, and she had no intention of giving it away now. It was better, by her reckoning, if her family could be kept out of the whole nasty episode until she could go home and explain everything to them.

The sultan sighed philosophically and descended the three steps of the dais to stand directly in front of Charlotte. "Very well, then. For now, you may keep your little secret. Tell me, what do you think of my palace?"

Charlotte narrowed her eyes, braced to defend her virtue, but Khalif made no unseemly move. "It's like something from a storybook," she said, in her straightforward way. "I have never seen such luxury, or such—"

Before she could finish the sentence, a servant appeared in a second enormous doorway and announced someone's arrival. A moment later, Charlotte saw Patrick striding toward them, looking for all the world like a pirate in his breeches and flowing linen shirt.

Her heart somersaulted, then seemed to spin dizzily with hope. He hadn't left her after all.

Patrick took in her wispy golden robe, with its splendid embroidery, and the thick plait of honey blond hair draped over her right shoulder. Alev had woven ribbons and strands of pearls through the braid, and she'd lined Charlotte's eyes with kohl and painted her lips, too.

The captain let out a long breath, then his quicksilver grin reappeared, and his indigo gaze sparkled with mischievous amusement. He took her hand, turned it, and kissed the palm lightly, and she hoped he didn't feel her responding shiver of pleasure.

"You're still here," she said, regretting the words the moment she'd uttered them.

Khalif interrupted the encounter then—Charlotte had quite forgotten his presence, magnificent though he was—and said, "You may attend the captain in his quarters, Charlotte. A servant will come for you when it is time to return to the harem."

The cavalier manner in which Khalif had spoken irritated Charlotte, but she was too anxious to question Patrick to protest.

Patrick turned and started toward the doorway through which he'd entered, and Charlotte scrambled to keep pace with him.

"You'd better walk behind me," he warned in a whisper, his eyes twinkling, "if you don't want a long lecture on etiquette after your return to the harem."

Charlotte flushed with indignation and annoyance, but she fell back a few steps all the same.

Patrick finally paused in front of a door, high and arched

like all the others, and gripped the knob. He watched Charlotte with both humor and uneasiness when she swept past him, nose high, shoulders rigid with dignity.

The room was dominated by an enormous round couch, upholstered in dark blue velvet, and there were large, brightly colored pillows scattered across the tile floor. On a small table in one corner, a brazier burned, filling the air with a smoky aroma of jasmine. A tray of food awaited on the wide stone ledge under the single window.

Patrick gestured toward a nest of cushions piled on the floor. "Sit down," he said gruffly, and even though Charlotte couldn't tell whether he'd issued an invitation or an order, she sat.

Her knees had gone a little weak. "When are we leaving?"

Patrick carried the tray to where Charlotte waited and set it down before her.

"We'll talk about that later," he said.

Although Charlotte was troubled by something in his manner, she was also ravenously hungry. She consumed her share of rice, fried eggplant, and pastries filled with a mixture of cheese and spinach.

When the gnawing in her middle had been eased, Charlotte sat up very straight and said, "One of the women in the harem said you were lying when you promised to take me with you."

Patrick looked away for a moment, then shifted his inky gaze resolutely back to her face. "I was telling the truth," he said quietly, "but I wonder if you're going to believe that after tonight."

The fine food made a tempest in Charlotte's stomach, and she felt the color drain from her face. "What do you mean?" she whispered.

Patrick made no further pretense of eating. "You'll be safer here, at least for the next few weeks. After I've completed my business in Spain and Turkey—"

"What business?" Charlotte demanded, starting to rise awkwardly from the pillows. "Have you procured another virgin, Captain? Someone to sell into slavery, the way you sold me to Khalif?"

Patrick's eyes narrowed, and suddenly he was standing

49

very near, towering over her, immovable, like some monument chiseled from marble. "Good God, Charlotte, you can't possibly believe I'd do such a thing!"

"Why shouldn't I believe it?" Charlotte cried, outraged and afraid. Until now, she'd managed to maintain her composure, for the most part, but she was rapidly losing ground. "You're breaking your promise! You're leaving me here, just as Alev said you would!"

He shook his head, and his eyes reflected an anger equal to or greater than Charlotte's own. "You were originally kidnapped at the order of a pirate called Raheem," he said, but Charlotte barely registered the words because she was swamped in panic. "Khalif thinks he'll try to get you back."

"You could protect me!" Charlotte realized, to her humiliation, that she was almost pleading, but she couldn't help herself.

"No," Patrick said gravely, after swallowing visibly. "I have things to do, in places you cannot go. I would have to leave you alone often, and I will not do that."

Charlotte felt tears sting her eyes. She raised her fists to pound Patrick's broad chest in helpless fury; he caught her wrists in his hands and stayed the blows with the merest contraction of muscle.

"Liar!" Charlotte sobbed, completely overwhelmed. "I hate you—how could you do this—?"

Patrick silenced her with a gentle shake, still gripping her wrists. "I could never hurt you," he said, in a raspy whisper.

"You're lying!" Charlotte insisted. "Why should I believe a devil, a white slaver, a pirate—"

"This is why," Patrick answered brusquely. Then he hauled her against him, tilted her head back by plunging his fingers into the hair beneath her braid, and kissed her.

Charlotte struggled for a moment, then sagged in temporary defeat as he touched her lips with his tongue, made them open for him. Their tongues battled, writhed together like lovers, and battled again. Charlotte couldn't breathe, didn't care if she never drew a breath again as long as the kiss didn't have to end. Her nipples pulsed against the fabric of her robe and the hardness of Patrick's chest, and there was a hot, melting sensation in her depths that promised some primal upheaval.

Patrick lowered her skillfully to the pillows, never breaking the kiss, until she lay supine and gasping beside him. "This is the reason, Charlotte," he reiterated, cupping one of her breasts with his hand and then teasing the hidden nipple with his fingertips. "I couldn't give you to any other man, because I want you for myself."

Charlotte's senses, so long attuned to this man by means of her fantasies, would not be denied by anything so mundane as logic. She wanted to give herself, even *needed* to give herself, to Patrick, be he pirate, rescuer, or avenging angel.

She trembled and gave a soft cry as he bent his head to kiss the pulse point at the base of her throat.

After an interval of almost excruciating pleasure, during which Charlotte untied the black ribbon that held back Patrick's hair and then entwined her fingers in the richness of it, he met her eyes again.

"I want to look at you, Charlotte," he said gravely. "Will you let me do that?"

She was lost, already adrift on a whirl of emotion and physical wanting, and she nodded.

Gently Patrick removed her robe, and she lay before him on the soft pillows, bare and vulnerable and feeling truly beautiful for the first time in her life.

At first he did not touch her, but he set her afire by letting his eyes travel slowly over her length. Then he caressed a curve here, kissed a hollow there, and Charlotte uttered a series of soft, jerky sighs.

When he simultaneously closed his lips around the peak of one of her breasts and laid his hand on the mound of moist curls between her legs, she arched her back and moaned.

Patrick's chuckle vibrated against her breast, but he continued to draw on her nipple, to tease it with the edge of his teeth, to lave it unmercifully with his tongue. In the meantime, he burrowed through the silken tangle to boldly touch the nubbin of flesh pulsing there.

Charlotte spread her legs, unable to stop herself, and her hips began to undulate under Patrick's hand, obeying him, letting him set their rhythm. He enjoyed her other breast as though it were a ripe fruit, then trailed kisses down over her quivering belly.

"While you wait for me, Charlotte," he murmured, "remember this. Remember that I taught you pleasure."

She felt the tiny curtain part between his fingers, and then he took the revealed treasure into his mouth, with the same brazen greed he had shown at both her nipples. She made a sound that was half moan and half shout, and felt her eyes roll back as Patrick lifted her legs over his shoulders and continued to suckle.

She began to babble in a delirium of pleasure, clutching the velvet pillows, then Patrick's shoulders, then his rich hair. Her heels dug into his back, seeking purchase, and she rolled her pelvis forward against his mouth.

Finally the sensations gathered into a single wild crescendo, and with a savage cry of surrender and triumph, Charlotte gave everything she had, everything she was, to Patrick.

She was dazed afterwards, and fully expected him to mount her and achieve satisfaction for himself, but instead he simply held her close against his side and stroked her with one gentle hand. At first she was touched at his unselfishness and restraint, but then another thought went through her mind like a shock.

Perhaps he simply wanted her to remain untarnished, so that Khalif would still desire her.

She stiffened, and he immediately subdued her with firm tenderness. "Trust me, Charlotte," he said, after a long time had passed. "Please. Just trust me."

"I'm sure the serpent said much the same thing to Eve," Charlotte replied, embarrassed that her voice still sounded shaky and breathless. Good grief, she'd never guessed that men could cause such cataclysmic pleasure, even in her wildest imaginings.

Patrick laughed and swatted her bottom. "You're probably right," he conceded. "Now, let's get you back in your clothes before the servants see you."

Charlotte snatched up her robe, mortified at the idea. Suppose someone had come in while she was bucking under Patrick's mouth like a wanton? Or heard her carrying on as he drove her from one glorious pinnacle to another?

Raising himself on one elbow, still fully clothed, his hair loose like an Indian's, he grinned at her. "Why are you blushing, Charlotte?" he teased. "Could it be because you liked what I did to you?"

She glared at him, infuriated that she couldn't deny his assertion. To do that would have been plain foolish, after the way she'd gasped and sobbed and pleaded with him for more, and more still. "Your arrogance doesn't become you, Mr. Trevarren," she said.

She was kneeling, about to rise to her feet, when Patrick reached beneath her robe and claimed the place where he had taken such liberties before. He slipped his middle finger unerringly inside her, while rotating his palm slowly against the flowering rosebud he had so thoroughly mastered earlier.

Charlotte groaned and let her head fall back, and Patrick chuckled again.

"Oh, goddess," he breathed, still working his wicked magic, "perhaps my arrogance is unbecoming, but your passion makes you even more beautiful."

He teased her a little longer, then withdrew, cupping that same hand under her chin. "Think of me as you lie on your couch tonight," he said, and then he kissed her eyelids and her mouth and the rounded tops of her breasts.

Charlotte was still disoriented, and wildly disappointed that he'd aroused her a second time and then left her unsatisfied. She was startled when he suddenly clapped his hands to summon a servant, then hoisted her unceremoniously to her feet.

"Why, Patrick?" she whispered. "Why did you make me want you all over again, then turn away?"

He smiled at her and touched the tip of her nose with one finger as a male servant hurried in. "I told you before," he answered, his voice low. "I want you to think of me, tonight and every night, until I come back for you."

Patrick spoke to the servant in deft dialect, then gave Charlotte's elbow a slight squeeze.

"Behave yourself while I'm gone," he ordered sternly.

Charlotte drew a deep breath, in order to keep herself from crying. "I won't promise you anything," she said, with a toss of her head, and then she followed the servant out of Patrick's apartments and into the hallway.

They hadn't turned more than one corner when another man appeared, wearing snug-fitting black breeches and an expensive silk shirt. He looked like Khalif, but was much smaller and thinner through the face.

"Who is this?" he asked, with disquieting delight, stepping between Charlotte and the servant, who stopped and waited uneasily. "Has my brother found yet another jewel to adorn his couch?"

Charlotte stepped back when he reached for her shoulders. "I don't know who you are," she said, operating solely on bravado, "but you'd better not touch me."

"I am Ahmed," the man said accommodatingly, his jet-colored eyes dancing with lust and mockery. "The sultan, may Allah continue to bless him, is my half brother."

Charlotte saw the servant slip away and prayed she hadn't been abandoned. "Please let me pass. I'm supposed to go directly back to the harem. I'll—I'll be in trouble with the *sultana valide.*"

Ahmed folded his arms, but other than that, he didn't move. "Yes," he said. "That withered old nanny goat will probably have Rashad bare your delectable little bottom and blister you in front of the whole harem, as an example, but I promise the memory of the pleasure I will give you will sustain you through even that."

Both fear and fury swelled in Charlotte's bosom, tangled in her throat. She stepped back, red-faced and trembling, her hands clenched at her sides. His suggestion so stunned and angered her that she could not have offered a response even if one had occurred to her.

"Enough, Ahmed. Leave the woman alone."

Ahmed tensed at the sound of the other voice, while Charlotte used all her strength to keep from sagging ingloriously against the wall in relief.

54

Khalif stepped from the shadows to stand at his brother's side, regarding Charlotte with a bemused expression. He spoke not to her, but to the servant who had surely summoned him, and the other man gestured for Charlotte to follow.

She started to obey, but Ahmed reached out and grasped her upper arm hard.

"Let me take her for just this one night, Khalif," he pleaded furiously. "You have so many women, you will not miss her."

Khalif removed his brother's fingers from Charlotte's arm. "Go," he told her gently.

Charlotte hurried away, staying close behind the servant. She didn't look back once, not even when she heard Khalif's and Ahmed's voices raised in anger.

When they reached the entry to the harem, the servant drew back, eyes lowered respectfully, and the eunuch came forward to collect her. He cupped her elbow lightly in his hand and said, "Be very quiet. The *sultana valide* will not be pleased if she thinks you've been wandering through the palace at this late hour."

Once again, Charlotte was taken by surprise, for she had not expected the eunuch to speak English, let alone be kind. She wanted to explain that Khalif himself had summoned her, and then sent her to Captain Trevarren's quarters, but she didn't dare attract that vengeful old lady's attention by speaking. She went crimson from hairline to toenails, just thinking about the scandalous things she'd let Patrick do to her on those soft cushions.

Rashad escorted her past innumerable couches, where the sultan's women slept, until they reached one in the corner, beneath a moonlit window.

"This is your place to rest," Rashad said. And then he moved away into the darkness, making no more sound than a soft spring wind ruffling new grass.

Charlotte unfolded a silky, shawl-like covering lying across the foot of the long, low couch, and stretched out, using the shawl as a blanket. She fell into an immediate sleep, though she had fully expected to lie awake half the night, remembering.

Instead, she relived her initiation into womanhood in her dreams, dancing with Patrick's tongue, feeling the release of some warm fluid deep within when he satisfied her. It was still dark when she awakened with a start, sitting bolt upright on the couch, breathing as hard as if she'd been running.

The soft, desperate sounds of passion she had heard in her dreams continued in the fragrant stillness. The noise culminated in a series of sighs that seemed to catch on one another, and Charlotte's cheeks burned as she realized what was happening.

She closed her eyes tightly and fell back on the couch, wondering how she could have lived twenty-three years and learned so little about the world in all that time.

Within three days, the *Enchantress* dropped anchor off the coast of Spain. Patrick was in the worst mood he could remember. Under other circumstances, he would have gone straight to his favorite brothel and satisfied all the yearnings Charlotte had so innocently aroused in him, but for some reason, his conscience wouldn't allow that.

Thus, he suffered, and so did everyone else who came within the broad range of his temper.

He sold the spices and silks he'd brought from Riz, and bought shipments of lace and wine to carry to Turkey. He could think of nothing and no one but Charlotte, and how badly he needed to bury himself in her and end the terrible tension of wanting her so much. Because of his preoccupation with a young woman who refused him her last name and yet rode his mouth in ecstasy, Patrick was not as careful as he should have been.

He'd had words with Cochran, the first mate, when his friend told him his nature had turned foul and he ought to take himself upstairs and let a whore work it out of him. Patrick had been furious, and he'd sent the others, Cochran included, summarily back to the ship.

He was jumped from behind as he left the shoddy waterfront tavern at a late hour, his loins still aching, his mind distracted by frustration. He felt the blade of a knife brush against his throat and turned sober between that moment and the one that followed.

Patrick brought one bootheel down hard on the instep of his attacker, making the other man scream in pain, but there were others, and they seemed to come at him from every direction. He had clutched one by the shirt collar and drawn his fist back for the kind of punch that loosens a man's teeth when he recognized his own cook.

"Damnation, Cap'n!" the man bellowed. "It's them you're supposed to fight! We're on your side!"

His friends had disobeyed his orders and stayed, then, he thought, turning his full attention to the battle at hand. He sensed Cochran and the others around him, saw only strangers through the red haze of fury that shifted and shimmered in front of his eyes.

Patrick had no way of knowing how long the fight raged; it might have been fifteen minutes, or two hours. When it was over, he crouched beside a supine body and wrenched the man upright.

"Who are you?" he demanded.

The man's eyes rounded, then drifted shut in a swoon. Patrick threw him roughly back to the ground and found another wayward soul to question.

This one babbled in rapid dialect, but Patrick deciphered enough of it to know that these were Raheem's men, and he said as much to Billy Bates, one of his sailors.

"Filthy lot they are, too," Billy said, dusting his hands off on his own none-too-clean garments.

Patrick hauled the frightened Arab to his feet and slammed his hard against the tavern wall. "Take me to Raheem," he said, in the dialect. "Now!"

The other man shook his head, his dark eyes full of fear and defiance. "He'll kill me," he said. "I would rather die here in the street than suffer Raheem's punishment."

Tightening his grip on the man's shirtfront, Patrick lifted him to his tiptoes and bounced him off the wall again. "Tell him I said he's a coward," he rasped. "You tell him that

Patrick Trevarren, captain of the *Enchantress,* called him a yellow-gutted sewer rat."

The Arab nodded fitfully and ran when Patrick released him.

If the insults he'd already offered didn't bring Raheem out from under some maggot-covered rock, Patrick could think of plenty more.

In the first days after Patrick's departure, Charlotte kept to herself as much as possible and did as she was told. The other women in the harem didn't exactly snub her, but they didn't pursue her acquaintance, either. Only Alev spoke to her; to her extreme gratitude, the *sultana valide* left her strictly alone.

A full week had passed and twilight found Charlotte sitting in the courtyard, her back to the trunk of the elm tree, which had come to symbolize all things familiar to her. Rashad had given her drawing paper and pencils, and she was making a sketch of the house she'd grown up in when Alev joined her.

"That's very good," the other woman said, shifting uncomfortably as she took a seat beside Charlotte on the bench. "Is it your home?"

Charlotte swallowed the knot that had filled her throat at the word "home" and nodded. "They'll be so worried when they hear about the kidnapping."

Alev laid both hands on her distended stomach and grimaced before giving Charlotte a sympathetic look. "You could write them, you know, and tell them you've run off to be married. Then they might be angry, but they wouldn't suffer so much."

"Who would mail the letter?" Charlotte asked, her heart beating faster.

"Rashad could arrange that easily enough," Alev said, her belly moving visibly beneath her robe.

"But if my father knew I was here—"

"You cannot tell him that," Alev broke in quickly, "and I will have to read the letter, of course, to make sure you do not say anything . . . improper. Rashad would then have it sent from somewhere in Spain or Morocco."

Charlotte imagined her father and Lydia reading the suggested missive. Papa would be angry that she'd married so far from home, but Lydia would quiet him soon enough. Millie would say she'd always expected her elder sister to do something reckless and romantic like eloping in a foreign country, and the boys would be too busy running in and out of the house to care one way or another.

The marriage would be a lie, of course, and Charlotte had never been untruthful with her father and stepmother. Even now, it wasn't an easy prospect to consider, but she couldn't let them fret and agonize over her if there was a way to comfort them.

"Write your letter," Alev said. "Rashad and I will take care of the rest."

Charlotte nodded with sad resignation.

Alev drew in a sharp, sudden breath and clutched her belly. Because her stepmother was a midwife, Charlotte knew the look of impending motherhood.

"Are you having pain? Shall I bring someone?"

Alev bit her lower lip for a long time before she was able to speak again. "Fetch Rashad, please. Tell him the time has come."

Charlotte hurried across the shady courtyard and into the harem, where she found the eunuch standing with his back to a wall, watching as he always watched.

"Alev's ready to give birth," she blurted. "She's in the courtyard, on the bench beneath the elm tree."

Rashad strode out of the harem without a word, and Charlotte followed on his heels. She had no idea how to assist with the delivery of a baby, but she wanted to be of help if she could.

The eunuch lifted Alev into his arms and carried her inside, where an immediate flurry began.

Most of the women of the harem scattered, chattering like brightly colored birds, but the *sultana valide* silenced them just by entering the room. She gestured to Rashad to follow her, and the eunuch, the old lady, and the pregnant woman disappeared.

Charlotte kept a vigil for a while, with the others, then

drifted back outside and climbed the elm tree to study the horizon. There was no sign of Patrick's ship, so she turned her gaze to the sugar white desert, bright as snow under the fierce sun, and wondered what was on the other side.

Later, in a quiet corner of the *hamam,* she wrote a long letter, full of lies, and addressed it to her family.

5

CHARLOTTE SENSED A DISTURBING UNDERCURRENT OF TEN-
sion in the harem, even though the other women seemed
unconcerned that Alev was about to give birth. They went
on laughing and bathing and reading and eating chocolates
and sweetmeats, just as if it were an ordinary day.

When Rashad came out of the *sultana valide*'s apartments, Charlotte was waiting for him. "How is Alev?" she
asked.

The eunuch sighed. "This will be a difficult day for her,"
he said, in his formal way. "But if she gives the sultan a son,
she will surely become a *kadin.*"

Charlotte gnawed at her lower lip, a quiet anger bubbling
within her—an anger toward a system that reduced women
to the status of pretty dolls, or brood mares. "And if she
gives the sultan a daughter?"

Rashad's dark eyes reflected understanding as well as a
gentle warning. "Female children stay with their mothers
while they're small, and if they're bright, they often go away
to school. A sultan's daughters are princesses, after all."

A loud cry sounded from within the *sultana valide*'s
quarters, and Charlotte shuddered to think what it would be

61

like to be at that old woman's mercy, particularly during childbirth. "I want to go to Alev," she said, starting to go around Rashad. "I could help—"

The eunuch stopped her by gripping her arm. While his grasp wasn't painful, she could not have escaped it by her own strength. "The sultana will not tolerate your interference," he said. "It is dangerous to flout her wishes."

Charlotte felt both desperation and fury as she heard Alev scream again. "I don't care!" she spat, trying to pull away.

Rashad would not release her. Indeed, his round, mahogany face set, he double-stepped Charlotte through the *hamam* and then past the baths. Beyond the marble and tile pools was a line of doors, and it was to one of those chambers that the eunuch took his captive.

He turned a latch and thrust Charlotte into a sumptuously furnished cell, containing a pallet covered in red velvet, an unlighted brazier, a large bowl of tropical fruit, and a carafe of water. Overhead, a huge window let in the light of day.

Charlotte was too frightened to take in more than the most cursory details, however. She stared at Rashad, overwhelmed.

"I will not hurt you," he said, in his authoritative voice.

She found her tongue. "Then let me out of this—this fancy jail!"

The eunuch executed a slight bow. "Of course," he agreed. "As soon as Alev has given birth, and you have calmed yourself, you will be free to join the others."

"Free," Charlotte mocked, folding her arms and beginning to pace. "I'm a prisoner in this place—a bird in a fancy cage—and I don't know why no one will admit it!"

Rashad surprised her with a deep, resonate chuckle. "You are a very rebellious bird," he observed, "and you'd better learn to behave before the *sultana valide* has your feathers plucked."

Heat pooled in Charlotte's cheeks. "That old woman has no authority over me!"

"This is not America," Rashad pointed out, his expression serious now. "You have no rights here. And the *sultana valide* has every authority!"

Charlotte swallowed. If she ever wished for an adventure

again, she thought miserably, she hoped she'd be struck by lightning. Assuming she survived this particular exploit, of course. "I want to go home," she said, after a long moment, her voice small and tremulous.

An expression of sadness moved in Rashad's features. "So do I," he replied hopelessly. "But I will never see my own country again, and neither will you."

With that, he went out, closing and locking the door behind him.

Charlotte rushed about the small chamber in a burst of panic, then forced herself to calm down and sank to her knees on the pallet. She thought with longing of the tall elm tree in the courtyard, and the liberty, however hazardous it was, that lay beyond the palace walls.

She had eaten a banana, taken a nap on the pallet, recited every poem and sung every song she knew, before Rashad came back at sunset and released her.

"The sultan celebrates the birth of twin sons," the eunuch announced. "He wishes you bathed and dressed and sent to his chambers to dance for him."

Charlotte gulped. "D-Dance for him? I'm afraid I don't know any steps . . ."

Rashad smiled. "Then I would suggest that you make some up," he replied, ushering her out of her luxurious prison cell. "The sultan will have his amusements."

She glared up at her companion, wanting to gall him because he was so arrogant, so officious, and because he'd held her captive so many hours. "You speak well for a slave," she said.

Rashad's dark eyes sparked, but Charlotte couldn't tell whether he was feeling anger or amusement. "I should. I accompanied the sultan to England when he took his schooling, and before that, I served his father."

They reached the baths, and once again a bevy of chattering women surrounded Charlotte, stripping away her robe, escorting her into the water. A thorough washing followed, and her hair was carefully shampooed. After that, she was dried and stretched out on a marble table, where a warm paste that smelled of sugar and lemon was spread on the skin of her legs, allowed to harden slightly, and then pulled off. The soft, fair fuzz covering Charlotte's lower extremities was being removed.

The process was almost painless, but its implications worried Charlotte right out of her fog of decadent pleasure. "What are you doing?" she demanded straightaway, trying to sit up.

She was immediately pushed back onto the table, and the spreading and pulling continued. Even Bettina Richardson, the eternal innocent, could have figured out that she was being prepared for the sacrifice, like a helpless lamb, and the realization filled Charlotte with panic.

"Let me go!" she cried, struggling.

"Enough!" Rashad said, appearing at the foot of the table and glowering down at her. "You will be silent!"

She subsided, but her mind sought a method of escape even as she ceased her struggles and lay glaring up at the women who attended her.

When Charlotte's legs and underarms were smooth and bare, she was washed again, then fragrant oils were massaged into her skin. She closed her eyes, willing her body to be tense, ready for battle, but all her muscles went loose with decadent abandon.

She was dressed in a dancer's garb: bright yellow harem pants with transparent legs and a tight-fitting bodice, sparkling with topazes, that revealed her stomach. Over these scanty garments went a brown silk robe, embossed with golden thread.

Charlotte's hair was carefully toweled, scented, and then brushed. One of the women wove tiny orange flowers through the tresses, and another lined Charlotte's eyes with kohl and painted her lips with pink rouge. With dignified resignation, she followed Rashad out of the harem and along the winding hallways.

"If Khalif thinks he's going to touch me, he's wrong," she said, to Rashad's broad back.

She thought the eunuch chuckled, but his bearing was stern. He didn't turn to meet her gaze as he boomed out, "You will do whatever the sultan tells you to do."

"In a pig's eye," Charlotte responded. She was whistling

in the dark and she knew it, but her pride wouldn't let her accept such a travesty meekly.

This time Rashad glanced back at her. "You will not last long," he said, with certainty and regret. "You are much too contentious and unruly."

Charlotte sighed, exasperated. "What are you going to do? Feed me to the sharks?"

The eunuch had resumed his rapid pace. "That fate would be preferable, I assure you, to angering the *sultana valide.*"

Charlotte made no response, for she was sure Rashad's comment was only too true. She followed the eunuch until they came to a huge chamber, where braziers filled the air with the aroma of incense. Here, there was another dais, this one glittering with thousands of tiny mirrors. There were cushions and couches everywhere, and other women, in revealing clothes like Charlotte's, danced to the music of the tiny bells tied around their ankles.

Khalif was seated on a cushion in the midst of the dancers, looking very much the sultan in his costly blue robes. A gigantic sapphire decorated the front of his turban, and his bright, dark eyes were speculative as he studied the new arrival.

"Charlotte," he said, and she thought she saw one corner of his mouth curl in a smile, though she couldn't be certain. He gestured with both hands. "Come forward. I would look at you."

Charlotte wet her lips nervously with the end of her tongue and took a few steps toward him.

"Turn around," the sultan instructed, not unkindly, but with the kind of casual dispatch only a potentate would have the brass to carry off.

She made a hesitant little circle in front of him.

"Ah," he sighed. "Sometimes honor is a great burden."

Charlotte frowned, perplexed.

"Sit," Khalif said, with another sigh, gesturing toward a nearby cushion. "Enjoy the dancing. Tonight we are joyous before Allah."

Relieved and confused, Charlotte took a seat on the indicated pillow without comment. A servant gave her *boza* in a golden chalice, and she actually began to relax as she watched the dancers whirl past like a flurry of brightly colored birds.

Charlotte had not been submitted to the training some of the other women in the harem were undergoing, but she had discerned enough about the culture to know she must not speak to Khalif unless he asked her a question. Baiting Rashad was something else—she'd already guessed that the eunuch had the patience of the Almighty—but the sultan held the power of life and death in his hands. Even though he'd been kind to Charlotte, rescuing her from his brother Ahmed that night when she was returning from Patrick's quarters, she knew he could be ruthless if he chose, even brutal.

"Have you seen my sons?" Khalif inquired, after clapping his hands and causing the dancers to disband. Talking among themselves, they went to the long, low table next to the dais and began sampling the staggering variety of food displayed there.

Charlotte was startled for a moment—her mind had been wandering, skipping over the courtyard wall and across the sea in search of one Patrick Trevarren—but then she smiled and shook her head. "I wasn't allowed into Alev's apartments, but I heard she'd given birth to twin boys."

Khalif nodded, and it seemed that his whole countenance beamed with pleasure. "It is good for a man to have many sons," he said.

Swallowing a demand to know what was wrong with daughters, Charlotte tried to look demure. "Are there others?" she asked. "Besides the twins?"

The sultan looked troubled. "Yes," he said. "But one can never be sure they are safe."

Charlotte felt a chill, despite the uncomfortable warmth of the room. "Surely your children are protected, here in the palace—"

"There are always spies," Khalif mused. "There are enemies, and small intrigues among the women." His pensive expression faded in the next instant, however; he summoned the dancers back from the refreshment table.

Once again they whirled around him, this man who was the hub of their world, reflections of their yellow and red and blue and green garments fragmenting in the mirrors on the dais.

Charlotte began to feel dizzy, and looked away. She immediately spotted Ahmed, leaning against a far wall, his arms folded, staring at her. Like Khalif, he wore a turban and robe, but his clothes weren't of the same grand quality.

She bit her lower lip and made herself watch the dancers.

The evening stretched on interminably. There was more dancing, more eating, more laughter. Finally Khalif made a selection from among the harem women who had attended him so faithfully, and sent the rest away with a perfunctory dismissal.

Charlotte hurried to join the others, vastly relieved that she had not been selected to remain with Khalif in his quarters. She felt Ahmed watching her when Rashad came to collect the women the sultan had sent away, and stayed close to the eunuch.

As she lay on her couch that night, tears of loneliness, fear, and frustration brimmed in her eyes. She might as well stop deluding herself; Patrick wasn't going to come back for her, and she would probably never see Quade's Harbor again.

Instead, she would live out her life in Khalif's harem. Eventually the sultan would send for her, and she'd have no choice but to obey his summons. Maybe she would have children eventually, and a measure of happiness, like Alev.

She wiped her cheeks with the back of one hand. She didn't want another man touching her the way Patrick had, planting his seed in her. She'd rather die in the desert . . .

Slowly, her heart pounding, Charlotte rose on her couch and sniffled. No one stirred; she knew the *sultana valide* was snoring in her quarters, exhausted from overseeing Alev's delivery, and she had not seen Rashad since her return to the harem earlier.

She groped beneath her couch until she found a pair of flat sandals the eunuch had given her and put them on. Then, rising, she carefully lifted the lid of the chest that held her belongings and took out the plainest robe and veil she had.

When she was dressed, she crept into the courtyard, where the elm tree rustled in the night breeze, its leaves ruffled in silvery starlight.

Charlotte made herself sit down on the bench and think, though her every impulse bade her to scramble over the wall and flee. She would need water and food to survive the journey.

As much as she wanted to, she knew she couldn't make her escape that night.

So it was that Charlotte began hiding bits of dried fruit in her clothing chest. She took hard black bread, too, and small cheeses with rinds to protect them from the air. She squirreled away dates and a variety of nuts, but water was still a problem.

Finally she stole a silver flask from one of the other women—Charlotte didn't dare even think what the penalty for thievery might be—and filled it with water the first chance she got. The fancy bottle didn't hold much, but it was better than nothing, and she couldn't wait around hoping a wine flask or a canteen would turn up.

One night, when Alev's babies were seven days old, Charlotte waited until she was sure everyone was asleep, then got up from her couch, dressed, took the flask and the bundle of food she'd gathered, and slipped out to the courtyard. It was bathed in the light of a million stars, though there was no moon.

Standing on the bench under the elm tree, Charlotte put the flask in a pocket of her robe, rolled the garment up around her waist, and held the bundle of food in her teeth. Then she shinnied up the rough trunk, nimble as a monkey.

She didn't let herself think about the things that would happen if she was caught; no, Charlotte kept her mind firmly focused on success. She could not fail, she refused even to entertain the prospect.

She crawled along a branch, selected for its sturdiness, until she reached the wall. Then, after a deep breath and a whispered prayer, she leaped over it and landed with a thump in the white sand.

Charlotte huddled in the shadows for a few moments, catching her breath, waiting for her heart to stop its wild palpitations. When she had herself under some control, she ran for the desert, as hard as she could go, promising God she would never indulge her penchant for mischief again if only He'd let her escape.

She ran until she was out of breath, until she was stumbling and falling in the sand, then forced herself to moderate her pace. Once or twice she looked back to see the palace receding grandly into the distance, but there seemed to be no one in pursuit.

Charlotte walked, hoarding her small supply of water, letting the stars guide her. Surely she would come upon a village or even a city soon, and someone would help her get back to the Continent, where she could find a British or American embassy.

Gradually the stars faded and the sun rose.

At first Charlotte was wonder-struck by the beauty of a crimson sunrise spilling over snow white sand, but as the splendor of dawn gave way to the bright heat of morning, she was forced to take a sip of her precious water. She stopped once, and nearly decided to go back, but the palace was no longer visible and the hot desert wind had wiped away her footprints.

An hour passed, and then another, and the sun was relentless.

Charlotte kept walking. The air shimmered and undulated, like an ocean, and for a while it seemed that Lydia, her strong, sensible stepmother, walked beside her. "You're never defeated unless you quit," Lydia said. She was wearing a sprigged cotton dress and carrying a parasol that cast cool shadows over her soft blond hair and beautiful face.

"You're only a mirage," Charlotte pointed out, opening the flask and taking her second drink since her departure. "But you're right."

Lydia faded, but after a while, Charlotte's father, Brigham Quade, took her stepmother's place. "You've gotten yourself into a hell of a mess this time, Charlie," he said good-naturedly.

"I know that," Charlotte said, somewhat shortly. Sun-addled as she was, she knew this vision wasn't really her father, and therefore she didn't have to be polite. "If you're going to talk to me, at least give me some sensible advice."

"Go easy on the water," Brigham complied. "You're a long way from the pump house."

Charlotte rolled her eyes and trudged on. She was in desperate trouble, and she knew it, but she still didn't truly regret leaving the palace. To her way of thinking, it was better to risk everything for freedom and die in the attempt than to spend the rest of her life in the harem.

Finally, just when she thought she would surely fall to the hot sand and fry like a sausage on a griddle, she spotted a series of dunes off to her right. Some of the higher ones were casting shadows—cool, dark ponds of twilight.

Charlotte stumbled into one of them, praying the shade wasn't a figment of her imagination, like Lydia and her papa had been. She sank to her knees, her fingers digging deep into the fine sand, and let the shadows hide her from the sun. As her consciousness slipped away, she knew for a fact that she was going to die.

When she awakened—because of the heat, she quite expected to find herself in someplace other than heaven— she was looking up into a familiar face. Khalif stared down at her, his dark eyes grim.

"Foolish one," he scolded gruffly, lifting Charlotte into his arms. She blinked, saw that there were half a dozen riders around them.

"Patrick?" she asked, but the name only trembled on her lips. There was no breath behind it.

Khalif set Charlotte on the back of an impatient sorrel gelding and swung deftly up behind her. When she was settled, he opened a canteen and held it to her lips.

"Slowly," he warned. "Drink very slowly."

Charlotte's craving for water was all-pervasive, but she managed to obey the sultan's command because she knew he spoke from experience. She drank as much as Khalif would allow, then sagged against his chest. She was barely conscious of the powerful horse carrying them back to the palace beside the sea.

She drifted in and out of awareness during the ride, and awakened briefly to find herself in the harem again. Alev and

Rashad were stripping away her clothes, which seemed bonded to her skin, but she could not find the strength to protest. If she came too close to the surface, she knew, she would feel the pain, and she wasn't ready for that.

Later, a cool, soothing cream was applied to her flesh. The pain drew nearer, snarling at her like a beast in the darkness.

Then her head was lifted, and some potion was poured onto her tongue. It was vile-tasting stuff, but it drove the dragon away, and soon she floated on a cloud woven of a thousand dawns and sunsets.

She heard Alev's voice. "Will she live?"

"I'm certain of it," Rashad responded. "Though I daresay the *sultana valide* will make her wish she hadn't."

Inwardly Charlotte flinched, not from fear, but anger. She hadn't escaped, she was still a prisoner in the palace, but that didn't mean she would let one mean old woman bully her. She was determined to recover, if only to spite the sultana.

Charlotte was awake a few minutes, then asleep for several hours. When the pain was bad, someone would always give her a dose of medicine and make it stop. Once, she opened her eyes and saw Alev standing over her.

"Your babies?" Charlotte whispered, filled with dread because she sensed that her friend had seldom left her side since Khalif and the others had brought her back to the palace.

But Alev smiled and touched Charlotte's forehead gently. "My sons are safe and strong," she said. "Rest now. You will be well soon."

Charlotte rested, but one day she rallied. She was weak but fully conscious, and when she lifted her arms she saw that they were spotted with new skin.

"My face," she cried, raising both hands to her cheeks. She was certain the desert sun had baked and melted her into some hideous creature fit only for sideshows and circuses.

Alev was sitting beside her couch, nursing one of the new babies while Pakize tried to placate the other one with a finger. "Your face will be fine in a few weeks, thanks to our almond cream," Alev said.

Pakize handed Charlotte a small hand mirror with an engraved silver back, and she looked warily into the glass. Her skin had peeled badly, but it was clearly renewing itself.

After moving the greedy baby to her other breast and then modestly covering herself again, Alev arched her eyebrows and asked, "Whyever did you do such a foolish thing, Charlotte? You're in very serious trouble, you know."

She closed her eyes and tried to will herself into oblivion again, but it was too late. She was definitely on the mend. "What kind of trouble?" she asked.

Alev leaned forward on her stool and whispered, "You ran away and endangered yourself and others. That is a cardinal sin. And you stole the little flask."

Charlotte swallowed. Wondering where Patrick was, feeling more certain than ever that he truly had abandoned her. "What will happen to me?"

"You will be punished," Pakize said, in halting, eager English, and the servant girl seemed to relish the prospect.

"How?" Charlotte demanded, looking at Alev instead of Pakize.

Alev sighed and looked away for a moment. "That will depend," she finally replied, "on what the *sultana valide* decides is fitting."

Charlotte decided not to ask any more questions for the time being, because her imagination was already running wild. Maybe she would be boiled in oil, or roasted inside a suit of armor, like some English knights were during the Crusades . . .

She was still imagining horrible fates when a stir of excitement swept through the harem like a fresh breeze and Khalif himself appeared at her bedside. He did not offer her a smile, but instead glared down at her with as much fury as if he'd had to ride into hell itself to perform the rescue.

"So," he said briskly, "you are recovering."

Charlotte managed a faltering smile. "Yes, thanks to you."

He narrowed his dark eyes at her. "You could have perished," he said. "What would I have told my friend, Captain Trevarren, if you had not survived?"

She felt a little spindrift of hope swirl up in her middle,

even though she was fairly certain she didn't matter at all to Patrick. After all, he'd left her in a harem without a second thought, and if he'd been planning to return, he would surely have been back by then.

"I don't think he would even have troubled to ask where I was," she said.

Khalif glowered. "It is suicide to wander alone in the desert! Did you wish to die?"

"No," Charlotte replied. "I wanted to be free, and I was willing to die trying to get away."

Khalif shook his head, looking genuinely baffled. "These strange American ideas are not good," he reflected. "Especially in a woman."

Charlotte hadn't the strength to argue, so she just smiled, hoping somehow to charm the sultan into showing mercy.

He did not look beguiled. "You have set a bad example for the others," he said. "When you are well, you will be disciplined."

Charlotte swallowed the rebellious words that leaped to the tip of her tongue. She was in no position to irritate the sultan, and besides, he'd saved her life. "In that case, I think it will be some considerable time before I'm myself again," she said sweetly.

Khalif's mouth twitched, and a light flickered in his eyes for a fraction of a moment, but then he hardened his jaw again and fixed her with an imperial look. "I can wait," he assured her coolly.

Charlotte squirmed. "It's cruel, the way you're all being so mysterious about this. Why, a person would think you meant to feed me to the sharks in one-inch cubes."

The sultan's white teeth showed in a smile that quickly disappeared. "The sharks have done nothing to deserve such a fate," he replied, and then he turned and swept grandly out of the harem, leaving Charlotte to stare up at the ornately decorated ceiling and go right on wondering what was to become of her.

"The rules cannot be suspended for one woman, Patrick," Khalif told his newly arrived friend, who was sitting cross-legged on a cushion, enjoying a cool drink. "If I allow such a

73

departure, the others will be in revolt before I know what is hitting me. It would be chaos."

Patrick smiled at his friend's convoluted phrasing, but he was worried about Charlotte. Discipline could be harsh in Riz, and it was true that Khalif would lose face if he allowed the error to pass. "I don't want her hurt."

"I warned you," Khalif replied, "that Charlotte would have to abide by our ways. She did not. She endangered herself, my men, and a number of good horses in her silly attempt to escape!"

Patrick lifted one hand, palm out, in an effort to establish peace. "I know what she did was foolish, Khalif, but she was raised in a place where there's plenty of fresh water as well as an inland sea, and trees stay green the year around. She knew nothing of the desert."

"There is only one way I can give the responsibility of this woman over to you," the sultan said seriously, after a long, pensive interval. "Do you know what that way is?"

Patrick gave a heavy sigh, full of long-suffering resignation. "Yes," he said. "I'll have to marry the little fool myself, God help me."

6

By THE TIME THE SUMMONS TO KHALIF'S APARTMENTS FInally came, Charlotte had mentally rehearsed her fate so many times that the reality seemed almost anticlimactic. She submitted to the usual bathing and anointment, buffing and brushing, with stoicism.

Alev and Pakize dressed her in white robes—symbolic, Charlotte decided, of a lamb being prepared for the slaughter. Her hair fell loose around her breasts and down her back, but flowers and strands of tiny golden pearls were woven through the tresses.

Finally Rashad signaled that it was time to go, and Alev solemnly kissed Charlotte on both cheeks. Unlike the other women, she wore no veil.

Shoulders straight, head high, Charlotte followed Rashad out of the harem with a tragic dignity reminiscent of Mary Queen of Scots on her way to the gallows.

When she and the eunuch had woven their way through the complicated system of hallways to finally reach Khalif's apartments, however, her heart began to pound. Would she be publicly beaten? Thrown into a rat-infested dungeon and forgotten? Turned out into the desert to wander until she died in an agony of thirst?

Khalif, resplendent as always in silks and jewels, greeted her with a curt nod of resignation. She was a problem to be dealt with, his manner said, like a stubborn mare refusing to take the bit, or a dog that wouldn't come to heel.

Despite her fear, which was suddenly profound again, Charlotte felt the sting of fury, too. She was about to tell Khalif what she thought of his pompous tyranny, but a quick look from Rashad made her bite her lip instead.

The sultan dismissed the eunuch with a gesture, and Rashad left the apartments.

It was all Charlotte could do not to run after him, pleading for protection. Instead, she looked Khalif straight in the eye and said, "Well, let's get on with it. I'm tired of dreading my punishment."

Khalif smiled, but Charlotte was not reassured by this small indication of goodwill. "Perhaps this day will not be remembered for bringing your punishment," he said mysteriously, "but someone else's."

Charlotte frowned and looked around, but the great, opulently decorated room was empty except for the two of them. "I don't understand," she said.

The sultan chuckled, but without humor. "That is true of many things, I think," he replied. He grasped a golden cord near the place where he stood and pulled. "For your own sake as well as that of others, my dear, I hope you will make an effort to overcome some of your more obvious shortcomings—like following your every impulse and speaking when you would be better advised to remain silent."

Charlotte's cheeks burned, and her heartbeat thundered in her ears. She knew Khalif had summoned someone by tugging on the bellpull—a servant bearing a whip or club? A swordsman to whisk off her head? A slave-master to drag her off to market?

She closed her eyes tightly, struggling to retain her composure, and when she opened them again, she saw Patrick stride through one of the great doorways. He wore his usual breeches, high boots, and pirate's shirt, and his dark hair was tied back, as always, with a narrow black ribbon.

Charlotte's knees went weak with relief and confusion when he smiled at her.

He approached, gripped her shoulders in his hands, and gave her an indulgent kiss on the forehead. "I hear you've been misbehaving, Charlotte. Why doesn't that surprise me?"

Her throat had closed; she forgot to breathe. How she loved this man, and how she despised him at the very same time!

Patrick let go of her—she barely kept herself from crumpling to the floor out of sheer shock—and turned to grin at his friend the sultan. Then he met Charlotte's bewildered gaze again.

"Here's your choice, goddess," he said. "You can either marry me or take a beating."

By some miracle, Charlotte found her voice. She was overjoyed at the prospect of spending her life with Patrick, but his nonchalant, take-it-or-leave-it manner was hardly the reaction she would have wanted. "This is a difficult decision," she replied. "After all, the beating would be over in a few minutes, but a wedding might be only the beginning of my grief."

Patrick narrowed his eyes at her. "Mind your tongue, darling," he said, with acid affection, "or you'll get both the wedding *and* the beating."

Charlotte swallowed, glanced warily toward Khalif. Then she took a subtle step nearer to Patrick. "Why do you want to marry me at all if you feel that way?" she demanded in a whisper.

He let his gaze travel over her, lingering at her breasts, then her narrow waist, then her softly curving hips. "I am something of an optimist," he said, looking into her eyes again, filling her with a delicious sense of softness. "I believe there is still hope that you can be salvaged, though it will take work and a lot of determination."

Charlotte would have kicked Patrick in the shin at that moment, if she hadn't needed him to escape Khalif's primitive disciplinary policies. She fluttered her lashes and made herself smile sweetly. "I will try to cooperate," she promised, hoping she wouldn't choke on her own words.

Patrick gave her a skeptical once-over, then turned impatiently to his friend. "Let's get on with it," he said, his tone clipped.

Khalif pressed his palms together, rolled his eyes upward, and murmured a chant in his own language. Then he smiled at Patrick and shrugged. "You are one flesh before Allah," he said. "Take your bride and—please, see that she stays out of trouble."

Charlotte glanced wildly from Khalif to Patrick. "Are we truly married?"

Her alleged bridegroom drew a deep breath, let it out, and then swept Charlotte up into his arms. "I'm afraid so," he said. "There's nothing to do now but make the best of it."

With that, he walked out of the sultan's apartments, carrying her with him like so much salvage from a wrecked ship.

"We didn't sign any papers," Charlotte babbled, full of terror and sweet anticipation. "Nobody said, 'You may kiss the bride' or 'I now pronounce you man and wife'—or 'Does anyone object to this marriage?'!"

Patrick favored her with a wicked smile as he strode down a familiar hallway. "Don't worry, Mrs. Trevarren—I mean to kiss you thoroughly, among other things. And here in Riz, Khalif's word is law—he can pronounce us anything he wants. Anyone who objected would probably have been beheaded for his insolence."

Charlotte's face throbbed with hot color, partly because Patrick had spoken so bluntly and partly because her body was already making preparations for fireworks. "Oh," was all she dared to say.

Patrick shifted her in his arms to open the door of his apartments, then crossed the threshold.

Charlotte saw the same nest of pillows where she had responded so scandalously to this man's attentions on another occasion and buried her face in the curve of his neck.

He laughed and set her on the huge round couch.

"What if someone comes in?" she managed to ask, drawing her knees up and wrapping her arms around them.

"No one would dare," her husband answered, tugging his shirt off over his head to reveal a muscular, sun-browned chest and a vee of dark, masculine down. "Everyone in the palace knows we've just been married."

Charlotte looked at Patrick's navel, then quickly away. "Everyone?" she echoed, annoyed. "Someone might have told *me* there was going to be a wedding. I thought I was about to be tied to a pillar and whipped or something."

"I'm sure that idea has already occurred to Khalif at least once," Patrick agreed blithely. Charlotte had half expected him to pounce on her and subject her to all those glorious sensations he had taught her to want so shamelessly. Instead, he turned away to stand looking out a window.

She retreated awkwardly to the center of the huge couch. "You needn't carry this charade any further, Captain—we both know you only went through with the wedding to save me from being beaten. You've done the chivalrous thing. Now, if you'll just take me back to the Continent, and direct me to an embassy . . ."

Patrick was facing her again, and the expression in his ink blue eyes was a disconcertingly determined one. "'The chivalrous thing'?" he asked, raising one eyebrow. "Charlotte, I'm no knight in shining armor. I married you because I wanted the privileges of a husband. All of them."

She swallowed, started to move into retreat again, but Patrick bent down and clasped her firmly by one ankle. His thumb moved in a small circle on the tender arch of her foot for a moment, then he pulled her toward him.

Bending over Charlotte, bracing his hands on either side of her, Patrick took her mouth boldly with his own. She resisted only until she felt his tongue seek entry, then parted her lips in surrender.

While he kissed her, Patrick molded her breast in one palm, then caressed her hips and buttocks. She clutched at his back, plunged her fingers into the thick, soft hair on his chest, ran her hands over his rib cage.

She lay breathless when he released her mouth, willingly submitting as he removed her gauzy robes and looked at her

79

with an expression of rapt passion. Then, muttering a hoarse word she didn't understand, he curled one strong arm under her waist and raised her off the couch so that he could take one of her nipples full into his mouth.

Charlotte cried out, enraptured, clinging to Patrick with both hands as he feasted on her. She wanted desperately to give herself, to be taken, but somehow she knew her husband would insist on preparing her first.

Patrick splayed his hands beneath her shoulder blades, holding her easily to his lips, like a chalice. He attended the first nipple thoroughly, then went on to the second.

His bride writhed in pleasure as he drank from her, whimpered with need when he let her relax against the couch and began undoing his breeches. He was half kneeling, half bending over her, naked and magnificent, when he spoke.

"Charlotte—"

She touched his splendid mouth with two fingers to silence him. "I know, Patrick—it will hurt a little because I'm—because I've never been with a man before—but I want you to take me fast and hard."

He groaned, and she had a glorious revelation that he wanted her as desperately as she wanted him. "Charlotte, I—"

Brazen in her desire, letting her yen for adventure guide her actions, Charlotte reached out and closed one hand tightly around Patrick's erection. She felt her eyes widen and her heart lurch as she comprehended his size.

Patrick gave her no time to wonder how she would accommodate him; he pushed her legs apart with one knee and lowered himself to her. "After the pain will come pleasure," he told her. "I promise you that."

She clutched at his lean hips, wanting him inside her, and with a moan of surrender he gave her his length in one smooth, irrevocable stroke. There was a tearing sensation and considerable soreness, and yet Charlotte felt as though some vital, long-lost part of her had been restored. Yes, the invasion hurt, for Patrick filled her completely with his masculinity, but beneath the pain coursed a river of incomprehensible joy.

Murmuring gentle, raspy, senseless words, Patrick began to move upon her, taking her, giving her up, taking her again. Their gazes seemed locked together, just as their bodies were, and a soft, crooning sound flowed from Charlotte's throat as she and Patrick found the ancient rhythm.

He conquered her, released her, conquered her, relentlessly.

"Patrick," she whispered, pleading. "Patrick—"

"Soon," he vowed. "Just keep rising to meet me—like that—oh, God in heaven, Charlotte—"

The conflagration began as a burst of flame in Charlotte's soul and quickly spread to the temporal part of her, knotting her loins into a hard, smoldering knot of fire, then releasing them in a storm of sensation.

Both her neck and back were arched as she convulsed in Patrick's arms. He guided her patiently through the experience, then delved deep inside as he made his own surrender.

Charlotte was stricken by the power of his body as it flexed against hers, by the glazed ecstasy she saw in his eyes.

"Patrick, I love you," she blurted out, before she could stop herself.

He fell beside her in sated exhaustion, arranged her so that he could kiss her nipple between periods of gasping to get his breath. Charlotte curled her hand behind his head to let him know he was welcome at her breast. She hoped that, in the delirium of his passion, he hadn't heard her foolish declaration.

Patrick slept, awakened to kiss her breasts for a few minutes, then slept again. Charlotte marveled that this strong, magnificent man could be so vulnerable, and want such a simple comfort from a woman's body. After a time, she shifted, and teased his mouth with the other nipple until she felt him drawing at her once more. She could blissfully have gone on attending her husband like that forever, but the time came when he wanted to take command.

Lying on his back, he set Charlotte astraddle of his hips and toyed idly with her well-suckled breasts. When he had her moaning softly and writhing a little, he spread one hand over her belly and found her magic place with his thumb.

With slow, circular motions, he teased her until she

stiffened, rising high on her knees, and then began to jerk helplessly against his hand. When the pleasure released her at last, she sagged forward, sprawled over his chest like a harlot.

And there wasn't another place on earth she'd rather have been—not the Continent, not Quade's Harbor, not even heaven itself. Finally, after years of imagining herself joined with this very man, she had experienced the reality, and it was better than any fantasy.

They lay still for a long while, not speaking. Patrick played idly with Charlotte's hair, removing the decorations one by one, while she marveled at the sheer glory of being a woman.

At dusk they ate fruit and cheese and pastry from a giant platter left for them earlier. Then, when Charlotte was hoping Patrick would make love to her again, he took her hand instead and led her outside, into a small, private courtyard. There, another tile-lined pool waited, the water comfortably heated by the sun.

Tenderly, almost with reverence, Patrick bathed Charlotte, purposely arousing her, pausing between latherings and caresses to kiss her until her knees seemed to dissolve. When she was dazed with need, he leaned against the side of the pool, turned her so that her back was to him, and teased her with the promise of another taking.

"Love me," she finally pleaded, curving her feet around the backs of his knees and rising high to offer herself.

Patrick lowered her slowly onto his shaft, nibbling her nape and the side of her neck as he guided her toward excruciating pleasure. He fondled her breasts as he filled her, rolling the nipples between his fingers like hard little berries, and Charlotte threw back her head and groaned as the bright desert stars began to play tag with one another.

She did not simply respond in Patrick's arms that night; she performed breathless operas, and he made no effort to muffle her cries of delighted submission. She had her vengeance, though, by disengaging herself before he'd been satisfied and repaying him for the bath he'd given her earlier. When she knew he was ready, that as strong as he was, he'd nearly reached the breaking point, Charlotte maneuvered him onto the smooth steps at the shallow end of the small pool and knelt between his knees.

The water seemed as warm and soft as a blanket around them.

"Charlotte," Patrick groaned, and she didn't know whether he wanted her to stop or go on, she only knew he was begging.

She remembered the exquisite, almost torturous pleasure he'd subjected her to the first time they were together, weeks before, and she had come up with a variation. After taking him firmly in her hand, she took him just as firmly with her mouth.

He gave a long, strangled moan, but Charlotte showed him no mercy. She worked his senses as ruthlessly as he had hers, running her hands over his belly, along his thighs, and under his buttocks while she tormented him.

At last, with a broken cry, he freed himself, hauled her onto the sun-warmed tiles surrounding the pool, and plunged into her. Charlotte had not expected to respond again, she'd thought he'd wrung every imagining of passion from her already. Still, when she felt Patrick stiffen violently, felt his warmth spilling into her, she was seized by a spasm of release so sudden and so violent that she actually lost consciousness for a fraction of a second.

They lay entwined on the tiles for a long time, until the breeze from the desert began to grow cool, then bathed each other again and returned to Patrick's room. After blotting herself dry with a towel, Charlotte reached for the white robe, understanding now that it had been chosen for its resemblance to a wedding dress.

Patrick stopped her by taking her wrist in his hand. He didn't need words to tell her he found her body too beautiful to cover; his eyes told her that.

Much later, on the velvet couch, with a covering of some gossamer fabric over them, Charlotte dared to ask the question that was uppermost on her mind. "You are planning to take me with you this time, aren't you?"

He hesitated before replying, "Yes. After tonight, I don't think I could be noble enough to leave you behind."

Charlotte might have raised herself on one elbow to look down into Patrick's face if he hadn't held her so close to his side. "Noble? You think it's *noble* to abandon a woman in a sultan's harem?"

Patrick chuckled. "I would leave you in only one harem in the world, Charlotte—Khalif's. Except when you took it upon yourself to strike out for the desert, you were safer here than you would have been anywhere else." He threaded the fingers of one hand through her tangled hair. "Remind me to scold you for that, goddess. You could easily have died out there."

"My intentions were good," Charlotte insisted, her hand spread comfortably over the hard, muscle-rippled surface of his belly.

"Exactly. Your intentions were good when you decided to visit the *souk* that day, too, weren't they? And I'll wager you've done a lot of other rash things in your time, as well, Charlotte Trevarren."

She liked the sound of her new name. Sighing, she cuddled closer to Patrick's side. "A few," she admitted. But the topic of Bettina had been brought up, however indirectly, and she couldn't ignore the terrible guilt that followed. "I can live with what happened to me," she confessed, in a small voice, "but I have nightmares about Bettina. She didn't want to leave the house, but I insisted, and now God only knows what kind of unspeakable things she's gone through."

Patrick cupped Charlotte's chin with a callused hand and turned his head to look into her eyes. "Is that your friend you're talking about? The one who was with you in the marketplace?"

His frown nearly stopped Charlotte's heart. Did he know something dreadful about Bettina? Perhaps he was about to confirm Charlotte's worst fear—that the poor girl had ended up in debauchery and degradation.

"Yes," she managed to say, her eyes burning with tears. "Bettina Richardson is her name. She's probably a slave somewhere now, thanks to me, if she's alive at all—"

Patrick gave her face a little shake and kissed her briefly

on the lips. "Miss Richardson is not a slave of any sort, goddess—except, perhaps, to fashion. I saw her myself, and paid a boy to take her home."

"What?"

"I was in the *souk* that day, too, remember? Apparently the kidnappers only needed one woman to fill their quota for the day, because they left Miss Richardson standing in the alleyway, screaming her throat raw. I looked all over for you, but by then it was too late. Then you turned up in my cabin like a captured mermaid." He smiled at the memory, and Charlotte punched him lightly in the ribs.

Her relief that Bettina was safe was dizzying. She took a few moments to absorb the knowledge, then poked Patrick in the side again, remembering something else about that day.

"You were consorting with that dancer," she accused, hating the idea of Patrick with another woman, even if it *had* taken place before they'd become close. "No wonder you failed to rescue me. You'd used up all your strength."

Patrick laughed. "Consorting," he echoed. "Yes. You could say that. As for using all my strength—you'd be surprised at how much I have." He bent, uncovered one of Charlotte's breasts, and kissed the rounded top, venturing perilously close to an already-straining nipple.

Charlotte wanted some assurances first. She wrenched the cover up again. "You're captain of a clipper ship," she pointed out. "Does that mean you have a woman in every port? I won't tolerate a faithless husband, Patrick Trevarren, and I don't care how fashionable it is!"

He kissed her again, very gently. "Fashionable?"

She nodded. "Yes. You know as well as I do that men in the United States and Europe—all over the world—think it's perfectly all right to take a mistress—"

"Does your father have a mistress?"

"Of course not," Charlotte snapped. "My stepmother would go after him with a hunting rifle. Besides, he's very happy with Lydia."

"Then why all this concern about philandering husbands?"

"I'm not as naive as you think, Patrick. I have a good education and I've traveled—I've even been thrown into a harem, for heaven's sake. I've seen enough of the world to know that my father and my uncle are exceptional men, at least when it comes to keeping their marriage vows." She paused for a breath. "Even Mr. Richardson was sneaking out of the hotels in France and Spain, when Mrs. Richardson was suffering from one of her sick headaches. More than once, I saw him walking with a strange woman."

"Maybe Mrs. Richardson gets a lot of sick headaches," Patrick suggested wryly. "Tell me more about your father and your uncle and this stepmother of yours."

There was no reason to keep the family name a secret anymore, as far as Charlotte could see. Now that she was actually Patrick's wife, just as she'd claimed to be in the letter Rashad had sent to America for her, she meant to make a real effort to trust him.

"I grew up on Puget Sound, back in Washington Territory —you don't remember it, but we met in Seattle one day—"

He interrupted with a low, hoarse burst of laughter and "You were the wench who climbed up in the rigging of my ship and couldn't get down."

Even then, all those years later, after the most intimate relations with Patrick, Charlotte blushed at the memory. "It's about time you recalled that," she said. "Now, do you want to hear about my family or not?"

He grinned. "Yes, goddess—tell me everything."

"My father is Brigham Quade. He owns a considerable stand of timber and a mill, among other things."

Patrick sighed. "I know Brigham, Charlotte—everybody who's ever ventured within a hundred miles of Seattle does. By now he's probably about to dock in Europe and tear the place apart, stone by stone, until he finds you."

"No," Charlotte said, somewhat sadly. She loved Patrick, and she knew in her heart that home was at his side, but she still missed Papa and Lydia and Millie and all her rambunctious little brothers and cousins. "I wrote and told Papa I'd married you."

That announcement garnered Patrick's full attention.

"What?" he demanded, raising himself on one elbow to frown down at her.

"I couldn't let my family suffer, Patrick, so I told them I was happy. Papa will yell and swear when they get the letter, but then Lydia will calm him down and he'll accept what's happened. Isn't that better than letting them believe I was forced into white slavery?" When he didn't answer, she went on. "Besides, what I said is all true—now. I did marry you, and for tonight anyway, I'm happy. And you needn't think I can be so easily distracted, either—I want to know if you intend to keep our wedding vows or not."

"I didn't make any vows, remember?" he pointed out, but there was a smile in his eyes as well as his voice. "Ours wasn't exactly a conventional ceremony, obviously. However, since it's important to you, I'll make a promise now. For whatever time we may have together, I will 'cleave only unto you.'"

"I'd better not catch you cleaving to anybody else," Charlotte warned. She was troubled by the words "whatever time we may have together," but decided to consider the implications of that remark later, when her mind was clear again.

Patrick laughed. "Fine." He moved to kiss her, but she stopped him by putting her fingers between his mouth and hers. "What?"

"You haven't told me about your family."

He frowned, shrugged one shoulder. "I'm the only son of a very wealthy man, whom I dislike intensely, and the feeling seems to be mutual. He sent me to school in England after my mother died, and when I was finished I apprenticed myself to my uncle, who was captain of the *Enchantress* until he died three years ago."

Charlotte moved her hand in a circle on Patrick's belly, intending to comfort him but soon discovering that she'd done something else instead. "What a lonely life you must have had."

Gently he lowered the cover again, so that Charlotte's breasts were bared to the moonlight and to him. "I have everything I want," he said gruffly. "A fine ship, a home so like Paradise that even Adam and Eve probably couldn't tell the difference, more money than one man could ever need—and now a sweet, fiery wife to warm my bed." He took one of her nipples into his mouth and suckled.

Charlotte stretched in luxurious surrender, her toes curling. "D-Don't you want a son?"

Patrick tongued her thoroughly before lifting his head from her breast. His indigo eyes looked black in the darkness, and somber. "Several," he replied, "and daughters, too." He lay between her legs now, and slipped himself an inch or so inside her, just to tease. His tone, however, sounded serious indeed. "Will you give me a baby, Charlotte?"

She was already fevered with wanting, even though he had done very little to arouse her. "Y-Yes—oh, yes . . ."

" 'Oh, yes, take me' or 'Oh, yes, I'll bear your children'?" Patrick asked, giving her only slightly more. His voice was full of mischief.

Charlotte arched her back suddenly and claimed him, delighting in the way he groaned in response and offered up a visible struggle for self-control. "Both," she replied, gripping his taut buttocks and holding him prisoner inside her for several long moments. "I want you to take me, and start a baby growing inside me this very night."

Patrick groaned again, and began to rock his hips, and Charlotte could say no more. The pleasure consumed her as quickly as wildfire.

7

Just before dawn, Patrick awakened his bride and then went to the door to summon a servant. Sleep-fogged, Charlotte bathed in the tiled pool and again donned her white robes.

"You're sending me back to the harem?" she asked Patrick, confused and a little alarmed when she returned to the bedchamber to find Rashad waiting patiently beside the door, his thick arms folded.

Patrick's manner was conciliatory, but his words did nothing to reassure Charlotte. "Just for a little while," he said. "Khalif and I have business to discuss."

Indignant color pulsed in Charlotte's cheeks, but she offered no protest, sensing that Patrick had made up his mind on the matter.

Reaching the *hamam*, the central gathering place within the harem, Charlotte encountered Alev. The other woman took her arm and hustled her out into the enclosed courtyard, and her manner was terse.

"Did you spend the night with Khalif, then?" she demanded.

Charlotte didn't like Alev's tone or the implication of her question. "No," she replied coldly, pulling free of Alev's hard grasp on her elbow. "I was with my husband."

Alev arched one eyebrow in a silent query.

"Patrick Trevarren," Charlotte explained, somewhat smugly. "Khalif married us in his chambers last night."

Alev's relief was apparent, but there was a spark of something else in her eyes, too. A sort of amused skepticism. "And already your 'husband' has sent you back to us?"

Charlotte's face burned, and she narrowed her eyes. "Patrick had business to discuss with the sultan," she said. "As soon as that's completed, I'm sure my husband will send for me and we'll leave."

Taking Charlotte's arm again, Alev sat down on the bench under the elm and pulled her companion after her. "This marriage—was it a Christian ceremony, or did Khalif simply utter a few words and make a pronouncement?"

Charlotte swallowed. The nuptials had not been performed by a priest or a minister or even a justice of the peace, which might well mean the marriage was binding only in the kingdom of Riz. It was even possible that the impromptu service had been nothing but a sham, cooked up between the two men, and designed to lure Charlotte to Patrick's bed . . .

"Well?" Alev prompted, when Charlotte was silent.

"Khalif married us himself," she said miserably. She couldn't bring herself to voice her suspicions; besides, the situation was probably obvious to Alev anyway.

Alev nodded, her brows knitted together in a thoughtful frown. "Then you and the captain are forever joined in the sight of Allah," she said. "Unless, of course, your husband decides he wants to divorce you."

Charlotte was still in shock from her earlier conclusions. "Divorce me?"

"If you displease your sea captain, Charlotte," Alev said importantly, "all he has to do is clap his hands together and say 'I divorce you' three times."

"That's awful!"

"Under our laws," Alev went on, "such a parting of the ways is entirely acceptable. And that's not all—a man can have as many as four wives, and all the concubines he desires."

Charlotte stood, then sat again, forlorn. She'd given herself to Patrick wholeheartedly, believing herself to be his wife. Matters had seemed so simple when she'd lain beneath him on his couch, and in the bath in the small courtyard outside Patrick's bedchamber. Now Charlotte was badly shaken.

"Patrick and I are Americans," she pointed out, her voice revealing her uncertainty. "Islamic laws don't apply to us."

"They do when you are living in an Islamic country," Alev said, without rancor. "And Trevarren sent you back to the harem, didn't he? Besides, that would mean the marriage wasn't legal either."

Charlotte's misery intensified. She rose and began to pace back and forth in front of the bench. "You don't suppose he lied to me?" she asked, speaking more to herself than Alev.

"It wouldn't be the first time a man had twisted the truth to lure a woman into his bed, would it?"

Charlotte stopped and glared down at Alev, who was still seated comfortably on the bench, her face and figure dappled by the shadows of the elm's many leaves. "Why are you trying to upset me?" she demanded. "What have I done to you?"

Alev sighed and stood. "I did not mean to be unkind," she said. "You don't seem to understand that things are very different here, and I was trying to warn you about having expectations that can only lead to disappointment."

With that, the other woman vanished inside the seraglio, and Charlotte once again peered speculatively up through the branches of the elm tree. Had Patrick merely used her? Did he intend to abandon her in the harem again, now that he'd taken his pleasure with her?

She had to find out.

Charlotte laid one hand to the rough bark of the elm tree. The last time she'd attempted an escape, she'd nearly perished in the desert, and she certainly didn't want to go through that ordeal again. No, if Patrick had indeed deceived her, she would learn of it prior to his departure and find a way to stow away on board the *Enchantress*.

Having a plan, however outlandish it might be, always made Charlotte feel better. She took a few more minutes to calm herself, then returned to the harem.

In the early afternoon, the other women stretched out on their couches to sleep, but Charlotte was far too restless to lie still. Her heart leaped with relief when Rashad caught her eye and gestured for her to come to him.

With unusual obedience, she hurried to meet the eunuch in the doorway.

"Your husband wishes you to join him in his chamber," Rashad said.

Charlotte's heart tripped over a beat, then fluttered wildly, like an excited bird beating against the bars of its cage. She was filled with dizzying joy and with an equal measure of resentment that Patrick had the power to treat her like a slave.

When they reached Patrick's quarters, the door was open. Rashad gestured for Charlotte to pass over the threshold and, when she had, left them alone.

Charlotte's temper simmered, though she managed a sweet smile. "Hello, Mr. Trevarren," she said.

Patrick had just popped a fat purple grape into his mouth, and he chewed and swallowed before answering, " 'Mr. Trevarren.' I like that. It sounds old-fashioned and deceptively obedient."

Charlotte's stomach seemed to do a somersault. "If you want obedience, I would suggest you buy a little monkey in the *souk* and train it to dance on its hind legs whenever you snap your fingers," she said. Her emotions were still in a wild tangle; one part of her wanted to fling herself into Patrick's arms, while another would have liked to claw his ears off.

He laughed and folded his arms. "You are either very brave or very foolish, my love. I haven't decided which."

She drew a deep breath and held it for a moment, but she could not hold back her greatest concern. "One of the women in the harem told me you can divorce me by clapping your hands three times. Is that true?"

Patrick's indigo eyes sparkled with some private mirth. "Absolutely," he replied.

Quiet rage set Charlotte's face aflame. "She also said you could have four wives if you so desired, and all the concubines you wanted," she ventured, struggling to keep her tone of voice even.

He nodded. "Here in Riz, I can take more than one wife if I choose, though the unions wouldn't be recognized outside the Arab countries, of course. As for concubines, there is no limit, here or in the Christian world." His mouth twitched almost imperceptibly at one corner as he paused, studying Charlotte. "Come here."

She wanted to resist him, but she could not. She moved toward him, stepped into his arms. "I will not be your concubine," she said, in pure bravado.

Patrick slipped one side of her robe down, revealing her shoulder and the rounded top of her breast. "You will be whatever I ask you to be, Charlotte," he said huskily. "And we both know it."

He kissed her, and although Charlotte fought to summon up some shred of rebellion from her beleaguered soul, she found herself surrendering instead. Patrick undressed her, touched and admired her exquisitely vulnerable body at his leisure, and finally arranged her like a feast on the velvet couch.

After that, he pleasured her unmercifully, with his hands and his mouth and finally, blessedly, his shaft. Charlotte was utterly spent when at last he let her rest, collapsed across his chest in a daze of satisfaction.

Patrick splayed long, sun-browned fingers through her tousled hair while, with his other hand, he gave her bottom a proprietary squeeze. In those moments, Charlotte would quite literally have given her soul to hear her husband say he loved her, but no such tender words were forthcoming.

"We'll sail with the morning tide," he said instead.

Using the little bit of frail strength that remained to her, Charlotte lifted her head to look into Patrick's ink-colored eyes. "I-I want to go with you."

He touched the tip of her nose with his forefinger and gave her an indulgent look. "I've already told you, Mrs. Trevarren—where I go, you go. Don't you trust me?"

She found some of her old spirit. "Of course I don't trust

you," she said, touching his lower lip idly. "Why on earth would I, when I might be just the first of four wives, or no wife at all?"

"No wife at all?" Patrick frowned. "What in the name of God's eyeballs do you mean by that?"

"Our marriage wouldn't be legal anywhere but here," Charlotte said. She sounded brave and even defiant, but inwardly she was on the verge of tears. "And even in Riz, all you have to do to get rid of me is clap your hands and say a few words."

Patrick lifted his head to kiss her lightly on the mouth. "I guess you'll have to behave yourself, then," he said.

It wasn't the answer Charlotte had hoped to get. "My father isn't going to appreciate this one bit," she warned. "When Papa and Uncle Devon find out how shamefully you've used me, they'll chop off your fingers and toes and make you eat them."

He grimaced, but mockingly. "Such threats, Mrs. Trevarren. I'm terrified."

"If you had the brains God gave a pump handle, Mr. Trevarren," she replied, "you would fear for your life. Brigham Quade is not a man to be trifled with."

Patrick's eyes smiled, even though his mouth was somber. "Then it would seem to be a good thing that it's you I want to trifle with, goddess, and not your illustrious sire." He rolled over, so that Charlotte was beneath him on the velvet couch, looking up at him with mingled irritation and desire. "Spread your legs, wife," he said. "I want to take you. Now."

Only minutes later, Charlotte was crying out, her body wrought with desperate convulsions of pleasure as Patrick reveled in her wildness and, at the same time, tamed her.

He did not send her away again, not that afternoon, or that night, when they'd bathed and eaten and then made love so many times that Charlotte lost count.

In the morning, after saying farewell to both Rashad and Khalif himself, Charlotte boarded the *Enchantress* with her husband. She wore bright yellow robes sent to her by Alev, and stood on the deck watching as the magnificent white palace was swallowed up in the sapphire distance.

"Go into my cabin," Patrick ordered in passing, busy with the workings of the ship. "I want you to stay out of the sun."

Charlotte obeyed, having little other choice. She was escorted to the captain's quarters by Mr. Cochran, who promised to bring tea and fruit once they were well under way.

Bored, Charlotte read the spines of every one of Patrick's books while she waited, then resorted to going through the ship's log. When that enterprise failed to turn up any interesting information, she opened the top drawer of his desk.

Inside, tucked discreetly to one side, she found a small packet of letters, tied with a narrow ribbon. The stationery was heavy vellum, soft blue in color, and the scent of gardenias rose from it.

Charlotte knew better than to snoop, but she was feeling bored and slightly rebellious, and now an undeniable stab of jealousy had been added to the mix. The name Pilar Querida was neatly scripted in the upper left-hand corner of each envelope, along with a street address and the name of a small city on the southern coast of Spain. Costa del Cielo.

She had barely returned the packet to the desk and closed the drawer when Patrick entered the cabin. He paused just over the threshold, looking at Charlotte in an odd way, as though he suspected her of some unsavory action but was at a loss to prove his claim.

She did not ask who Pilar Querida was, for the faint hint of perfume permeating the letters had answered that question already. The discovery left Charlotte feeling as though she'd been struck behind the knees by a runaway log.

Putting her hands behind her to clutch the edge of Patrick's desk, she asked, "Where are we going now, please?"

Patrick crossed the room to the bed, sat down on its edge with a purely masculine sigh, and kicked off one of his boots, then the other. "Spain," he answered, collapsing onto his back and offering no indication whatsoever that he expected Charlotte to join him.

She sank into the desk chair, her fingers knotted in her lap. "Are you ill?" she asked, because all the other questions that came to her mind were inflammatory ones that could only start trouble.

Her husband sighed again, just as heavily as before. "No, Charlotte," he answered patiently, "I'm just exhausted. I don't think I've slept more than two hours in succession since you and I were married."

Charlotte blushed, and when Patrick yawned, she gave an involuntary yawn of her own. She waited until his breathing had settled into a deep, even meter, then removed her slippers and crawled onto the bed beside him. She had no more than closed her eyes before the sweet darkness of slumber overtook her.

"How long before we reach Spain?" Charlotte asked hours later, as she and Patrick stood looking out at a dark sea and a sky full of stars.

Patrick was leaning against the railing, and it seemed that he was somehow taking sustenance from the quiet waters and the creaking of the ship's timbers. "We'll be there tomorrow, if the winds are good," he replied, somewhat distractedly.

Charlotte had agonized over the mysterious Pilar, fearing that the woman held some unshakable place in Patrick's heart, but now, for the first time, she recognized that he had other mistresses as well. There was the sea, for one, and the *Enchantress,* for another. Perhaps he would never love a woman with such quiet reverence.

She felt an oddly sweet sadness fold over her spirit as she linked her arm with his. "And after Spain, where will we go?"

He turned his head, looked down at her with those wondrous eyes. "Where would you like to go, Charlotte?"

She let her cheek rest against his muscular upper arm for a few moments, reflecting on the question. Charlotte had often marveled at her stepmother's devotion to Brigham Quade; now she was beginning to understand how deeply a strong woman could care for an equally forceful man. Such love was an elemental thing, beyond blithe definitions and even poetry; to grasp it fully might take every moment of a lifetime. Or an eternity.

Finally, softly, she echoed, "Where would I like to go?" Charlotte paused again, drinking in the slumbering sea, the multitude of silver stars. "Wherever the wind takes me." Bold as she was, she couldn't quite make herself reveal the full truth and say, *Wherever you are, Patrick. That's where I want to be.*

He might laugh at her for thinking their marriage was anything more than a game to him.

Patrick gazed down at Charlotte in silence for a long time, his eyes reflecting the starlight and the deep, primal secrets of the ocean itself. "I have business in Spain," he said at long last, his voice gruff. "After I've finished with that, we'll sail for the island—we'll have cargo to deliver there. Then, after the *Enchantress* has been made ready again, we'll set out for Seattle."

Charlotte gripped the ship's rail tightly. She wanted most desperately to be reunited with her family, but she feared that Patrick meant to leave her in Washington Territory, to sail on without her.

She grasped what she hoped was a safe topic. "The island?"

Patrick's teeth flashed in a spontaneous grin. "I believe I've mentioned the place once or twice—it's in the South Pacific. I raise sugar cane there, but mostly Hidden Island is a place to think and restore myself."

Charlotte was enchanted and, momentarily at least, distracted from her worries. "Hidden Island," she repeated dreamily, imagining palm trees and blue lagoons and gloriously colored orchids growing wild. "What a mysterious name."

Above them, the masts creaked in a light breeze, and sailors called to one another from fore and aft. Patrick was silent, and Charlotte was homesick for a place she'd never seen.

They stood on the deck awhile longer, then went below to Patrick's quarters, where a large tub brimming with steaming water was waiting.

Charlotte was delighted. "A bath!"

Patrick gave her a sidelong look as he closed and latched

97

the door. "Yes, Mrs. Trevarren. And it's mine, so don't get any ideas about taking it over."

She put out her lower lip and sat down on the end of the bed, her arms folded. "You aren't being very gentlemanly, I must say."

Her husband hauled his shirt off over his head, revealing a well-sculpted chest and back. "I've made no claims to good manners," he said. "I like my comforts and pleasures, and I've been pretty straightforward about that."

Charlotte blushed and averted her eyes for a moment. When she looked back—she tried to resist and failed miserably—she saw that Patrick had kicked aside his boots and was in the process of removing his breeches.

"Ministers preach sermons about men like you," she observed. "They say you're nothing but tools of the devil."

Patrick stepped into the large, ornate copper tub, sighed hedonistically, and lowered himself into the water. "So you listened in church, did you?" he asked, settling back and cupping his hands behind his head. "That's amazing. You strike me as the sort to wool-gather from the first note of the opening hymn to the last word of the benediction."

Charlotte coveted the feel of warm water against the skin, and she was vaguely insulted as well. "I'm not the scatter-brain you seem to think I am, Mr. Trevarren," she said, somewhat tersely, while fighting a quite contrary urge to strip off her clothes and join her husband in his bath. "Furthermore, I was attentive in church. My stepmother, Lydia, was very strict about our spiritual development. She says people need fellowship and ritual to be healthy in their minds."

He reached for a bar of soap and the washcloth one of the sailors had laid out, along with several towels. "Are you a believer?" he asked offhandedly, as though it were normal to have such a discussion stark naked, in a lantern-lit ship's cabin dominated by a rumpled bed.

"Yes," Charlotte answered, "though I must admit I share my father's doubts about organized religion. Too many people are looking for an excuse to let someone else do their thinking for them—like their pastor, for instance. Or the deacon."

Patrick lathered the washcloth, looking thoughtful. "Not everyone is a leader, Charlotte. Plenty of people need somebody to look up to and follow, and there's nothing wrong with that. Would you mind washing my back, please?"

The change of subject was so quick and so unexpected that Charlotte's tongue tangled around the words she'd planned to say.

"No," she finally managed.

He frowned. "Why not?"

Charlotte took a few moments to cast about for an answer. "Because I'm annoyed with you, that's why not. First, someone dumps me out of a sack at your feet like a litter of unwanted kittens, and you immediately start ordering me about. Then you leave me in a *harem*, for pity's sake, and after that, you offer me a choice between marriage and a beating. Now you don't even have the common decency to let me take the first bath!"

Methodically Patrick soaped his chest, making the dark hair lie against his skin in swirling patterns, like frost on a window. "You're welcome to join me," he informed her, after lengthy consideration.

He was so arrogant, Charlotte thought furiously. Not only had Patrick dismissed her list of complaints concerning his behavior without so much as a shrug—now he seemed to think she should be honored to share his bathwater!

"Thank you so much," she said, with acid sweetness. "You are extremely *generous, sir.*"

Patrick laughed and sprang up out of that copper bathtub as suddenly and sleekly as a dolphin breaking the surface of the sea. He gripped Charlotte's arm, while she was still stunned, and dragged her, robe, slippers, and all, into the water.

The gossamer fabric of her gown turned transparent and clung to her every curve. She struggled wildly, and the floor of the cabin was awash, but Patrick held her easily, her back to his chest.

"You wanted a bath, Charlotte," he reasoned, his lips close to her ear. "Now you're going to get one."

She kicked and twisted. "Let me go this instant!"

Patrick sighed but did not slacken his hold. "There is just no pleasing you," he said, with philosophical resignation. "We're going to have to do something about your contrary and, yes, downright shrewish temperament, Mrs. Trevarren."

Charlotte calmed herself, but it took a series of several deep breaths and a mental count to twenty-seven. Her hair had come down from its pins and was plastered to her shoulders and breasts in sodden strands, and the robe, the only garment she possessed, was almost certainly ruined. "This is reprehensible behavior, Patrick. Release me at once."

Instead, he turned her to face him and brazenly admired her breasts, which were entirely revealed by the filmy fabric. "Certainly, my dear—anything you say. You have only to wash my back, as a good wife could surely be expected to, and then you may do whatever you wish."

Once again, Charlotte began to count, making no sound but shaping the numbers with her lips.

Patrick laughed. "By God, you must be the stubbornest woman ever created. It will be a challenge to tame you."

Charlotte knew her eyes were shooting fire. If she'd dared, she would have spit in Patrick's face, but even she wasn't quite that courageous. "You will see angels dance the minuet in hell first," she hissed.

He brought her close to him, raised her a little way out of the water, and scraped one fully visible nipple lightly with his teeth. "No, Charlotte," he argued, after subjecting her to sweet torment for several moments. "But I will see *you* dance beneath me, in my bed, this very night. Your own cries of pleasure will be the music."

She trembled, awed by the power this man held over her, outraged by it, as helpless against it as she would have been against an earthquake or a hurricane. "Patrick—" she gasped, loving him and hating him, both at once.

Gently he peeled away Charlotte's wet robes and tossed them aside. Her slippers had come off during the battle, and while one was submerged, the other floated. These, too, were retrieved and discarded.

Patrick positioned Charlotte astraddle of his hips, and

soon water splashed rhythmically over the sides of the tub as she rode him.

Charlotte was sleeping like a rock beside Patrick, and he willed her not to awaken when the alarm bell up on the main deck began to clang steadily. He reached for his clothes, found that they were soaked with the overflow from the bathtub, and cursed as he splashed to the chest for fresh breeches and a clean shirt.

"Patrick?" Charlotte muttered as he dressed. "Are we sinking?"

"No, goddess," he answered. "Go back to sleep."

She sighed. "All right," she replied, with unusual compliance, and Patrick felt a strange twisting sensation somewhere deep in his chest. It was purely remarkable, he thought, as he took his pistol from a desk drawer, how a little amber-eyed minx like Charlotte could complicate an otherwise orderly life.

Quickly, more by instinct than by sight, Patrick loaded the gun's chamber and then strode across the dark cabin and out. No more than a few minutes had passed when he reached the wheelhouse.

"What is it?" he demanded of Cochran, who was on night watch.

"There's a ship approaching, sir—off the starboard side. She's moving fast, and I don't think she's just passing close by for a friendly hello."

The night was silvered with the light of the stars and moon, and Patrick snatched the spyglass from Cochran's hand and raised it to one eye.

Sure enough, another vessel was coursing toward them. Patrick couldn't make out her colors or emblem. "Tell that idiot to stop ringing that bell before I stuff his head into it and strike every note in the 'Star-Spangled Banner,'" he muttered, still studying the intruder.

"Yes, sir," Cochran responded, and immediately carried out the order.

Patrick's well-developed instincts told him the visitors weren't friendly. Under different circumstances, he would have relished the challenge of a good fight, but Charlotte was belowdecks, warm and well loved in his bed, and that put a very different light on the situation. He had taken on a weakness as well as a wife, he reflected, and he'd never felt more vulnerable.

He saw the flash of cannon fire, and his experienced crew rushed to their battle stations. The *Enchantress* fired on her attacker, and the salty air was suddenly pungent with the smells of gunpowder and smoke.

A ball struck the ship's hull and she quivered under the impact, but her timbers, heavy oak from the oldest forests in New England, held firm. Patrick felt her strength through the soles of his feet, for the clipper was as much a part of him as his stomach or his soul. She had breath and a heartbeat of her own.

The cannon on both vessels fell silent, but only because the intruder had drawn up alongside. As pirates poured over the rails from the other craft, Patrick concentrated on defending his ladies—Charlotte, the wife he had not intended to wed, and his beloved and faithful mistress, the *Enchantress* herself.

8

THE SOUNDS OF A RAGING BATTLE WERE UNMISTAKABLE, EVEN to Charlotte's relatively naive sensibilities. She bolted out of bed, trembling, and scanned the small chamber for something to wear. Her robe, the only garment she possessed, was sodden, and there was nothing to do but commandeer some of Patrick's clothes.

She found gray kidskin breeches in the trunk at the foot of his bed, along with a very dashing linen shirt. The breeches were too loose in the waist and too snug through the hips, but Charlotte wasted no time worrying about the way they fit. She might be called upon to defend herself at any moment.

After more searching, she finally found a mean-looking dagger among Patrick's belongings. Uncertain that she would be able to wield the blade against another human being, Charlotte nonetheless carried it with her when she left the cabin.

The din of warfare was deafening by the time she sneaked cautiously onto the main deck, and smoke curled everywhere, like a blue-gray fog, making it difficult to breathe. All around her, male bodies clashed in hand-to-hand combat.

103

Charlotte gripped the handle of the dagger in slippery palms and crouched behind a large crate to assess the situation. There was another ship bobbing alongside the *Enchantress*, and it required no particular genius to work out that the attackers were pirates.

Closing her eyes briefly, Charlotte swallowed and, once again, silently cursed herself for ever wishing to find adventure.

A hard, familiar body tumbled backwards against the crate. Patrick bent his knees and kicked the pirate hard in the chest, sending the other man sprawling.

"What the hell are you doing up here?" Patrick yelled, without even looking at Charlotte. "Find a place to hide and stay there until I tell you otherwise!"

With that, he sprang back into the fierce battle, and Charlotte did not pause to wonder how he'd known she was crouched behind that crate. She looked around carefully, then made a dash for the doorway leading to the lower deck.

She had barely gained the top step when she felt ironlike arms clamp around her from behind. A jolt of pure terror shot through her system, petrifying her for a moment, but then some deeper, more primitive part of her mind took over. She fought like a tigress, wildly thrusting the dagger behind her, against her assailant's torso.

A bellow of furious pain presaged her release; Charlotte did not pause to look back, but scrambled down the short flight of stairs and hurtled along the companionway. She was pulling open the door to the storeroom, where she intended to hide until she was either rescued or murdered, when a hairy hand reached past her head to slam it shut again.

She whirled, her back to the hard oak panel, and found herself face-to-face with a leering pirate. The smell of him, coupled with the terrible fear she felt, made bile surge into the back of her throat. He clutched one bloody thigh, his fingers stained crimson, and glared at her.

"Cut into my hide like a joint of venison, will you?" he rasped, revealing himself to be an Englishman of very low social standing. He knotted his other fist in her hair, slammed the back of her head hard against the doorjamb.

"You'll have to pay for that, little lady, and the price will be a dear one!"

Charlotte moved to knee him, but he saw the attack coming and shifted sideways to avoid it. She was left with no choice but to use the knife again, and she did, pretending the pirate was a roast chicken and aiming for the breastbone.

The blade bounced off, but not before it sliced the man's filthy shirt and the flesh beneath. He gave another shout of animal fury and sprang at her again, but at that instant, God be thanked, he was wrenched away.

Patrick sent him headlong into the wall, and the misguided wretch folded to the floor, unconscious.

"Damn it all to hell, Charlotte," Patrick blazed, bending to get the pirate by the back of the collar and drag him toward the steps, "I don't have time to play nursemaid to a puddingheaded woman! Do as I told you!"

"I was trying!" Charlotte couldn't help pointing out, before she ducked into the storeroom and bolted the door behind her.

The place was dark and the air was hot and close. She stood still for a long while, struggling to calm her nerves, and when her eyes had adjusted to the near-total absence of light, she crawled behind a tall crate.

Muffled shouts and gunshots seeped through the deck over her head, and Charlotte started to tremble, now that she had time to review her situation. When she heard a body thud hard against the storeroom door, her heart leaped into a beat so fast that it left her with no strength to breathe. She lifted the lid on one of the barrels and climbed inside, sneezing as a cloud of flour rose around her.

Squatting down, she tried to be grateful that the cask was only partially full and at the same time prayed her hiding place wasn't marked by a circle of white.

The interval to come was like something out of Dante's *Inferno*—more than once, the storeroom door literally rattled on its hinges as it was struck from outside. The battle, confined to the upper deck before, was now being waged in the lower confines of the ship as well.

Charlotte's bravado was all gone. The dagger's handle was literally glued to her hand, since she was perspiring, and clumps of paste formed on her cheeks when she finally gave way to tears. If the pirate siege was successful, the results would be too horrible to contemplate.

She waited, too frightened even to pray.

At least an hour had passed, by her fevered reckoning, when she heard a thunderous knock.

"Charlotte!" The voice was Patrick's. "Open the door!"

Relief swept through Charlotte—he was still alive!—followed by the purest rage. He had sounded impatient, as though he would rather be doing almost anything besides looking for his wife.

"How do I know you're not being coerced? This might be a trick—a pirate could be holding a knife to your throat!"

"You've been reading too many silly books," the captain responded irritably.

She climbed out of the flour barrel, went to the door. She stood with her ear pressed to the panel, listening. Then, driven by her longing for light and safety, Charlotte took a chance and lifted the latch.

Patrick stood alone in the companionway, glaring at her. His dark hair was rumpled, his face was bruised, and his shirt was torn, but there was no visible blood anywhere on his person.

"Thank God," Charlotte rasped.

Patrick leaned against the doorjamb and let his indigo gaze move over Charlotte's figure. She must have looked like a ghost, she thought, her hair wild, her countenance covered in flour from head to toe.

It didn't help when Patrick chuckled.

"Don't you dare laugh at me!" she warned, trying to push by him.

He barred the way, as impassable as the stone wall that enclosed her stepmother's rose garden back home in Quade's Harbor. "Everything is all right, Charlotte," he said, with gruff gentleness. "There's no need to be afraid."

With a little cry, Charlotte flung her arms around Patrick's neck and clung to him, shaking with residual fear. "I thought you were surely dead—I was certain the pirates would make me walk the plank . . ."

She felt his smile as his lips moved against her hair.

"The *Enchantress* doesn't have a plank," he said reasonably. "And, as you can see, I'm very much alive."

Charlotte slid slowly down Patrick's chest, but she couldn't quite bring herself to step away. "Are they gone?" she whispered. "The pirates, I mean."

He smiled and brushed her hair back from her face. A cloud of flour rose and dissipated between them. "Yes, goddess," he said. "Come along and we'll see about getting you cleaned up."

The cabin was still awash in spilled bathwater, and all hands were needed above decks since the ship had sustained damage during the attack, so Charlotte was given a mop and told to swab the floor. By the time she was finished, and the cook's helper could be spared to bring fresh water so she could wash, her skin, eyebrows, and hair were crusted with dried flour. She felt like a plaster statue.

"Will there be anything else, Mrs. Trevarren?" the lad from the galley asked, once he'd poured the last bucket of hot water into the tub. He was no older than fourteen, by Charlotte's accounting, and doing a poor job hiding a grin.

"Yes," she answered, pretending to great dignity. "You may stand guard outside the door. I don't want anyone to come in while I'm having my bath."

The boy went out, and Charlotte stuffed the end of a pen wiper into the keyhole just in case he turned out to be of less than sterling character. Then she removed the clothes she'd purloined from Patrick's trunk, peeling the cloth carefully away from her flesh like bandages from a wound.

For the second time that day, she scrubbed her skin and hair, and she was just rising out of the water, a towel bunched against her bosom, when Patrick suddenly strode in.

He eyed her naked form brazenly as he closed the door, and Charlotte flushed with annoyance and the damnable attraction she could not deny.

"I specifically instructed that young man to guard the door," she said, arranging the towel around her like a toga.

"I am the captain of this ship," Patrick said offhandedly. "I will not be barred from any part of it—particularly my own cabin."

Charlotte swallowed. The events of the day had been harrowing, to say the least, and she had just about exhausted her personal resources. She hoped Patrick could not see that she was shaking as she stepped over the side of the tub.

"What am I supposed to wear now?" she asked, sitting down on the edge of the bed with an angry little bounce. "Or must I go naked from now on?"

Patrick grinned. "As appealing as I find that prospect," he replied, "I'm a jealous man. I'd have to confine you to the cabin until we reached Spain, and you probably wouldn't like that." He went to the armoire, opened one of the glistening walnut doors, and plundered through various well-tailored garments until he found what he sought—a dreadful dress covered in purple lace ruffles. "I'd forgotten about this," he said. "Who'd have thought it would ever come in handy?"

"I wouldn't have guessed that violet was your color," Charlotte remarked tartly.

He tossed it to her and it billowed on her lap, a riot of ugliness smelling of cheap perfume. "Put it on and keep your mouth shut," he said.

Charlotte stood, holding the frock in front of her and frowning at it. As if she had a choice whether to wear the thing or not. "Apparently I wouldn't have been the first to wander about the *Enchantress* in a state of nakedness," she observed, though she didn't really want to hear about the strumpet who had entered the captain's cabin wearing that awful dress and then went off without it. "Perhaps the poor creature was plucked straight from your bed by pirates?"

Patrick folded his arms, and his gaze was level. "I believe she left wearing one of my shirts," he answered. "This was after she poured tincture of opium into my brandy and relieved me of my watch and all my money, if I remember correctly."

Charlotte couldn't help smiling. "It's good to know that not every woman responds to your charms as shamelessly as I do," she said sweetly. She was angry with herself for succumbing to petty jealousy, and with Patrick for being able to inspire the emotion in her in the first place.

He lifted one eyebrow. "I did not say the lady didn't enjoy

herself thoroughly in my bed before robbing me," he informed her.

A hot blush bloomed in Charlotte's cheeks. It seemed grossly unfair that she had come to Patrick as a virgin, while he had probably bedded women of every station from princess to belly dancer.

"How modest of you to say so," she snapped.

Patrick laughed and, to her profound relief, left the cabin without another word.

Charlotte put on the hideous dress, which was too small in the bosom and made her feel like a streetwalker. The neckline was low, and she had to keep tugging it upward to hide her cleavage.

For all of that, Charlotte's curiosity was greater than her commitment to propriety, and she couldn't bear to stay in the cabin. She had to go up on deck and see what damage had been done to the *Enchantress.* Some of the crewmen were undoubtedly wounded, too, and would need medical care.

First thing after reaching the deck, Charlotte looked up and saw that the mainsail had been torn from top to bottom. There were smears of blood everywhere, and part of the railing had been shattered, probably by cannon fire. The ship listed slightly to one side, and the smell of gunpowder still lingered in the air.

Looking out to sea, she saw the other vessel moving slowly toward the horizon.

"You look even better in that dress than Monique did," Patrick said, startling Charlotte so badly that she jumped. It was uncanny, the way he could sneak up on her, given his size. He moved with the grace of a circus performer on a high wire.

Charlotte seethed. From the looks of things, the ship was probably going to sink at any moment, and Captain Trevarren wanted to discuss past conquests. "I'm surprised she kept it on long enough for you to take notice," she retorted.

Patrick laughed. "I suppose it would be useless to send you back to my cabin," he said, "so I'll just tell you not to get underfoot."

She gave him a haughty look and glanced around, searching for wounded crewmen. "I used to help my stepmother and Dr. McCauley tend the sick and injured sometimes, back home. Was anyone hurt?"

He gestured toward the port side. "Yes," he said, and all the humor vanished from his expression in an instant. "Over there," he told her, already moving in the opposite direction, toward the rigging. Moments later, he was climbing the net of ropes as deftly as a spider on a web. Charlotte felt a pang as she recalled their first meeting, a decade before, in the harbor at Seattle.

After a moment's reverie, she broke free of her thoughts and started for the other side of the ship.

Only about half a dozen men had been hurt, she was relieved to find, and none of them seriously. Charlotte tried to ignore the sailors' vocal appreciation of her borrowed purple dress while she helped Mr. Cochran and Mr. Ness to wash and stitch their wounds.

When all the men had been treated, there was nothing to do, and Charlotte would have been the first to admit that idleness generally had an unsavory effect on her character. She returned to Patrick's cabin long enough to wash her hands and select a book from the captain's collection, then returned to the deck.

Patrick was still high in the rigging, working with several other men to mend the rent sail. It seemed to Charlotte that the ship was limping toward the coast of Spain, and her vivid imagination delivered up a series of disconcerting pictures. She saw the *Enchantress* sinking, encircled by sharks and other creatures of the deep. She even felt the water closing over her face . . .

"Mrs. Trevarren?"

She started slightly, clutching the borrowed book to her bosom. Mr. Cochran was standing before her, his expression mild and polite.

"Excuse me," the first mate said, "but you look a little on the peaky side. I was thinking that perhaps you might want a cup of strong tea with a little brandy added."

Charlotte put Patrick's precarious position in the rigging firmly out of her mind. She was struck by Mr. Cochran's

110

refined way of speaking. "That was very thoughtful," she said, with a prim nod. "Thank you."

Mr. Cochran nodded and walked away, and Charlotte sat down on the very crate she'd hidden behind just over an hour before. Although she was wearing a harlot's dress, the first mate's kind attentions made her feel like a lady again. She looked up at Patrick, saw him pull off his shirt and drop it from the rigging to work bare-chested in the sun.

She sniffed. Her husband had a few things to learn about being a gentleman.

The next day, just before sundown, land was sighted. Charlotte stood at the rail, watching purple shadows dart and waver across the water. A welcoming committee of dolphins greeted the ship, jibbering and showing off like rowdy children.

Charlotte hadn't slept at all the night before; she'd been too busy trying to keep the ship afloat by the power of her will. Patrick's lovemaking might have diverted her mind from her fears, but he had never come to bed. In fact, he hadn't even joined her for supper.

Now, watching the dolphins frolic, Charlotte acknowledged the duality of her emotions, at least to herself. She would be overjoyed to feel solid ground beneath her feet again, and to be in a country where a man was entitled to only one wife, but she felt a peculiar, niggling dread, too. She sensed another great change approaching, as ominous and powerful as one of the wild windstorms that sometimes ravaged the shores of Puget Sound.

The cook's helper, Tipper Doon, appeared beside her. The young man sighed as he regarded the olive groves and the red tile roofs of the stucco houses clustered close to the shore. He was very young, and Charlotte wondered, not for the first time, if someone somewhere was worrying about him and praying for his safe return.

"What's the name of that village?" she asked, hungry for conversation.

"Costa del Cielo," he said. "Coast of the Sky. Sometimes the water and the heavens are just the same color, and the town looks like it's floating in midair."

Charlotte smiled. "You're a poet, Mr. Doon," she told him. "Tell me—where were you born, and are there people there waiting for you?"

He turned and regarded her with eyes as blue as the coastal sea. His sandy hair just brushed his collar, and he dressed much as Patrick did, though his plain-spun breeches and muslin shirt were not so costly as the things the captain wore.

"I boarded the ship in San Francisco," he answered. "My ma was all I had, and I figure she was too busy with whiskey and men to notice I was gone."

"You've had some formal education," Charlotte persisted, with a note of affectionate suspicion in her voice.

Tipper lifted one shoulder in a shrug. "A lady from the church came around when I was little and asked if I wanted to go to school. I went most days, because the place was warm and the teacher usually brought me something to eat." He shrugged again and gave Charlotte a lopsided grin. "While I was there, I happened to learn a few things."

Thinking of her own sheltered childhood, in comparison to Tipper's, made Charlotte feel both gratitude and sadness.

"Where did you grow up, Mrs. Trevarren?" he asked, a little shyly.

She smiled. "In a little town in Washington Territory called Quade's Harbor. My sister and I were wild as monkeys in the jungle until I was thirteen and Millie was ten. Then Papa, who had been a widower for some time, remarried. Lydia—my stepmother—changed all our lives for the better."

Before Tipper could offer a reply, the cook bellowed his name and he had to leave. After a nod of farewell, he sprinted belowdecks to the galley, leaving Charlotte alone again.

She was in a nostalgic mood, having spoken aloud of her home and family, and a sense of deep loneliness bruised her heart. She wished Patrick would appear, but he didn't, not until after dinner, when members of the crew had dropped the anchor and a sizable skiff was being lowered over the side. A rope ladder was flung after it.

112

Patrick dropped a carpetbag into the bobbing dinghy and smiled at his wife.

"I'll go down first," he said.

Charlotte looked over the side and, all of the sudden, began to feel seasick. The fact that she was about to descend a rope ladder in full skirts was the least of her problems.

She swallowed. "I d-don't know if I can . . ."

He seemed to be remembering the episode a decade before, when Charlotte had frozen high above the decks of the *Enchantress* and he'd had to climb up to fetch her. There was no mockery in his manner or his expression.

"I'll be with you the whole time," he promised. Then he swung over the rail and climbed down just far enough to leave space on the ladder for Charlotte to fit within the sheltering circle of his arms.

She clutched her skirts as close to her legs as possible, and Mr. Cochran very politely lifted her over the side.

Patrick's breath was a warm temptation near her ear as he spoke. "Don't look down. We'll be in the skiff before you know it."

Charlotte clung to the rough hemp ladder and simply took one step downward after another, her eyes squeezed tightly shut. Just as Patrick had promised, she soon found herself seated in the small boat, clutching the bench and battling nausea.

Several more crewmen joined them, and then Patrick and the others began rowing toward shore. Charlotte drew a series of deep breaths and reminded herself of all the times she and Millie and Lydia had gone out on the Sound in a rowboat, fishing for cod.

It didn't help much, and Charlotte knew she was green by the time they finally reached the wharves. The dock shifted and swayed under her feet, and she fairly scrambled onto the cream-colored sand covering the bank.

The first stars were popping into view, and a pleasant breeze blew in over the water.

Charlotte began to feel better. Now she would be able to purchase appropriate clothes, and sleep in a room where the floor didn't move. In the morning she would have a fine breakfast of fruit and biscuits, then she'd write another letter to her family and post it immediately.

"Is that the hotel?" she asked, pointing to a gracious white building looming just ahead, at the end of a street paved in brick.

Patrick smiled. "There is no hotel in Costa del Cielo," he replied.

Charlotte could not hide her disappointment. "No hotel?" she echoed.

"There are two taverns with rooms for hire," he told her, his blue eyes sparkling, "but I think you'll be happier staying with my friends, Señor and Señora Querida."

Querida. The name caught in Charlotte's spirit like a fishhook in tender flesh. She recalled the elegant handwriting on the perfumed envelopes she'd found in Patrick's desk. *Pilar,* she thought.

In that moment Charlotte was more ashamed than ever of the purple dress she wore. She yearned to ask about Pilar, but she didn't dare because she wasn't ready to admit that she'd seen the letters.

"I wouldn't want to impose," she said, with all the dignity she could summon. The sailors who had come ashore with them took their leave and headed toward the center of town.

Patrick smiled at Charlotte, giving her gown an amused assessment. "You can't stay at either of the taverns, even though I have to admit you're dressed for it."

Before they had reached the tall iron gates of the Querida compound, a servant appeared, holding a lantern. A beautiful young woman in a glowing white dress stood waiting, the light of the stars and the gas streetlamps flickering in her dark hair.

Seeing Charlotte, the other woman narrowed her brown eyes for a moment. In the next instant, however, she turned all her attention on Patrick, uttering a joyous little cry and hurling herself into his arms.

He set her away from him with a slightly stiff motion.

"Hello, Pilar," he said.

The girl looked at Charlotte again, her eyes widening with disbelief when she saw the purple dress.

Charlotte was thinking of the letters this beautiful young

woman had written to Patrick, and all that might have passed between them. She held her breath, waiting.

"This is my wife, Charlotte," he said.

Pilar's dark eyes flashed. She muttered something in rapid Spanish, turned on one delicate heel, and swept away into the gathering darkness like a ghost.

Patrick didn't seem at all ruffled by his mistress's displeasure. He chatted with the servant in amicable Spanish while the man led the way through a courtyard, past a tall, whispering fountain, and through a set of double doors.

The room beyond was a small suite, dominated by a huge bed with a blue velvet canopy and a white eyelet spread. There was a marble fireplace at one end of the chamber, with a large mirror above the mantel. Behind the gleaming brass andirons on the hearth stood a lush green plant in a ceramic pot.

Charlotte saw herself and Patrick—indeed, the whole of the room—reflected in the looking glass over the fireplace. He stood behind her, this husband she loved so desperately and knew so slightly, and laid gentle hands on her shoulders.

"Look at you," he scolded gently. "You have shadows under your eyes." He began unfastening the buttons at the back of her dress, and Charlotte shivered, partly from anticipation. "Tomorrow will be a busy day, goddess. You need your sleep."

He had already taught her to need something else even more than sleep, but she could not speak so boldly of her desire for him. Her emotions were too near the surface.

"Will you stay with me?" she asked.

Patrick bent his head to kiss her lightly on one temple. "I will be back later," he replied. "Are you hungry?"

Charlotte was still a little seasick, and meeting Pilar Querida had been something of a shock. She shook her head, her gaze linked with that of the man in the mirror. Her pride kept her from begging him to stay until she'd fallen asleep.

He turned her in his arms then and touched her lips with the tip of his forefinger instead of kissing her. "Good night, Mrs. Trevarren," he said.

Charlotte was sure he was going off to make peace with

Pilar, and the knowledge was like poison in her soul. The thought of Patrick charming another woman was nearly unbearable.

"Good night," she said, lifting her chin.

When he was gone, Charlotte found water and soap in a small dressing room adjoining the bedchamber and washed as best she could. Someone had laid a soft cotton nightgown with an embroidered bodice across the foot of the bed and set a tray on one of the bureaus.

Charlotte put on the gown and ignored the food. Drawing back the covers, she tumbled into bed, expecting to lie sleepless as she had the night before, waiting for Patrick. Instead, she tumbled head over heels into a dark well of exhaustion, and when the bright light of morning awakened her, she remembered no dreams.

9

C OCHRAN WAS INDULGING IN THE WATERFRONT TAVERN'S specialty, a particularly potent red wine, spiced and heated, but it was too early for Patrick to take strong drink. Instead, he sipped from a mug of overbrewed tea.

"How bad is the damage to the ship?" Cochran asked, as sympathetically as if he'd asked about the health of a beloved relation.

Patrick let out a raspy sigh, weary to the core of his spirit. He had spent a sleepless night in a room down the hall from Charlotte's suite at the Queridas' home, ensnared in a conflict between his conscience and his desires as a man. He needed a shave, he was still wearing yesterday's clothes, and he was exhausted.

None of these factors did anything to improve his mood.

"I was waiting at the gates when the boatyard opened this morning," he finally replied. "The *Enchantress* will be in dry dock for at least a month."

Cochran cursed under his breath. He enjoyed shore leave, like the other members of the crew, but Patrick knew the first mate was always happier at sea. "I'd say we have a score

117

to settle with those pirates," Cochran said, after a few moments of silence. "Any idea who they were?"

Patrick nodded grimly. "Raheem was leading that crew of bilge rats," he replied. He was certain the notorious outlaw of the Mediterranean had had two goals in mind: to capture Charlotte, whom he surely regarded as his rightful property, and to avenge Patrick's interference in the matter. Even now it chilled the very marrow of his bones to think of Charlotte falling into the bastard's hands.

"Raheem," Cochran reflected, rubbing his stubbly chin. "I've heard of the fellow, but never made his acquaintance. Did you catch a glimpse of him during the fight?"

Patrick shrugged. "I don't know. I was pretty busy, all things considered."

Cochran smiled. "It was quite a scrap, wasn't it?" he said, obviously relishing the memory.

Privately Patrick wondered at his own personal reaction to the incident. He'd always enjoyed a good fight himself, but during Raheem's attack on the *Enchantress*, he'd been so worried about Charlotte's safety that he'd hardly been able to think straight. In fact, he was lucky the distraction hadn't gotten him killed.

"I must be getting old," he confessed. "The whole time it was happening, all I could think about was my wife, and whether she'd done what I told her to do and hidden herself, or if she was wandering around the deck in the midst of it all, looking to get her throat slit."

The other man laughed and raised his mug of spiced wine in a wry salute. "To love," he said.

Patrick glared at him. He thought of Charlotte constantly, and whenever he did, he wanted her with an embarrassing intensity, and he would willingly give his own life to protect her. Still, he couldn't credit the idea of romantic love. That was the province of schoolgirls and comsumptive poets.

"Don't be maudlin," he snapped. "Charlotte and I are playing a game, that's all. When we tire of it, I can set us both free with a few words and a gesture."

Cochran's smile faded. He sighed and pushed back his chair. "If this is a game, Captain," he said seriously, "Mrs.

Trevarren is winning. Have a care that you don't take your feelings for the lady too lightly."

Patrick stood too. Although he was confused by his friend's words, and the attitude behind them, he didn't pursue the subject. He simply tossed a coin onto the table and followed Cochran out into the hot brightness of a Spanish morning.

Ten minutes later, when Cochran had gone to the boatyard to oversee the repairs on the ship, Patrick walked back to the Querida compound. He planned to stretch out on his lonely bed and catch up on some of the sleep he'd lost the night before.

A servant appeared in Charlotte's room almost immediately after she'd awakened, carrying a pretty yellow cotton morning gown. Probably it was a grudging donation from the beautiful Pilar, but Charlotte accepted the offering with grace and gratitude. After all, her alternative was to wear that hateful purple thing Patrick had unearthed for her.

When she had washed and dressed, another maid came to brush and arrange Charlotte's hair. Then she was served a delicious breakfast of flaky pastries, fruit, and coffee in the small courtyard outside her suite.

She ate heartily, and felt restored as she sat sipping her coffee at the end of the meal, enjoying the chatter of birds and the warmth of golden sunshine. Then Patrick strode into the courtyard, looking weary and not a little despondent.

Charlotte's heart constricted when she saw him, even though she had every reason to suspect that their marriage, so real and so sacred to her, was no more than an amusing diversion to him. She did not ask where he'd been, but simply said quietly, "Good morning, Mr. Trevarren."

He came to a reluctant stop next to the white iron table where she sat, folded his arms, and tilted his head to one side. "Hello, Charlotte," he responded gravely. He swept his gaze over her soft, upswept coiffure, her face, her shoulders, left bare by the borrowed dress. "Did you sleep well?"

She smiled serenely. "As soundly as the dead," she replied. "You?"

Patrick scowled down at her, then, with that same diffidence he'd shown before, he dragged back a chair and sat. "Charlotte, I—"

Charlotte never found out what he'd meant to say, for just then Pilar joined them. He stood again, as quickly as he'd taken a seat.

Pilar favored him with a soul-rending smile, her dark eyes shining, her ebony hair bound into a single heavy plait woven through with gardenias of the palest cream shade. As she had been the night before, the girl was dressed entirely in white—this time the fabric of her gown was a gauzy organdy.

The daughter of the house was startlingly beautiful, a Spanish angel, and yet as Pilar and Patrick talked, Charlotte underwent a revelation of sorts. The night before, in the more whimsical light of the moon and stars, Pilar had seemed older. Now, however, in the sun-flooded courtyard, Charlotte could see that she was really a child, no more than fifteen or sixteen, and she was clearly suffering from a colossal crush on Patrick.

Charlotte frowned, ignoring their conversation to refill her coffee cup from a small bone china pot. Patrick had kept Pilar's letters, it was true, but now Charlotte suspected that he meant to return them someday. She could imagine him teasing Pilar good-naturedly, sometime far in the future, of course, about her tender *amor.*

"We'll be here for a month or more," Patrick was saying as Charlotte turned her attention back to the here and now. "You'll need all sorts of clothes, so see that you don't stint when the dressmaker comes to call."

With that, Patrick bent down to kiss Charlotte's cheek, which was instantly aflame at his touch, nodded to a pouting Pilar, and went into the house.

"I do not see why he must be so blind and bull's-headed," Pilar said, in stilted, boarding-school English.

Charlotte smiled, feeling much calmer—not to mention more charitable—now that she realized Pilar was no threat, and gestured toward the chair Patrick had just abandoned. "I think most men are blind and 'bull's-headed,'" she replied.

Pilar sat, with a little flounce of her voluminous skirts, and tears of frustration and youthful heartbreak brimmed in her lovely eyes. "You are from America," she said, and there was a vague accusation in her tone. "Patrick, too, is an American. Is this why he married you?"

Not knowing how to answer, Charlotte simply shrugged.

Pilar dashed away her tears with the heel of one palm, then narrowed her eyes at Charlotte as if to see past some murky veneer to the reality beneath. After that, she gave a theatrical sigh. "I shall never marry," she said tragically.

Charlotte bit her lower lip for a moment, to keep from smiling. She suspected now that Pilar wore white often, because she so wanted to be a bride.

"Nonsense," she replied, when she could control her expression. "You are young and lovely and you obviously come from a very good family. You will fall in love with some devastatingly handsome rake—when you're older of course—and have the grandest wedding Costa del Cielo has ever seen."

"What is this 'rake'? Is it not a tool for digging?"

Charlotte squeezed one of Pilar's hands, touched by the girl's fragile naiveté, and defined the word as best she could.

Pilar gradually warmed toward Charlotte as they talked, though it was easy to see she wouldn't have chosen that course if she could have helped herself.

When the same servant who had brought Charlotte the dress she was wearing reappeared and spoke with Pilar in rapid Spanish, the girl listened, then dismissed the maid.

"Manuella says Mama's dressmaker has arrived. She has brought samples of cloth and many drawings of gowns she can make for you. Come, we are to meet with la señorita in the sun-room."

Charlotte followed Pilar back into the house, through the suite, and along several wide hallways. Soon Charlotte was poring over books full of beautiful, hand-colored illustrations, and she and Pilar were chattering like old friends.

Although Charlotte would have settled for a half dozen sensible day dresses, Patrick had evidently left orders that she was to be outfitted for all contingencies. She selected morning and afternoon gowns, gowns for parties and operas, gowns of silk, with embroidered bodices, for sleeping. Her feet were measured for shoes and dancing slippers, and the dressmaker showed her exquisite lace trims for delicately stitched drawers, camisoles, and petticoats.

Charlotte's family was prosperous, and she'd always had fine clothes. She hadn't realized how much she'd missed all her pretty things. Unlike her younger sister, who had always been something of a ruffian from infancy, Charlotte appreciated fashion. Back in Paris, before she'd gone adventuring, she'd filled drawing tablet after drawing tablet with sketches of lovely French clothes, intending to have some of her favorites made up when she arrived home.

Sadness touched her spirit. Life could be uncertain and perilous, she'd discovered; she might never see her family again. She hurried to her private courtyard, overcome, and stared blindly out at the dancing sea, struggling to regain control of her emotions.

She didn't hear Patrick approaching, didn't realize he was there until he laid his hands on her shoulders.

"What is it?" His tone was gentle, as much a caress as the touch of his hands.

Charlotte turned, looked up into the beloved face—the face she so often wanted to slap. "I was just feeling a little wistful, that's all," she answered.

Patrick took her chin in his hand, passed the pad of one thumb lightly over her lips, as he sometimes did as a prelude to kissing her. "Then we'd better try to lift your spirits," he said. His voice found its way inside Charlotte, resonated there, like a note played on some inner harp.

Her heartbeat quickened, a flush rose in her cheeks, and both occurrences made her feel silly. Even as her pride rebelled, however, her all-too-human body yearned to make the sweet, silent music Patrick alone could bring forth.

He chuckled at her expression, bent to kiss her lightly on the nose. "What you need, Mrs. Trevarren," he said, "is a diversion. An elegant party, I think, with lots of dancing and laughter and food."

Charlotte swallowed. She loved parties, but she'd had another kind of celebration in mind. She looked up at Patrick uncertainly, caught in the age-old dilemma of whether to speak forthrightly of her feelings or keep them to herself.

Again Patrick caressed her mouth with his thumb. "What?" he prompted quietly.

Frankness won the hour, being so integral a part of Charlotte's nature. "You didn't come to our bed last night," she said, faltering but determined.

He grinned. "Did you miss me?"

Charlotte wanted so to say she hadn't, but it was a lie she couldn't manage. She skirted the question, countering with one of her own. "Do you have a mistress in Costa del Cielo?"

Patrick arched one dark eyebrow. "Only a wife," he replied. His expression was very serious, although Charlotte thought she saw merriment lurking far back in the depths of his eyes. "As unconventional as our wedding was, my dear, I'm afraid we *are* married."

She met his gaze directly, bravely, hoping he could not see how crucial the whole matter was to her. "You could end it just by clapping your hands together three times and repeating, 'I divorce you,'" she reminded him.

"Is that what you want?"

Charlotte looked away for a moment, found her courage. "No. But it seems to me, Mr. Trevarren," she said, "that all the advantages of this union are on your side. I have no assurance that you won't take up with another woman, or sail away and leave me on some wharf—"

"Those things could happen even if we'd been married in a church in Quade's Harbor, with all your family looking on," Patrick pointed out reasonably. "Besides, it isn't only husbands who stray, Charlotte. You could leave as easily as I could."

She opened her mouth, realized she didn't have a sensible response prepared, and closed it again.

Patrick laughed and bent his head to give her a tantalizing kiss. "I will be very busy, tomorrow and the next day and for a lot of days after that," he told her, while she was struggling to catch her breath again, "but I won't neglect my duties as a husband."

Charlotte was at once elated and embarrassed. "Until this

123

morning, when I saw her clearly in the light of day," she confessed, "I thought Pilar was your mistress."

Her husband uttered a long-suffering sigh. "Pilar is a child," he said.

"She's old enough to send perfumed love letters," Charlotte argued.

Patrick was obviously trying to look stern, but the laughter in his eyes gave him away. "You've been going through my desk," he accused.

She bristled. "It was an accident," she said.

"Umm," Patrick said thoughtfully, frowning as he considered. His hands rested low on the small of Charlotte's back, pressing her close with graceful insistence. "Did you read the letters?"

Charlotte's face warmed. "No."

"Because they're written in Spanish?"

She was deliciously aware of Patrick's proximity, of the scent and power and sheer substance not only of his body, but of his spirit as well. "I didn't need to read them," she faltered, and although she'd intended to sound defiant, her words seemed petulant instead. "The perfume told me quite enough."

Idly Patrick lifted one hand to cup her breast. "Pilar is convinced she adores me," he said. "At some point, she'll come to her senses and I'll give the letters back to her."

A web of delicious sensation, centered in the plump breast Patrick was caressing, unfolded into every part of Charlotte's being. It was a struggle to keep her mind on the subject of their conversation. "You could simply destroy the letters, couldn't you?"

Patrick shook his head, sighed, and deftly drew down the neckline of her borrowed gown, as well as the muslin camisole beneath, baring her. "No," he answered. "She would always wonder if I had really destroyed them, or if they would turn up later to embarrass her. A lady shouldn't have to worry about things like that."

Charlotte trembled as his thumb moved across her nipple, lightly shaping and preparing it. Her reason was fleeing rapidly, but she clung to a few remnants. "In that case— why not give them back now?"

He sighed again, focused his attention on the breast he was clearly hungry for. "That would be unkind," he answered, his voice slow, sleepy-sounding. "Pilar's adoration is harmless, after all. She'll grow out of it sooner or later."

Charlotte was in an anguish of wanting, although the courtyard certainly wasn't the proper place for the playful intimacies of a husband and wife. She let her head fall back in helpless surrender, moaned when Patrick leaned down to take her nipple between his lips.

He took his nourishment freely, with no apparent concern that they might be interrupted, then put Charlotte's camisole and bodice back in place and gave her well-attended breast a fond little pat.

Charlotte's need had risen to a fever pitch. "Patrick—" she pleaded, hating her weakness and his strength, stunned once again to know how easily he could stir a violent tempest within her. A storm only he had the power to still.

He touched his fingers to her lips. "I'll be back tonight," he said, and then he left her, striding across the courtyard, disappearing through a gate.

Charlotte sat down on a stone bench, unable to stand because of the riot of emotions besetting her. She loved Patrick, she hated him. She wanted to obey him, and to rebel against him.

When she'd recovered somewhat, a process that took considerable time, she took a pen, a bottle of ink, and some stationery from the desk in her room. Then she sat down at the table in the courtyard again, and wrote a second long letter to her family.

Rashad had insisted that he'd mailed the first missive, composed while she was still a member of Khalif's harem, but Charlotte was taking no chances. Her loved ones were probably frantic with worry as it was.

She spent the afternoon laboring over her letter, only nibbling at the midday meal of fruit and cheese and dark bread a servant brought. During the hottest part of the day, while most citizens of Costa del Cielo enjoyed a leisurely siesta, Charlotte wrote pages, crumpled them, and composed others. It was important to make her father and Lydia understand that she loved Patrick and truly wanted to be with him, despite their strange courtship.

Charlotte had fibbed in the first letter, for she'd been a captive then, without hope of escape, wanting to protect her loved ones from the pain the truth would have caused. Now, excluding only the most intimate details of her relationship with Patrick, she recounted the adventure incident for incident. In the end, she had such a thick sheaf of pages that her writings would have to be sent in a packet instead of an envelope.

That night, wearing yet another borrowed dress, this one cream-colored, with touches of antique lace decorating the bodice and cuffs, Charlotte dined with the Querida family. It was a pleasant meal, although conversation was awkward, due to the differences in language. And there was no sign of Patrick.

After the meal, there was music in what would have been the drawing room in England, or the parlor in America. Señora Querida played the harpsichord, while the señor offered a hand to his daughter, with teasing formality, and drew her into a dance.

Charlotte watched in delight, but there was a bittersweet ache in the center of her heart. Often, while Lydia played piano, Millie and Charlotte had taken turns dancing with their father in much the same way. Again, still, she missed her dear ones with a painful poignancy.

Just when she would have made a polite excuse and fled to her room, Patrick appeared. He had exchanged his usual garb of trousers, high boots, and a flowing shirt for a finely fitted evening suit, complete with a gray-and-charcoal-striped ascot and a stickpin.

Charlotte had thought she'd grown used to his magnificence, for he was heart-stoppingly handsome even under ordinary conditions. On that magical night, however, the pirate was posing as a prince. When he took Charlotte in his arms and began to whirl her gracefully around the room, in time with Mrs. Querida's sprightly assault on the harpsichord, she forgot everything that had troubled her before.

During that single dance, it was as though Charlotte's soul and Patrick's touched and then fused into one. Not a word

126

was said, and all the dictates of propriety were observed, and yet the experience was somehow more profound than their most intense lovemaking had been.

Charlotte realized, with glorious despair, that her heart had gone to this man for sanction, to remain with him not only throughout their mortal lives, but throughout eternity as well.

If Patrick had felt this fundamental shift in the course of things, he gave no sign of it. He danced with Charlotte twice more, and then with Pilar, who was obviously charmed. The señora beamed from her bench at the harpsichord, while her husband leaned against the mantel over the marble fireplace, watching fondly.

Not even a whisper of envy moved against Charlotte's heart, but she was overwhelmed by her emotions, and she needed time and solitude to sort them out. She'd been so certain, before that night, that it wasn't possible to love Patrick more than she already did. Now she was reeling from the sudden expansion of her sentiment; the vast ocean had, without warning, taken on the dimensions of a universe.

She slipped out of the richly furnished drawing room, hoping to go unnoticed, and hurried along the corridors to the suite.

There, in the wash of moonlight flowing in through the windows, she paced, full of reckless, elemental energy. She could not accommodate these new feelings, she fretted silently, wrapping her arms tightly around herself. In those treacherous moments, Charlotte feared her very soul would burst.

"Charlotte."

She whirled, saw Patrick standing in the doorway of the suite, cloaked in shadows. She couldn't read his face, because of the darkness, but she heard concern in his voice, and quiet understanding.

She began to cry, and snuffled out, "What's happening to me?"

Patrick lifted her easily into his arms. "I couldn't tell you, goddess," he confessed, in a raspy whisper. "I'm feeling pretty dazed myself." He kissed her, and Charlotte felt the universe begin to unfold again, doubling and redoubling at a dizzying speed. He broke away finally, and carried her to the bed, and Charlotte couldn't separate his trembling from her own. "I want you so much," he said, taking down her hair with awkward fingers, "that I'm afraid of what will happen when I have you."

She peeled away his tailored coat, pulled the stickpin from his ascot, clawed at his shirt buttons. Just as frantic, Patrick stripped her to the skin, in a matter of moments. There were no sweet preliminaries that night, no tentative caresses, for their yearning for each other had melded into a single, primitive desire, as unstoppable as an earthquake.

Patrick laid Charlotte on the bed and thrust himself into her, and she welcomed him with a passion older than the stars.

Their loving had been like some kind of joyful battle that night, Patrick thought as he lay staring up at the ceiling, a sleeping Charlotte curled against his side. From their first encounter, she had been like a spirited jungle cat, responding with ferocious abandon to the things he taught her. Still, something new had happened between them tonight, even before they had tumbled into bed. While they were dancing, so innocently and circumspectly, something within him, long disjointed, had been wrenched back into place.

Patrick was glad of the darkness and Charlotte's deep slumber, because suddenly there were tears in his eyes, tears of the most profound, poetic wonder. After the wonder came fear of the purest sort, for he loved this woman—for the moment, at least, he couldn't deny that—and by loving her, he had opened himself up not only to happiness, but to incomprehensible pain.

Even as he drew Charlotte closer, her body warm and supple against his, he wished he'd never seen her, wished she'd never left Quade's Harbor, never ventured into the marketplace and gotten herself kidnapped. His old life had been a lonely one in some ways, but he hadn't been unhappy. Despite his many and varied adventures, during which his body had been in indisputable danger, his soul was always safe.

No more, he thought grimly. If he lost Charlotte, whether to death or indifference or the love of another, he would never be whole again. He would have to live out his days with a crippled and twisted spirit.

She stirred beside him, this woman who was both his rescuing angel and his conqueror, and spread her fingers over his bare belly. Patrick moaned when those same fingers clasped his manhood and brought it to instant and rather painful attention.

"Come here," she purred sleepily. "I'm not through with you."

Helpless to resist, Patrick rolled onto her, resting the weight of his upper body on his forearms, and positioned himself between her warm thighs. "You might show me a little mercy," he pointed out, only half in jest.

"Not tonight," Charlotte teased, lifting her hips and taking him inside her easily, drawing him deep. "Perhaps, if you're very good, I'll let you sleep tomorrow."

Ever since he'd had his first woman, at the age of thirteen, Patrick had always done the taking. Now, incredibly, he was *being taken,* and he couldn't begin to comprehend the emotions the fact stirred in him. He moved in rhythm with Charlotte, following her lead, unable to stop himself. The response was instinctive, the needs behind it as unfathomable as the sea itself.

She crooned senseless words of encouragement, and he was frantic to obey her. When she bucked beneath him, then stiffened and cried out in triumph, Patrick misplaced his soul. He flexed wildly against her, reaching deep, and the walls of her feminine channel clenched around his shaft.

He cried out as he spilled his seed, the pleasure almost beyond bearing, and Charlotte spread her hands over the taut muscles of his buttocks, urging him, comforting him, commanding him. Finally she allowed him to collapse—he no longer had a will of his own, he knew—but as soon as his breathing had evened out, she wanted him again.

She got a basin of water and a cloth from somewhere and slowly, gently washed him. "Sit up," she said, and somehow he obeyed her, even though he had no strength.

"Charlotte," he pleaded raggedly, tilting his head back,

knowing he could not escape. Nor could he rebel, because as she kissed and fondled him, he grew hard again, his staff resting against his belly like an oak.

"Hush," she scolded, and then she took him into her mouth and began to work him over so thoroughly that before a minute had passed, he was out of his mind.

10

PATRICK HAUNTED THE BOATYARD FOR THE NEXT TWO WEEKS, overseeing every aspect of the repairs to the *Enchantress*. Before Charlotte, the matter would have consumed his every waking thought, as well as commanding his physical presence; now his mind strayed often to the energetic little temptress he'd married in Riz.

Charlotte, he reflected, not once but a thousand times, was part lady of the manor and part lioness. Every day new gowns arrived from the dressmakers' shops, and Charlotte was as cool and regal as a duchess as she modeled them for him. When Patrick joined her in their bed at night, always at a late hour, she showed him the wild side of her nature, giving and taking pleasure with the same degree of ferocious passion.

Standing at the stern of the *Enchantress,* Patrick stared at the sun-spangled waters of the blue-green sea and wondered if tender feelings were turning him into a nervous old woman. Things were going too damn well, by his reckoning, and he was profoundly uneasy, as well as restless.

Experience had taught him to expect challenges, *especially* when life seemed to settle into a pleasant routine.

A stir of voices and a clatter on the dry dock made him turn, and there was Charlotte, stepping down from one of the Queridas' coaches, a pink and white striped parasol shading her from the bright glare of the sun. Her dress, full-sleeved and trimmed with lace, was rose-colored, a splash of femininity in starkly masculine surroundings.

Charlotte spotted Patrick, waved cheerfully, and proceeded along the plank-way and onto the main deck. He was not entirely pleased, for the wharves and the boatyard were rough places, yet he couldn't help being glad to see his wife.

He greeted her with a frown, however, and a brisk "What are you doing here?"

"I came to see how the work on the ship was progressing," she replied, and by the way she lifted her chin and stood her ground, Patrick knew Charlotte was undaunted. As usual.

She gave the parasol a little twirl and treated Patrick to a smile that took the starch out of his knees. "Spain is lovely," she went on sweetly, "and the hospitality of the Querida family cannot be faulted. However, I believe I've been infected with your wanderlust, Mr. Trevarren. I find that I'm eager to travel on from here, and see what lies over the horizon."

Patrick was in a misery of lust, even though Charlotte had not done anything overt to tempt him. He wondered if the workmen and his crew would notice if he spirited her off to his cabin for an hour or so, then dismissed the idea. If he didn't watch himself, his reputation as a scoundrel would be ruined, and word would spread throughout the seven seas that Patrick Trevarren had become a *husband*.

"I've told you not to come here," he scolded, taking Charlotte's arm and hustling her to the railing. "The waterfront is no place for a decent woman!"

She looked up at him and batted her eyelashes in a way that could only be described as insubordinate. "What is there to fear," she drawled, "when I have *you* to look after me, Captain Trevarren?"

He wanted to shake her. "After being kidnapped in the marketplace and ending up in a harem," he whispered furiously, "I'm amazed you can ask a question like that!"

"You can't protect me?" Charlotte simpered, still baiting

him. Her otherwise guileless golden eyes were filled with laughter. "Mercy, Patrick, are you confessing to a *weakness?*"

Patrick clamped his jaw down tight for a moment. He had but one frailty—his fascination with this woman. He glared at her, offering no reply to her question, knowing she didn't really expect one.

She smiled, enjoying her minor victory, and opened her beaded handbag. "As it happens, I do have legitimate business. This message was delivered this morning." She extended an envelope of heavy, cream-colored vellum.

A premonition swelled in the pit of Patrick's stomach as he took the envelope. The front bore only his name— anyone in Costa del Cielo would have known where he was staying. On the back, however, was Khalif's distinctive seal, pressed in green wax.

He broke the seal, took out a single sheet of paper. The message was written in a plainly feminine hand, in perfect English. *Ahmed has taken the palace by treachery and imprisoned Khalif. He will kill the true sultan, and his heirs, and we have no means to fight him, as Khalif's own men are away on a desert campaign. Please come quickly, if you truly are his friend.*

Patrick read the letter a second time, crumpled it in his hand. Despite the differences between their two cultures, Khalif and Patrick were closer than most brothers, and he could not ignore such a summons, even though it might well be a trick of some sort.

"Cochran!" he yelled, startling Charlotte so badly that she flinched.

"What is it?" she asked, taking the wrinkled page from his hand and smoothing it on the polished oak railing. "Oh, no," she breathed, when she'd read the message.

The first mate appeared instantly, more excited than alarmed. "Yes, sir?" His tone was eager.

"Get me a ship!" Patrick ordered. "Round up all our own men and any others you can find. We're going back to Riz!"

Cochran had the good grace to look puzzled. "Where will we get a ship, sir?" he reasoned.

Patrick snatched the letter out of Charlotte's hand and

133

thrust it at Cochran. "Damn it, I don't care if you have to shanghai a fishing scow—just do as I told you!" He turned his attention back to his wife now, and firmly linked her arm with his own. "You will go back to the Querida compound," he told her, "and you will stay there until I come to get you."

Charlotte blinked, then stubborn color rose in her cheeks. "I want to go with you!" she protested.

He ushered her toward the boarding ramp. "At the moment, Mrs. Trevarren," he replied, "your preferences are the least of my concerns. This time, if you value your lovely hide, *you will obey me!"*

She began to sputter, but Patrick propelled her over the ramp and then thrust her into the waiting carriage. When he slammed the door shut and barked an order at the driver, in impatient Spanish, Charlotte put her head out the window and called furiously, "I won't forget this, Captain Trevarren!"

Patrick might have laughed if he hadn't been so worried about Khalif. Ahmed, the sultan's half brother, was ruthless, and his taste for power was no secret. There was every chance that Khalif was already dead, and his execution would have been a brutal one, not necessarily swift. Worse, the princes, Khalif's young sons, all too young to leave their mothers, would be murdered too, just as the letter writer had said.

The crew of the *Enchantress* rallied within minutes, and listened in eager fury as Patrick related his plans.

They would not approach the palace by sea, because Ahmed and his band of thieving rebels would be expecting that, and any approaching ship would surely be sunk by cannon fire before shore could be gained. After they'd crossed to the island kingdom of Riz, and made port in the city of the same name, they would buy horses and other provisions in the marketplace and attack Ahmed from the desert side.

The outcome would, of course, be in the hands of God.

Reaching the guest suite in the Querida mansion, Charlotte flung her pink and white parasol across the room in a

134

fury. She was not given to tantrums as a general rule, but in this case she could not be gracious. Patrick was her husband, and her place was by his side, no matter where he might go.

Now he was off to Riz, imperious as some Greek hero, bent on rescuing his friend, and he planned to leave her right there in dull Costa del Cielo for the duration. As far as Charlotte was concerned, there was only one thing worse than being in mortal danger, and that was for *Patrick* to be in mortal danger without her! Suppose he got himself killed, and she never saw him again?

Charlotte bit down hard on her lower lip and paced faster. Patrick hadn't listened when she'd practically begged him not to leave her in Khalif's harem, and he had grown no more tractable since. There was absolutely no sense in trying to reason with her hardheaded mate, even if she did encounter him before he left on his crusade, which was unlikely.

Her thoughts took a wild turn. She'd read about a woman once who had dressed up in men's clothes and gone off to fight in the American Civil War, just to be near her husband. Perhaps she could disguise herself, and stow away on whatever ship Patrick had managed to purloin for the journey . . .

"No," she said aloud, with a sigh. No one would be fooled by such a gambit, for there was nothing boyish about Charlotte's figure. Following her abduction from the *souk*, when she'd been delivered to Patrick with only a burlap sack to provide cover, she'd worn one of his shirts and a pair of his trousers. She'd simply looked like exactly what she was—a woman wearing a man's clothes.

For all of that, Charlotte had no intention of giving up and staying meekly behind while Patrick sailed grandly into the sunset. She had friends in Khalif's palace, too—Alev and Rashad. And there were Alev's little sons to think about, and the other princes who stood between Ahmed and the throne of Riz.

Deliberately Charlotte calmed herself. She sat on the edge of the bed she'd shared so happily with Patrick and tried to think. Only a single idea came to her, though she racked her

135

brain, and it was a desperate one, hardly better than stowing away. Still, since it was the only plan she'd been able to come up with, Charlotte decided to follow through.

She waited until the household had settled down for siesta, then sneaked out, carrying a pouch of gold coins Patrick had given her one day, for incidentals. The sun was mercilessly hot as she walked down dusty, stone-paved streets toward the waterfront.

There were plenty of boats moored in the harbor; surely she would be able to hire someone to take her across the water to Riz.

Charlotte paused outside the first in a row of shoddy-looking taverns, working up her courage. She hadn't thought to bring her parasol, and the skin on her nose was starting to tickle with the beginnings of a sunburn.

She was just about to climb three stone steps and enter the place when a barmaid came out and hurled a bucket of slops into the street, barely missing Charlotte's pretty skirts. "You might look where you're throwing things!" she protested.

To her amazement, the barmaid replied in English. "I might," the dark-haired woman said pertly, "and then again, I might not."

Charlotte placed her hands on her hips and stared at the woman resolutely, but her tone was moderate when she spoke again. After all, she was there seeking a favor. "I need passage to Riz," she announced, "and I can pay. Is there anyone in this . . . establishment who can take me across?"

The servant turned, addressed the interior of the tavern in strident Spanish. Her words brought seedy-looking sailors of all sizes, shapes, and nationalities to leer at Charlotte from the filthy windows and crowd the doorway.

"You choosy about the sort of people you sail with?"

Charlotte swallowed. "Well, I wouldn't want a criminal," she replied.

The raggedly dressed woman shrugged. "Then there's nobody here—or anywhere on the waterfront, probably—who can help you." She started to close the door, though the grizzled faces remained at the windows.

"Wait!" Charlotte cried. She couldn't bear the thought of staying in Spain, watching and waiting, full of fear that

Patrick might never return. "I'll hire anyone who's never raped or committed murder."

The barmaid translated, and subsequently the crowd thinned. There were murmurs. One man stepped forward, however.

Charlotte retreated a step herself, and tried to smile. "Hello," she said, as cheerfully as she could.

"Hello," the sailor answered, smirking a little, and Charlotte recognized his accent as American. He was of medium height and indeterminate age, with a wiry build and short brown hair that bristled around his head like the quills of a porcupine. "What business do you have in Riz, miss?" he asked.

Charlotte was scared, but she was also eager to be on her way. After all, the sooner she set out, the sooner she would be able to catch up with Patrick. "It's quite personal," she said. "All you need to know is that I want to go there and that I can pay for my passage. What is your name, please?"

He looked surprised—evidently he had assumed he was the one in control of the situation. Charlotte would waste no time in disabusing him of that notion. "Mabrey. Jack Mabrey."

"My name is Mrs. Patrick Trevarren," Charlotte replied, with a cordial smile. She enjoyed watching the color drain from Mabrey's pockmarked face. "You may call me Mrs. Trevarren, if you have cause to address me, though I imagine you'll be too busy steering your ship to chat."

The feral gleam had faded from Mabrey's small eyes, and his throat worked visibly. "Why are you tryin' to hire a boat, if you've got a rich sea captain for a husband?"

Charlotte sighed philosophically, and her collected manner was pure sham. "His ship, the *Enchantress,* is in dry dock for repairs. I'm sure he's already commandeered a craft—no doubt he wasn't nearly as polite about it as I—and sailed without me."

Mabrey rubbed his chin, which was as bristly as the top of his head. "How much?"

Charlotte brought out two gold pieces, held them up for the seaman's perusal. "I'll pay half when you agree to take me across, and half when we arrive," she said. She had other money in the pouch, but she expected she might need that in Riz, particularly if it took her a while to locate Patrick.

"You leavin' your man or somethin'?" Mabrey persisted, though he quivered visibly with the yen to reach out and snatch away the first coin. "I don't want no trouble with the likes of Trevarren, not even if the job brings in a month's drinkin' money."

"He'll never know who brought me across, I promise you." Charlotte assessed the man again; he wasn't at all presentable, and under ordinary circumstances, she wouldn't have crossed the street with him, let alone a body of water. "Let me warn you, however, that if your behavior toward me is at all questionable, before, during, or after the journey, the captain will learn of it. And he will not rest, I assure you, until you've paid for the error in blood."

Mabrey wet his lips with his tongue, hesitated a moment, then nodded. "He'll not find cause to come after me," he said, and Charlotte felt she had no choice but to believe him.

"Where is your vessel?" she asked, shading her eyes from the sun as she turned to gaze at the fleet of disreputable scows and fishing boats in the harbor.

Mr. Mabrey led the way down to the shore and pointed out the worst-looking craft of them all. The boat was barely bigger than the dinghy she and Millie had used for fishing on the pond back home, when they were little girls. It listed to the starboard side, and even from that distance, Charlotte could see that its timbers were rotting.

She almost backed out, so intimidated was she by the thought of passing through shark-filled waters aboard such a pitiful affair, but at that moment she spotted a clipper moving toward the horizon. It was a smaller ship than the *Enchantress,* sleek and fast, and somehow Charlotte knew Patrick was at its wheel. She had to act immediately, and with boldness; if she did not, she might well spend the remainder of her life wishing she'd followed her husband.

"Quickly!" she cried, tugging at Mabrey's filthy sleeve.

Mabrey summoned one of his drinking companions to row them out to his boat in a dinghy. Charlotte hesitated again when she saw the vessel at close range, then set her teeth and climbed up the rope ladder behind Mabrey, careful to keep her skirts close around her legs for modesty's sake.

The boat smelled even worse than it looked, and the single mast creaked ominously as Mabrey set the sail, but by that time there was no going back. Charlotte gave the man one gold coin, as agreed, and stood in the bow, trying to keep the clipper in view as they lumbered awkwardly in its wake.

All too soon, the fleet vessel disappeared, however, and Charlotte's courage faltered a little. Suppose she failed to catch up with Patrick in time? Even worse, what if she *did,* and he was furious, and he sent her back to Spain, or locked her up in the house of some friend in Riz?

The farther they traveled from shore, the rougher the water became. Charlotte's stomach shivered as the boat pitched and rolled upon the waves, and she feared she would retch. After a while, however, she settled into a sort of rhythm, and her midday meal stayed down.

It was full dark by the time they completed the crossing, but Charlotte figured that was a good thing. She would need to buy shawls to cover her arms, head, and face if she didn't want to be arrested for indecent exposure.

Since the tide was in, Mabrey was able to moor the craft at the wharf, and there was no need to row ashore. Charlotte hid behind some barrels and crates while her unlikely protector went off in search of the garments she needed to move about in an Islamic society.

The marketplace was nearby, and like the waterfront, it was lit by torches. While she waited for Mabrey to return with her veils, she craned her neck and squinted, looking for the fast clipper that had brought Patrick across. She couldn't make out the ship, but at the sound of a familiar voice, she turned her attention back toward the *souk* and there was Captain Trevarren himself, arguing loudly with a horse merchant.

Charlotte wanted to call out to him, but she didn't. She wondered now which fate would be more dangerous— traipsing around Riz without the required covering or facing Patrick.

She was still in the throes of indecision when Mabrey came back, bearing two tattered, moth-eaten shawls made of mud-colored cloth. Charlotte hastily draped herself, gave the old sailor the other gold coin, as agreed, along with the price of the wraps, and hurried toward the horse merchant's tent.

There was a corral beside it, filled with horses of broadly varying quality. Evidently a bargain had been struck, for Patrick was paying the merchant, and his crewmen were bridling the animals and mounting them.

Charlotte came to what she hoped was a modest and unassuming stop at Patrick's right elbow, keeping everything but her eyes veiled. Still, she knew she must have been conspicuous in that pink dress.

"Captain Trevarren?" she said, hoping the effort at politeness would work in her favor.

Patrick froze—for a moment, even the noisy *souk* seemed silent as the remotest desert—then slowly turned his head to look at her. His blue eyes looked black as night, she thought, and not just because of the darkness.

"Charlotte?" he rasped, after a long, shocked interval.

She nodded. "I'm afraid so," she said, in a quiet but bright voice.

He muttered a string of colorful words, took her arm, and shuffled her into the shadow of the horse merchant's tent. "How dare you disobey me like this?" he demanded, in a terrifying whisper. "Are you completely fearless, or just plain crazy?"

Charlotte swallowed. "There's no need to be rude," she pointed out, assembling her dignity. "I'm not a person who sits and waits, Patrick. I'm a person who goes out and does things."

"I can see that," he snapped, and then he swore again.

Charlotte figured she might as well press on toward the mark. "Furthermore, if you try to send me back or leave me behind again, I will simply find another way to follow you."

"I ought to turn you over my knee!" Patrick growled, giving her a shake.

She smiled, sensing that she'd won. "But you won't," she replied reasonably. "If you were the sort to strike a woman, even on the . . . bottom, you would surely have done it by now."

His nose was almost touching hers, and his eyes glittered with torchlight and fury. "Don't be too sure of that, Mrs. Trevarren," he told her. "If I weren't in a hurry, I'd take down those ruffly drawers of yours and give you a blistering you'd never forget!"

Evidently Patrick had finished his lecture, for the time being at least. He dragged her back toward the paddock without requiring an answer to his remarks, and Charlotte didn't have a reply ready anyway.

An Arabian stallion had been saddled for him, and he hoisted Charlotte onto the animal's back without ceremony, then swung up behind her.

"Give me trouble, Mrs. Trevarren," he challenged, through his teeth, "and I'll make good on my threat. Here and now, in front of God and everybody else!"

Charlotte believed him. Besides, she'd used up her allotment of bravado for the day, just hiring Mr. Mabrey and crossing to Riz in his leaky, stinking boat. She sat still and kept her mouth shut, and even though there was no telling what perils she might be facing, her spirit soared with joy.

Whatever happened, she would participate, and that was so much better than waiting in some dull, safe place to hear a secondhand account. Charlotte leaned back against Patrick's chest, absorbed the strength of the arms that encircled her, and slept.

When she awakened, it was near dawn, and the party was far out in the star-washed desert. Arabs, probably guides Patrick had hired, were setting up tents in the white sand, while the other riders drank from flasks and speculated on the difficulty of taking the palace back from Ahmed.

Patrick lifted her down from the stallion, and even though he wasn't rough with her, there was no tenderness in the motion, either. Without speaking, he propelled her toward one of the tents.

Skins had been laid out on the floor of the tent, soft and smooth as kid, and Charlotte stretched out to sleep again, exhausted. Still, on some level she was aware of the war council being held outside.

As the night turned to dawn, the air grew hotter. Charlotte squirmed fitfully out of her clothes.

"Here," Patrick's voice said, with grudging gentleness. "Have some water."

She was barely conscious, but her thirst was as real as her weariness, so she sat up and sipped slowly from the canteen he held to her mouth. The heat was intense, even in the shadowy shelter of the tent, and Charlotte saw that Patrick had taken his clothes off, too.

He stroked damp tendrils of hair back from her forehead when she sank to the skins again. "What am I going to do with you?" he asked, in a hoarse whisper. "You're completely incorrigible."

Charlotte sighed, squirmed to make herself more comfortable. Her camisole was wet with perspiration, and felt sticky against her bosom. "I won't be left behind," she said sleepily. "Let that be a lesson to you."

Patrick chuckled, and something in the sound made Charlotte open her eyes and look at his face. He was lying on his side, his head propped on one hand. "I give the orders in this family," he replied, untying the ribbons at the front of her camisole and idly peeling the cloth away from her breasts. "And if anybody's going to learn a lesson, Mrs. Trevarren, it's you."

All of Charlotte's muscles ached from being on horseback most of the night, and she couldn't remember a time when she'd been more tired. Even so, when Patrick leaned down to touch one of her nipples with his tongue, she was instantly ready for him.

"And you called *me* incorrigible," she gasped.

Patrick took his time answering. He enjoyed her breast for a good long interval, then gently parted her legs and aligned himself between them.

Charlotte whimpered, raising her hips, wanting him inside her. They could save the preliminaries for another day.

He chuckled and moved to her other nipple, drank stubbornly from it, ignoring her low, frantic urgings. Finally, finally, he slanted his mouth over hers and kissed her deeply, swallowing her cry of welcoming passion as he lunged inside her.

It seemed to Charlotte that all the heat of the desert had

142

gathered in her body. Every stroke of Patrick's hips drove her closer to madness, and she pitched violently beneath him. They came together, their tongues battling, not daring to break the kiss until the last moan of pleasure had been sounded.

When it was over, Charlotte cried *because* it was over, because it had been so beautiful, because she loved Patrick so much. He kissed her eyelids until she quieted, and then they both slept.

At sunset, Patrick awakened Charlotte. They ate a meal of nuts and pitted dates, accompanied with small amounts of water, and then they made love again.

Charlotte was weak-kneed and a little dazed as she dressed for another night of hard riding, but Patrick seemed to have energy to spare. He whistled as he helped break camp, and Cochran and the other members of his crew teased him in low voices.

While Charlotte blushed to imagine what they were saying, Patrick laughed at their jokes.

All too soon they were traveling again, and the muscles in Charlotte's thighs throbbed in protest as the stallion galloped tirelessly over the sand. She would have died before complaining, though. Patrick would surely gloat and say he'd been right to leave her behind if she grumbled at all.

The hours passed with the leisure of decades, it seemed to Charlotte, and when they reached an oasis and stopped, she wanted to sob with joyous relief. Instead, she found a small pail and filled it with water from the spring, which was fringed with palm trees and lush grass. Keeping her shoulders as square and straight as she could, she waited until the tents had been set up, then went inside the one she and Patrick had shared the day before.

She was naked, having just bathed herself, when Patrick tossed the tent flap aside and came in. His gaze was arrogant as he looked at her, but his words were humble.

"You are so remarkably beautiful," he marveled, in a broken whisper.

Charlotte did not try to hide herself; she stood before Patrick, feeling as pure as Eve before the fall from grace. In those moments, she could believe that they were the only two people on earth, and that the oasis was the fabled Garden.

She went to him, opened his shirt, kissed the hard, salty flesh beneath.

Patrick drew in a sharp breath, gripped her shoulders as if to push her away, then entangled his fingers in her hair and held her close instead. "I haven't forgotten that you disobeyed my orders," he warned breathlessly as she continued to taste him. "If we get through this without being killed, I might well murder you myself."

Charlotte touched his nipple with her tongue, smiled when he groaned in response. "I'll remember that," she whispered, trying to sound properly chastised.

11

O N THE THIRD NIGHT, AFTER THE TENTS HAD BEEN ERECTED, one of the Arab scouts rode out of camp. Returning within the hour, his expression excited and grim, he told Patrick that Khalif's palace was nearby.

Patrick's crewmen were heavily armed, and it was plain to Charlotte that they were spoiling for a fight. As for Patrick himself, well, he just looked resolute.

"Since I would only be wasting my breath if I told you to stay behind," he told Charlotte, his features chiseled and hard in the cold light of the stars and moon, "you will ride with me. But be warned, Mrs. Trevarren—if you undermine my authority over these men by disobeying me, you will be punished. That, my beloved, is a solemn vow."

Charlotte shivered, well aware that Patrick was serious, that his tender regard for her would not stop him from disciplining her if she interfered with his plans. She was frightened of the upcoming battle with Ahmed, being no fool. At the same time, however, Charlotte could barely stand still, so great was her anticipation of an adventure.

It was like living out one of the splendid, romantic fancies she'd indulged in as a child, far away in Quade's Harbor.

"I promise to be a good soldier," she told Patrick. She looked around at the men, who were ready to ride and armed to the teeth. "Don't I get my own gun or a sword or something?"

The question brought a low ripple of laughter from the riders, but Patrick only rolled his eyes and mounted his horse. After regarding Charlotte for a long moment, his expression unreadable, he reached down and hauled her up behind him.

It was plain she wasn't going to have a weapon; she would simply have to depend on her wits. She did wish, however, that she could trade her torn, dirty pink dress for a pair of trousers and a shirt.

The party was made up of around two dozen men, but Patrick, Charlotte, and the two scouts rode ahead, their horses moving almost soundlessly over the ancient sands. Finally they saw the palace, glowing like alabaster against the dark sea.

Charlotte tugged at Patrick's sleeve to get his attention, then whispered, "If you'll give me a boost, I can climb over the courtyard wall, outside the *hamam,* and let you in through the south entrance."

Patrick turned in the saddle to look back at her, and she could see by his bearing that he wanted to reject the idea, that he was searching his mind for a reason to do just that.

"Do you have a better strategy?" Charlotte demanded, annoyed. "The main entrances will be locked and guarded, and if you storm the gates, you'll pay a heavy price for the folly!"

He scowled at her for a long moment, then said, "I'll climb the courtyard wall myself—"

Charlotte sighed with frustration. "And stride right through the harem? *That* would raise a commotion that would be heard from here to Costa del Cielo."

"She's right, sir," Cochran put in cautiously. "Mrs. Trevarren knows her way around in there. She could probably find a robe and veils and move about without raising suspicion."

Patrick's jawline tightened, and he glared at Charlotte while he considered. Finally he nodded. "All right," he said.

146

"But once we're inside, you're to return to the harem and stay there. It's probably the safest place in the palace."

Charlotte remembered her frightening encounter with the sultan's half brother that night, in the hallway outside Khalif's quarters, and wondered. Ahmed was the sort to abuse both power and privilege, and as the new ruler of Riz, the harem and its women were his property.

"I'll do whatever I have to do," Charlotte said. That was the closest she was going to get to any promise, and Patrick knew it as well as she did.

He looked at her for a long moment, as if to memorize her features, and then rode on.

As they approached the courtyard wall, Charlotte looked up at the branches of the elm tree she'd once climbed to escape. At the time, she'd hoped never to see the harem again, and now she was about to risk her life to get inside.

Cochran and the guides hung back, watching for guards, while Patrick rode close to the wall, then hauled Charlotte forward, so that she sat in front of him in the saddle. He kissed her deeply, thoroughly, and then looked into her eyes.

"For God's sake," he whispered, "be careful."

Charlotte smiled bravely, but she was no fool and she was terrified. "Steady me so I don't slip," she replied, and then she stood on the horse's back like a trick rider in the circus, while Patrick held her legs.

Blessing the days when she and Millie had scrambled up and down trees like monkeys, she swung gracefully onto the wall and perched there for a moment, staring down at Patrick. Then she blew him a kiss and lowered herself silently to the courtyard below.

There, in the shadows, she paused, waiting for her heart to stop pounding and her breathing to slow down. She listened with all her concentration, then made her way slowly toward the arched doorway leading into the harem.

Inside, she paused again, letting her eyes adjust. After a few seconds, she could make out couches, and the women sleeping upon them. Some snored, others muttered as they dreamed, but no one stirred.

Charlotte appropriated a robe and veils from a bench at the foot of one of the couches and hastily removed her ruined dress. Once she'd put on the garment and hidden her discarded gown behind a tall chest, she crept across the harem to the inner doorway.

If there was a guard, Rashad or a replacement appointed by Ahmed, he would be there. Charlotte had to get through that portal, as well as a series of hallways and a large chamber, in order to reach the southern entrance to the palace, where Patrick and the others would be waiting.

She made herself a part of the shadows, hardly daring to breathe, and peered into the passage. She saw no one and, after a moment of gathering her courage, stepped over the threshold.

An instant later, strong arms clamped around her, and a hand was pressed over her mouth. She struggled, and her assailant pressed her against the wall of the palace, holding her throat with the steely fingers of his left hand while reaching up to light an oil lamp with his right.

The glow revealed Rashad's face, and Charlotte was so relieved that she nearly fainted. Although she couldn't be absolutely certain, of course, instinct told her that the eunuch was loyal to Khalif. He might be willing to help.

"You!" he rasped, his hand still encircling Charlotte's throat like a manacle.

"For heaven's sake," Charlotte croaked, "let me go. I can't breathe!"

Reluctantly Rashad released her, but his gigantic body still made a barrier every bit as daunting as the palace walls. "What are you doing here?" he demanded, keeping his voice low.

Charlotte swallowed. She had no choice, she concluded, but to risk everything by taking him into her confidence. Rashad was a very intelligent man, and he would accept nothing short of the truth.

"Patrick—Captain Trevarren and his men are outside the south entrance," she whispered. "They've come to help Khalif."

Rashad's expression revealed nothing of his thoughts, and Charlotte waited in an agony of suspense. What if she'd been wrong about the eunuch's loyalties? What if he was in league with Ahmed, and he'd been in on the plot against the true sultan from the first?

Finally he spoke. "I will go and let them in," he said. "You stay here."

Charlotte's relief was rivaled only by her irritation. After all she'd been through, she wasn't about to sit quietly in the harem, twiddling her thumbs and missing all the action. She smiled and folded her arms. "I can't," she answered, somewhat smugly. "Patrick is expecting *me* to open the outside doors. If you go instead, he may not recognize you in the darkness. He has a sword and he wouldn't hesitate to run you through—he's that intent on finding Khalif."

Rashad sighed. "All right," he agreed, in a hiss, after what seemed like an interminable interval. "Follow me, and be silent!"

Charlotte offered a private prayer of gratitude as she followed the eunuch along the stone passageways and through the gigantic formal chamber beyond, where the floors were made of marble.

There was a guard watching the entrance; Charlotte could see his shadow and the red tip of the cheroot he was smoking. She held her breath while Rashad reached back to stop her in her tracks with one massive hand.

He spoke to the guard companionably, in Arabic, while Charlotte hung back in the darkness, watching. Praying.

The sentry hesitated, then offered a friendly response. Rashad clasped the back of the other man's neck, and the guard groaned and sank to the floor, unconscious.

"Did you kill him?" Charlotte whispered, moving past Rashad to unlatch the outer door.

The eunuch offered no reply.

Patrick and the other men entered immediately, and Charlotte was quick to say, "This is Rashad, Khalif's servant. He's loyal to the true sultan."

After giving her shoulder a squeeze—the simple gesture communicated a great deal—Patrick smiled. "Yes, I know Rashad well. Where is Khalif?" The smile faded. "He is alive, isn't he?"

Rashad looked haggard, but he nodded. "According to

those who prepare his food, the sultan is alive. This may not be a blessing, though, for there's a rumor that Ahmed means to unman his brother. He may have already done so."

Patrick closed his eyes for a moment, and Charlotte watched in fascination as a new strength welled up in him, as clear and as mystical as the starlight shining on the snowy sands of the desert.

"Come," Rashad said. "He is being held in the oldest part of the palace. I will take you there."

Patrick nodded, then pulled a handkerchief from his pocket. Before Charlotte had time to suspect, let alone react, he had snatched her close and gagged her. Following that, he pulled a length of decorative gold cord from one of the tapestries on the wall and promptly bound her, hand and foot.

"I apologize for the indignity, goddess," he told her as he carried her along the hallway, "but this was the only way I could think of to keep you from following me right into battle and getting yourself killed."

Charlotte struggled, even though it was hopeless, and she thought she would burst with frustration and fury.

Rashad paused and opened an ornate door, grinning as he gestured. "She'll be safe in this closet," he said.

Patrick set Charlotte carefully inside, patted her on the head, and closed the door, shutting her up in utter darkness.

At first, Charlotte was so upset that she couldn't think, she could only squirm and twist in her bonds. After several minutes, the futility of her situation came home to her and she was still. One angry tear slipped from her eye and trickled down onto the gag.

In principle, she understood that Patrick was only trying to protect her, but he had done an injury to her pride that would not be easily forgiven. Charlotte was, after all, the product of untold generations of Quades, and she had been bred to be a participant, not a bystander.

As much as she loved Patrick, she would have vengeance —provided both of them lived through the night, that is.

Patrick and the others had proceeded only a little way before they were seen and the alarm was sounded. Adrenaline rushed through his veins—it didn't matter that they'd been discovered, now that they were inside the palace. If it hadn't been for Charlotte, his beloved weakness, he would have relished the prospect of a fight.

He tossed a pistol to Rashad, and he and the others formed a large circle, their backs to one another, as Ahmed's men flowed into the open chamber, brandishing swords and knives.

The battle was ferocious, and there were times when it seemed they were hopelessly outnumbered, but the circle held, and eventually the onslaught slackened.

Patrick had not been conscious of the passing of time, but dawn was flooding the palace with crimson light when Rashad led him down into the torchlit passages leading to the cellars. Rats scurried past at intervals, but there were no guards posted at the heavy wooden door where the eunuch finally paused.

"Here," Rashad said sadly, gesturing.

There was a steel lock affixed to the door. Patrick grabbed his pistol back from Rashad, took careful aim, and fired, splintering the metal. Although he was afraid of what he would find when he stepped over the threshold, Patrick didn't hesitate.

The chamber was dark, the air thick and fetid.

"Khalif?"

There was a groan in the darkness. Rashad struck a match, but the light was small, flickering and faltering in the gloom.

Patrick strained his eyes, found his friend tied by the wrists to rusted rings embedded in the wall. Khalif had been beaten and starved, and probably tortured, but his smile flashed white as Patrick cut his bonds.

"You have always had a good instinct for timing, my friend," Khalif said as Patrick put an arm around his middle to support him.

"Not good enough, from the looks of you," Patrick muttered. Now that Rashad had found and lit a lamp, he could see that his friend was in bad shape indeed. A combination of despair and rage sent bile rushing into the back of his throat. "Cochran will tend your wounds," he said hoarsely. "In the meantime, I'll see to that brother of yours."

Khalif made a sound that might have been either a sob or a burst of bitter laughter. "I owe you my life—not to mention my manhood," he labored to say as he and Patrick followed Rashad out of the stinking cell. "Still, I must ask you to swear that you will leave vengeance for me. Ahmed's sins go beyond what he's done to me, my friend—he murdered my mother, the *sultana valide.*"

"Jesus." Whether the word was prayer or plea, Patrick could not have said. Asking the next question took all his strength. "What about your children? Are they safe?"

Khalif stumbled beside him, his breathing ragged and hard. "My mother hid them," he said, and now it was plain that he was weeping. "That is why Ahmed killed her, because she would not tell him where they were. Still, my wives might have known, and they might have been weaker than the *sultana valide.*"

Patrick wanted to weep himself, so great was the pain he felt for his friend, but Khalif was depending on his strength now. "Where will I find him?" he asked.

Khalif folded, unconscious, and Rashad rushed to help. Between the two of them, Patrick and the eunuch supported the sultan.

"Ahmed will be in the sultan's private chambers," Rashad said, his voice harsh with bitterness. "Every night he beds another of his brother's wives."

Ahmed was indeed in Khalif's room, and there was a woman sharing his couch. He sat up, blinking in amazement and terror, when he saw Patrick and Rashad carry his brother into the room.

While the eunuch settled the insensate sultan gently on another couch, Patrick pulled his knife, which was bloody from the earlier confrontation in the chamber near the harem, and approached the larger bed.

"Get out," he said to the woman, who immediately bounded from beneath the sheets. Out of the corner of his eye, Patrick saw her snatch her robes from the floor, wrap them around her naked torso, and flee.

Ahmed had recovered his aplomb somewhat, and he

glared up at Patrick in defiance. "This does not concern you. You have no right to interfere."

Patrick pressed the sharp edge of the blade against Ahmed's throat. "Nonetheless," he replied, "I'm interfering. In fact, if your brother hadn't asked me to save you for him, I would be cutting you into thin slices right now."

Ahmed glanced at his senseless half brother, and a gray pallor appeared under his bronze skin. "It would be kinder if you cut my throat!" he gasped.

Patrick smiled. "I know," he answered.

Within an hour, Ahmed and all his surviving henchmen were locked away in the small cell where Khalif had been imprisoned earlier.

Charlotte slept for a while, there in that cramped space, and when she awakened, her energy was restored, and so was her outrage. The bindings on her wrists and ankles were too tight, and she needed to pass water.

When the closet door suddenly opened, filling the closet with light, however, it occurred to her that Patrick might be dead, along with all his men and Rashad, too. She looked up to see Alev's face.

"There you are," the other woman said, squatting to remove the handkerchief that had silenced Charlotte all this time. "Rashad said you were in a closet, but he didn't say which one, and there must be twenty of them in this part of the palace alone—"

"Did you see Captain Trevarren?" Charlotte blurted. As angry as she was with that man, she couldn't take another breath until she knew whether he was alive or dead.

Alev smiled, though the sadness and fear of recent events showed plainly in her eyes. "He is with Khalif. The Englishman, Cochran, is tending the sultan's wounds." She untied Charlotte and helped her to her feet.

Charlotte was amazed at how unsteady she was. "What about Ahmed? Is he running loose somewhere?"

Alev shook her head and slipped an arm around Charlotte to steady her. "Ahmed and his men are in the cellar, according to the servants."

A horrible thought came to Charlotte, and she stopped,

feeling the chill of the marble floor rise up inside her. "The princes—" she began, and was able to go no further.

The other woman embraced her and smiled, not quite so sadly as before. "They are all alive and well, thanks to the *sultana valide.*" Alev looked somber again. "It is she, the sultan's mother, who is dead. Ahmed strangled her, in front of all of us, when she refused to tell where the princes had been hidden."

Charlotte was ashamed to recall how actively she'd disliked the old woman. She marveled over the sultana's courage now, and her eyes filled with tears as she imagined what it must have been like to stand by helplessly while another human being was murdered.

"You've been through so much, Alev," she said softly. "How did you bear it?"

"Khalif is alive, and so are my fine sons. I try to be grateful for what is good and not dwell too long on what is evil."

Alev took Charlotte to the harem, where the other women were abuzz with excitement over the morning's adventures and the news that Khalif still lived. Charlotte took off her stolen robe and stepped into one of the huge tile-lined baths, letting the water, which was heated by braziers beneath the floor, soothe her aching muscles.

The others pelted her with questions, most of which had to be translated by the patient Alev, and Charlotte gave a thorough and slightly embellished account of her travels over the water to Riz and across the desert. She told as much as she knew about the actual rescue operation, and added a little that was only speculation.

Towels and a clean robe were provided when she was finished with her bath, and Charlotte dried off and got dressed. While she ate a large breakfast of fruit, sherbet, coffee, and cheese, Alev brushed the tangles from her hair.

"Where will you go after you leave here?" Alev asked, and there was a certain wistfulness in her voice.

"Back to Spain, I'm sure," Charlotte answered confidently. Although she still wasn't certain of Patrick's feelings for her, she knew he would never abandon the *Enchantress.*

"We were attacked by pirates when we left here, you know, and Patrick's ship was damaged. It's being repaired now."

Alev repeated the words in Arabic, her tone tremulous with excitement, and soon Charlotte was telling another story—how the pirates had boarded the *Enchantress* at sea and all about the battle that had ensued. By the time she was finished, she felt as weary as if she'd actually relived the entire experience.

She yawned, and Alev pointed her gently toward one of the couches. Soon Charlotte was stretched out, sound asleep.

It was Rashad who awakened her, sometime later.

"Captain Trevarren is asking for you," he said. He made it sound as though God had just issued an eleventh commandment.

Charlotte flushed and sat up. "Is he?" she asked sweetly. "Well, far be it from me to keep my master waiting."

Rashad narrowed his eyes, studying her suspiciously, but he didn't question her behavior. He simply led the way out of the harem and through familiar hallways, finally stopping in the doorway of Khalif's quarters.

He bowed slightly, then turned and walked away.

Charlotte lingered in the hall for a few moments, marshaling her fury. She had several bones to pick with Patrick Trevarren, and she would start with the fact that he'd tied her up and thrown her into a closet. Shoulders squared, chin high, she marched over the threshold.

Khalif lay on an enormous round couch, naked except for the sheet that covered him to the waist. His bare chest was covered with welts and burn marks, and Cochran had bandaged each of his fingers individually. There were deep shadows under his closed eyes, and even from across the room, Charlotte could see that it was a struggle for him to breathe.

Patrick stood at one of the windows, his back to the room, his shoulders stiff beneath his torn and blood-spattered shirt.

Between Khalif's visible injuries and Patrick's hidden ones, Charlotte forgot all about her personal grievances.

She went to Patrick first, standing at his side, looking up into his face. His expression was stony and rigid.

"Are you hurt?" she asked, and he flinched when she touched his arm. Clearly he hadn't realized she was there.

His face was bruised and there was blood in his hair as well as on the front of his shirt. He shook his head. "I lost two men in the fight," he said. "One of them was only nineteen years old."

Charlotte rested her forehead against his shoulder and put her arms around his waist. "I'm sorry, Patrick," she said gently. She held him for a long time after that, without speaking, trying to absorb some of his grief into her own spirit, so that the burden could be shared. "Will Khalif live?" she asked, much later.

Patrick looked back at his friend. "Yes, I think so," he replied gruffly. "God in heaven, Charlotte, what that bastard did to him . . ."

Charlotte had drawn conclusions of her own from the bandages on Khalif's fingers and the burns on his midsection, but she let Patrick tell her what had happened because she knew he had to give voice to the knowledge or be driven insane by it. She wept as she listened, but she didn't speak until Patrick was finished.

"You need to rest," she said, reaching up to place her hands on either side of his wan face. "You're exhausted."

Patrick's gaze sliced to Khalif. "No," he said simply. "Someone has to keep watch."

"Cochran is someone," Charlotte reasoned gently, taking Patrick's hand and gently leading him toward a nearby couch. "And I'll stay, too." She began unbuttoning his ruined shirt. "If Khalif needs you for any reason, I promise to wake you immediately."

Patrick's blue eyes darkened with pain and a profound weariness. His smile was so fragile, and so fleeting, that just a glimpse of it nearly broke Charlotte's heart.

"Why does it always surprise me to see what a man will do to someone he calls 'brother'?" he asked.

Charlotte wanted to weep, but she kept up a brave front for Patrick's sake. She pressed gently on his shoulders and he sank to a sitting position on the edge of the couch.

"You're forgetting the blessings," she said, kneeling to pull off one of his boots, then the other.

His voice was ragged. "What blessings?"

"The princes are safe," Charlotte said, thinking fast and speaking somewhat recklessly. "And Khalif will recover and rule over his kingdom once more. When we get back to Spain, the *Enchantress* will surely be herself again, and we'll sail off to your island. Besides that, I think I'm going to have a baby."

Patrick sat there for a long time, immobile, and then suddenly clutched her shoulders with his old strength. "What did you say?"

Charlotte smiled into his battered face. "I said Khalif will recover," she teased. "I said—"

He shook her, albeit good-naturedly. "You're carrying my child?"

Having nothing else to do while confined in the palace closet, Charlotte had fumed and cried, prayed and cursed, slept and dreamed, and still had plenty of time to think. It was during that quiet interval that she did some counting.

"It would seem so," she said. "Lie down, Patrick."

Amazingly enough, he obeyed, but he still clasped her arm with one hand, so that she couldn't pull away. "Are you sure?"

"As sure as one can ever be," Charlotte replied. "I'm . . . well . . ." She paused and glanced toward Cochran, who was sitting by Khalif's bed. "I'm very late."

Patrick's eyes drifted closed, but there was a smile on his lips. "A baby," he said. He fell into an exhausted sleep soon after, but some time passed before his hold on Charlotte's arm slackened enough for her to pull away.

She went to stand next to the bed, opposite Mr. Cochran. "Is there anything I can do?" she asked softly.

The first mate looked up at her, glanced in Patrick's direction, and then smiled at Charlotte. "Plenty, I think. It would do the captain's soul good if you sat by him, Mrs. Trevarren. He's a fine man, and the treachery he's seen today left its mark on him."

Charlotte looked at her tattered, sleeping husband and thought she would surely die if she came to love him even a little more than she already did. Then she found a hassock, dragged it close to Patrick's couch, and sat down beside him, holding one of his hands in both of hers.

He stirred in his sleep, and Charlotte bent to brush her lips lightly over his knuckles. Looking down at Patrick, she marveled at the complexities of the man. He was so strong, so arrogant and bullheaded, and during their lovemaking he was nearly always dominant. Now, however, he was like a child, needing nothing more than the comfort of her presence.

12

PATRICK SAT IDLY ON A LOW WALL IN THE COURTYARD OUTSIDE the bedchamber he and Charlotte had been sharing since their return to the palace two weeks before. His manner was easy—he was peeling an orange with a small fruit knife— but his words were earnest and quietly forceful.

"For once in your life, Charlotte, listen to reason. You're in a delicate condition, and I would be a fool to let you cross the desert on horseback. It's a miracle, in fact, that you didn't miscarry the first time."

Charlotte sighed. Khalif had a long way to go before he was fully recovered from his ordeal, but he seemed to be on the mend. Patrick was eager to get back to Spain and take command of the *Enchantress,* since the repairs were surely finished by then. "I don't suppose it would do any good if I promised to be careful?" she ventured.

Patrick folded the knife blade and then popped a section of juicy orange into his mouth. "You're absolutely right, Mrs. Trevarren," he said, after a chewing and swallowing process that proved to have a disturbingly sensual effect on Charlotte. "It would do no good at all. For one thing, you don't have the faintest conception of what it means to 'be careful.' For another, your promises are worth two to the penny."

Indignation pulsed in Charlotte's cheeks. "I may be tricky, but I'm not dishonest," she protested.

Her husband grinned and enjoyed another piece of sweet, succulent fruit. "Oh, I'm not denying that your heart's generally in the right place," he replied. "It's your judgment that leaves something to be desired."

Charlotte was not used to giving in on any point she felt strongly about, and she wanted to go to Spain with Patrick in the worst way, but she sensed that it would be futile to press the point. He would make sure she stayed behind even if he had to lock her up to do it, and Charlotte had no desire to spend the next fortnight as a prisoner.

"Would I have to stay in the harem, like before?" she asked. It must have been the timid note in her voice that caused Patrick to narrow his gaze and squint at her suspiciously.

"Hardly. Do you think I've forgotten that last time you bolted over the wall and nearly fried yourself in the desert before Khalif found you?"

She thought of Ahmed, the sultan's vicious brother, locked up in the small cell in the ancient part of the palace, along with his compatriots, and shivered as she approached Patrick. The conditions were very different, of course, but the principle was the same. She was a captive.

"Where would you keep me, then? In a box, like a pet mouse?"

He drew her to him by holding out a morsel of fruit, touching it to her lips. It lay spicy and cool on her tongue. "As foolhardy as it sounds," he answered, "I believe I could trust you if you had something to keep you occupied."

Charlotte savored the tart flavor of the orange even as she fought against the odd feelings of arousal Patrick had generated by feeding her. "Something to keep me occupied," she repeated. "Like what?"

He lifted her up to sit beside him on the wall. "Cochran will be coming with me, so he won't be able to doctor Khalif.

I'd feel better, knowing you were here to look after my friend."

Maybe the captain was serious, *or* maybe she was being hornswoggled, but Charlotte was pleased to be appointed keeper for once, instead of being the one who had to be kept. "Really?"

Patrick touched her nose, and his fingers smelled pleasantly of citrus. "Really," he answered, somewhat hoarsely. "I'll come back and carry you off before you've had time to miss me."

Not likely, Charlotte thought. Her husband's impending absence was already a sore spot in her heart. "I believe that a woman belongs with her husband, especially if she's expecting," she told him, "but since I don't seem to have a choice this time, I'll promise to stay here."

He leaned close, gave her a brief, flirting kiss. "Thank you."

His words so surprised Charlotte that she swayed slightly and nearly fell off the wall. Gratitude was the last thing she'd expected from him; after all, he'd won that skirmish and could afford to be a little smug.

He laughed at her look of wide-eyed surprise and kissed her again, this time in a more lingering fashion. They *both* nearly toppled to the stone floor of the courtyard when a voice sounded from the doorway of their chamber.

"Excuse me, sir," Cochran said, in embarrassed tones, "but there's a ship out in the harbor and she looks questionable."

Patrick immediately jumped to the ground, and Charlotte felt the tension in his forearms as he lifted her after him.

"Did you recognize her?" he asked. He turned to fix Charlotte with a brief, quelling glare that told her plainly enough what he wanted—for her to stay out from underfoot and keep her opinions to herself.

"Couldn't venture a guess, Captain—except that I don't like the look of her, or the feeling in the pit of my stomach."

Patrick strode past his first mate and disappeared, and even though Charlotte was burning with curiosity about the vessel in question, she stayed behind. It wouldn't do to defy her husband at this juncture; he might decide to take away her freedom if she did.

Cochran touched his forehead in an affectionate salute and followed Patrick.

After a few moments of pure agitation—just because she'd complied with her husband's terse orders didn't mean she had to like being left behind—Charlotte decided that the best course was to make herself useful. She went into Khalif's quarters.

Rashad was there, keeping a watchful and worried eye on the sultan. "Is there some disturbance?" the eunuch asked, having heard the commotion in the passageway. His brown fingers were curled around the pearl handle of a knife, and it was plain from his stance that he would fight to the death to defend his master if the need presented itself.

Charlotte wondered at such loyalty; it was a peculiar trait in a slave, especially one who had been emasculated by his captors. She met his gaze. "There's a strange ship coming into port, and Mr. Cochran's uneasy."

Rashad set aside the blade, but he still looked troubled as he took the wet cloth from his master's head, soaked it in a basin next to the bed and wrung out the excess, then spread it over Khalif's brow again. "Pirates, perhaps," he speculated, "or friends of Ahmed, expecting to pay their respects to a new leader."

Khalif groaned in his sleep and muttered something unintelligible.

"Pirates?" Charlotte asked, after swallowing. She'd already had one dramatic encounter with a band of seagoing outlaws, and she had no desire to repeat the experience. "Surely they wouldn't be bold enough to attack the palace—"

"I must go and see what is happening," Rashad interrupted. He picked up the knife again, pressed the handle into Charlotte's hand. "Please stay here with the sultan. If anyone else comes near him, kill them."

Charlotte was chilled by the cold directness of the order. "You can't be serious. What if Alev visits, or one of the other women?"

Rashad's dark eyes were hard as jet. "There are traitors and spies in the whole of the palace," he said. "The harem is not immune to treachery. *No one* other than myself, the captain, or Mr. Cochran is to set foot in this room."

"And Patrick thinks this place is safe for a pregnant woman," Charlotte muttered, once the eunuch had left her alone with the sleeping Khalif.

The sultan moaned again and stirred, and Charlotte drew up a hassock to sit beside him. "There now," she said, as if comforting one of her younger brothers after a bad dream. "Just rest. You're perfectly safe." She inspected the knife, then set it aside with a shudder.

Khalif opened his eyes, looked at her in puzzlement, then smiled. "Rashad, how you have changed," he teased.

Charlotte put on a front, not wanting the sultan to guess that his palace might be facing a siege, and touched his bare arm. She tried to smile at his joke. "How do you feel?"

The sultan sighed. "As though I've been lying unclothed in the desert sun for three days," he said. "Could I please have some water?"

She poured some from a crystal carafe and held a cup to his dry lips. There was a look of confusion in his brown eyes that dismayed her. "Would you like something to eat? I could send for some nice fruit and cheese."

Khalif shook his head, collapsed against his pillow of brightly colored, striped silk. "No," he said grimly. "I am not hungry." He reached for her hand.

Now that a fortnight had passed, his fingers were no longer bandaged, but there were ugly scabs and the new nails were just beginning to grow in.

"Please," he muttered. "I do not wish to be alone."

She smiled and shook her head to reassure him, hoping he wouldn't end up with a lot of marauding pirates for company.

But that was silly, she thought. Even if the mysterious ship *was* carrying a pack of cutthroats, Patrick and the others would be able to hold them back.

Probably.

"I'm not going to leave you," she said gently, remember-

163

ing how her stepmother, who was a trained nurse, had comforted the sick and injured merely by speaking tender words and staying close by through the worst. Just then, Charlotte missed Lydia with a special keenness.

"Talk to me," Khalif pleaded, like a fitful child. "Tell me about the place where you lived."

Charlotte blinked back unexpected tears, waited for a sudden lump in her throat to subside before she replied, "I grew up in a small town called Quade's Harbor," she said.

"Quade's Harbor," Khalif repeated, clinging to her hand and emitting a long, exhausted sigh.

After a sniffle and a deep breath, Charlotte regained control of herself. When she got back to Washington Territory, she would gather her brothers and young cousins around and tell them all about the sultan's palace, and Patrick's ship, and what it was like to deal with pirates. In the meantime, she would simply have to be especially brave.

"It's such a beautiful place," she said dreamily. "There are trees—so dense, you wonder how a squirrel could pass between them. They're evergreen—mostly fir and cedar and pine—and in a certain light, they take on an inky cast. And the water! It's blue as can be sometimes—Puget Sound, I mean—"

"Are there mountains?" Khalif's voice was hoarse, and Charlotte touched his forehead with her free hand, a gesture she'd learned from Lydia. She frowned because his skin was hot beneath the backs of her fingers.

"Yes," she said. "You can see the Olympics, out on the Peninsula. They're covered in snow in winter, and even in summer they wear white caps. Sometimes the slopes look purple." She paused, hearing a vague rattle in Khalif's breathing. "When you turn inland—if it's a fair day—you can see the mountain the Indians call Tahoma."

"I would like to meet an Indian," Khalif murmured. Then he drifted off into what appeared to be a shallow and restless sleep.

Charlotte went on holding his hand for a long moment, sensing a peril that had nothing to do with pirates, and when she turned she was startled to see Patrick standing in the doorway, watching her. His expression was troubled.

She placed Khalif's hand gently on the bed before rising and crossing the large room to speak softly to her husband.

"Are we about to be invaded by pirates?"

Patrick went on staring somberly, as if she were speaking a language he didn't understand.

"Patrick?" Charlotte finally prompted. If she was about to have her throat slit or be carried off to some other harem, she wanted to know about it.

"No—I mean, I'm not sure. They're sending a skiff ashore with two men on board. Cochran and I will be waiting for them on the beach." Patrick's eyes strayed toward his sleeping friend, came back to Charlotte's face. "How is Khalif?"

Charlotte folded her arms and met Patrick's gaze, puzzled by his behavior. "He's not well," she replied honestly. "He's fevered, and I don't like the sound of his breathing."

Patrick moved silently to Khalif's bedside, reaching down to touch the other man's forehead. "Damn," the captain muttered. "Do you suppose he's caught some infection of the blood or something?"

She went to the basin and lifted it from the marble-topped table; the liquid was tepid now, and would bring little comfort to the patient. "It's more likely to be pneumonia," she said. "I've seen injured lumberjacks succumb to it, and women after they've been in childbirth. The malady attacks when the body has been weakened."

The captain's glare was as intense, in that moment, as the desert sun. "Khalif could die." His hissed the realization aloud, and from his manner anyone would have thought the fault was Charlotte's. "After living through everything else, *he could die.*"

Charlotte touched Patrick's arm, but only after several seconds of hesitation. "We don't know that it's pneumonia," she said. "I was only guessing, and I'm certainly no authority."

Patrick glowered down at Khalif, as if to challenge the affliction to assemble itself into something solid and come forth to do battle. A long, silent interval passed, and then the captain looked into Charlotte's eyes, and she saw his despair.

"I've got to join Cochran on the beach," he said, laying his hands on Charlotte's shoulders. "I'll be back as soon as I can."

She nodded, still holding the basin. When Patrick had left the chamber, she emptied the brass bowl in the courtyard and pulled a cord to summon a servant.

Rashad returned before Patrick did, and found Charlotte bathing Khalif's head, chest, and upper arm with cool, fresh water.

"What is happening?" she asked, barely speaking above a whisper. It was late afternoon by then, and the palace was quiet, as it generally was at that time of day.

The eunuch edged Charlotte aside and took over the task of tending the sultan. "I'm only a slave," he grumbled, his concern for his master making him surly. "I do not know all things."

"Nonsense," Charlotte scoffed. "You're privy to every whisper of gossip in this palace. What are the servants saying about that ship out in the harbor?"

Rashad tried to intimidate her with one of his scowls. "The servants know even less than I do."

"Very well," Charlotte said, following the words with a sigh of long suffering. She straightened her hair and smoothed her robe. "I will simply have to go out there to the beach and find out for myself."

The eunuch stopped her before she was halfway across the room. Charlotte was amazed at his grace and speed, since he was a man of considerable bulk. "The captain wouldn't want you interfering," he said.

Charlotte seethed. She was getting damn tired of hearing what the captain wanted. She wrenched her arm free of Rashad's grasp. "Perhaps you are willing to live as a slave," she blurted out, "but I am not!"

A bleak look flickered in Rashad's eyes, and Charlotte regretted her words.

"Some of us," he replied coldly, "were not given the choice."

She bit her lower lip and started to apologize, but she stopped when she saw Rashad's pride glittering in his eyes. She returned to Khalif's bedside without another word,

166

which was enough of a concession as far as she was concerned.

After an hour of awkward silence, a servant appeared, bringing a summons from Patrick, and Charlotte joined her husband in their nearby bedchamber.

He looked distracted, impatient, and oddly remote as he tossed the few belongings he'd brought with him into an Arab version of saddlebags.

Charlotte was alarmed. "You're leaving?" The words shaped themselves into a combination of accusation and demand. "What about Khalif's condition? What about those pirates out there, waiting to pounce and murder us all in our beds?"

Patrick slung the leather bags over one shoulder, and a sort of dour humor moved in his eyes. "They're fishermen," he sighed, "not pirates. They've been becalmed for a week and they wanted to take on fresh water, that's all. As for Khalif, well, I'm depending on you and Rashad to take care of him."

She was stricken with a kind of grief at the thought of being separated from Patrick, even for a short time. Staunchly she resisted the temptation to use her own vulnerability and that of their unborn child to force the issue. "I see," she said, with consummate dignity.

Patrick studied her thoughtfully for a while. Charlotte waited for him to say he loved her, or even that he hated to leave, but in the end, he did neither. He took her into his arms and kissed her, and then he left, without offering any other farewell.

For Charlotte, Patrick's departure was a painful tearing away, but she was determined not to wilt like some fragile spring flower. Being Charlotte meant being strong, and she could not lose her courage without sacrificing her self as well.

Still, with Rashad keeping watch over Khalif, she lingered at an upstairs window of the palace, watching forlornly as Patrick and his party of men set out across a twilight-shadowed desert.

Charlotte had heard somewhere that it was bad luck to watch loved ones until they were out of sight, but she kept wanting one more moment to look at Patrick, and then another. When he rode onto a high dune and turned to raise a hand to bid her good-bye, her heart surged into her throat and a soft sob escaped her.

She returned his wave, whirled, and rushed into the palace.

Khalif awakened about an hour later. His fever had risen and he seemed disoriented, but Charlotte coaxed him to swallow a few spoonfuls of broth and some cool water. After that, he rested fitfully.

Rashad startled Charlotte out of a half doze by materializing behind her and laying one hand on her shoulder. "Go and get some rest, Mrs. Trevarren," he said. "I'll wake you if there is any change."

Charlotte was tired, and she had to think of her baby's well-being in addition to her own. She nodded and left the sultan's chamber, but before retiring, she made her way to the seaward side of the palace to look out on the moon-washed water.

The dark ship still rode the shadowy waves, and as she studied it, Charlotte felt a chill, despite the warmth of the night. *Fishermen,* she insisted to herself, remembering that Patrick and Mr. Cochran had met with the strangers and been convinced there was no danger.

Although her stomach was still flat, Charlotte had already developed the habit of laying her hand against it, as a way of communing with the tiny life growing inside her. She took a last look at the vessel, shivered again, and then reminded herself that pregnant women were full of strange fears and fancies.

Her baby was safe, they were all safe, for even if the fishermen *were* really pirates, or clever military enemies of Khalif's, the sultan had more than enough trustworthy men guarding the palace.

Charlotte finally retired to the bedchamber—how lonely and vast it seemed without Patrick—where she quickly washed, polished her teeth, and collapsed. She dreamed of horsemen crossing the desert, the moon lighting their way, and her heart followed even if the rest of her had to stay behind.

In the morning Khalif was better, though still very weak.

Charlotte read aloud to him, badgered him to drink cup after cup of spring water, and told him stories about her father and uncle and her sister and brothers. When the sultan slept in the early afternoon, Rashad came to take his turn at keeping the vigil.

He was clearly ill at ease.

"What is it?" Charlotte demanded in a whisper.

To her surprise, Rashad did not try to evade her question. "It's that ship," he reflected, frowning. "They have the water they needed. There is no good reason for them to linger."

"Surely Khalif's men are keeping an eye out."

Rashad nodded. "Still, I don't like this. Ahmed has powerful friends, for all his treachery—inside the palace as well as out."

The fine hairs at Charlotte's nape seemed to bristle. She had disliked the sultan's half brother in the first place, because he was a scoundrel and a boor. Now that she had seen the evidence of his brutality—Khalif's injuries—she knew Ahmed was a fiend in the bargain.

"We'll just have to be vigilant," she said finally.

Wanting the company of women, even though some members of the harem weren't particularly friendly, Charlotte set out for the part of the palace where only females, eunuchs, and Khalif himself were permitted.

As soon as she entered the *hamam*, however, Charlotte found herself surrounded by the sultan's women. All were eager to know how Khalif fared, though many were plainly resentful and envious of Charlotte's privileges as well.

Alev translated, then quickly shuffled the visitor outside, into the private courtyard where the great elm tree grew.

Charlotte touched its rough bark fondly, remembering her daring escape. Of course, some would call the enterprise a failure, but at least she'd *tried* to reach freedom, instead of just sitting about bemoaning her fate.

With surprising strength, Alev clutched her arm. "It is said that you are Khalif's favorite now, that you no longer live in the harem because you're sharing his bed. Is this true?"

Outrage stung Charlotte's heart and spread through her like venom. "I am married to Captain Trevarren," she pointed out, "and I'm a faithful wife. I have been staying in the room Patrick and I shared."

Alev blinked, then had the good grace to look embarrassed. After a moment, however, she put the awkwardness behind her and went on. "Will you take a message to the sultan for me? Will you tell him his sons are fine and strong, and that I beg to come to his rooms to see for myself that he is recovering?"

Charlotte's anger softened. If Patrick had been the one to be so grievously injured, she would hate being kept from him. "I'll give him your message," she agreed gently. "But Rashad will allow no one to visit Khalif except Patrick and me. He seems to have made up his mind on the matter."

Alev's blue eyes flashed. "Rashad is too full of himself," she fumed. "He is a eunuch, a slave, and I am a favorite—soon to be a *kadin*—the mother of two of the sultan's sons! Khalif will permit me to come to his chamber if you ask him personally."

Charlotte simply nodded and averted her eyes, knowing Alev's request would be refused and feeling nothing but sympathy for the other woman.

That afternoon Charlotte bathed in scented water, put on a clean robe provided by Alev, ate chocolate and sweetmeats with the others. One of the concubines played a beautiful melody on a harp, while another sang an accompaniment in sad, haunting notes.

It was the forlorn song of a wild creature captured, and Charlotte's heart ached as she listened.

13

CHARLOTTE WAS SITTING WITH KHALIF, THREE MORNINGS later, when the roar of cannons firing echoed through the palace. Servants and soldiers alike rushed along the passageway outside, but although Charlotte was very worried, she did not feel compelled to run after them and investigate. The strange ship was still at anchor in the harbor; plainly, its captain had finally made a hostile move.

Khalif did not react so calmly. In fact, he bolted upright, nearly displacing the embossed silk sheet that covered the lower half of his body. "Rashad!" he shouted. "Get me my sword!"

From the first volley of cannon fire, Rashad had been looming in the doorway like Gibraltar, knife at the ready. He turned at the sultan's words, a protest brewing in his eyes, but in the end he did not dare defy his master.

With furious reluctance visible in his every motion, Rashad found the requested weapon and brought it to Khalif.

Charlotte was not so intimidated. "Are you mad?" she demanded of the sultan as he accepted the brass-handled

171

sword and, at the same time, swayed with weakness. "Go back to bed and let your men defend the palace!"

Khalif was practically naked, clad only in a loincloth, but he was either unaware of the fact or unconcerned with it. His dark eyes glittered with annoyance as he glared at Charlotte. "Enough!" he shouted. "I do not take orders from women!"

Rashad tried to intervene, although his attitudes toward the female gender were no more enlightened than the sultan's. It was obvious that he feared for Khalif's safety and well-being. "Your Majesty—"

Not to be shunted aside, Charlotte shook her finger in Khalif's face. "You'll never reach the outer courtyard, let alone the beach," she warned. "Your injuries have left you weak!"

The sultan's complexion had already turned gray, and he glistened with sweat just from the rigors of rising from his bed and taking up his sword. "Silence!" he bellowed, wavering again, then blinking his eyes rapidly as if his vision had clouded.

Charlotte folded her arms and maintained a stubborn stance. "Don't raise your voice to me," she said tersely. "I won't put up with it." Out of the corner of her eye, she saw Rashad staring at her in dumb wonder, and the cannons continued to thunder in the dense heat of the morning.

"Take her to the harem," Khalif told his slave, seething. Then he reached for a robe, which was lying across a bench at the foot of his couch, and nearly collapsed.

Rashad hesitated, then reached out to help the sultan, only to be bellowed at for his trouble.

"Be gone—you have your orders!" Khalif shouted, obviously struggling to hold himself upright. "Unless you wish to join my half brother and his companions in the dungeon, you will do as I say!"

The eunuch glared at Charlotte, grabbed her arm, and hustled her out into the passageway.

"I cannot leave him unguarded," the angry slave rasped. "Do as the sultan wishes and go to the harem. You will be safer there."

Something struck the outside wall of the palace with a

reverberating impact, and Charlotte swallowed the refusal she'd already formulated in her mind. The harem was the last place she wanted to be, especially if the attackers managed to breach the walls, but arguing would be a waste of precious time.

She nodded curtly and set out in the proper direction. As soon as she was beyond Rashad's range of sight, however, she turned and hurried toward the seaward side of the palace.

Patches of fire flared orange from the gunwales of the ship, while Khalif's men fought back with cannon of their own. As Charlotte stood watching at a window that was ten times her height, skiffs were lowered to the turquoise water, bobbing, fragile as leaves on a storm-struck pond.

In the next instant, the invading vessel swayed drunkenly, her stern tilting, and then began to sink.

It all seemed to happen so slowly. The men on the balconies and parapets of the palace continued to fire, and some of the skiffs went under, taking their passengers with them.

Charlotte recalled the sharks that populated the harbor and closed her eyes for a moment, imagining them circling under the small boats, waiting, darting to the surface with vicious grace . . .

The men in the remaining skiffs fought back with rifles and pistols, and miraculously, some of them made it through the rain of cannonballs and bullets to the shore. Charlotte decided she'd seen enough and raced through the palace to the harem.

Alev rushed toward her, holding one of her babies. Khalif had not allowed the woman to visit him when Charlotte had relayed Alev's frantic request, probably because he did not want her to see him in a state of weakness.

"What is happening?" she cried, almost accusingly, her face pale with fear. The other women clustered around too, voices buzzing.

Charlotte attempted to steady Alev by grasping her upper arms. The young servant girl, Pakize, stood nearby, carrying the second of Alev's newborn twins. "There is an attack under way, but the sultan's men have already sunk the pirates' ship. The battle will be over at any moment, I'm sure."

Although Alev translated Charlotte's words to the others, she did not seem reassured, and neither did the rest. Just then another devastating blast shook the ancient walls, and the women rushed in every direction, screaming.

"Dynamite?" Charlotte speculated aloud as Alev grabbed her arm with one hand and started dragging her toward the inner part of the *hamam*.

"Come!" the other woman cried, panicked. "The enemy has surely gained the inner courtyards—we must hide!" She addressed the others as well, but in their own tongue. An elder wife, who had her own apartments and was seldom seen in the harem, flattened both hands against one of the inner walls and pushed, revealing an opening.

Charlotte and all the rest of them passed through the chasm inside, and the panel closed again, with a fierce grinding sound. They were in a stone cubicle, and bars of dusty light fell from narrow openings in the roof, two stories above.

"Fascinating," Charlotte said. She'd read about secret rooms, but she'd never seen one, even when touring castles in England and Scotland.

Alev gave her a quelling look and patted the fitful bundle resting against her shoulder, but said nothing.

Charlotte was unfazed. "This must be where the *sultana valide* hid the princes when Ahmed took over the palace," she speculated.

Her friend nodded, shuddered at the memory.

All around, babies and small children were crying, and their nervous mothers tried in vain to calm them. Gently Charlotte took the infant prince from Alev's arms and held him while her friend struggled to keep her composure.

"Does anyone else in the palace know about this room?" Charlotte asked, raising her voice above the snuffles and wails. It seemed unlikely to her that anyone would hear the noises, since the walls were so thick, and yet she wished they would all be quiet for a moment.

Alev looked weary, and she wrung her hands as she nodded. "Rashad knows," she answered. "Pray that he's able to hide himself, if the invaders succeed in overrunning the palace."

"He would never tell them where to find us," Charlotte said quickly. The baby she held had settled down a little, but she continued to pat his tiny back.

"You are right," Alev agreed sadly. "And they will kill Rashad for his silence."

Charlotte felt the color drain from her face. She and Rashad had not been friends, exactly, but neither had they been foes. It made her ill to think of the pressures he might face. "The princes were hidden here when Ahmed overthrew Khalif. Why didn't the would-be sultan try to force Rashad to show him how to get in?"

Alev's smile was wan, and Charlotte noticed that faint shadows were already forming under her eyes. Or perhaps that was just a trick of the light.

"Ahmed was mad with power. He was too preoccupied with playing sultan to recall that the harem was overseen by a eunuch." She looked grim, snatched her child back from Charlotte and held him so tightly that he began to whimper again. "Oh, Charlotte, what if someone releases Ahmed in all the confusion? Who is protecting Khalif?"

Charlotte didn't have the heart to tell Alev about the sultan's fierce determination to guard his home and family. She simply said, "Rashad was there when I left."

An hour passed, and some of the women and children sat down on the floor, leaning back against the stone walls. Alev nursed the baby she held, having already fed his brother, then arranged him in her lap to sleep. Pakize still held the other child.

The air in the secret room became hotter, thicker, harder to breathe. Charlotte needed a chamber pot, and her muscles were beginning to cramp. She thought of Patrick, and his boneheaded determination to "protect" her, and giggled half-hysterically at the irony of it all.

Alev gave her a strange look, as did several of the others.

Charlotte felt a need to make it clear that she wasn't losing her reason. "I was just thinking," she began, a little defensively, "how funny it is that Patrick insisted on leaving me here in Riz so I would be *safe.*"

175

Her friend clearly didn't see the humor.

Another hour passed, then another, and the light coming in through the roof began to thin. Finally darkness fell, and a few candles were brought from pockets and pouches and lit, and the children began to fuss in earnest.

Charlotte could bear the waiting no longer. She stood, dusted off her robe, and announced, "We've got to take this situation in hand."

Alev stood, awkwardly, after jostling her sleeping baby into the arms of one of the other women. "What can you be thinking of?" she snapped, her hands resting on her hips. "There is no better place to hide—even the Turks did not find this room when they invaded Riz during the time of Khalif's grandfather!"

Charlotte was struck by the odd, old-fashioned meter of Alev's speech. Even though her friend had been born and raised in England, she had clearly absorbed the culture of Riz, and made it her own.

"We will need food and water," Charlotte reasoned. "Besides, there weren't all that many pirates left, once the sultan's soldiers sank the ship and several of the skiffs that remained. It's quite possible that things have returned to normal and Rashad and the others have simply forgotten that we're in hiding."

Alev had an argument at the ready. "It is also 'quite possible,' Madame Trevarren, that you are wrong. The very act of leaving the hiding place might well reveal the rest of us to the enemy."

Charlotte sighed, looked around the shadow-filled cubicle. "There must be another way out, besides grinding open a part of the wall," she reflected aloud. "We need to find out what's going on out there, and I could bring back some food and water, too."

In rapid, hushed Arabic, Alev consulted with the senior wife, who had stood apart from the others from the beginning, looking haughty and aloof. Finally the wife, or *kadin*, grudgingly indicated a place in the floor where the stones were broken.

Upon investigation, Charlotte was surprised and pleased to find an underlying board, which had been covered with smooth rocks. Beneath that was a narrow tunnel, burrowing away into darkness.

"Where does it lead?" she asked, already preparing herself inwardly for the forthcoming expedition.

More consultation followed, then Alev replied, with a shiver, "To the passageway behind the dungeons." She looked gray as death in the gloom. "Oh, Charlotte, don't do it, please—just stay here with the rest of us and wait."

Charlotte looked at the tunnel and thought of all the different sorts of vermin that surely lived inside it, and for a moment her resolve wavered. When she weighed the dangers of the unknown against the prospect of sitting passively by and waiting for someone to come and rescue them all, however, she hesitated no longer.

"I'll return as soon as I can." She lowered herself to her stomach and peered inside the hole. The best course of action would be to crawl in headfirst, she decided, and slowly grope her way toward freedom. She looked directly at Alev. "If the palace is clear of enemies, Rashad or I will come and open the secret panel. If it is not, I'll return by way of the tunnel. Whatever happens, though, I won't tell anyone besides the eunuch where you are."

Alev must have guessed that Charlotte's mind was closed to further persuasion; she nodded grimly, and the two women exchanged a brief embrace.

The tunnel was dark and musty, and at times it narrowed to such a point that Charlotte feared she would not be able to squeeze through. She had more than one moment of paralyzing fear, imagining what it would be like to get stuck and die of hunger and thirst in the bowels of an ancient palace. Once, she encountered a rat; she saw its red eyes glowing in the darkness and felt its fetid breath upon her face. Her heart thudded in her throat while she tried to project an attitude of unremitting menace, and finally the rodent retreated into some cubbyhole farther along and did not trouble Charlotte again.

Still, she knew the memory of the creature would not soon leave her. There would surely be nightmares in which the animal grew bigger and bigger, until it filled the tunnel.

Charlotte wept, though she wasn't consciously aware of it, as she inched on toward an uncertain fate.

Whether an hour or a day had passed since she'd left the secret chamber, Charlotte had no way of knowing. Her courage stirred, however, when she caught the first faint murmur of voices ahead of her.

She crawled on, elbows and knees scraped, hair tangled, and at one point the tunnel grew so constricted that Charlotte had to let out all her breath to squeeze through. Then, reaching a wider place, hearing a conversation clearly, she rested, catching her breath, wishing she spoke the language of Riz even one tenth as well as Patrick did.

The speakers were men; that was all she could determine without getting a look. New terrors presented themselves. She might be heard moving within the wall, and captured. Or—and this fate was still worse—she could find herself in one of the cells, at the mercy of Khalif's prisoners. Not only would she be cruelly used, and probably killed long after she'd begun to pray for death, but Ahmed and his followers would escape through the tunnel and find the hidden women and children.

Charlotte made herself take a deep breath and hold it. She had come this far; now was no time to lose her mettle. Besides, there was no room to turn around and retreat. Taking great care to be silent, Charlotte shinnied forward, toward the rumble of voices.

Finally she found herself looking out into a dark passageway, through a crack in the sandstone wall. The stench emanating from the cells on either side of the torchlit hall—urine, vomit, excrement, and mold—brought acid surging up from her stomach. She retched silently, convulsively, then lay still, thinking of Lydia, who had seen and smelled much worse during her service as a nurse during the Civil War. *Physically,* her stepmother had said, *one builds a tolerance, but a part of the spirit never forgets the horror.*

What would Lydia do in my place? Charlotte asked herself. She did not have to wait long for the answer; Mrs. Brigham Quade believed in going forward, never back.

Charlotte crept close to the wall again and put her eye to the thin vein of light to look out.

Two Arabs entered the passageway at the far end, talking between themselves. Their clothes were not fine, but dirty and poor and wrinkled, and one man laughed raucously at some comment of the other.

Behind them came two more men—like the first pair, they were strangers to Charlotte, but the half-conscious prisoner they dragged between them was not. Even in the gloom, Charlotte recognized Rashad, and she could tell that he'd been savagely beaten.

Her heart sank, for a moment, into a mire of unutterable despair. Somehow the worst had happened, the unthinkable —the invaders had managed to prevail against Khalif's soldiers. But how?

A cell was opened, Rashad was thrust onto its filthy, straw-covered floor, and metal clanged against stone as the door was slammed. It was locked, and then the jailer hung the keys from a spike and he and his companion left the dungeon.

Blood pounded in Charlotte's ears as she waited, marshaling her thoughts and praying devoutly for courage and guidance. Then, as quietly as she could, she began picking away at the sandstone rocks that hid the tunnel from plain view.

Moans and coughs sounded from the shadowy depths of the cells, but no one seemed to notice when Charlotte finally cleared the way and writhed out of the entrance like a snake leaving its hole. She landed on the hard floor with a bone-jarring *ker-thump,* waited in an agony of suspense for the guards to burst in and find her.

Nothing happened.

At first Charlotte was unsteady on her feet, having been wedged into the tunnel for so long, and she stood for a time, gripping a bar of one of the cells, struggling against a cowardly urge to abandon her mission and shinny back to relative safety.

In the end, however, she could not bring herself to leave Rashad to further sufferings. She walked slowly to the end of the passageway, took down the ring of keys, and returned to his cell.

He groaned as she ground the ancient key in an even more primitive lock.

"Hush," she whispered, "it's only me. Charlotte."

The straw rustled as Rashad sat up, making a mountainous shadow against the inside wall of the cell. "Allah preserve us," he muttered in disbelief. "How did you get here? Did Ahmed's friends find the hiding place?"

The lock finally gave, though it made rather more noise than Charlotte would have liked. "The women and children are still safe, as far as I know," she assured him in a whisper, entering the stinking chamber and crouching beside him. "For you and me, my friend," she went on philosophically, "the outlook is not so encouraging. I didn't expect to find you here and I have no plan for getting you out. Being a portly man, you would never be able to pass through the tunnel."

Rashad sighed, labored to his feet. "You must go back the way you came. I will look after myself." He swayed, and Charlotte steadied him, feeling the sticky warmth of blood under her hands.

"You've been doing a fine job of that so far, haven't you?" she mocked, though not unkindly. It was apparent that Rashad had suffered enough already. "Is Khalif alive? Have they taken him prisoner?"

Rashad's teeth flashed in an unexpected grin. "Khalif was drugged by a faithful servant, then bound and gagged and deposited in the back of a deep closet."

Charlotte knew that Patrick's method of keeping her out of trouble, when they'd first returned to the palace, had inspired the eunuch, but she had no time or energy for resentment. "The palace has fallen, then?"

The grin was gone. "Yes," Rashad answered. "The men in the ship had spies inside. The traitors helped them get past the gates, and Ahmed was immediately released."

Creeping to the cell door, Charlotte peered cautiously into the passageway. "I wish Captain Trevarren were here. He'd know what to do."

"He'd tell you the same thing I did: Go back where you came from. I will cover the opening in the wall after you."

"I can't just go off and leave you," Charlotte replied

impatiently. "You're hurt. Besides, there is no food or water in the secret chamber. I promised to bring some back."

Rashad leaned close, his low voice thundering in the darkness as he replied, "Sometimes promises must be broken."

"What about your wounds?"

"The very pain itself will serve to drive me past the obstacles in my way. Go now. If you are found here, there will be nothing I can do to save you or the others who depend upon us."

Before Charlotte could reply, the latch of the outer door clattered. Quickly Rashad pushed Charlotte back into the shadows of the cell and stood there with her. One of the guards ambled along the hall, eating an orange with a total lack of grace. He saw the open door first, and then the opening of the tunnel, but even as a shout of alarm formed on his lips, Rashad was upon him.

Charlotte winced at the cracking sound she heard, watched wide-eyed as the sentry folded to the floor. Rashad took both a gun and a knife from the man's belt and handed the former to Charlotte.

It was a small, shiny pistol.

"Take this," Rashad said, clearly expecting Charlotte to follow his earlier dictates and climb back into the tunnel. Instead, she put the gun into the pocket of her robe and hastened to replace the stones that would hide the opening in the wall. Whatever happened to her and Rashad, Ahmed must not learn of this passage.

Rashad had taken the keys earlier, and with only one glance back at Charlotte and a disgusted shake of his head, he began unlocking the doors of the other cells. Many of the prisoners were wounded and remained inert, but a good number poured out to await orders from the eunuch. Charlotte, having finished covering the tunnel entrance, blended in with the men, marveling that they'd been so quiet while she was speaking with Rashad.

She would have followed the others out of the dungeon and into the thick of conflict had it not been for a pitiful groan coming from one of the newly opened cells. The need to be in the center of things drew her forward, but duty pulled her back. She could not ignore human agony, not when there were things she might do to combat it.

Full of frustration as well as compassion, Charlotte lingered in the cell block. The din of battle arose outside as Rashad and the freed soldiers confronted their captors.

Someone moaned.

Charlotte sighed and went to the opposite end of the passageway. Beneath the hook where the keys had been stood a bucket of water with a ladle inside.

She squatted, dipped a finger into the pail, and touched it to her tongue. The water was tepid, but fresh enough.

Charlotte picked up the bucket and carried it into the first cell.

Sleep eluded Patrick, and his cabin aboard the *Enchantress* was too small for adequate pacing, so he left it and went up on deck. The night sky was star-washed, and the ink black waters reflected its silvery glow.

Patrick gripped the railing and silently castigated himself, yet another time, for leaving Charlotte behind in Riz. Traversing the desert a second time would have been a trial for her, to be sure. Then there was the crossing to Spain, and the ever-present possibility of a pirate attack.

Being parted from Charlotte had been pure anguish this time, perhaps because he knew she was carrying his child under her heart. To make matters worse, during their separation he had developed a mysterious sixth sense, and that faculty was telling him that she was in far worse danger for staying in the palace.

Cochran appeared beside him, and Patrick was startled.

The first mate chuckled. "There now, Captain, it's only me. Since this isn't your watch, would you mind telling me what you're doing up here on deck?"

Patrick scowled at his friend. "I don't have to explain my actions to you," he snapped tersely.

Cochran sighed and leaned against the railing, seeming to breathe the sight of the sea into his soul just as he breathed air into his lungs. "That you don't," he answered good-naturedly. "Don't fret yourself, Patrick. We'll reach Khalif's harbor before sunrise, and you'll find the Mistress Trevarren as well and sassy as ever."

An involuntary shudder moved up Patrick's spine. "Something is wrong," he said gruffly, watching the starlight shimmer on the water. "I should never have let her out of my sight for a moment!"

"That last part is probably true," Cochran conceded. "Your lady does tend to get herself into dutch when she's left unsupervised. But she's as strong-minded and wily as any man, and my guess would be that she can take care of herself and half the palace without working up a sweat."

"I hope so," Patrick whispered. "God in heaven, I hope so." He was still uneasy, though, and his unborn son or daughter was so small, so vulnerable . . .

Cochran slapped Patrick on the shoulder and then walked away without another word.

There wasn't much Charlotte could do for the men who had been wounded in the uprising against Khalif. She gave water to those who could sip from the ladle and whispered soothing words she knew the patients could not comprehend. She held their hands and told the lost ones it was all right to die.

She had probably been in the cells for two hours or so when she heard the door opening at the far end of the passageway.

It never occurred to Charlotte that the visitor might not be Rashad, coming to tell her that the palace had been taken back again. She stepped out of the cell, feeling weary to the core of her spirit, and encountered a shadowy figure in Arab dress.

She would have sworn her heart stopped beating.

The man lifted a lantern, and Charlotte saw the too handsome face, with all its marks of debauchery and weakness. Ahmed laughed.

"I will not live to see nightfall," he said, and his madness shone as plain as the lantern light in his ebony eyes. "For all of that, Allah has seen fit to make my last day a pleasurable one."

Charlotte retreated a step. "Stay away from me," she warned.

Ahmed reached out, closed one hand around her wrist before she could escape. "What a pity it is," he breathed, "that I won't have time to train you properly. Still, your spirited nature should offer a delectable challenge. Come with me, and I will show you what a woman is made for."

She struggled, clasped one of the cell bars with one hand, but Ahmed was stronger. He wrenched her free and propelled her ahead of him, toward the outer door.

14

Ahmed had grasped Charlotte by her hair, and he propelled her along in front of him with cruel force. Since they moved along rarely used passageways, they did not encounter Khalif's men, and from that quarter, rescue seemed impossible.

Charlotte was far from despairing, however, for she still had the pistol Rashad had given her, secreted in the pocket of her robe. If matters came to such a dire point, she would shoot Ahmed without hesitation, just as her father and uncle had shot mad dogs and infected rats during an outbreak of rabies several years before.

Finally, after traversing a maze of passages and dusty, long-unused rooms, Ahmed thrust Charlotte through the high arched doorway of a large chamber.

The room was clean, and scented smoke wafted from several brass braziers. A male slave played softly on an instrument resembling a lyre, his eyes downcast, his brown body fairly quivering with tension. In the center of the space was a great couch, piled high with pillows of all colors, and the walls were hung with fading tapestries that must have been centuries old.

If she hadn't been in such untoward circumstances, Charlotte would have taken pleasure in exploring the place. As it was, she felt compelled to keep her wits gathered solidly about her.

"No one will think to look for us here," Ahmed told her, with a smarmy smile, giving her hair a vicious little wrench before flinging her into the heart of the chamber. "At least, not for some time." He ran dark, insolent eyes over Charlotte's dirt-smudged person. "You look like a street urchin," he scolded. "You must be bathed before our time of love."

" 'Time of love'?" Charlotte scoffed, sounding braver than she felt. "If I had anything in my stomach, I would surely vomit."

Ahmed laughed. "Ah, Charlotte, sweet Charlotte. You are indeed a spitfire, as the westerners say. This heartens me." Having said this, he clapped his hands together and spoke to the slave in rapid Arabic.

"I hope that doesn't mean we're married or something," Charlotte said stiffly, referring to the hand-clapping gesture. "I already have a husband—not that such a fact would trouble a polecat like yourself."

"A polecat," Ahmed echoed thoughtfully, rubbing his chin. He was gaunt from his time in prison, and his eyes gleamed, as if from some fever of the soul. "This is an insult, I am sure."

"You're damn right it's an insult," Charlotte replied, caught up in the flow of her own bravado. "A polecat is a skunk."

Ahmed glared at her, letting all his hatred show. "Your insolence is wearing on me, Mrs. Trevarren. I would suggest you stop talking before you earn yourself a taste of the lash."

Charlotte would not willingly have shown trepidation for anything, but she felt the color drain from her face and knew from Ahmed's expression that he saw and savored her fear. "Let me go," she said, with dignity, after a long silence. "I have done nothing to you."

The sultan's treacherous half brother rolled his eyes in an apparent bid for patience. "It is not a matter for revenge," he replied. "I want you and therefore I am entitled to you."

The slave had quietly filled an ornate brass hip bath from tall urns of sun-warmed water while they were talking. At a nod from Ahmed, he went back to playing his lyre.

"And my feelings have no bearing whatsoever?" Charlotte inquired saucily, needing to challenge Ahmed's complacent barbarism and prejudice even though she knew it would do no good at all.

"None," Ahmed confirmed flatly. "Now, undress yourself, and wash, and make certain that your hair is clean as well."

Charlotte folded her arms. "You can go straight to hell," she said.

Ahmed gave a raspy sigh of exasperation; then, his movement as quick as mercury set free from a vial, he reached out and slapped Charlotte so hard that she staggered backwards. Her hand went automatically to the pistol in her pocket; an instant after she'd made the gesture, she regretted it.

Before she could draw the weapon to defend herself, Ahmed had guessed at its presence, wrested it from her, and backhanded her a second time. Again she glimpsed a madman looking out of the ebony-dark eyes.

"This is not America," he told her, his voice drawing tighter as he spoke, like a string on an instrument that has been wound too far. "Nor is it England. Here, women do not speak impudently to their superiors."

Charlotte refrained from comment, since the things she wanted to say were sure to get her another slap at best and a painful death at worst. But she did not move toward the hip bath, nor did she avert her gaze from Ahmed's.

The would-be sultan raised one eyebrow. "Why do you hesitate?" he asked, his voice lethal in its very softness.

"I don't want you—" she paused, gestured toward the slave, who was still quivering with fear "—or him . . . to watch me as I remove my clothing."

Ahmed laughed, then shrugged. His indulgence came as a definite surprise. He spoke to the slave, and the poor man left the room. For his own part, Ahmed simply turned his back, the pistol still clasped casually in one hand.

"Do not even consider trying to escape," he said, with acid cordiality. "If you make a move toward either door, I will hear you and I will kill you for your disobedience—but not before punishing you thoroughly, of course."

Charlotte had no doubt that he was serious. She slowly stripped off her ruined robe, then the chemise beneath, and stepped naked into the hip bath. Her mind raced as she washed herself clean of tunnel dirt, cobwebs, perspiration, and the rank smell of the dungeon itself. She had still not come up with a solution when Ahmed turned and handed her a musty cloth to dry her hair and body.

She glared at him, ferociously proud even in her nakedness. In the privacy of her heart, however, she was uttering frantic, wordless prayers for help. The unthinkable was about to happen; a cruel man meant to lay hands on her in violence, to rape and probably kill her. If she'd had only herself to defend, she might have given up at that point, but she was carrying a child. She could not bear the thought that their son or daughter would never get a chance to live and grow, to feel sunlight and rain on his or her skin.

"Wouldn't you like me to dance for you?" she asked, crooning the words. Charlotte had no idea where the question had come from; she hadn't the wits for cunning because her fear was so great. "Just as the harem women dance for Khalif?"

A tense interval passed while Ahmed considered. He was certain to die this day himself, which meant he had little or nothing to lose. Perhaps, too, in some corner of his wasted mind, he wanted to savor this final triumph over his brother, to make it last.

"Very well," he said hoarsely. Then he went to a chest beside the wall, beneath a tapestry showing an ancient battle against English crusaders, and brought out a gossamer garment of pale lavender, along with a beautifully beaded vestlike top. "You will dance."

Charlotte took the garments, amazed that her hand didn't shake when she reached out for them. She had never been more terrified, not even during the battle on Patrick's ship, when the pirate had cornered her outside the storeroom.

She turned her back to put on the full, see-through

trousers, with their girdle of embroidered brocade, and the vest, which laced in front and barely covered her bosom.

Her hair, freshly washed and unbrushed, hung down her back in twisting tendrils.

Ahmed took a moment to admire her before summoning the slave back with a shouted order and a clap of his hands.

Soon the slave was making music again, and Charlotte danced to it, slowly, like a creature under a night spell. She realized that sunrise had arrived when trails of crimson flowed in through high palace windows and glittered in the gold and silver threads of her clothing.

Ahmed watched her as if transfixed, seeming to lose track of time, but Charlotte was not so naive as to think she could forestall the inevitable forever. Now that her captor had taken her pistol away, she was depending upon Rashad to find her, or perhaps Khalif. Both were familiar with the palace, with all its hiding places and cubbyholes, and this out-of-the-way chamber would not be unknown to them.

"Again," Ahmed said shortly, when the slave stopped playing out of what was probably sheer weariness.

Charlotte's heart was beating fast, and she was perspiring slightly, but she kept dancing. Indeed, she would whirl and twist until she dropped, if that would save her.

After a while, however, Ahmed's eyes began to harden as he watched her. Finally he raised both hands, palms out, and said, "Enough." He turned to the terrified slave. "Leave us!"

Charlotte stood still, catching her breath. She braced herself to fight, with all the wildness of a cat that has grown up on its own, living on field mice and garden snakes.

Before Ahmed reached her, however, her prayers were answered. Khalif and—dear God, was she hallucinating?— *Patrick* burst into the room, both carrying swords.

"He has a gun!" Charlotte shouted as Ahmed reached for the weapon.

Khalif sent the pistol flying from his half brother's hand with one swing of his rapier. The sultan looked fierce, somehow more than human, as if he'd risen above his weakness and conquered it, however briefly.

"Give my brother your sword, Patrick," Khalif said, his

eyes fixed on Ahmed. "I would not have him face me unarmed."

Patrick didn't hesitate, though Charlotte saw reluctance in every line of his body and face. He tossed the sword to Ahmed, who caught it deftly.

While the two brothers faced off for what would undoubtedly be a fight to the death, Patrick came to Charlotte and enfolded her in his arms. His strength flowed into her, like spiritual medicine, heightening her own powers.

"It's high time you got back, Patrick," she scolded as they watched Khalif and Ahmed engage each other in graceful battle. "As you can see, I have not been safe."

Patrick squeezed her briefly, but said nothing. He was watching the sword fight, and Charlotte knew he was ready to jump to Khalif's defense if the need arose.

Khalif had been ill, and he was not as fit as he would normally have been. The match seemed equal, however, probably because Ahmed himself had spent days languishing in prison.

The thin blades of the rapiers clanged together, and the sound reverberated horribly. Ahmed sliced open Khalif's upper arm, Khalif drew blood by drawing the point of his sword across his half brother's middle.

Charlotte shuddered and turned her face in to Patrick's chest, clutching at his shirt with both hands.

The battle seemed to go on and on, but finally there was a scream of mortal agony, and Charlotte forced herself to turn her head and look. Ahmed, struck through the heart by his brother's rapier, was dead before he'd folded to the floor.

Charlotte gave a little moan of horror and relief, steadied herself when Patrick left her to go to his friend's aid. Khalif wavered on his feet as he gazed down at Ahmed, bloody sword in hand. His eyes brimmed with tears.

"This terrible day has been stalking Ahmed and me since we were boys," he said gruffly. "My brother could not bear for peace to exist between us. Even as a child, he hated me."

Patrick took the rapier gently from Khalif's hand. "It's over," he told his friend. "Ahmed is gone and now you will have peace again."

Khalif nodded, but he still stared at the corpse lying on the floor at his feet, his face gray with blood loss and grief.

Charlotte had recovered enough to think of practical matters. "The women and children are still in hiding," she said. Guilt assailed her because she had not had the opportunity to return to Alev and the others with news and supplies, as she had promised.

"Rashad has released them," Khalif said, turning away at last, staggering to a velvet-upholstered bench and sitting down.

Patrick tore a strip of cloth from the sheets on the bed where Ahmed had meant to rape Charlotte and made a tourniquet for the sultan's cut arm. For all his efficiency, however, his indigo gaze fixed itself on his wife and not his patient.

"Are you all right, goddess?"

She considered for a moment, then nodded. "How did you find me?"

Patrick sighed, crossed the room to take her in his arms. "You've got a ghost, even though you're alive," he told her. He paused, brushed her temple lightly with his lips, tightened his embrace for a moment, as if to reassure himself that he was really holding her again. "I've been haunted by thoughts of you ever since I left for Spain. When I got here, Rashad and Khalif and the others had already taken the palace back, and when Ahmed didn't turn up after a quick search, the eunuch directed us here."

Charlotte rested her forehead against his shoulder and sighed. "Once," she confessed, "I wished for adventure. Now I believe I've had quite enough excitement to last into my old age."

Patrick chuckled, kissed her forehead. "I have a feeling, Mrs. Trevarren," he said, "that our adventures have just begun. You draw trouble the way a summer picnic draws bees."

Khalif had recovered enough to speak by then, and he did so, staring at Charlotte in weary bewilderment. "Rashad assured me you were safe with the harem, in the secret room—just before he drugged and imprisoned me. Did he compound his transgressions by lying, too?"

Quickly Charlotte shook her head. "No, he was telling the truth. I *was* with Alev and the others—until I found the tunnel under the floor. It seemed to me that, unless we were all content to grow cobwebs in that hidden chamber, somebody had to venture out and see what was happening. I managed to get to the dungeons and release Rashad."

"Who then released me," Khalif reflected, with a sigh, rubbing his temples. "I shall forgive my servant Rashad, then, for taking matters into his own hands as he did. There can be no question of his loyalty."

"None at all," Charlotte agreed.

Moments later, Rashad himself arrived, bringing a party of soldiers with him. When he saw that Ahmed had been killed, the eunuch gestured for two of the men to come forward and carry away the body.

"We have captured the traitors," Rashad said to his sultan, his tone grave and formal. "What shall be done with them?"

"Behead them," Khalif replied. "Let it be done now, in the main courtyard, under the bright light of the morning sun. Let all who live within these walls see the fruits of treachery."

Charlotte's eyes had gone round and her stomach had risen to the back of her throat, then plummeted into place again. She started to step forward, to protest, but Patrick stopped her by grasping her arm. An eloquent look and a shake of his head further discouraged her.

"Come, Mrs. Trevarren," he said. "We're not needed here." With that, Patrick took Charlotte's hand in a bone-crunching grasp and led her past Rashad and the soldiers and out into the passageway.

"You can't let this happen!" she whispered.

Patrick didn't even slow down. He just strode toward the main part of the palace, dragging Charlotte along behind him. "I can't stop it," he replied abruptly. "And neither can you. This is an ancient society, with rules of its own."

Charlotte knew he was right, but it still went against her principles to see violence answered with violence. "I want to leave this place," she said breathlessly, rushing to keep up with her long-legged husband, "and never come back."

192

He looked back at her over his shoulder. "That's one wish I can grant," he said. "As soon as I know things are under control here, we'll sail for the island."

A surge of joy welled up inside Charlotte, but in the next moment she was overwhelmed by the backlash of all that had happened to her in recent hours. She let out a wail and burst into unceremonious, un-Charlotte-like tears.

Patrick stopped, lifted her easily into his arms, propped his chin on top of her head, and proceeded through the passageway. "Go ahead and cry," he told her, with hoarse gentleness. "You've earned it."

While the executions were taking place, Patrick and Charlotte were alone in his chamber, oblivious to everything and everyone except each other. They celebrated life, even while death held savage sway in the center courtyard.

Charlotte lay curled against Patrick's side, her bare body glistening with perspiration, one finger playing idly with the hair on his chest. "I love you," she said.

Patrick sighed and held her a little closer, but he did not offer the same pledge. He just closed his eyes and went to sleep.

Although she was happy to be with Patrick again, and although her body had certainly been satisfied, Charlotte's soul still hungered. What would it matter—what would anything matter—if Patrick didn't love her?

She laid one hand to her abdomen and closed her eyes. No matter what the cost might be to her, she would never raise her child in a loveless household. She would take her baby back to Quade's Harbor first, to grow up in the light and warmth of her father and Lydia's marriage . . .

For the next three days, Khalif remained in his quarters. Various members of the harem visited him at different times, Alev included, but he did not show himself publicly.

Charlotte was standing at one of the upstairs windows, gazing toward the sea with undisguised yearning, when Patrick slipped up behind her and put his arms around her waist. He bent, gave her a nibbling kiss on the side of the neck.

"Could it be, Mrs. Trevarren," he teased, "that you have a yen for wandering, just as I do?"

She turned in his embrace and looked up into his eyes. "Yes," she answered. "When will we leave?"

He touched her chin with an index finger. "Tomorrow, I think. Were you beginning to fret that I might send you back to the harem and sail off without you?"

Charlotte's cheeks flared. "Considering that you've done it before, it wouldn't be unjust of me to think such thoughts."

Patrick laughed, bent his head, tasted her lips. "Not this time, my love. Once the *Enchantress* is under way, I may not even allow you to leave the cabin." He touched her breast, making the nipple go taut against the fabric of her muslin camisole.

She smoothed the skirts of her sprigged cambric dress, one of the multitude of garments Patrick had brought from the dressmaker's shop in Costa del Cielo. "You've spent too much time in countries like Riz," she said loftily, hoping he hadn't detected the slight shiver of anticipation his touch had stirred in her. "I was not designed to lie naked in your cabin and provide you with a never-ending supply of satisfaction, you know. I am an intelligent woman with a will and a life of my own."

Patrick grinned and pulled her into a deep, shadowed crevice in the wall on the other side of the passageway. "I don't begrudge your satisfaction," he teased in a whisper, caressing her breasts as he spoke. "Why, pray tell, do you begrudge me mine?"

It took all Charlotte's strength to reply, for the familiar, sweet weakness was flooding through her veins. "I don't," she said. "Perhaps I will confine *you* to the cabin and come to you whenever I want."

He kissed her with leisurely command and great tenderness. "I will gladly be your prisoner," he replied. He was lifting her skirts.

She leaned back against the stone edge of the dark alcove, closed her eyes. "Patrick, please . . ."

Patrick chuckled. "You needn't beg, goddess," he said.

He slipped gracefully to one knee, his hands under her petticoats, on her muslin-covered thighs. "If I were you, though, I'd try to be quiet. We wouldn't want to scandalize the servants."

Charlotte gave a soft cry of surrender as he brought her drawers down and off and nuzzled her once before taking her boldly into his mouth. She had meant to fight him, because the place of his conquering was so outrageous, but instead she ended with her knees over his shoulders and her back braced against the wall, in a near faint of ecstasy at his plundering.

The palace courtyard was strung with paper lanterns, and the women of the harem floated about like brightly colored birds, laughing and chattering. A small band of musicians played in a corner, and a series of tables, set end to end, held food and drink of every description.

Khalif had recovered, for the most part, and the insurrection had been dealt with, once and for all. He wanted to celebrate.

"I will be sorry to see you go, my friend," the sultan said to Patrick as they stood drinking *boza* and watching one of the women dance, her pale blue dress floating as she turned, as insubstantial as fog. "I sense that you will not be returning to Riz in the near future."

Charlotte was on the other side of the courtyard, talking with her friend, Alev, and Patrick felt a swell of happiness in his heart when his eyes found her. "It's time I had a family and a home of my own," he answered. "After this, I'll be a planter, not a sea captain. The *Enchantress* will be at anchor, except when there are crops of sugarcane and indigo to be transported."

Khalif cleared his throat. "While I was ill, and Charlotte cared for me, I began to love her."

Patrick met his friend's earnest and uncomfortable gaze. "I know," he said, laying a hand on Khalif's shoulder. "If you drink a lot of fluid and get some rest, you'll get over the virus."

The sultan blushed, something Patrick had never seen

him do before. He started to speak, and stopped himself, looking miserable and tongue-tied.

Patrick kept his hand on the sultan's shoulder. "She carries my child," he said gently. "Still, ask Charlotte to stay if that's what you want to do. Should she agree—and I warn you, my good friend, that she won't, because she could not bear to be just one of many wives—I will release her. Her happiness is more important to me than anything else."

Khalif sighed, touched Patrick's hand with his own. "I would not broach such a subject," he said, "if I did not know that the marriage ceremony I performed will not be considered valid in your own culture. There has been no Christian service, am I right?"

A strange, defensive feeling gripped Patrick, but he replied evenly. "Yes." He paused, studying his friend with a pensive frown. "I'm surprised you would want a woman you know is carrying another man's child, Khalif. For all its good points, your society is not exactly progressive where such matters are concerned."

"It makes a difference," Khalif said, "that the child's sire is as close to me as a brother." The ghost of Ahmed moved plain in his dark eyes for a moment, then evaporated. "Closer," he amended.

Patrick's regard for Khalif had not lessened—they had been friends too long and the habit was entrenched—but that didn't mean he didn't want to knock the sultan through the nearest wall for lusting after the woman he loved. The captain gestured toward Charlotte. "Tell her what you feel. You're going to go mad if you don't."

Khalif searched Patrick's face for a moment, then proceeded across the courtyard. Patrick wanted to look away, but he could not. He leaned against the stone wall and watched.

It was true enough that he'd never told Charlotte how he felt about her, and when he'd had the opportunity to marry her properly in a Christian country, he hadn't. Maybe he was still as much a rascal as ever. Maybe he would grow tired of her after a while, and hurt her.

The sultan took Charlotte's hand and led her off into the dusk, and Patrick sprang away from the wall, remembering what *he'd* done when he'd lured her into the shadows and lifted her dress.

In the next moment, however, he stopped himself. Charlotte deserved to make her own choice, he thought. Besides, surely she wouldn't want to stay in the palace, to live with the other women and be summoned to Khalif like a servant when he wanted her.

Patrick bit his lower lip. Not a few of the female sex were actually happy as members of a harem. They had every luxury, after all, and the attentions of their husband were rare enough not to become tiresome. If Charlotte married Khalif, she would have jewels, carriages, the grandest of clothes—

He made a mental note to buy her a string of pearls or maybe a diamond necklace if she chose to remain with him. There would be no need of a carriage on the island, but maybe he could have a boat built for her. Yes, a fancy barge, worthy of a modern-day Cleopatra.

Charlotte emerged from the darkness as he watched, and approached Patrick with a determined step. "Khalif has proposed marriage," she told him, with a solemn gravity he had not expected. "Do you have anything to say, Mr. Trevarren?"

Patrick gaped at her for a moment, then barked in a furious whisper, "Of course I have something to say! I want you with me, where you belong."

"Enough to marry me?"

"We *are* married."

"Here, perhaps. But once we get beyond the borders of Riz, we'll be living in sin."

Patrick looked for some sign of humor in her face, but she seemed totally serious. "I see no reason to change things," he told her. "Our arrangement has worked very well up until now."

"It just stopped working," Charlotte answered. "Unless you promise to marry me, before a priest or a minister of the gospel, I'm staying here."

"You can't be serious," Patrick challenged, angry at the realization that she held a winning hand. "You hate this place. Even as a *kadin*, you would only be one of several—"

197

Charlotte interrupted with an eloquent sigh. "I would not have to live here," she said. "Khalif promised to buy me a house in Paris and have a magistrate marry us legally."

The heat of anger surged into Patrick's face. Khalif hadn't said anything *to him* about setting Charlotte up in France and offering her a wedding! "Why, that—"

Charlotte blocked his way when he would have gone around her. "Fighting will solve nothing," she said, in a tone that made him want, just briefly, to throttle her. "Besides, if you attack the sultan, his men will play croquet with your head. Do I have your promise, or not?"

It was blackmail, as far as Patrick was concerned, but some well-honed instinct warned him not to say so. "All right," he said. "You have my promise. We'll be married as soon as possible."

15

AT LAST, CHARLOTTE THOUGHT, STANDING NEAR THE BOW OF the *Enchantress* and gazing toward the horizon, they were at sea. The misty salt air was like medicine, and even the sway of the deck beneath her feet was a welcome sensation. She did not look back at the palace; the place was imprinted on her memory for all time.

Patrick appeared beside her, bracing himself with his forearms against the railing, the wind ruffling his raven hair. "There's a surprise for you in our cabin," he said.

Charlotte studied his profile for a long moment, marveling at the power of the emotions his very presence could rouse in her. She drew a deep breath and took a plunge every bit as dangerous as if she'd dived over the side of the ship to swim with the sharks. "I don't think we should share a cabin," she replied, ignoring the mention of a surprise even though she was wildly curious. "It isn't precisely proper, under the circumstances."

He turned slowly, his eyes narrowing as he looked at her. "What circumstances?" he queried, in a dangerously low tone. "We are married, in case you've forgotten."

"We aren't," Charlotte argued softly, squaring her shoulders. "There is no written record of a union between us anywhere in the Christian world."

Patrick sighed, leaned a little more heavily against the rail. "That didn't seem to bother you when we were in Spain," he pointed out.

"I had other concerns then," Charlotte replied. "I think you should bunk with the crew until we make port and find a judge or minister."

He was ominously silent, and Charlotte was reminded of the great hush that sometimes descended on the land around Puget Sound just before a violent windstorm. "It seems to me, Mrs. Trevarren, that you are slightly tardy in your virtue. Have you forgotten that my child is growing inside you?"

Charlotte drew herself up in valiant resolve. She could not force Patrick to love her, she knew that. But if she didn't have his respect, there would be no hope for them. "I haven't forgotten," she said, at length. "I will not be your mistress, Patrick."

He glowered down at her. "You were willing to go to Paris and live in a house Khalif provided."

"Khalif offered me a real marriage. Besides, I never considered accepting his proposal. I just wanted to illustrate to you that my affections are not to be trifled with. It would be most unwise to take me for granted."

When Patrick didn't respond, but simply glared as if he would dearly love to fling her overboard, Charlotte turned in what she hoped was a dramatic and graceful swirl of skirts and marched off to investigate the surprise awaiting her in the captain's cabin.

On the bed she found a stack of high-quality sketching books, tied together with a wide blue ribbon. There was also a fine set of water-mixed paints, colored chalks, some special pens, and half a dozen bottles of ink in various shades.

Charlotte was charmed and delighted, but she was also determined not to let gratitude overcome good sense. Patrick was a willful man, and if she did not set adequate boundaries for their relationship, great unhappiness would result.

With a smile, she took up one of the drawing pads and the box of bright chalks and returned to the deck. She was not one to keep a journal, not in the common fashion at least, but Charlotte liked to put her dreams and memories down on paper in the form of sketches. She had not had much opportunity to draw since her abduction in the *souk* in Riz, and the prospect of making pictures was a wondrous pleasure to her.

She found an out-of-the-way place on the upper deck, sat on a crate with her limbs curled gracefully beneath her, and began to record her experiences in detail. She drew harem dancers, and men fighting with swords, and a desert camp beneath an enormous moon. She rendered Patrick's likeness more than any other, however, showing him as he'd looked in profile that morning, standing at the railing.

"That's very fine work, Mrs. Trevarren," a voice observed.

Charlotte looked up, startled, and smiled to see Mr. Cochran standing before her. She turned to a fresh page in the pad and began to sketch his image as they talked.

"Thank you," she said. "I've always drawn, you know, and I was trained in Europe."

Mr. Cochran crouched before her, reminding her of an Indian at ease beside a campfire. "You should take steps to preserve those pictures," he said amiably. "You'll want to show them to your grandchildren, when you tell of your adventures in Riz."

Charlotte sighed. "I haven't thought that far ahead," she confided, still sketching. "At the moment I'm still trying to sort it all out for myself."

They lingered in companionable silence for a time, then Mr. Cochran said, "I was sent to tell you that your dinner is waiting in the captain's cabin."

Charlotte was hungry; the fresh sea air and sunshine had given her a hearty appetite. She closed her sketch pad, gathered her chalks back into their box, and stood.

There was no sign of Patrick when she reached the cabin,

now crowded with trunks containing all the new clothes made for her in Spain. Although Charlotte told herself quite firmly that she was relieved to be alone, a deeper and more insistent part of her nature was disappointed.

She poured water from a brass ewer into a basin and washed her face and hands, then sat down at Patrick's desk to survey the contents of her tray. There was fresh fish, riced potatoes, green beans cooked with bacon, and hot tea.

Charlotte ate with exuberance.

She was finished, and replete, when Patrick swept in like a fierce wind scouring a canyon. He stood just inside the doorway, arms folded, regarding her in a way that made her distinctly uneasy. Especially since she had left the desk to sit on the bed, with her back to the wall and her legs outstretched, the sketchbook in her lap.

At last the captain spoke. "You haven't changed your mind about our sleeping arrangements, I presume?"

Charlotte shook her head, struggling to put down the rebellion of emotion stirring in her heart and soul. She would miss Patrick's lovemaking, for she had reveled in it, but she knew she must make every effort not to show her feelings. If Mr. Trevarren were to take her into his arms and kiss her, for instance, or simply touch her in some of the ways he had, her fortitude would surely melt like so much candle wax.

"That is correct," she said formally and at some length. She kept the sketchbook in front of her like a shield and primly smoothed the skirts of her dress.

"You completely discount our marriage, then?"

Charlotte lifted her chin. "We have no marriage," she said stubbornly.

Patrick looked at her in silence for a long moment, then sighed philosophically and said, "Very well." With that, he clapped his hands together. "I divorce you," he said. He clapped again. "I divorce you." And a third time. "I divorce you."

Even though she herself had denied the existence of a marriage between them, Patrick's gesture came as a severe shock to Charlotte. She knew she'd gone pale, and that her lower lip was trembling, and that she was going to cry at any moment.

Patrick nodded politely, opened the door, and walked out of the cabin without another word.

Charlotte sat stunned, staring at the place where he'd stood, as if by concentrating she could conjure him back. Tears brimmed along her lower lashes and coursed down her cheeks.

Her unreal marriage seemed very real indeed, now that it had been terminated. What had she done?

Patrick did not make another appearance that night; he sent the cook's helper, Tipper Doon, for the toiletries and fresh clothes he needed.

Feeling especially lonely, Charlotte took out pen and ink and paper and drew her father's image, then added Lydia's deceptively delicate-looking personage at his side. On succeeding pages she sketched Millie and each of her brothers, and her beloved uncle Devon as well.

The dear faces were both a comfort to her and a reminder of how very far from home she really was. She had pinned the drawings to the walls of the cabin to dry, and she cried as she washed, cleaned her teeth, put on her nightgown, and brushed her hair. After lying abed for a long time, the sea rocking the ship as gently as a loving mother would rock a cradle, she drifted off into a fitful and restless sleep.

The first dream came that night.

Charlotte awakened with a cry, sitting bolt upright in bed, groping wildly for Patrick before she remembered with dismay that she had banned him from the cabin and he had subsequently "divorced" her.

She tried to remember what had happened in the nightmare, in order to dismiss it as mere fancy and thereby calm herself, but she recalled nothing except a sense of doom and helpless horror. The feeling lingered long after she had lain down again, long after her breathing and heartbeat had slowed to their normal meters.

It was the pregnancy, she finally concluded, laying her hands protectively over her abdomen, one above the other. Lydia had sometimes been very testy and emotional when she was carrying her children. Her stepmother had had dreams, too, and nights that were altogether sleepless, and once she'd left the family dinner table in tears because Brigham had announced his intention to vote for a Republican president.

Charlotte sighed again, then tossed and turned for a while, trying to get comfortable. She missed curling up in the warm shelter of Patrick's embrace, and feeling his hard chest against her back.

Finally, beset by pure exhaustion, Charlotte slept.

They passed Gibraltar early the next morning—it was a breathtaking sight, and Charlotte's pencil flew over her sketch pad. Patrick might have anchored the *Enchantress* there, at the busy port, long enough for them to be married at least, but he made no effort to do so.

Charlotte avoided him, which was relatively easy because he was making every effort to stay out of her path. She considered going to him and trying to institute some sort of peace, but that idea went wholly against the grain. After all, *he* had been the arbitrary one, with his summary hand-clapping divorce.

Still, Charlotte missed Patrick, and not just in her bed. She mourned the silent, secret language that had grown between them, the shared laughter, even the rousing disagreements.

The *Enchantress* coursed gracefully along the coast of Africa, the wind warm and ample in her sails. Charlotte stood at the railing for hours at a time, watching the tropical shoreline for any sign of an elephant or a zebra or a lion. From a practical standpoint, she knew such exotic animals would only be seen far inland, but that didn't stop her from hoping.

Every night she ate alone in the cabin and slept alone in the overlarge bed. Sometimes she would return and find evidence that Patrick had been there, to retrieve a book or fresh clothes or some other personal belonging probably, but for the most part he managed to stay on the opposite end of the ship.

The dreams continued and always left Charlotte with a

vague feeling of impending disaster, although she could never remember clear details when she awakened.

They had been at sea a full ten days, and the *Enchantress* was headed in an easterly direction, toward the South Seas, when they found the first rat.

Cochran himself had stumbled upon the corpse while on night watch. The rodent had retched up most of its insides, and was still bleeding from its ears. It was too much, even for Cochran's iron stomach, and he staggered to the rail.

He was weak when he came away, and he took care not to step on the vile mess on the deck as he hurried past it to awaken the captain.

Patrick was in a foul mood. He had not exchanged a civil word with Charlotte in nigh on two weeks, let alone shared her bed. He hated sleeping in the cramped cabin reserved for the occasional paying passenger; the ceiling was too low and he was continually bumping his head.

He was awake, nursing a glass of brandy, when the pounding sounded at his door and he heard Cochran's voice.

"Captain! Open up, quickly!"

Alarm spiraled in the pit of Patrick's stomach at the urgency of the man's plea. Cochran had been everywhere and seen everything, and it took a great deal to shake him.

Patrick raised the latch and drew back the door. "Good God, man, what is it?" he grumbled. He wasn't drunk exactly, but his head was fogged and he was a little unsteady on his feet.

"Come with me," Cochran ordered, and even though the night was cool for the tropics, a fine sheen of perspiration gleamed on his skin. "Now."

"What—?"

"Now," the first mate insisted.

Patrick followed him along the passageway, up the steps, onto the main deck. On the starboard side, Cochran took one of the lamps down from its hook and held it over a disgusting mass of gore that had once been a rat.

The stench was worse than the sight, and Patrick turned

his head for a moment, swallowed the bile that rushed into the back of his throat. "What do you make of this?" he asked, in a hushed voice, after a long interval had passed. "Is it plague?"

Cochran was keeping his distance. "I don't know if it's plague or not, Captain. I do know that we're in trouble, every last man jack of us."

"And Charlotte," Patrick whispered, closing his eyes briefly. *And our baby.* "Have somebody get rid of this thing and swab the deck with lye soap. In the morning we'll search the ship from one end to the other to see if there are others."

"There will be more," Cochran assured his captain. He sounded like a man talking in his sleep.

Patrick roused the cook and set him to boiling water. Then he went back to his cabin, stripped off his clothes, and scoured himself from head to foot. Of course, he couldn't wash away the memory of the diseased rat; it was an image that would haunt his mind for a long time.

When he was through washing, he dressed in fresh clothes and left the cabin again, going straight to the place where Charlotte slept.

She had locked the door, and even though that was the only prudent thing for a woman to do on a ship full of men, he was annoyed.

He closed one hand into a fist and pounded on the heavy panel until it shook.

Finally Patrick heard the latch rattle on the inside and the door creaked open a little way. Charlotte peered around the edge.

"Patrick?" It sounded as though she would have been less surprised to encounter Lincoln's ghost. "Wh-What is it?"

He pushed the door open, stepped over the threshold, and stood looking down at her. She was wearing one of his shirts for a nightgown, and her maple-sugar hair tumbled loose down her back and over her shoulders. Her golden eyes were wide and troubled, but if he wasn't mistaken, there was a triumph in them, too.

Patrick couldn't tell her about the rat, and the possible meaning of such a gruesome event. After all, it wouldn't do to frighten her without just cause. Still, he couldn't leave her, either.

"I've missed you," he confessed gruffly, and that was true. He'd regretted his impulsive divorce many times, especially in the depths of the night when he'd needed so badly to turn to her for that sweet solace only she could offer.

She folded her arms, tilted her head to one side. "And I've missed you," she admitted. "But—"

He thought of epidemics he'd seen, men dead of the plagues and strange fevers so rife in the tropics. "Just let me hold you," he interrupted.

To his infinite relief, Charlotte did not make him beg. She simply took his hand and led him to their bed. Deftly she began unfastening his shirt.

"You look dreadful, Patrick," she said gently. "What is it that's frightened you so?"

Patrick pulled her near, held her very tightly for a moment, his eyes closed. He could not explain, not yet. "Charlotte," was all he said.

After a few minutes, he took off his shirt and boots, then his breeches, and crawled into bed. Charlotte came readily into his arms and tucked herself up close against him. Her heart seemed to beat in rhythm with his.

"I need you," he said, after a long time, fully expecting her to rebuff and even revile him.

Instead, Charlotte ran her hand over the hard muscles of his stomach, then clasped his rod with strong fingers.

Patrick moaned in an agony of joyous relief and passion as swift as a riotous western river. Then he caught hold of her wrist and held it for a moment.

"I'm warning you, Charlotte," he rasped. "If you're only teasing me, stop. Now."

She kissed the edge of his jawline. "Whatever it is that's tormenting you, I'll make you forget it," she promised.

And she did.

Charlotte was humming to herself as she washed and dressed the next morning, recalling how she'd put Patrick through his paces the night before. There had, of course, been no small amount of personal satisfaction in the task, and for the first time in days, she hadn't been troubled by nightmares.

She breakfasted in the cabin, as usual, then took a sketch pad and pencils and went out on deck.

The sun was bright against a robin's-egg sky, but there was no wind, and the water seemed smooth as blue ice. Tension lay over the vessel like an unseen shroud, and when Charlotte looked up, she saw that the sails were limp against the masts.

"We're becalmed," Tipper Doon told her as he passed with a bucket of steaming water. "And there're dead rats all about. You'd best go back to your cabin and stay there, Mrs. Trevarren."

Charlotte scrambled to catch up with him. "What do you mean, 'there're dead rats all about'?" she insisted.

The boy stopped, met her gaze. His young face looked grim, even in the golden beauty of that strange day. "It's some sickness, ma'am," he said patiently. "The rats got it first, but chances are they'll spread it to us people soon enough."

Charlotte shrank back for a moment, automatically sheltered her baby by putting one hand to her abdomen. "Dear God," she breathed. "Isn't there anything we can do?"

"Doon!" bellowed a voice from farther along the deck.

"I'd best go now, ma'am," Tipper hastened to say. "'Fore this water is too cold to do any good."

Charlotte hunted until she found Patrick. He was aft, searching the horizon through a gleaming steel spyglass trimmed in copper.

It was obvious that he'd sensed her presence, but he took his time acknowledging her.

"If you've come seeking an apology for last night," Patrick informed her brusquely, keeping his eyes trained on the distance, "you'll be disappointed."

"Last night be damned," Charlotte sputtered. "Look at me!"

He slanted his gaze in her direction. "You've found out about the rats," he said, with a note of resignation in his voice.

"What does it mean?" Charlotte was filled with dread, and she well knew that the disaster her dreams had warned about was upon them.

"They're diseased. Cochran came across the first one last night, turned inside out on the deck. Since sunrise, the men have found a dozen more in like condition."

Charlotte swayed ever so slightly, reached out and gripped the rail to steady herself. "There will be sickness, then."

"Without question," Patrick answered grimly. He made no move to touch her, but she so wished to be sheltered in his arms.

"Perhaps we could go ashore somewhere—"

"Even if there were land within a hundred miles—and there isn't—we couldn't bring a plague like this on innocent people, Charlotte."

She trembled, hugged herself. "My baby," she whispered. "Oh, dear God in heaven, my baby."

Patrick took her into his arms at last, but he sounded angry when he spoke. "And mine," he pointed out in sharp tones.

Charlotte embraced him, rested her head against his shoulder. "God help us," she said brokenly. "God help us all."

The first sailor went down with the malady the crew had named the bloody fever the next morning. The ship was still becalmed, and it seemed to Charlotte that the *Enchantress* and all her passengers were adrift in the palm of the devil's hand.

By noon, two more men had been carried to their beds, and at twilight, the first victim died. A prayer was offered and he was put overboard, wrapped in the blanket from his bed. The man's meager belongings were put into a tin box and locked away until they could be given to his family.

In the beginning, Charlotte was practically inert with fear. Then she got hold of herself, and her mind cooled. She went below to help tend the sick and was quickly and fiercely ordered away.

Desperate to be doing *something,* she tried to draw, but all her pencil would produce were gargoyles and specters and other horrible monsters.

When night came, the deck seemed utterly deserted. Charlotte stood looking up at the stars, praying for her baby's life. A cool breeze whispered through her hair, and she heard a shout from a man high up in the crow's nest.

"There's a wind coming up!" he cried, and sailors rushed on deck, eager to set the sails and be under way again. Charlotte suspected they were entertaining fanciful hopes of outrunning the pestilence somehow, just as she was.

There were more funerals the next day, and still others the day after that. Charlotte remained hearty and strong, though even Patrick could not keep her from the sick. She bathed fevered faces, wrote letters to mothers and sisters and sweethearts, spooned broth into unwilling mouths, and emptied slop jars. She sang soft songs, held hands, prayed that departing souls would be received in heaven.

"You must go back to your cabin and rest," Cochran told her, late one night, when she'd just covered the slack face of a boy barely older than the eldest of her brothers. "You have the baby to think of, and the captain."

Patrick had been working as tirelessly as Charlotte, if not more so, since the members of his crew had begun to diminish and the winds had picked up. Far into the night, he would collapse beside her on their bed, fully clothed, sleep for two hours at the most, and then get up and start over again.

"There's nowhere I can go to hide from this fever," Charlotte said. "Patrick says it's got into the very timbers of the ship herself."

Cochran nodded. He was gaunt, and his beard stood out, bristly, on his gray cheeks. "I've seen vessels come ashore without a living soul aboard, once they've been struck by the pestilence."

Charlotte shivered, folded her hands in her lap. She couldn't remember which of her dresses she was wearing, and didn't take the trouble to look. "I refuse to die," she said, addressing the fates as much as Cochran. "I haven't done all my living yet."

Remarkably, considering the circumstances, Cochran smiled. "If anybody can survive a plague like this one, it would be you," he said. "It does seem that the faeries and spirits love you with devotion."

Tipper Doon, fallen sick these three days past, groaned fitfully in his sleep. Tears of despair stung Charlotte's eyes as she moved her stool to the side of his hammock and began to bathe his face. "Don't you go and die, Tipper," she scolded, so weary that she forgot her conversation with Cochran in midstream. "You haven't done all your living, either."

With that, Charlotte began to weep in earnest, bending forward until her forehead touched Tipper's chest. "Lydia," she sobbed, beyond the bounds of reason now and unable to pull herself back. "Oh, Lydia, please help us!"

Strong hands lifted her from the stool, steely arms encircled her. Patrick had come for her, and she wept helplessly, hopelessly, against his shoulder as he carried her out of the hold where the sick men lay.

In their cabin, he undressed her and put her to bed. When she wouldn't eat, he spooned weak tea into her mouth instead.

"If only Lydia were here," she said, aware that she was raving, unable to stop herself. "She would know what to do—"

"Hush now," Patrick said. He was beside her in bed, holding her. "We're only a few days from the island. You can go ashore there, and old Jacoba will look after you until you're strong again."

The words made little sense to Charlotte, but she understood one thing: that the island was near. She held on tightly to the hope of reaching it.

Charlotte slept until the middle of the next afternoon, and awakened feeling stronger. She was even a little embarrassed that she'd surrendered so thoroughly to exhaustion the night before, and allowed Patrick and the others to see her fall apart.

After nibbling at a piece of dried bread and some fruit, she dressed and went off to the hold to see how the sick were faring. If she didn't spell Mr. Cochran, she feared he would not take the time to eat or sleep, and much depended upon him.

Reaching the hold, Charlotte saw no sign of the first mate, but the ship's captain sat in a straight-backed chair beside a patient's berth, his face buried in his hands.

She stood behind Patrick, touched his shoulders. She knew his despair, knew he felt responsible for the sufferings of his crew. "This isn't your fault," she pointed out, with gentle reason.

He bolted from his chair, as if her fingers had burned his skin, and staggered out of her reach. His back was still turned to her; she had yet to see his face.

"We'll reach the island soon," she said, in a quavering voice, trying to offer him the same hope he had extended to her the night before.

Patrick turned, swayed slightly, and waved Charlotte away with a distracted motion of one hand, as though she were an insect. "Tomorrow," he confirmed, in tones she barely recognized. "But I won't be leaving the ship until the last man can be brought ashore, and that might be weeks."

"But you said—"

He looked at her at last, and she saw the sickness move in his features, like a second entity. "I said you would be going ashore, and you will. To send you is to risk every life on the island, but I can do nothing else. The rest of us will stay until the danger is past."

Charlotte moved toward Patrick, sensing what was about to happen, but before she reached him, his knees buckled and he sank to the deck with a crash. She screamed once, and fell across Patrick's chest in abject sorrow, and it took Mr. Cochran and several other men to pull her away.

16

TORCHES BURNED ALONG THE SHORE OF THE ISLAND, SHINING like golden stars of welcome in the dark night. To the crew and passengers of the *Enchantress,* however, the land might have been beyond the far side of heaven, rather than within shouting distance, for they dared not leave the ship.

Charlotte stood on deck, exhausted and haggard from battling the tenacious illness that had felled Patrick and a number of the other men, and looked with yearning at the flickering lights and the shadows of trees.

"Oh, Mr. Cochran," she said to the man standing at her side, "I do long for fresh food and solid ground beneath my feet. I want to sleep beside my husband in a bed with crisp, clean sheets, and smell the scents of flowers instead of the stench of this plague."

The first mate nodded with glum agreement. "Aye, Mrs. Trevarren," he said, with a sigh. "Sometimes it seems we're condemned to sail back and forth across the River Styx, you and I, while Satan himself laughs at our predicament."

Charlotte sagged slightly against the railing, nearly at the end of her strength. By some miracle, she had not fallen sick, but Patrick had been unconscious for several days, and she could not know whether or not her unborn baby had been affected by the malady. There would be no peace for her until she felt the child move, and until its father was his old arrogant and irascible self again.

She lifted her chin, determined that, for the sake of her man and her baby, as well as herself, she would not fold.

Charlotte spat overboard, furiously and with vigor, and shook her fist. "That's for the devil," she said, with purpose. Then she shouted into the gloom, "You're not going to win, Lucifer, so go back to hell, where you belong, and leave us be!"

Mr. Cochran chuckled, and there was grief as well as amusement in the sound. "Are you truly so intrepid, Mrs. Trevarren, that you would challenge the evil one himself?"

"Yes," Charlotte replied firmly, but in the next moment her resolve deflated a little. "It's easier if there is someone to fight, even if that someone is the devil himself," she told her friend sadly. Then she took up her skirts and turned back, making her way quickly along the deck, down the steps, through the passageway to Patrick's cabin.

He lay insensate, his skin gray as death and at the same time drenched in sweat, upon the very bed where he had made such vital, tireless, explosive love to Charlotte only days before. Candle flames provided the only light, a dim, funereal glow that made Charlotte shiver.

One by one she lighted the kerosene lanterns and blew out the candles. Then she went to the bedside and began, for the thousandth time, to bathe Patrick's face and upper body with cool water.

"Patrick?" She had whispered his name again and again, and he had not responded, even with the flicker of an eyelash or the twitch of a muscle, but this time he actually opened his eyes.

Charlotte was not comforted by this, for she viewed his soul through those indigo windows, and it appeared to be receding, drawing back from life. Tears brimmed along her lower lashes and she smiled and took one of his hands in hers.

"You're home," she said gently. "We're at anchor, just a stone's throw from the shore of your island."

Patrick sighed. "Good," he said. For some moments he fought visibly to gather strength. "You're well, Charlotte? The child—?"

She bent, kissed his pale forehead. "I'm fine, Mr. Trevarren, and your baby is just where you left it."

He smiled at that, and the sight broke Charlotte's heart as smoothly as a piece of seasoned wood coming under the ax. "That's good," he struggled to say. "And the men? How many survive?"

Charlotte's instinct was to protect Patrick from the truth, but she knew that could not be done. "Twenty-six," she answered.

"Fourteen perished then," Patrick said. He closed his eyes once more, and a single tear slid down over his right temple to glitter in his hair.

She squeezed his hand. "Yes," she told him softly, "but it seems the worst is over. Five of the men who fell ill are recovering now."

Again Patrick looked at her. "If I die, bury me on the ridge behind the island house—Jacoba will show you the place."

"You'd better *not* die, Patrick Trevarren," Charlotte scolded quickly, holding on to his hand with a tighter grasp, fearing he meant to go right that minute. "I'm depending on you, and so is this child of ours." She pressed his hand against her belly, hoping to emphasize the reality of the new life they'd conceived together even though there was still no evidence to be felt.

He brought her fingers to his lips, kissed the knuckles. Then he closed his fever-bright eyes and slept.

Charlotte did not let go of his hand, but clutched it in her own as she prayed fervently for Patrick, for their baby, for herself. When there were no words left, no dreams and hopes and pleas that had not been brought before the Almighty, Charlotte stretched herself out beside the man whose soul was joined to hers and slept.

A knock at the cabin door awakened her; she sat bolt upright, fresh from the deepest regions of slumber, and it was a moment before she realized where she was. She turned to Patrick, saw that he was breathing still, and swayed under a crushing flood of gratitude.

"Just a moment," she called quietly to the visitor waiting on the other side of the door. Rising, Charlotte smoothed her hair and her hopelessly rumpled dress. "Who is it, please?"

"It's Miss Jacoba McFaylon," came the reply, in a burr as thick as cold oatmeal. "I've come for my beloved captain, and no one will keep me from him, miss, neither you nor that fatheaded Mr. Cochran nor anyone else on this ship."

Charlotte opened the door and found a plump woman, late in middle age, standing in the outer passage and looking every bit as determined as she'd sounded. She wore a crisply starched housekeeper's dress and had gray hair and one lazy eye. The other orb, brown and bright as a bird's, regarded Charlotte with testy curiosity.

"Mr. Trevarren has given orders that he's not to be taken ashore until all danger is past," Charlotte said, somewhat lamely, stepping back to admit Mrs. McFaylon, who entered like the fiery breath of God.

"I've never followed his damn orders anyway," the Scotswoman said. She bustled over to the bed, lifted one of Patrick's eyelids, and peered beneath it.

"Good God, Jacoba," he blurted out, with more strength than Charlotte had seen him evidence since before his illness, "you'd scare a man straight into perdition without giving it a second thought!"

Jacoba nodded wisely. "I told Mr. Cochran as how you'd come round soon enough, if I could just lay a hand to you, and I was right," she said. She gestured toward Charlotte. "And who's this pretty bit, pray tell?"

Charlotte smarted under the older woman's words and tone; they combined to make her feel like a stray mongrel with mange and a bad smell.

Patrick's eyes seemed to dance, just for a moment, as he looked past his housekeeper to Charlotte. "She's my wife—sort of. It's a long story, I'm afraid—one I haven't the strength to tell just now. I want you to take very good care of Mrs. Trevarren, Jacoba—no matter what happens."

The old woman turned to look at Charlotte with that single, plainly discerning eye. "Mrs. Trevarren, is it? Well, the others will not be pleased to hear that, now will they?"

"The others?" Charlotte inquired.

Conveniently Patrick closed his eyes and descended into another deep sleep.

"What others?" Charlotte persisted, drawing closer to Jacoba.

Jacoba waved the question aside. "No time for such silliness," she said. "We must get the captain to his bed now, where he can be looked after in a proper fashion."

Not even an hour had passed before Patrick had been put on a litter and taken ashore by boat. Charlotte rode with him, carrying her art supplies and staying stubbornly close to his side. She couldn't help looking around here, though, for the sea and the island and the sky made a great spectacle, with their violent blues and greens, crimsons and golds.

Parrots and other, smaller birds added dizzying colors of their own—reds and yellows, pinks and whites; the variety seemed endless. Flowers bloomed everywhere, in even more audacious shades, and a sugary scent filled the air.

The small boat was manned by black-skinned natives, and when they reached the shore, they leaped out into the surf and lifted Patrick's litter between them, like pallbearers carrying a coffin. The captain was only half-conscious, but in a moment of lucidity he barked, "Jacoba!"

The Scotswoman, who had been waiting on the beach, stepped forward, but there was nothing in her manner to indicate that she was in any way cowed by the thunderous summons.

"Here I be, Captain," she said, with awe-inspiring dignity.

"I gave an order," Patrick pointed out, struggling to rise from the litter and failing. "I was to remain on board ship until there was no danger of bringing this fever ashore!"

"So you did," Jacoba conceded, "but there are lots of your orders I don't pay a mind to, sir, and this be one of them." She turned her single eye to the two men standing at either end of Patrick's litter. "Take him to his rooms in the big house, and be quick about it. I've got a kettle of my special soup bubbling on the stove, and the sooner we get some down that gullet of his, the better."

Charlotte was at once relieved and disquieted. She felt a new hope for Patrick's recovery, and it was an almost holy joy to feel the solid ground under her feet. Still, Jacoba was obviously a force to be reckoned with, and Charlotte did not know whether the older woman was friend or foe.

She scrambled through the deep, soft sand to keep up with the litter bearers, all her attention fixed on Patrick. He was very weak, and the bones of his face showed too plainly under his skin, but he flashed her a brief smile before drifting off again into sleep.

Patrick's house stood high on a hillside, overlooking the turquoise waters of the cove, a gigantic place with white Grecian pillars supporting the roof of the front veranda. Charlotte was too weary to be impressed, though her arms did tighten around her drawing supplies as she regarded it.

They crossed a great lawn, as green and manicured as any in England, and entered through a great double door. The floor of the entryway was of priceless green marble, and there was a tapestry on one wall that surely dated from the sixteenth century.

The work portrayed a number of nymphs in gauzy dresses, lounging around a pool, and Charlotte made herself a silent promise that she would return later and study the scene more closely. While it was beautiful, something about the tapestry troubled her, and she was frowning as she climbed the wide, curving stairway with the others.

Patrick's quarters took up the entire front of the house, and the enormous bed, with its graceful folds of mosquito netting, overlooked the sea. Three sets of French doors separated the room from a stone terrace large enough to accommodate a table and chairs and numerous potted plants.

The island men took Patrick from his litter and laid him on the bed, dirty clothes and all. Charlotte set her art things on an exquisite table topped with gray marble and approached him, unaware until the moment of impact that Jacoba had the same thought.

"I won't leave him," Charlotte said bluntly when she saw the look of challenge in Jacoba's eye.

Patrick had rallied himself again, however briefly. "Charlotte stays," he decreed.

Jacoba gave a great sigh. "Very well," she said, although it was clear from her tone that the concession was against her better judgment. She regarded Charlotte thoughtfully, and at length. "You look as weak and spindly as a baby bird," she finally announced. "You won't be much help to the captain if you don't get some rest and some flesh on those bones, and a hot bath wouldn't hurt you none, either, if you don't mind my saying so."

Charlotte lifted a corner of her mouth in a weary smile. "Would it matter if I did mind your saying so?"

Jacoba narrowed her eye for a moment, then let out a booming laugh that did much to ease the tension. "No, miss, not so's you'd notice. There's a washroom that way, and I'll see what I can find you in the way of fresh clothes."

"I have plenty of dresses on board the ship—"

Jacoba interrupted with a shake of her head. "Won't do. We'll boil the fever out of what things we can, but the rest will need burning."

Charlotte did not want to think of her beautiful, custom-made garments being tossed into a fire, but she knew no unnecessary chances would be taken lest there be a new epidemic among the people on shore.

"What about the crew?" she asked. "Many of them are still sick."

Jacoba spoke distractedly, her mind evidently fixed on the next task awaiting her busy, competent hands. "There be an old homestead just down the beach; the captain's men will be looked after there until we're sure the plague has passed."

Charlotte nodded and made her way toward the indicated washroom, too weary to think further.

The luxury of the chamber startled her, for she had not seen its like even in Khalif's palace. There was a great, tile-lined pool, set directly into the floor, and even one of those modern commodes with the pull-chain for flushing. Lush plants, thriving in priceless crockery urns, lined one wall, and there was a high, arched window to let in the vision of the sea.

Charlotte stripped away her ruined dress and washed carefully with scented soap. Presently a smiling woman with beautiful coffee-colored skin entered, bringing towels and a white cotton dress.

"Hello," Charlotte said, pitifully grateful for the smile. She was a stranger in paradise, and not entirely sure of her welcome. "My name is Charlotte Trevarren." A frown creased her forehead. Or was she still Charlotte Quade?

The maid executed a curtsy, averting her eyes. "I be Mary Catch-much-fish," she said. "Miss Charlotte wants food?"

Charlotte's stomach grumbled at the prospect. "Oh, yes, please." She took one of the towels from the stone bench where Mary had set them and covered herself modestly as she climbed the steps out of the pool.

Mary bobbed again. "I bring plate to table outside, now Mr. Sun go to other side of house." With these words, she turned and went out again.

Charlotte put on the white dress, which was too large for her but clean and otherwise comfortable, found a comb and carefully worked the tangles from her wet hair. When she went out into the master bedroom again, Jacoba was spooning some sort of broth into Patrick's mouth. His eyes, so hollow before on the rare occasions when he'd opened them, brightened when he saw Charlotte approaching the bed.

He held out one hand, and Charlotte went to him, ignoring Jacoba's palpable disapproval.

"He'll be needing a bath of his own now," the housekeeper interceded, her voice blustery.

Patrick actually chuckled, an event that made Charlotte's beleaguered spirits soar in celebration. "I probably smell like a camel," he said.

"Worse," Charlotte assured him, bending to kiss his forehead. A moment later, she raised her eyes to meet Jacoba's gaze straight on. "I'll see to my husband's bath," she said. "You may go as soon as you've finished giving him the soup."

Jacoba opened her mouth to protest, darted a quick look at Patrick, and then thought better of speaking.

Mary entered, carrying a tray, and Charlotte kissed Patrick again, then followed the good-natured maid out onto the terrace. "I'll need lots of hot, clean water for the captain, please," Charlotte said as she sat down at the table in a pool of soft sunshine. An array of fresh and exotic fruits awaited her, along with cold chicken and a delicately flavored rice dish.

"Yes, Miss Charlotte," the maid replied, with another curtsy.

Charlotte was so hungry that she was tremulous, but as she ate, the weakness subsided and she felt steady again, if tired. The view of the sun-dappled sea revived her a little too, though she was glad to be back on shore again.

Restored, she left her tray for Mary and went inside. The requested water waited in tall ewers, still steaming, and cloths, basins, and towels had been laid out as well. There was no sign of Jacoba, and Patrick had drifted back into one of his fitful sleeps.

Gently, tenderly, Charlotte undressed this man who was her soul mate if not her true husband, and began to bathe him. The process took some considerable time, and Patrick did not awaken, though he sometimes stirred. Maybe it was Jacoba's special herbal soup, maybe it was being in a safe and comfortable place again, but color was rising under his pale skin, and Charlotte could sense a growing strength in him.

When he was clean again, when even his rich, raven-dark hair had been washed and gently combed and pulled back the way he liked it, Charlotte curled up beside him in her borrowed dress, yawned, and followed him into the solace of slumber.

She awakened when she felt a familiar hand on her breast. Her senses leaped in response, pulling her suddenly to full consciousness, and she raised herself on one elbow to look into Patrick's face.

The room was filled with moonlight, and someone, probably Mary or Jacoba, had lowered the mosquito netting into place, giving the bed a misty sort of privacy. The air was warm, the night filled with a soft symphony of cricket-song, an ocean breeze rustling in the palm trees nearby, and the combined heartbeats of two lovers.

"Charlotte," Patrick said, and it was as though the name had cost him everything to say, and yet been worth the price. With the same hand that had caressed her breast, he lowered the neckline of her dress and bared her.

221

She knew what he wanted, and yearned just as deeply to give it. Charlotte moved close to him, brushed his mouth lightly with her hardening nipple, and he took it hungrily and suckled hard, as though starved for her.

Charlotte crooned with involuntary pleasure, for attending Patrick in this particular way always excited her, always filled her with a sense of sweet power. She entwined her fingers in his hair and urged him closer. After a time, she gave him her other breast, and he drank greedily from that one as well.

Finally he broke away, making a sound that might have been a groan or a laugh. "I've started something I'm not strong enough to finish," he lamented, his eyes glittering in the darkness as he regarded Charlotte, who lay trembling beside him now with her dress down around her waist. "Still, I want to see pleasure in your face as much as I want to watch the sun rise tomorrow."

Charlotte's eyes were stinging with tears, for there had been many hours when she'd thought she would lose this man who meant more to her than her next breath. Now it was plain that he was going to live. "Another time," she said softly.

But Patrick shook his head. "Now," he answered. Then he took her hand and pressed her own fingers firmly to the soft curls at the apex of her thighs. His hand moved atop hers, setting the rhythm and at the same time preventing escape.

Charlotte groaned, her legs widening involuntarily. "Patrick," she gasped, breathless, her head already tossing back and forth on the linen-covered pillow. "This is— scandalous—"

"Ummm," he agreed. "Scandalous. You're beautiful, Charlotte."

She convulsed softly under his fingers and her own, but the tide of passion only rose higher. "For an almost-wife?"

He increased the pace, made a low sound of approval as she responded. "For a saucy little vixen," he replied.

Her pelvis bucked and she cried out as a particularly keen shaft of pleasure went through her. "Dear God, Patrick—I can't bear it—it's too strong—"

"And getting stronger," he said.

Charlotte was fevered with delicious desperation. "I'm going to come apart . . ."

"Yes," he agreed, and when he bent to tongue her nipple briefly, Charlotte's prediction came true and she splintered into a million fiery pieces. While she thrashed in Patrick Trevarren's vast bed, he watched and savored her every response.

Morning found Patrick stronger but also distracted and more than a little distant. He sent Charlotte out of the room and spent a long time conferring with Mr. Cochran. When the first mate had gone, looking grim as he passed along the hallway, Charlotte hurried back to her husband's bedside.

Patrick was sitting up, his chest bare, his broad back resting against a mountain of pillows. He was gazing out through the center set of French doors, which had been opened earlier to the sea and the fresh air, and he did not look away when Charlotte came in.

She followed his gaze, saw the *Enchantress* bobbing on the tide at some distance from shore, her sails pristine against the varying blues of the water and sky. Although the scene was almost unbearably beautiful, or perhaps *because* of that, Charlotte felt an unaccountable dread.

"The crewmen—are they recovering?"

Still Patrick did not turn his eyes from the ship, the "she" he loved beyond all others. "Yes," he answered. "There have been no more deaths."

The room was comfortable with that soft, moist warmth typical of the tropics, but Charlotte shivered all the same. "Then why do you look like that?" she dared to ask. "Anyone would think you'd lost your most cherished friend."

"Maybe I have," Patrick answered, and she saw pain move in the strong lines of his face. Even gauntness and the lack of color could not disguise the aristocratic set of his features. "Maybe I have."

Charlotte glanced uneasily toward the beautiful clipper ship gracing the harbor. "What are you saying?" she whispered.

At last he turned his indigo eyes to her, and she saw

despair in them, along with returning health and that innate arrogance she both loved and hated.

"There will be one more victim of this cursed plague," he said, in a raspy whisper. Then he looked at the *Enchantress* again, as though to memorize every line of her, every sail and board.

Charlotte felt her knees go weak. She put both hands to her face as she recalled Patrick telling her that the dreaded plague had gotten into the very timbers of the ship. "Oh, no," she said. "No!"

"She'll go down after sunset," Patrick said in a toneless voice, his gaze remaining with his beloved mistress, the graceful ship that had served him so faithfully.

The rest of the day was tense. Patrick slept and awakened, slept and awakened. Always, when he was conscious, he looked upon the *Enchantress*, devouring her as hungrily as he had taken Charlotte's breasts the night before.

When night had fallen, Patrick dressed himself, at least partially, refusing all help, and staggered out onto the terrace to grip the stone wall in both hands. Charlotte was at his side, ready to break his fall if his strength gave way.

All day, small boats had moved back and forth between the ship and the shore, carrying charts and maps, bells and fittings, anything that could be saved. Now the little crafts converged on the greater vessel again, alight with torches.

The *Enchantress* was boarded; the small patches of fire told them that. She was doused with kerosene from stem to stern, for that had been Patrick's order, and then set aflame.

Men scrambled down ropes and even dived, shouting, over the sides as the proud clipper's decks flared with fire. Charlotte linked her arm with Patrick's, ignoring his resistance, as crimson flames licked at the masts, danced along the rigging, and finally caught the sails.

The ship was a sight of glorious tragedy as it burned against the blackened sky, and in its reflected light Charlotte saw a tear slide down Patrick's pale cheek to lose itself in the dark stubble of his beard.

"The Vikings used to burn their ships when they could no longer serve," he said hoarsely, after a long time. The worst of the roaring had subsided; the *Enchantress* was now a flaming skeleton, barely afloat.

Charlotte let her head rest against his upper arm, unable to restrain the sob that escaped her throat. "Oh, Patrick, it's like watching a loved one die," she whispered. "What will you do without her?"

"I don't know," he replied bleakly.

The ship burned most of the night, and Patrick refused to leave the terrace until her trial had ended. When she tilted gracefully forward and went under, he uttered a low sound woven of the purest grief, turned, and stumbled back into the house.

He collapsed on his bed, sprawled sideways, and immediately gave himself over to the solace of sleep. His vigil had left him exhausted, and Charlotte knew his spirit was raw with despair.

She made an awkward place for herself at Patrick's side, laid one hand lightly on his back, and closed her eyes.

She awakened the next morning to find herself in the company of a stranger who only looked like Patrick. The soul, the essence of him, seemed to have withdrawn, leaving a cold void in its place.

"Patrick?" Charlotte said, sitting up, alarm thick in her throat.

He was sitting up against the headboard, regarding her as though she were a troublesome stranger, and not the woman he had fought with, loved with tender fire, and gifted with his child.

"Go away," he said coldly.

Charlotte sat up, sleep-rumpled, confused, and thoroughly wounded. "Patrick—"

He leveled his lethal, ink blue gaze on her. "I said go away," he growled.

Determined that one of them should be rational, Charlotte rose, with dignity, and kept her chin high and her voice even. "You need to grieve for the *Enchantress* in private," she said, "and I can understand that." She reached out to touch his face, but he turned his head to avoid contact. Still, she found the courage to finish, "When you realize that it's a real woman you need, with a mind and a heart and hands and breasts, and not a wooden one with masts and sails, I'll be nearby."

Patrick said nothing, nor did he so much as glance in her direction.

Charlotte straightened her shoulders and walked out without looking back.

17

HAVING NO DESIRE TO REMAIN IN THAT ROOM AND ENDURE Patrick's moody silence, Charlotte decided to explore her surroundings.

Downstairs, in a large, sun-filled kitchen, she found Mrs. McFaylon arranging sliced bananas in a pie shell. The dour housekeeper gave Charlotte a thorough once-over before asking, "How is himself today, then?"

Charlotte sighed. "The man would have to cheer up to be melancholy," she said, and thought she glimpsed the merest hint of amusement in Jacoba's eye.

"It'll pass, miss," the older woman said gruffly. "The captain loved that ship better than any of his women, and he needs to grieve for her for a time."

Suspecting that the phrase "any of his women" had been dangled before her like bait, Charlotte refused to rise. "I'd like to explore the house and grounds a little," she said, being careful not to sound subservient. She did not ask if Mrs. McFaylon had any objections, but simply turned to walk away.

"See you don't go wandering in the sugarcane, miss. There be poison snakes there."

Involuntarily Charlotte shuddered. She would indeed avoid the fields, but she looked back over one shoulder and spoke with lofty disdain. "I doubt that any serpent could be more venomous than Patrick Trevarren in his current mood," she said. Again she saw the shadow of a smile in Jacoba's stern countenance.

The downstairs portion of Patrick's house was spacious and elegantly simple in both structure and decor. The rooms were flooded with light, and the windows offered sweeping vistas of sloping lawns, tropical foliage, and turquoise seas. Charlotte was stricken by the beauty of her surroundings, and by the way the indoors and outdoors seemed to blend with each other.

A sense of homecoming possessed her, and she felt tears sting her eyes. She had never been to the island before, and yet her soul remembered the place, and had yearned for it.

She found Patrick's study, which boasted walls and walls full of leather-bound books, along with expensive Persian rugs, leather furniture, and a marble fireplace. The massive desk was made of fine mahogany, expertly carved, and Charlotte sat in the matching chair for some time, just absorbing the personality of the room—which was purely Patrick, of course.

The very atmosphere gave her new hope, reminding her by its very essence that the captain was a strong man, physically and mentally. He would be himself again once the loss of the *Enchantress* had settled itself in his mind.

Restless, Charlotte let herself out through the French doors on the opposite side of the room and entered a quiet garden. Here, there was a patio made of ancient gray stone, and a gracious marble fountain, dappled with moss. Profusions of bright tropical flowers nodded in the sunlight, brazen as dance-hall women in their reds and pinks, yellows and oranges, pale blues and deep violets.

Charlotte approached a bush burgeoning with orchidlike blooms of the most flagrant pink and sniffed one of the blossoms, only to find that it had no fragrance. She was troubled by the discovery, and frowned as she walked away.

Beyond the garden were the lawns, then the snow white beach, then the sea, with its spattering of glittering daylight.

Charlotte put all thought of the flower's deception behind her, lifted the skirts of her cotton dress, and headed for the shore.

The sand there was fine, very different from the heavy, coarse, brown stuff of Puget Sound, where Charlotte had played as a child. It was warm and dry, too, prompting her to take off her slippers and walk barefoot, the breeze playing in her hair.

The serenity Charlotte had found in Patrick's study grew as she walked, listening to the music of the tide and the spirited, raucous cries of the birds hidden in the lush foliage. After about fifteen minutes had passed, Charlotte came to a small cove, a piece of Eden, a place so beautiful that she had to sit down on a large, flat rock to take it all in.

While she sat watching the water, knees drawn up under her chin, an odd-shaped, shiny head suddenly jutted up out of the water, just a few yards from shore. The creature made a cheerful gibbering sound, and Charlotte laughed in delight, then cautiously approached the sea, wanting a better look.

The dolphin greeted her with laughter of its own, rose partway out of the water, and skidded backwards with effortless grace.

Charlotte clapped her hands, unable to contain her pleasure. "Show-off!" she cried good-naturedly.

The shimmering, pearl gray beast chattered a response, and then, as quickly as it had appeared, it was gone again.

"Come back," Charlotte whispered, crestfallen, but she knew that such magic could not be summoned at will. She rested her chin on her knees for a minute or so, hoping the dolphin would choose to show itself just once more, but it did not.

Eventually Charlotte went on.

She marveled at the trees lining the beach, some heavy with coconuts, others with ripening bananas. Charlotte helped herself to one of the latter, which had fallen to the sandy dirt. As she was pulling back the thick yellow peel, a bloodcurdling screech sounded high in the leaves of the great tree.

Charlotte stopped, curious and alarmed at one and the

same time, and looked up to see a small, furry brown face peering down at her. The monkey shrieked again, bouncing on its branch.

The message could not have been clearer had the little animal actually spoken.

Charlotte took a resolute bite from the banana, bringing on another round of banshee-shrill cries, and then placed one hand on her hip.

"Try to put this into perspective," she told the monkey. "It isn't as if you're going to starve without this one banana, you know. The trees are full of them, and you can have all you want."

The wiry little beast shinnied partway down the tree, then dropped at Charlotte's feet with as much drama as a pirate in a cheap music-hall production.

Smiling, Charlotte lowered herself to her haunches. "Hello, there," she said, offering her free hand.

The monkey looked petulantly at her partially eaten banana.

"Oh, all right," Charlotte said, holding out the fruit.

"Mathilda," an unexpected female voice put in, "that is no way to treat a guest."

Charlotte looked up in surprise and saw a very pretty young woman, with bright violet eyes and blond hair, standing just a few feet away. She wore a simple brown dress, clean and of sterling quality.

"Hello," Charlotte said, feeling a strange fear as well as joy at encountering another female of approximately her own age. Jacoba was too prickly and inscrutable for her presence to be a comfort, but this person wore a receptive smile. "I'm Charlotte Trevarren."

The other woman paled slightly, it seemed to Charlotte, but recovered quickly. Her smile never faltered. "So he's married, then," she said, with a sigh. "Well, that was to be expected, I guess. My name is Eleanor Ruffin, but I like to be called Nora."

Charlotte felt an impulse to explain the complicated relationship between Patrick and herself, but did not give in to it. "Do you live near here?"

Nora nodded, indicating a place somewhere behind her

right shoulder. "Just down the beach. My friends and I are caring for the sick ones from the *Enchantress* in a cottage there. You'd best go no closer."

The monkey was tugging curiously at Charlotte's skirt and eating the extorted banana. "The men haven't gotten worse, have they?" she asked, worried.

Nora shook her head. "No," she said, with a little laugh. Her accent was a rhythmic Scots burr. "Patrick and Mr. Cochran have both ordered that the crew must be kept in relative isolation until we're sure the infectious period has passed, that's all."

Charlotte would have liked to see the first mate again, and Tipper Doon as well, but she was willing to wait. She smiled down at the monkey, whom Nora had addressed as Mathilda. "Is this a friend of yours?"

The other woman laughed. "Yes. Mattie has adopted us, for reasons known only to herself. She's a pest—and much too wild to suit as a pet—but we love her."

"We?" Charlotte asked. Along with interest, and natural curiosity, she felt a certain uneasiness, remembering Jacoba's reference to "the others" only too well.

Nora folded her arms and leaned back against the trunk of a tree. Her pale hair fell loose around her shoulders, and a creamy white flower was tucked behind her right ear. "Patrick hasn't told you about us, then," she said, with resignation but not rancor. "I guess that's not surprising, considering that he's a typical man."

Charlotte thought Patrick was anything but typical, but this was no time to argue. "No, he hasn't mentioned you," she said, with dignity. "But I'd like to know everything."

Nora frowned, thinking. "There are four of us," she said, "besides Jacoba, of course. Stella, Jayne, Deborah, and I. We're all hopelessly in love with Captain Trevarren, not that it does us a great deal of good."

The sand seemed to shift violently beneath Charlotte's feet, but she kept her balance, outwardly at least. "Patrick— *keeps* the four of you?"

The pretty blonde laughed again. "I guess that's an apt description of the situation, but we're not exactly a harem."

The very word "harem" stung Charlotte, for she under-

231

stood firsthand what such an arrangement entailed. She swallowed hard, overcome, then, without another word to Nora, who must have been perplexed, turned and rushed back toward the house.

Charlotte did not go directly to Patrick with her questions and concerns about Nora and the others, but instead sat on the stone bench next to the fountain in the garden until she'd managed to calm herself.

When she was breathing evenly again, and her angry, fearful heart had settled back into its normal meter, Charlotte smoothed her hair and skirts and entered the house. She went to Patrick's room and found him sitting in the center, on a great chair, looking as imperious as a king on a golden throne.

He wore a pair of fawn-colored breeches and nothing else, and Jacoba was barbering him with a pair of shears.

Charlotte loved Patrick's luxuriant hair and gave a cry of dismayed protest.

Patrick fixed her with a searing look. "I thought I told you to go away."

Charlotte was no stranger to conflict and confrontation, having come from a large, energetic family, and she held her ground. "Everyone else on this island may jump when you snap your fingers, Captain," she said coldly, "but I'm not afraid of you."

He narrowed his eyes and leaned forward slightly, while Jacoba continued to clip and snip. "What do you want?"

Subtly Charlotte bent and picked up a lock of dark hair from the floor, tucking it into her pocket. "I want," she answered tartly, "to be treated with a modicum of courtesy, if you don't mind. After all, I am 'sort of' your wife, and I am carrying your child, in case you've forgotten."

Patrick's gaze dropped to Charlotte's still flat middle for a moment, then he raised a despotic hand and Jacoba promptly left the room.

"Has the child moved?" Patrick asked, when he and Charlotte were alone.

A new understanding came to Charlotte in that moment. Patrick was afraid for the baby, as she was herself, and it seemed likely that at least a part of his attitude stemmed from a need to distance himself.

"It's too early for that, Patrick," she said gently. The lock of his hair, hidden in her pocket, felt silky as she rubbed it between two fingers. "The baby is still very small."

He scowled and turned his head, and Charlotte waited in silence as he grappled with this information. Finally he looked at her again.

"I'm sorry, Charlotte," he said.

The apology terrified her. "Why?"

"How can you ask that?" Patrick countered, sounding exasperated. "You've been through hell because of me."

Charlotte nodded toward the window, where the sea and sky and sand were framed in all their magnificence. "It looks like Paradise to me," she said.

Patrick sighed. His hair lay sleekly against the sides of his head, and Charlotte longed to plunge her fingers into its richness. "You don't belong here, any more than you belonged in Khalif's harem or on board the *Enchantress*."

"Fine," Charlotte agreed. Her voice sounded even and calm, which was strange because she felt like weeping and raging in frustration and fear. "Where is it, exactly, that I *do* belong?"

He closed his eyes for a moment, and a tiny muscle along his jawline tightened and then relaxed again. "Ships drop anchor here with some regularity," he said, after an extended silence, his voice raspy. "It would probably be best if you went home to your family."

Charlotte felt an earthquake, even though she knew the floor was steady under her feet. She clasped her hands together in an almost imperceptible bid for balance. "And what about our child?" she asked, with what she thought was remarkable composure. "Don't you even want to see your own baby, Patrick?"

At this, Patrick bolted out of his chair, then, in sudden weakness, lowered himself again. All the color seemed to fade from his face, and his broad chest moved visibly with the rapid meter of his breathing.

"If the child is male," he said, after several moments, his

gaze fierce as he looked at Charlotte, "I will come for him when he's sixteen or so. He'll learn to run this plantation, and captain a ship."

Now it was Charlotte who went pale. A volcanic rage pumped inside her, and her voice came in a hiss, like steam from a fissure in the earth. "I'll see you in hell before I'll turn any son of mine over to you to be ruined, Patrick Trevarren! And how dare you express a preference for a son over a daughter?"

"*Damn* it, Charlotte," Patrick ground out, "I have no such partiality—a girl belongs with her mother, that's all!"

Charlotte folded her arms and braced herself for battle. Later she would weep because Patrick obviously didn't want her, but only the heir she might give him. For the time being, however, she was determined to comport herself with dignity. "And a boy should be with his father?"

"That's right." Patrick set his jaw.

"I can't imagine surrendering my child, male or female," she said. "And if you're worried that your son might be deprived of the proper masculine influences, don't be. My father and Uncle Devon are authorities on raising boys."

Patrick levered himself to his feet again, this time more cautiously. "*I* will raise my son, and no one else," he informed her.

"If that delusion is a consolation to you," Charlotte replied obdurately, "then go ahead and cling to it." With that, she turned to leave the room.

"Charlotte," Patrick growled, his tone full of warning.

She did not pause until she'd reached the doorway. There, she turned to look back at him, and felt a painful tug in her heart, as ornery as he'd been, to see him looking so broken.

"What?" She deliberately gave the word a saucy twist.

"Do not walk away when I am speaking to you."

Charlotte laughed, hoping Patrick hadn't noticed the strain woven through the sound. "I am not your servant, Mr. Trevarren, nor am I your pet. If I find what you are saying unacceptable or insulting, I shall walk away without hesitation."

At this, Patrick glared at her ominously and then bellowed

234

a curse word and slammed one fist down on the arm of his chair.

"Kindly control yourself, Patrick," Charlotte scolded, speaking lightly and with impudence even though she was quaking inside. "You have no earthly right to vent your black moods on me."

He glowered and Charlotte left the room, closing the door quietly behind her.

When he was alone, Patrick swore roundly. Here he was trying to do the best thing for Charlotte, as well as for their unborn child, and she was treating him like a villain. Damn it, couldn't she see, after all that had happened, that it was a dangerous thing to be loved by Patrick Trevarren?

From the moment Charlotte had been dumped at his feet like a sack of potatoes, her perils had only increased. She'd nearly died in the desert, trying to escape Khalif's good intentions, and lived through a pirate attack on board the *Enchantress*. After that had come the little adventure in the palace, when Ahmed had been freed from the dungeon by his friends and had been about to rape and kill her. And if those thrilling dramas hadn't been enough, Charlotte had promptly become a passenger on a ship of death.

True, she had escaped the sickness herself, but that didn't mean the tiny life within her had fared so well . . .

Sometimes death came before birth, instead of long after, and Patrick could not bear to think of his son or daughter suffering such a fate.

He rose and made his way slowly, awkwardly, toward the French doors leading out onto the terrace, still damnably weak from the fever. Jacoba had returned with a broom and dustpan, and she fussed as she swept up the snippings of dark hair from the floor, but she was an old and faithful retainer and she knew better than to harass him directly.

Patrick steadied himself against the thick stone railing and gazed out at the spot where the *Enchantress* had gone down with all the fiery glory of an ancient warship. He imagined her settling into the sand at the bottom of the bay, beginning to disintegrate, and once again pain lanced through him.

Such was the fate, he feared, of things and people he loved.

He waited until he knew Jacoba was gone, for he felt as though his skin had been stripped away, leaving every nerve exposed, and only solitude could save him.

Then, with the same shattering difficulty as before, Patrick returned to his room, sat down on the edge of his bed. From the drawer of his nightstand, he took a stack of pen-and-ink drawings, all Charlotte's work.

A rueful smile lifted one side of his mouth as he looked at the profiles of Brigham Quade, of his beautiful wife, Lydia, of the winsome sister, Millie, of the uncle and the brothers and the cousins. They were strong and decent people; Charlotte would be safe with them, and so would the child.

Patrick set the pictures aside again and stretched out on his bed, too weary to sit up any longer. He put his hands behind his head and stared up at the ceiling, imagining himself sailing into Quade's Harbor some sixteen years hence.

Charlotte would be no less beautiful than she was this very day, he reasoned. Her character, already something to be reckoned with, would be fully developed by a variety of experience, adding the special grace of maturity to her face and figure. His heart constricted, just to think of first seeing her after a long separation; the daydream was painfully real.

He broadened the vision in his mind to include a lovely daughter, with Charlotte's golden eyes and, perhaps, his dark hair. The girl would naturally be spirited, and she'd have little use for a father who had sent money and presents from all over the world but never visited, he supposed. He winced to consider her youthful, idealistic scorn.

Maybe Charlotte would give him a son, instead.

Patrick pictured a handsome lad, broad in the shoulders as he was, and as the Quade men were. The boy would have Patrick's own dark blue eyes, he decided, playing God, but Charlotte's maple-colored hair. It was probably too much to hope that his son would be named for him, since Charlotte would surely hold the lad's father in low regard from the moment of her exile.

He decided the boy would probably be called Quade, and he liked that. Quade Trevarren.

What would Quade think of his father, after growing up without him?

The idea made Patrick tighten his jaw. If the boy was worth his salt, he'd spit in Patrick's eye and tell him to go straight to hell. His mind would be shaped by his grandfather and his uncles, not by the man who had sired him.

Maybe Charlotte was right, Patrick conceded miserably. Maybe it would be better if he just stayed away from Quade's Harbor, and from his child, forever.

The prospect filled him with fresh despair, and he slept to escape it.

Charlotte went to the garden and cried until she'd vented her emotions. Then she sent Mary Catch-much-fish up to the master suite for her drawing pad and some pencils. The young woman brought the supplies to her promptly and said, "Mr. Captain, he be sleeping. His mind need rest to mend, that's what Miss Jacoba say."

Although she hadn't asked for a report, Charlotte was pleased that Mary had taken it upon herself to offer one. Maybe, she thought, Patrick would change his mind about sending her away once he'd recovered from the lingering effects of the fever and the shock of having to sacrifice his beloved ship.

Yes.

He would surely realize, when he was better, that he and Charlotte were meant to be together, for always, whether on land or on the high seas. In time he'd understand that their child, whether boy or girl, needed them both.

She took her drawing paper and went back to the magical place farther along the shoreline where she had encountered the dolphin earlier.

The animal did not reappear, to her disappointment, but after a while Mathilda came and cozied up beside Charlotte, who was sitting comfortably on the rock, as if they'd always been the most intimate of friends.

Though Patrick's rejection had bruised her heart sorely,

Charlotte couldn't help being amused and uplifted by the monkey's visit. When Mathilda kept trying to snatch away Charlotte's pencil and paper, she finally gave her some of her own.

Mathilda was comical in her efforts to mimic Charlotte and draw a picture, and in spite of her heartache and confusion, the erstwhile Mrs. Trevarren was soon laughing so hard that tears came to her eyes.

That night, when the moon was high and Mathilda had long since disappeared into the foliage along the shore, Charlotte consumed a lonely, if delicious, dinner and then returned to the master bedroom.

She wasn't sure why she made that choice, except that something inside wouldn't allow her to abandon Patrick, even though that was clearly what he wanted.

In Charlotte's heart, Captain Trevarren was her lifelong mate, if not her legal husband, and the fact that he'd fathered her child created a bond that could not be severed. She put on one of her own nightgowns, which Jacoba and Mary had boiled for her and dried in the afternoon sunshine, and pulled aside the thick netting to approach the bed.

Patrick was sleeping soundly, his head tilted back, his imposing chest bared to the moonlight. Even in his weakened state he looked so magnificent that Charlotte's breath caught and she thought she would suffocate before she got it back again.

Gently Charlotte drew back the light covers and crawled into bed beside him. He was arrogant and impossible and bull-stubborn, it was true, and yet she seemed to love him more for his foibles rather than less. Her pride was intact, and so was her formidable sense of honor, and Charlotte felt no shame in loving this man who evidently did not love her in return, but only a deep, poignant sorrow.

He stirred but did not awaken, and Charlotte lay close to him, one arm resting protectively across his middle. In the morning, Patrick might well rant and rave and send her away again, but tonight she would take her rightful place beside him.

238

She was a long time drifting off to sleep, and in the depths of the night Patrick awakened her with leisurely, methodical kisses. When she responded, he mounted her, gently spreading her limbs with a motion of one leg.

"Charlotte," he whispered, and the name contained a tangle of meaning. It was at once a plea, a reprimand, a surrender, and a challenge.

His strength was returning, he wanted her, and to Charlotte and her eager body, those things were cause enough for celebration. She ran her hands over the taut, damp flesh of his back and replied with an age-old invitation that required no words.

Patrick groaned and sought her entrance with his manhood.

Charlotte sighed and arched her back to receive him.

"I need you so much," he said unwillingly as she took him smoothly inside her and held him captive for a long, delicious interval. He braced himself, pressing his hands into the mattress on either side of Charlotte, withdrew, and then slowly lunged.

Charlotte gave a soft sob of pleasure and welcome, for in this singular and private arena, Patrick was her master. She spoke to him quietly, eagerly, as he began to move upon her, inside her, encompassing her.

She threw her arms back over her head in utter surrender as her hips began to rise and fall under his, and she chanted his name over and over again, in an untamed litany.

She wanted to give Patrick everything she had, and take all he had to give, she wanted the loving to go on forever and to culminate in merciful satisfaction. She was contradiction itself, pitching under Patrick with wanton abandon and at the same time feeling certain she'd been transformed from a mortal woman to a favorite angel.

Charlotte was heaven's own in those moments, and the long cry of release she gave when Patrick finally appeased her was also a prayer of passion.

His powerful body flexed against her a moment later, and he uttered a low shout as his essence spilled into her warm depths. When he'd spent himself, he collapsed beside her, kissing her eyelids. He must have felt her tears, found their salty flavor on his lips, but he made no direct mention of them.

"Oh, Charlotte," he said, with infinite sadness, "what are we going to do?"

She knew he didn't expect an answer, and she didn't have one to offer. She laid her hand on his hard stomach, still moist from their exertions, and caressed him in tender silence. Soon, sleep claimed them both.

The next morning, Charlotte awakened to find Patrick glowering at her, as grumpy as ever. He acted as if she'd spoiled his virtue or something, and she decided to punish him.

Boldly she took him into her hand.

She saw both desire and stubbornness battle in his face; he wanted to resist her seduction and yet his body was already surrendering, already welcoming the delicious discipline of her strong, nimble fingers. When she lowered her head to lash him with her tongue, he muttered a beleaguered curse and stiffened.

Charlotte looked up, saw his Adam's apple climb his neck and descend again. His eyelids came down and he moaned her name, pleading, but she was not inclined toward mercy.

18

CHARLOTTE LEFT PATRICK LYING DAZED IN HIS BED THAT morning and matter-of-factly went into the next room to take her bath. Mary and Jacoba had washed and pressed more of her clothes, brought ashore before the *Enchantress* was set ablaze, and she put on a pretty dress of cambric embroidered with small pink flowers. Without so much as a glance in Patrick's direction, she moved haughtily through the bedroom to stand on the terrace and brush her hair in the sunlight.

She could feel his impatience and irritation building, and she smiled when he finally shouted, *"Charlotte!"*

She took her time responding to the summons. When Charlotte went to stand at the foot of Patrick's bed, she was pinning her braided tresses into a coronet, her arms upraised for the task.

Patrick focused his eyes on her breasts, swallowed visibly, and then barked, "If you think what you just did to me is going to change my mind about sending you home to Quade's Harbor, you're wrong!"

Charlotte blushed. Pleasing Patrick in the way she had

was a particularly private matter, and she was embarrassed by his voluble reference to it. "I didn't think any such thing," she said. And it was true that she had not been scheming, but simply indulging an instinctive desire.

"Please put your arms down," he snapped, "you're driving me insane!"

She paused for a long, deliciously defiant moment before granting his request, then placed her hands on her hips. "My, but you *are* in a fragile state of mind this day, Captain," she mocked.

He struggled visibly for control of his temper, then grated out, "Any woman can do what you did. Remember that."

Charlotte stood still as a post, though she wanted with all her heart to fling herself onto his bed like a wild beast and claw him to ribbons. "And any man can do what *you* did," she responded evenly. *"Remember that."*

A crimson flush rose in Patrick's neck. "Fair enough," he said, but grudgingly and after a long, charged silence.

Charlotte sat on the end of the mattress, making a great show of arranging her skirts just so. "I met Nora Ruffin yesterday," she said conversationally, watching him through lowered lashes.

Patrick closed his eyes, as if to fling up a barrier between himself and Charlotte, and that was when she knew she had him by the proverbial short hairs. "Is she well?" he asked.

Not for a million tropical islands or a million ships like the *Enchantress,* all her own, would Charlotte have let him know how that simple question injured her. "Yes," she said. "And so are Stella and Jayne and Deborah. They're looking after the men who fell ill on shipboard."

Patrick sighed, met Charlotte's unflinching gaze. "I suppose you have questions about Nora and the others."

Charlotte was surprised by his readiness to speak of so inflammatory a subject, but she didn't let that show. "It would seem that Khalif is not the only one to keep a harem," she said moderately.

He rolled his magnificent eyes. "Would that it were so," he said, moments later, with a twinkle of amusement. "Nora, Stella, Jayne, and Deborah are my wards."

242

Charlotte lowered her head, lest Patrick catch a glimpse of the disbelieving relief she felt. "Oh?" she asked, plucking at the fabric of her skirts.

"They came into my care in various ways," Patrick explained wearily. "Nora's father sailed with me, and died of gangrene after a leg injury in Fiji. Deborah and Jayne are sisters, alone in the world except for each other, and I bought them from a pirate I met two years ago, in Riz. As for Stella, well, she was left here by her father, a sailing man of my acquaintance, who never bothered to come back for her."

At last Charlotte looked up. She knew Patrick would not have embroidered the truth with pretty stitches to spare her feelings; he obviously didn't believe he owed her that much consideration.

"You don't have a mistress on the island then?" she asked bravely.

"I didn't say that," Patrick replied, with brutal frankness.

Before she could weigh the wisdom of the action, Charlotte had risen to her feet. "You keep a woman here?"

He studied the ceiling. "Suppose I do," he countered.

Again Charlotte was moved to violence, but by supreme effort, she forestalled the compulsion. She did not move, except to raise her chin a notch. "Suppose *this,*" she answered coolly. "If you betray my trust, Mr. Trevarren, Rashad will not be the only eunuch in my circle of friends."

Patrick startled her with a burst of hoarse laughter. "Ah, Charlotte, Charlotte. You vex me to my limits at times, but no one could ever describe you as dull."

She was in no frame of mind to appreciate humor. "You once promised me fidelity," she said evenly.

"That," he answered with a sigh, "was when we were still married."

Charlotte's exasperation was overwhelming. "Yes, I remember. It was also while we were married that you fathered this baby I'm carrying."

To his credit, Patrick looked chagrined. "I keep forgetting about that."

"I've noticed," Charlotte rejoined tartly.

He leaned forward, frowning. "Exactly what do you want from me?" he demanded. "Unflagging faithfulness? Fine. As long as we're together, sharing a bed, you'll have that."

"And after you deposit me in Quade's Harbor?"

"Don't be naive," was the succinct reply. "Do you really expect me to be celibate for the rest of my life?"

Yes, Charlotte thought miserably. "Of course not," she said aloud. "Nor do I intend to wither away on the vine like a spring violet on the hottest day of August, once you've sailed merrily over the horizon and left me on shore. For better or worse, Patrick, you've taught me to enjoy a man's intimate attentions, and I will naturally want to take a lover. Don't fret, though—I'll be discreet."

He reddened again, unable to hide the irritation her remarks had engendered in him. "That would hardly be proper," he pointed out. "Do you think I want my child raised by a woman with a—a reputation?"

Charlotte smiled smugly. It was all an act, of course, but Patrick didn't have to know that, and it was clear that he wasn't smart enough to guess. "I don't give a damn if it's proper, and what you want or don't want matters even less. I intend to be positively *notorious.*"

"Charlotte!" Patrick was obviously scandalized, a fact that delighted her.

She began to sweep back and forth at the foot of his bed, a pensive expression on her face. "I don't suppose it would be right to advertise," she mused.

"Advertise!" Patrick gasped. *"Advertise?!"*

"Oh, yes," Charlotte replied distractedly, drumming the fingers of her right hand against her left upper arm. "I'd want a certain sort of man, handsome, discerning, but wholly devilish when it comes to pleasuring a woman—"

"Good *God,* Charlotte!" His shout fairly rattled the windows. "If you're saying all this to raise my hackles, you're succeeding brilliantly!"

She smiled, catlike. "Am I to understand," she began sweetly, pausing to look straight into Patrick's eyes, "that you are to have unlimited rights when it comes to entertaining other women in your bed, but *I* am expected to guard my virtue until the day I dissolve into dust?"

Patrick pondered. "Yes," he finally said, sounding petulant, like a small boy.

"I'm afraid that's impossible," Charlotte replied warmly. With that, she turned and left the room. Humming.

Patrick sent something crashing against the doorframe and bellowed something quite unintelligible.

Alone, Patrick thrust himself out of bed, too furious to languish for another moment, but still too enervated to return to his normal way of life. He swore as he made his way into the adjoining washroom and began stripping away his clothes.

He'd intended to make things easier for Charlotte—and, admittedly, for himself—by alienating her with talk of other women. He had supposed that she would weep, and be furious for a time, and then resign herself to living out her life safe in the bosom of her well-known family.

Naked, Patrick lowered himself into the tepid waters of the bathing pool. Instead of reacting the way he'd expected, Charlotte had come back at him with all that talk about taking a lover and being notorious.

He fumed as he reached for a cake of soap, squeezed too hard, and sent the bar skidding across the tiled floor. There was no denying it, Patrick thought miserably, his spectacular plan had exploded in his face like a cheap pistol, and his very bones were still quivering with the impact.

He raised himself out of the tub, retrieved the soap, and began to wash. When he was clean, and had dried himself off with a towel, Patrick dressed in fresh breeches and one of the flowing shirts he loved. He did not favor the garments because of the dashing appearance they made, but because he could move freely in them, with no sense of confinement.

He brushed his shorter hair, polished his teeth, and went back to the bedroom to pull on his favorite pair of boots. Then, with uncertain but determined steps, Patrick made his way out into the hallway.

He had to stop twice before he reached the top of the stairs, leaning against the wall and dredging strength from some well deep inside him, but finally he managed to descend to the first floor.

In his study, Patrick sank gratefully into the leather chair behind his desk and began going over the records his overseer had been keeping concerning that year's crop of sugarcane. During that brief time of absorption, he didn't think of his lost ship, or of Charlotte, and that was a mercy.

After a day spent exploring the island and sketching, Charlotte had dinner on the downstairs veranda, with Mr. Cochran. Following that, she sat alone in Patrick's study, reading a spicy novel purloined from a high shelf.

It was late when she returned to Patrick's room, and through the French doors she could see a bright, silvery moon spilling its light over dark waters.

The captain was in a quiet but nonetheless foul temper, wearing a pair of wire-rimmed spectacles she had not seen before and reading grimly from a volume of Chaucer.

At the sight of Charlotte, he slammed the book closed but made no move to rise from his chair facing the empty fireplace.

"Have you come to plague me again?" he asked.

Charlotte raised her eyebrows, contained the giggle that rose in her throat, then replied, "Anyone who would read Chaucer on purpose is quite capable of plaguing themselves, without assistance from me."

Patrick's mouth twitched at one corner, but he was clearly not about to let humor get in the way of a good sulk. He narrowed his eyes and leaned forward slightly. *"What* are you doing here?" he demanded.

"I should think that would be obvious, even to someone as deliberately obtuse as you are. I plan to extract my rights as a wife and then get a good night's sleep." Sometimes Charlotte was as amazed at her audacity as anyone could have been, but she was careful to hide her personal surprise and chagrin.

"Your *rights* as a wife," Patrick repeated, in angry marvel. "May I remind you, *Miss* Quade—" he put a purposefully unkind emphasis on the word "Miss" "—that we are no longer legally married?"

"Maybe not legally," Charlotte agreed, "but we have a moral bond, and I'm not about to let you forget it." All of the sudden, she was enjoying herself. She gestured toward the bed. "Lie down, Patrick. I want you."

She almost laughed at the crimson flush that surged into his neck and then flooded his face. He was clearly flabbergasted, and when he attempted to speak, the words were garbled.

"Very well," she said in a light tone, turning away for a moment to hide the sparkle in her eyes. "If you won't cooperate, then I'll just have to take . . . matters . . . into my own hands. So to speak."

The book clattered to the floor and at the same moment Patrick uttered a low, growling shout of amazement and fury. He approached her from behind, caught her shoulders in his hands, whirled her around to face him.

"Are you *trying* to infuriate me?" he demanded, in a stunned whisper.

"No," she replied. She was intimidated, and that was precisely why she raised her chin and did her utmost to appear undaunted. "I'm just treating you the way men treat women every day, in every part of the world."

Patrick looked baffled now, as well as outraged. "What has that to do with—"

"It has everything to do with what's happening between us, Mr. Trevarren," she interrupted. "And you know it quite well." She found a nightgown, spread it neatly on the bed, and began unfastening the buttons of her dress. She neither showed nor felt the slightest self-consciousness as she took off her clothes. Knowing that he was completely off balance, she changed the subject. "I had a nice chat with Mr. Cochran this evening, at dinner. He says the men are all recovering nicely."

Patrick obviously wanted to look away, and just as obviously could not make himself do any such thing. His throat worked visibly as he stared at Charlotte, and his voice came out sounding gruff. "I know that. Cochran gives me a daily report."

Charlotte was bare of all but her good intentions by that point, and she took her time covering up. She reached for the nightgown she'd selected earlier and held it out, as if reconsidering its appeal. She felt Patrick's gaze as surely as if he'd been touching her, and she secretly reveled in his fascination.

"Did he tell you, then," she began distractedly, "that barrels and lengths of rope and other such things have been washing up on the beach for the last day or so?" Out of the corner of her eye, she could see that Patrick stood with his arms folded, and there was an element of suppressed energy in his bearing.

"Yes," he answered, drawing nearer now. "It would seem to indicate a ship in trouble, since none of the debris is from the *Enchantress.*"

Charlotte turned and looked up into his eyes, her expression serious. "Shouldn't someone go out there and look?"

"In what?" Patrick retorted impatiently. "A native fishing boat? We're all stranded here, Charlotte, until another ship comes in." He ran splayed fingers through his sleek, newly shortened hair. "It might be months or even years before we lay eyes on an outsider."

To Charlotte's way of thinking, the prospect was not without good points. "Hmmm. That will make it difficult for you to palm me off on my family, won't it?"

"So we're back to that, are we?" He was glowering.

Charlotte laid her hands against his chest, felt a slight trembling and then the acceleration of his heartbeat against one palm. "I've said all I have to say on that subject. Kiss me, Patrick."

He looked at her mouth, leaned his head toward hers in a motion so slight as to be nearly imperceptible, then drew back and scowled. "You're not turning into one of those blasted 'new women,' are you?"

She smiled, sliding her palms lightly upward to his neck, knitting her fingers together at his nape. "Oh, no, Patrick, I'm not turning into 'one of those blasted new women.' I was *raised* to be one."

He sighed. "All right," he said, exasperated, spreading his arms wide of his body and then slapping his hands against his sides in resignation. "You win—I don't have the strength or wit for your games. Have your way with me."

The seriousness of this speech made Charlotte laugh out

loud. Then, her hands still caught together at his nape, she drew him downward into a leisurely kiss.

After that, there was no way of telling who had their way with whom.

Charlotte was breakfasting alone on the veranda the following morning when Cochran came hurrying up the walk, a look of intent concern on his face.

"Good morning, Mrs. Trevarren," the first mate said. Although he sounded distracted and a little rushed, she was pleased that *someone* was still willing to recognize her bond with Patrick. "Is the captain up and about?"

Charlotte had risen from her chair and stood gripping the porch railing now. Over Mr. Cochran's right shoulder she could see several natives just emerging from the thick foliage to the east of the house. They were carrying an inert, half-naked man.

"Captain Trevarren decided to breakfast in his—our room this morning," she said. She was already making her way down the steps. "What's happened? Has that poor man been drowned?"

Mr. Cochran shook his head. "No, ma'am, and more's the miracle. Two fishermen found him on the sand this morning. He's been in and out of his proper mind." The first mate paused, hat in hand, and cleared his throat. "We wouldn't have brought him here, Mrs. Trevarren, but he's in such poor shape that I didn't figure it would be wise to put him in the cottage with the others. He's surely too weak to stave off infection."

Charlotte nodded, lifting the pretty skirts of her pink lawn dress so that she could hurry across the grounds to greet the approaching party.

Mr. Cochran went inside the house.

Charlotte studied the unconscious man who had washed ashore like so much driftwood, her heart twisting with sympathy. He was unlike Patrick in every way, with his delicate build and pale brown hair, but something about him touched her all the same.

Jacoba arrived before the group had reached the front

veranda, sputtering and fretting like a mother hen who's just found a chick far afield of the coop.

On orders from the housekeeper, translated by a wide-eyed Mary Catch-much-fish into their own language, the fishermen laid the stranger out carefully in a downstairs bedroom. He'd lost one boot, and the few shreds of his brown trousers that had not been torn away were sodden. He began to shiver violently as Mary and Jacoba stripped him, as though the ruined clothing had offered him some warmth and protection.

"Be easy in your spirit, traveler," Jacoba told him, in a soothing voice Charlotte had not heard before. "You're among friends now and we'll take care of you." She looked at a hand-wringing Mary with her single eye. "Fetch warm water and towels and some of that rum I keep for the Christmas cakes."

Charlotte drew nearer the bed when Mary bustled out. "Is there anything I can do to help?"

Before Jacoba could answer, Patrick's voice sounded from the doorway, as low and ominous as approaching thunder.

"You can leave this room immediately," he commanded coldly.

Charlotte glared at her erstwhile husband. "I have experience as a nurse," she reminded him.

Patrick came to the foot of the bed and looked down at the poor shipwreck victim with dispassionate curiosity. His words, however, were plainly directed at Charlotte. "Jacoba was tending the sick and injured before you graduated from diapers to drawers. She doesn't need your help."

Jacoba looked from the captain to Charlotte and smiled. Charlotte was infuriated at first, but then she recognized the older woman's expression as one of knowing amusement, not triumph.

"I will not have you in here yammering and getting underfoot, Patrick Trevarren," the Scotswoman said. "Facts be that I'd rather the both of you got out of my way so I can work on this poor devil proper-like. Why, look at him. What parts of him isn't blue is gray, like a corpse."

If it hadn't been for the gravity of the situation, Charlotte would have laughed at the look on Patrick's face. Clearly he wasn't used to being dismissed like a troublesome child, and Charlotte wanted to ask how he liked getting back some of his own.

She didn't quite dare. It was one thing to disobey Patrick and quite another to go against Jacoba's alarming authority. The older woman was an unknown quantity, and Charlotte wanted her friendship.

She swept out in a rustle of skirts, her chin held high, and was followed, at a much slower rate, by Patrick.

The captain had been most friendly during the night, but he had returned to his surly and recalcitrant mood upon awakening that morning, which was why Charlotte had taken her breakfast in solitude.

She returned to the veranda, sat down, and poured lukewarm tea into the china cup she had left behind in the excitement.

Patrick joined her, to her secret pleasure, not taking a chair at the white iron table but instead leaning back against the porch railing, his arms folded.

Charlotte hoped her trembling didn't show as she lifted the cup to her lips and took a ladylike sip.

"What do you make of this?" Patrick asked, almost grudgingly, when she failed to initiate a conversation.

She raised her eyebrows, as if puzzled about his meaning, though she knew full well, of course, that he was referring to the man being tended with such fierce efficiency inside the house.

Patrick seemed annoyed. "There can be no doubt that there's been a shipwreck."

Charlotte sat back in her chair, dabbed at her lips with a linen napkin, and reached for another of the light, sugary biscuits Jacoba had baked that morning. "Perhaps," she agreed, after stretching the silence as long as she dared. "But perhaps our visitor was captured by pirates and thrown overboard for some reason."

"You have a wild imagination," Patrick accused, clearly irritated.

Charlotte took her time in eating the biscuit, then

shrugged one shoulder and replied, "I won't deny that. But it isn't as though recent events haven't given me cause to expect the unexpected."

Patrick narrowed his eyes at her. He looked different, with his shorter hair and his somewhat gaunt features, but Charlotte realized in that moment, with a searing jolt, that she would love him forever and ever. The knowledge comforted her but, at the same time, filled her with an elemental and fathomless fear.

His words came as an even greater shock than her insight had. "You know, of course, that you and my child will never lack for any luxury, even though I may be a world away from you?"

She averted her eyes, unwilling to let him see the pain he'd caused her. *Damn him,* she thought brokenly. *Is he so dense that he can't guess the truth—that I'd rather go hungry at his side than live in luxury on another continent?*

"My father is a wealthy man," she said, wanting to wound Patrick, wanting to attack him bodily, but forcing herself to speak in a quiet, ladylike tone. "Neither the child nor I will want or accept so much as a bent penny from you, Patrick Trevarren. Once you leave us, you'll do better to stay gone."

A difficult silence followed, during which Charlotte's heart seemed to tremble, crack, and then break into two badly bruised pieces. Finally she made herself look up at this man she loved so thoroughly, so desperately, and so hopelessly.

"Who knows?" she said, with a lightness of manner that was wholly feigned. "Perhaps I'll fall in love with that stranger who washed up on the sand this morning. That would be romantic, don't you think?"

Patrick spat a curse word, thrust himself away from the railing, and stormed into the house, slamming one of the great double doors behind him.

Charlotte supposed she should have felt triumph, for she'd obviously gotten Patrick's goat, but instead she just lowered her face to her hands and breathed deeply until the urge to sob uncontrollably had passed.

Once she'd recovered her composure, Charlotte stood and

began to clear the table, only to be shooed away by a scandalized Mary Catch-much-fish.

When Patrick left the house minutes later, in the company of a sheepish Mr. Cochran, and with a protesting Jacoba trailing after them, Charlotte refused to give in to her own feelings of apprehension. Instead, she took the opportunity to look in on the patient.

The sleeping man was waxen, his rest fitful, and he gave a cry of despondency that wrung Charlotte's heart. She went to the bedside and gently took one of his hands in both her own.

"Susannah!" he screamed suddenly, bolting upright on the mattress, with its crisp linen sheets. "Dear God, *Susannah!*"

Charlotte's throat tightened in sympathy. "There now," she said softly, "you're safe here. Nothing is going to hurt you."

The stranger looked at her, frantic, in the grip of a living nightmare. His eyes were a spring green. "She drowned—I tried to save her, I tried so hard—"

"Shh," Charlotte said, smoothing sweat-dampened hair back from his forehead. Despite her outward composure, she was filled with visions of the unknown Susannah, crying out for help, sinking beneath the waves of an angry sea before she could be reached. "Of course you did everything you could. Rest now. You need your strength."

He did not relax, however, but instead flung his head back on the pillow and gave a harrowing cry of grief. It was worse than a sob, worse than a scream of pain, that sound, for it came from the very depths of his soul.

Instinct warned Charlotte not to allow the patient to withdraw into his agonies if she could stop him, and she gripped his shoulders hard.

"Tell me your name!" she ordered.

Again that haunting moan of despair came.

"Don't you dare give up now!" Charlotte yelled, kneeling on the mattress, digging her thumbs into the man's sparely muscled upper arms. "It's a bloody miracle that you're still alive—do you hear me? A miracle! That means you've got things to do before you go on to your rest, important things! Damn it, mister, you *get back here right now!"*

Amazingly, he stilled, staring up into Charlotte's face as if he were just returning to himself from some far distant place. "Who are you?" he asked, the words sounding a rusty rasp in his throat.

She smiled, released him, scrambled off the bed, and smoothed her skirts. "My name is Charlotte Quade Trevarren," she said.

"Susannah?" He looked past Charlotte's shoulder. "Is my wife here?"

Charlotte shook her head, swallowed, and made herself keep smiling. "I'm sorry."

In the next few minutes, Charlotte learned that the visitor's name was Gideon Rowling. He was an Englishman, and he and his new bride, Susannah, had been sailing to Australia when their ship had been set upon by pirates. Some of the passengers and crew had escaped in lifeboats, the Rowlings among them, but most had been murdered outright. The vessel had been looted and set ablaze.

The lifeboats had eventually become separated one from another during a storm, and in the end the skiff the Rowlings had shared with an old man and two crewmen had been overturned. The last time Gideon had seen Susannah, she'd been holding out her hand to him, screaming for help.

When the story was finished, Gideon lapsed into sleep again, no doubt because he found reality unbearable, and Charlotte couldn't say she blamed him.

19

"T HAT FEVER MUST HAVE BURNED UP YOUR BRAIN," COCHRAN observed, with his usual dry bluntness, as he stood beside Patrick at the porch railing. Both men were gazing out to sea, and both were yearning for the feel of a deck beneath their feet. "Once in a lifetime—provided the gods and all the fates have agreed to favor him, that is—a man encounters a woman like Charlotte. Yet here you are, ready to drop her off on her papa's doorstep like a lot of dusty baggage." The first mate paused, sighed deeply. "If Brigham Quade doesn't shoot you like a mangy stray for this, he's not the man I think he is."

Patrick gave a sigh of his own. Would no one ever understand that he was being *noble*, giving up Charlotte and the child this way?

He had been fooling himself before, thinking he could be happy as a planter, confined to one place all his life; he'd faced that. He needed excitement, experience, even the occasional brawl.

Plainly his life would consist of one dangerous adventure after another, and he thrived on the fact, could not give it up for a safe, quiet existence. By his reckoning, it followed that

255

a woman and baby could not rightly be expected to live in such a manner.

"Perhaps, Mr. Cochran," he said grimly, his eyes still fixed on the horizon, his fingers tightening as he gripped the railing of the veranda, "you would be better off minding your own affairs and leaving me to mind mine."

Cochran took a cheroot from his pocket and lit it, and the rich, fruity scent of the smoke encircled them. "You know," he replied, at his leisure, "I never took you for a fool. Now I'm forced to admit that I was wrong."

Patrick was stung, but he wouldn't let Cochran see that. He gave his friend a wry look and said, "A rare enough occasion—your owning up to a mistake, I mean."

Unruffled, Cochran simply smiled, shrugged, and drew deeply on his cheroot. "As if the sky wouldn't fall if *you* confessed to a failing or two," he replied.

It seemed to Patrick that a change of subject would be advisable just then. He liked Cochran and didn't want to do battle with him, verbal or otherwise. "What do you make of it, this Rowling character washing ashore?"

"I'd say it means trouble," Cochran answered readily, and with a hint of relish. "Not from Rowling, of course—he seems like a good enough sort. I figure Raheem—or some other dung bug just like him—is probably out there somewhere, waiting to hit this island like a squall. God help us all if they've learned that the *Enchantress* is at the bottom of the bay. And there've been signs that a big storm is brewing out to sea, too."

Patrick felt a stab of grief at the mention of his ship; he mourned her as he would a woman, or a child, or a beloved friend. For the moment, however, he had to think of practical matters; the half dozen cannon salvaged from the *Enchantress* had to be set up on the high ground behind the house, facing the bay. His wards and the sailors still recovering from the fever must be brought to the main house. Also, plenty of food and water would be required, in case of a siege by either nature or pirates.

Or both.

"Damn," Patrick murmured, but mixed in with the

undeniable dread he felt was a sense of excitement. Even the prospect of a challenge made him stronger.

In the days to come, the last vestiges of Patrick's illness fell away, for there was no time to languish on the veranda or in a sickbed. More debris from the shipwreck washed ashore, but there were no passengers, dead or alive, in the mix. And Patrick could feel trouble closing in, despite the calm waters of the sea and the soft, fragile blue of the sky.

A rising wind teased the tops of the palm trees, and Charlotte finally had to give up the idea of sketching, at least for that day. The pages of her drawing book fluttered so that she couldn't concentrate, and in any case, she had other pressing matters on her mind.

The mysterious, tragic Gideon Rowling, for one. Although Charlotte felt none of the attraction toward him that Patrick could stir with a glance in her direction or the mere lift of an eyebrow, Mr. Rowling was still a romantic and appealing figure. He slept most of the time, and broke Charlotte's tender heart by crying out repeatedly for his Susannah, and he had the thin, haunted beauty of a starving poet. He was a Christian missionary, as it happened, and he and his wife had intended to devote the remainder of their lives to the task of saving the Aborigines from damnation.

To Charlotte, it seemed a splendid undertaking, though ambitious.

Then there was Patrick, who was always in her thoughts, on one shelf or another. Charlotte hoped that the captain loved her—he did not attempt to hide his feelings when, in the warm, fragrant darkness of the tropical nights, he moaned her name and swore by all the saints that she owned his soul—and yet Patrick persisted in being difficult by day. He scowled at Charlotte whenever they encountered each other, which was a rare occurrence because he'd developed an uncanny ability to avoid her. When they did speak, an even more uncommon event, he made it clear that he still intended to relegate both her and the baby to Quade's Harbor.

In addition, Patrick's wards had moved into the main

house, along with the few seamen who were still ill enough to be confined. Cannon had been set up on the hilltops, and sailors and natives alike had been busy for several days, boarding up the windows of the house.

All in all, it was a lot to sort out, even for Charlotte's agile mind.

Wandering back into the house, which seemed shadowy and somewhat oppressive now that the windows were covered, she decided to look in on Mr. Rowling. He, unlike Patrick, could always be counted on for civil conversation, though he was still quite melancholy, of course.

He was seated in the downstairs parlor, listening quietly while Stella, one of Patrick's wards, played fairylike, oddly sorrowful music at the pianoforte. Charlotte would have retreated, seeing that her friend was not alone, but he smiled in a forlorn way when he saw her, and beckoned.

She approached, ignoring a scathing look from the pretty, dark-haired Stella, and crouched beside his chair. "Hello," she said gently.

He touched her hair, a gesture that, made by nearly any other man on earth, would have been sure to bring Patrick's wrath down on all their heads. "Charlotte," he said, his voice gruff and fond. His gaze dropped to her bare toes, which were just visible under the hem of her skirts. He grinned crookedly. "Where are your shoes?"

"I'm not certain," she confessed. "I don't recall exactly where I left them."

Mr. Rowling laughed, but the sound was oddly painful to hear.

Stella ended her musical recital with a crashing chord, rose from the piano stool like a geyser shooting out of the ground, and swept out.

Charlotte winced. "I'm sorry if I interrupted," she said.

Her friend sighed. "The young lady has decided to court me, I think," he confided, forlorn amusement shining in his eyes. "I don't imagine there are a great many eligible men on this island."

Charlotte looked away for a moment, because his words had brought Patrick's image surging to the surface of her mind like some magnificent creature rising from the sea.

258

"It's quite soon, isn't it—for you to be interested in another woman, I mean?"

He shrugged. "Being interested in a woman is quite another matter from being in love with one," he said, in grave tones. "I'll cherish the memory of Susannah until the day we are reunited in heaven, but the great weakness of my character is that I cannot abide loneliness. I have no doubt that I'll remarry at the first opportunity, and Stella is as likely a candidate as anyone."

She rose from her crouching position and took Stella's seat on the piano stool, idly spinning this way and that, just as she'd done as a child, back home in her father's parlor. "Men are fickle creatures," she observed, without rancor.

"And what prompts that observation, may I ask?" The question was pleasant in tone, and quietly offered.

Charlotte tried to smile, faltered, and gave up the effort. "It hardly comforts a woman, knowing the man she loves could replace her so easily."

"We are talking about the captain now, I think."

She lowered her eyes for a moment, but her cheeks felt hot and she knew Mr. Rowling could see her embarrassment. "Yes," she admitted. "I could be torn to pieces by rabid monkeys and scattered all over the island in bloody bits, and Patrick would probably say, 'Poor girl, what a pity,' and then start looking about for someone to take my place."

"You underestimate your station in Mr. Trevarren's heart, I think."

"Then you're quite wrong, Mr. Rowling."

"Gideon," he corrected.

Charlotte felt tears sting her eyes and ascribed them to her pregnancy and the changes it had wrought in both her body and spirit. "Gideon," she repeated, getting used to the name. Finally, after some seconds of awkward silence, she forced herself to meet his gaze again. There was something about him, some gentleness in his nature, that invited confidence. "I'm in a terrible fix," she said, wiping her eyes with the heels of her hands and then sniffling once. "I was married to Captain Trevarren, you see, and now I'm *not*, and there's a baby."

Gideon held out a hand to Charlotte, and she scooted the

259

piano stool closer, on its green crystal rollers, and clasped his fingers. "Go on," he said.

She told the whole story, starting with her first meeting with Patrick, long ago and far away, in Seattle. She'd loved Mr. Trevarren from the moment of their original encounter, high in the rigging of the *Enchantress,* she confessed. She'd become his true wife, in her own heart at least, when Khalif had pronounced them married. Patrick had ended their union—a fresh torrent of tears came when she related how easy it had been for him, just clapping his hands and repeating the phrase "I divorce you" three times—but for Charlotte the ties were far more binding. Now, she confided miserably, Patrick meant to abandon and forget her.

When Charlotte finished the wretched tale, leaving nothing out except the most intimate details, she saw a new fire in Gideon's light green eyes. A muscle tightened in his jawline. "By all that's holy," he breathed, in a furious undertone, "the man has gall, flouting the very laws of God!"

Charlotte swallowed, wondering if she'd said too much. It certainly wouldn't have been the first time. "I don't think he exactly meant to do *that*—" she began, but Gideon immediately cut her off.

"It's unconscionable," he declared. "Charlotte, if Patrick Trevarren won't marry you properly and give you and your child his name, then *I* will."

She felt the color drain from her face. Gideon was a fine man, good and gentle and handsome in the bargain, but wonderful as he was, Charlotte feared she could never grant him the privileges of marriage. Despite her brave words to Patrick earlier, about taking a lover and becoming notorious once he deserted her in Quade's Harbor, she found the thought of another man touching her abhorrent.

Gideon half rose from his chair and planted a brotherly kiss on Charlotte's forehead. Then he drew back and smiled again. "So that's the way of it, then," he said quietly. "Send your captain to see me, Charlotte. I'll put the fear of God into him."

Charlotte's eyes widened. "I wouldn't want Patrick to be *forced* into marrying me," she whispered.

260

Gideon patted her hand. "Don't fret, Charlotte. I don't think it's going to be necessary to use force."

Charlotte immediately sought Patrick out and found him in his study, going over a series of charts with Mr. Cochran. The wind rattling at the windows and mourning on the roof made an apt accompaniment to his sour expression.

Can this, Charlotte thought, with amazed resentment, *be the same man who held me so tightly last night in our bed, who took such eager solace in my body and invaded my very soul with the tenderness of his words and his touch?*

"What is it, Charlotte?" Patrick asked, his tone testy, his gaze as cold as the fiercest winter. "I have things to do, and not much time."

She stood as tall as possible in the great double doorway, her shoulders straight, her chin high. Even barefoot, her hair tumbled from a brief interval outside, Charlotte knew she was the very picture of dignity. It was a knack she had cultivated from early childhood.

"Gideon—Mr. Rowling—wishes to speak with you."

Patrick frowned, perhaps because she'd used the visitor's Christian name, and let the chart he'd been examining roll back into a cylinder with a whispery sound. "I'll see him later."

"Fine," Charlotte agreed sunnily, with a slight shrug. She turned to walk away, knowing she'd nettled Patrick, pleased by the fact.

To her surprise, he stopped her with a single terse demand. "Where are your shoes?"

First Gideon had wondered why her feet were bare, and now Patrick wanted to know. She looked back at him, somewhat coyly, over one shoulder. "I wouldn't think of interfering with your important business by answering such a silly question," she said. And then she walked away.

She heard him swear and smiled as she proceeded along the hallway leading into the back of the house. The kitchen was in a separate building, and Charlotte had a sudden yen for a handful of Jacoba's special biscuits. She hummed as she crossed the yard, hardly noticing the wind that made her hair dance and pressed her skirts against her legs.

* * *

261

Patrick tried not to think about the summons from his guest, the missionary who'd washed up on the beach some days before, but the caressing way Charlotte had said the man's name echoed in his head. He couldn't afford to plan the defense of everyone on the island while in a distracted state of mind.

He finally cursed, muttered an excuse to Cochran, who wore an irritating smile, and went in search of Rowling.

The man was in the parlor, and Stella and Jayne were both there, fussing over him, pouring his tea, chattering like a couple of tropical birds. Patrick was fond of the pair—they were like the sisters he'd never had—but just then their youthful eagerness to please Rowling annoyed him.

"Out," he said, without preamble or explanation.

Jayne and Stella exchanged pouting glances and then left the room.

Patrick closed the doors and leaned back against them, his arms folded across his chest, his expression anything but charitable. By his reasoning, he'd saved the man's life by offering the sanctuary of his home and the benevolent aid of his servants, and he owed him nothing more. He didn't speak, since by his presence it was obvious that he'd answered Rowling's summons.

The other man sighed, and Patrick was surprised and irritated to find himself wondering if Charlotte was attracted by Rowling's delicate features and polite, gracious manner. He put the idea resolutely out of his mind.

"Sit down, please," Rowling invited, as though this were his parlor and Patrick were there only on suffrage of some sort.

Patrick's pride offered him no option but to remain standing. He kept his gaze leveled on the smaller man and waited, letting his thunderous mood show in his bearing.

Rowling only smiled. "Stubborn, then," he commented, as if to himself. Because of his British accent, he sounded . refined when he spoke, and Patrick hoped Charlotte had enough sense to look beyond such superficial niceties.

"My time is valuable," he pointed out, and because of his thoughts, the words sounded sharp and impatient.

The clergyman gave another sigh. "Yes. Well, there's

nothing for it but to launch right in, now is there? You're taking sore advantage of an innocent young woman, Captain Trevarren, and as a man of God, I must protest."

Patrick thrust himself away from the doors, feeling as though he'd just been slapped across the face with a glove. "Are you talking about Charlotte?" It was a stupid question, he knew that even as he uttered the words, but Rowling's accusation had caught him so off guard that he hadn't paused to think.

"Yes. Lovely creature, isn't she?"

Patrick thought of the way Charlotte nurtured him every night, both body and soul, and spared Rowling an abrupt nod. "Go on, Reverend. I don't have the day to waste."

Rowling's smile didn't waver, but neither did it displace the grief so plainly visible in his eyes. "You led her to believe she was your wife, and then you got her with child. Is that not so?"

Patrick swallowed, started to speak, stopped himself. He hadn't felt this awkward since the first time he'd been asked to recite in school. "It wasn't quite that simple," he finally managed to say.

"Then," Rowling went on, as if Patrick hadn't spoken at all, "you proceeded to divorce her. Am I correct?"

"It was a pagan marriage and a pagan divorce," Patrick said tersely.

"Not to Charlotte, it wasn't," replied Rowling. "And now there is to be a child."

Patrick felt weary, and the brittle wall he'd built around his heart cracked a little. "Yes," he said, all his despair mirrored in that single word. He wished sorely that he were the sort of man to live out his life on land, in the rooms of a single house and the arms of just one woman, but he knew he wasn't. His wanderlust was as much a part of him as the color of his eyes or the alignment of his teeth.

"I have offered to marry her myself," the missionary said. "There can be no question of love between us, of course, but at least that way honor would be served and the little one would have a surname."

Pictures flooded Patrick's mind. He saw Charlotte lying naked in this man's bed, arching beneath the thrusts of his hips, her skin glistening with the singular exercise of passion, her glorious hair spread over the pillows. He heard her give the familiar half sob of release, and the sounds and images gave him such pain that he wrenched his thoughts in another direction. He saw a little girl, an exquisite miniature version of Charlotte, running across a green lawn, flinging herself up into Rowling's arms with a burst of musical laughter and a delighted "Papa!"

Patrick closed his eyes. "Has Charlotte agreed to the marriage?" he asked, the words coming hoarse from his throat.

"Not yet," Rowling answered, but Patrick was anything but reassured. The visitor's tone indicated that he fully expected to persuade Charlotte to become his wife, and soon.

"But?"

"But I expect she'll come around, once her condition is fully apparent. Even on a remote island, Mr. Trevarren, an obvious pregnancy would be an embarrassment to a woman without a husband." Rowling paused, rubbed his chin as he pondered. His next remark exploded in the room like dynamite. "Since you're officially the captain of a ship, sir, you have the authority, both legal and moral, to perform a marriage ceremony. I'd like you to bind Charlotte and me in holy matrimony—once she comes around to my way of thinking, that is."

Patrick felt as though some great, subterranean force were about to channel itself through him and erupt with a fiery violence. His voice came out in a hiss, like escaping steam. "I'll see you in hell first!"

Rowling laughed. "You may very well end up in the pit, given your arrogant, self-serving nature, Captain, but I can assure you that you will not encounter me there." He stopped, watching Patrick, letting his statement sink in. "Charlotte will marry me. I will give her child my name and love it as my own."

"You are very confident of your charms," Patrick growled, when he could trust himself to speak—which was only after he'd stridden across the room to the teakwood liquor cabinet and poured himself a brandy. "But you forget that we are essentially stranded here, for all practical intents and purposes. It may be months or even years before another ship drops anchor."

Rowling waited until Patrick met his eyes again before replying. "I have a calling to preach in Australia," he said, "and I will answer it. I have already prayed for a ship to carry me there, and one will be along shortly."

Patrick made a low, rude sound of amazement. "You *prayed—*"

"Yes," Rowling broke in, benevolently enough. "And with rare exceptions, God honors my requests."

Later, Patrick would regret the unkindness of what he said next, but at the moment, he was feeling too angry and cornered to say anything other than just what he did. "Did you pray for your drowning wife, or was that one of those 'rare exceptions' when God saw fit to ignore you?"

The color drained from Rowling's face, but he recovered quickly. He was strong; Patrick had to give him credit for that. "In His infinite wisdom, God must have decided that Susannah had done her work here and thus called her home to her reward."

Patrick looked away. An apology rose in his throat, but he swallowed it.

Rowling went on, his voice mercilessly cheerful now. "Charlotte will make a fine missionary herself, I think—"

Patrick didn't need theological training to know that he'd just been forgiven, in a very magnanimous fashion, and he was furious. He slammed the brandy snifter down onto the top of the liquor cabinet with such force that the stem cracked and the glass went over like a tree felled on an open hillside. "Enough!" he bellowed, interrupting Rowling's ongoing discourse on Charlotte's innate suitability for converting the unchurched.

The other man smiled again, in that damnably wise and gentle way Patrick was beginning to hate.

"Is there something wrong, Captain?"

"You're damn right there's something wrong!" Patrick yelled. "Charlotte is mine, and she will *remain* mine!"

Rowling spoke with an infuriating gentleness. "Then you had best marry her properly, Captain," he said reasonably.

Patrick narrowed his eyes at the preacher and spoke in a low, lethal voice. "Did she put you up to this?"

"Charlotte confided her troubles to me, that's all," Rowling answered. "It seemed only practical to offer her marriage—with my wedding band on her finger, she would be safe from scandal and I would be spared a crippling state of loneliness. Believe me when I tell you, Captain, that I was quite sincere in my suit, and if I were to pray accordingly, the tide of romantic fortune would surely turn in my direction."

It was galling, this Briton's confidence in the sway he held with the Almighty. Who did he think he was—Moses? David? "And you called *me* arrogant," Patrick bit out.

Rowling smiled, yet again. "'The prayer of a righteous man availeth much,'" he quoted, with blithe confidence. "And I *am* a righteous man, Captain. If I ask God for Charlotte's favor, He will almost surely give it."

"Don't trouble yourself—or God, for that matter," Patrick snapped. "If Charlotte will have me for a husband, I'll marry her. Today. Tomorrow. As soon as it can be arranged. And you, Mr. Rowling, may concentrate your prayers on a ship to carry you away from this island before I lose my patience and feed you to the fish!"

The man of God was unruffled, even amused. "You and I have seen each other's souls," he said. "From now on, it would be more seemly, I think, if we were on a first-name basis."

In that moment, just when he most wanted to explode with impatience, Patrick was confounded to make the discovery that he *liked* Rowling. Damn, but he wanted to despise the man, with his whole being, just as he had once hated a cruel headmaster at school, but he couldn't manage it.

The fronds of palm trees hammered at the windows, torn loose by the now shrill winds coming in from the sea. Patrick and Gideon stared at each other, one man seated, one standing, as much a part of the tempest as the elements themselves.

* * *

Charlotte was helping Jacoba and Mary Catch-much-fish in the kitchen when Stella stepped in, laboring to pull the wind-caught door shut behind her.

"Patrick wants to see you," she said, somewhat petulantly, looking at Charlotte with accusing eyes. "This minute, in his study."

Charlotte felt a leap of triumph, certain that Gideon had shown Patrick the error of his ways, that everything would be all right from then on. "Well," she said, rather flippantly, "I happen to be busy. *Patrick* will simply have to wait a little while. You may tell him that."

Stella stood her ground, arms akimbo. "I would sooner take tea with the devil," she responded, with spirit. "The captain is in a vile mood, and I'll not be the one to defy him."

With a long-suffering sigh, Charlotte wiped her hands on her borrowed apron—she'd been kneading bread dough— and swept Stella up in a look. In truth, she liked Stella and the others, but she was cautious about showing her feelings because she knew they resented her. "All right, then, I'll speak to him."

Patrick was alone in the parlor when she arrived, standing in front of the massive marble fireplace, his broad back turned to her. He lifted his gaze, saw Charlotte's reflection in the mirror, and froze her in place with an unreadable stare.

"Would you marry Gideon Rowling and go off to Australia to save souls, if he asked you?"

Charlotte considered, still looking into Patrick's eyes. Still, he had not turned to face her. "Yes," she said, after a long interval of careful and honest thought. Before, she'd been certain she could never bear the touch of another man's hands on her body, but she'd had a chance to ponder the matter practically since then. "Maybe I wouldn't accept the first time Gideon proposed, or the second, or the tenth. But he's a good man, and I know he would be patient with my . . . natural reluctance. My life with him would be interesting and fruitful, I'm sure."

At last Patrick faced her, though he made no move to

approach. He braced his back against the carved mantelpiece and regarded Charlotte for a long and suspenseful interval. "You could turn to another man, after what we've shared?" he asked, in a grave and quiet tone.

"Not as easily as you could turn to another woman, perhaps," Charlotte answered calmly. "But yes, in time, I think I could give myself to Gideon."

The storm howled at the walls of the great house and rattled the tall, deep-set windows in their frames. For a long time, Patrick and Charlotte were silent, listening, waiting. Lightning struck in the garden, and its pale glow moved in the room, even though the glass panes were boarded over.

"I want you to be my wife," Patrick said, when some time had passed.

Charlotte felt both exultation and anguish, in the space of one and the same moment. She wanted, yearned for, a real marriage to Patrick, and yet she knew he was not offering willingly. "And I want a proper proposal," she countered, with an airiness she didn't feel.

For an instant, the storm seemed to center itself in Patrick's very soul. He approached her, dropped to one knee, and glared up into her face. "Will you marry me?" he asked, in the most grudging of tones.

20

Y ES," CHARLOTTE SAID, FOLDING HER ARMS AND THEN TURN-
ing away so that Patrick would not see in her eyes what
injury he had done her by proposing so callously. "I will
marry you." *For our child*, she added in her mind.

She sensed Patrick's graceful rise from his knee to his full
and intimidating height. "The wedding will not change my
mind about leaving you in Quade's Harbor," he warned, his
voice low and cold. "You and the child will have my name,
however, along with the house and financial support I
promised you."

Charlotte whirled, driven by her pain. The shrieks of the
wind filled the room, as shrill and harrowing as if a hundred
ghosts were dancing on the roof. "Why are you agreeing to
the marriage, Patrick, when it's plain your feelings haven't
changed?"

He raised his hands, haltingly, as if to touch her shoulders
or frame her face, then let them fall back to his sides. "No,
Charlotte," he replied, "my feelings haven't changed. And
God help me, I don't believe they ever will."

With that cryptic statement, Patrick turned and strode
over to open the study doors and call to Mr. Cochran. That

done, he looked back at her and, with typical arrogance, made a royal pronouncement. "When the brunt of this storm finally strikes, it will level the cane crop and uproot half the trees on the island. Anyone foolish enough to be out wandering will almost certainly be killed. See that you stay inside and occupy yourself with selecting a wedding dress." His indigo gaze dropped to her feet. "And I would like you to wear shoes for the ceremony. I trust you will obey me, just this once?"

Charlotte smiled sweetly and took great care to speak in a voice too soft to carry to Patrick's ears. "I'd die first," she said.

He studied her for a long moment, then held the door open wide. "Kindly go on about your business, then. Cochran and I have things to do."

Charlotte moved regally past him. She encountered Mr. Cochran in the hallway and was much heartened by the sly wink he gave her.

Proceeding upstairs to the master bedroom, Charlotte began going through the splendid clothes Patrick had had made for her in Spain. Those that could stand boiling had been spared the fire, and fallen under Jacoba's efficient hands to be aired and pressed and hung in the enormous armoire that had been brought in from another room.

The impending storm and her own churning emotions were distracting to Charlotte, but she finally chose a soft ivory dancing gown decorated with tiny pearls and crystal beads. She decided to fashion the matching silk shawl into a veil of sorts, and was standing in front of the bureau mirror, experimenting, when a knock sounded at the door.

"Come in," Charlotte called, expecting Jacoba or perhaps Mary Catch-much-fish, with tea.

Instead, she saw all four of Patrick's pretty wards reflected in the looking glass. She turned to face Nora, Stella, Jayne, and the very shy Deborah, who had avoided her until then.

Charlotte braced herself, expecting some sort of confrontation. It was Stella, the dark-haired girl who had been courting Gideon, who stepped forward from the group.

"Jacoba says there's going to be a wedding," she said.

Charlotte nodded, waiting.

Stella looked back at her companions and then met Charlotte's gaze head on. "Patrick Trevarren has been like an elder brother to us, protecting us when we had no one, making sure we had everything we needed and much of what we wanted. I guess what we're here to say is that you'd better not hurt him, because if you do, you'll have us to deal with."

Having expected something quite different, Charlotte was relieved. "What makes you think I would deliberately do Patrick any sort of injury? I love him."

"You spent half the morning locked away in the parlor with Gideon Rowling," Stella reminded her.

Charlotte wasn't about to explain; she had done nothing wrong. She simply waited, arms folded, watching the others.

Something crashed hard against an outside wall, and Deborah, the youngest and smallest of Patrick's wards, started violently and gave a terrified cry. Nora, the vivacious girl who had first introduced Charlotte to the monkey, Mathilda, put a protective arm around Deborah's shoulders and murmured reassurances.

A moment later, Nora stepped forward to stand beside Stella.

"Patrick thinks we should all be sent away to live in England and America," she told Charlotte. "Although Stella wouldn't be averse to leaving the island, the rest of us want to stay right here. Would you speak to Patrick for us?"

Charlotte sighed. "I'll try, but the captain is not in an especially malleable mood just now. He's concerned about the storm—"

"And the pirates!" Deborah broke in, her cornflower blue eyes big with excitement and fear as she huddled closer to Jayne. "Jacoba says if those men get us, we'll be slaves to sin for the rest of our natural lives!"

Charlotte was exasperated that the housekeeper would plant such frightening thoughts in such an obviously naive mind. "Jacoba says too much sometimes," she said. "You needn't be afraid. There probably aren't any pirates nearby anyway."

Jayne, a redhead, tossed her head and spoke for the first time. "That's how much *you* know," she said, with good-natured scorn. "Mr. Rowling told us himself that his ship was boarded by rogues—"

"Those dreadful men are long gone by now," Charlotte reasoned, wanting to reassure the group. "And if they are nearby, by some remote chance, the storm will surely finish them off."

Jayne rolled her eyes. "Nonsense. There are a dozen smaller islands within spitting distance of this one, with any number of sheltered coves just right for hiding a ship."

"She's right," Nora said.

Before anyone else could speak, Patrick strode imperiously into the chamber and sent his wards out again. They left, though not happily, all four of them casting meaningful looks back at Charlotte.

She looked into Patrick's eyes and decided to delay presenting her arguments for letting Deborah, Nora, and Jayne stay on the island instead of going away to rejoin society.

"What do you want?" she asked coolly, returning to her experimentations with the shawl-turned–wedding veil.

She felt his smile like sunshine on her nape, heard it in his voice. "Regrettably, there is no time now for what I want," he replied. "We will marry within the hour, but the delight of consummating the union will have to wait until later."

Charlotte felt a blush rise in her cheeks and turned to look at him, the veil falling gracefully over her hair and shoulders. "Now? We're being married now?"

Patrick made a show of taking a watch from the breast pocket of his loose linen shirt and looking at its face. "In approximately fifteen minutes. Rowling has written up a certificate. He can say the words, we'll sign the paper, and the whole task will be over and done with."

"The whole *task?*" Charlotte echoed. "God in heaven, Patrick, haven't you the decency even to *pretend,* for my sake, that this is a real wedding?"

"It's quite real," Patrick said, with a distracted sigh. "Hurry it up, goddess. I have other things to do."

Charlotte rolled her eyes, knowing there was no sense in arguing. Patrick Trevarren was obviously about as sensitive

272

and romantic as any one of the oxen that dragged her father's timber down the mountain to the mill.

He looked at his watch again, frowned as though surprised to see that it hadn't changed in some fundamental way, and went out again.

Charlotte went into the bathing room, took her time with her ablutions, and put on a fresh camisole in light blue taffeta. She added matching drawers and voluminous petticoats, and then drew her ivory dress on over her head.

Mary Catch-much-fish appeared, as if by conjuring, to fasten the row of tiny buttons up the back, and her manner was nervous. "This big wind," she fussed, "it goin' to lift us all right off this island and fling us in the water!"

"It is noisy," Charlotte agreed. For hours, everyone in the household had been raising their voices to be heard above the commotion. "But we'll be right here when it's over."

Mary sat Charlotte down in a chair and began dressing her hair with uncanny skill. Her quick black hands flying, she made a soft knot at the back of Charlotte's head, while the sides and top billowed softly around her face. Deborah hurried into the room with a basketful of pink orchidlike flowers just as Mary was pinning the improvised veil into place.

Although Charlotte was delighted with the gift, she also feared the girl might have taken a serious risk to supply it. "Oh, Deborah," she whispered, "these are so lovely! But surely you didn't go outside to pick them?"

Deborah smiled shyly and flushed. She was small, with pale hair and delicate features, and someday, when she'd had a chance to mature, she would be beautiful. "Oh, no. I wouldn't dare defy Patrick that way—he would have made me stay in my room and read the entire book of Leviticus out loud if I'd done such a thing!"

Charlotte smiled to learn of Patrick's method of discipline. She knew he would have preferred for her to think he was far more severe in his dealings. "Then where did you get these lovely blossoms?" she asked as Mary deftly arranged them around the edge of her veil.

"Nora got them," Deborah answered in a breathless

whisper, obviously in awe of the other girl's daring. "When she went to look for Mattie the first time. You know, the monkey."

A jolt of alarm went through Charlotte's being. "The first time?" she echoed. Mary stood motionless now, her hands suspended in midair, listening with as much interest as Charlotte did.

"You won't tattle, will you? Nora has already been through Leviticus five times, so Patrick might make her read the entire Old Testament if he hears about this!"

Charlotte and Mary exchanged a look.

"Deborah," Charlotte said evenly, trying not to frighten the timid girl, "are you saying that Nora has gone out into this storm not once, but *twice?*"

Deborah's soft eyes filled with tears. "I've gotten her into trouble, haven't I?"

"Deborah," Charlotte insisted.

"Yes!" Deborah cried. "Yes, she's outside—I begged her not to go, but she said she couldn't leave Mattie to die in the storm—"

Charlotte spoke softly to Mary Catch-much-fish. "Go and tell Captain Trevarren about this, please. Someone will have to go after Nora and bring her back."

Mary nodded and rushed anxiously out of the room.

The world seemed to go dark as Charlotte sat there, listening to the furious banshee screams of the wind. There might have been a great commotion going on downstairs as word reached Patrick that one of his wards was not only flouting his orders but risking her life in the process, but Charlotte didn't hear it.

Perhaps half an hour had passed when Jacoba came for her, carrying a candelabra in one hand and looking as serious as if they were holding a funeral in her master's house that day, instead of a wedding.

"Was Nora found and brought back?"

"She and that dratted monkey came in just five minutes ago," Jacoba answered as she led the way out of the master bedroom and along the hallway. "The beast is safe, but I do believe the bridegroom is this minute giving Miss Nora a lecture she'll recall even when she's been a hundred years in heaven."

Charlotte sighed. She felt sorry for Nora, having been on the receiving end of Patrick's ire once or twice herself. If her own experiences were anything to judge by, the other girl would come away with blisters on her ears.

When she and Jacoba reached the main parlor, where candles had been set about to give their soft, flickering light, Nora was huddled near the pianoforte, sniffling, looking like a colorful bird with its feathers ruffled. Deborah, Jayne, and Stella stood around her, stalwart in their support even though they surely agreed that Nora had been foolhardy to leave the house for the sake of a monkey.

For his own part, the groom looked more ominous than ever. He glared at Charlotte, as if daring her to rebuke him for correcting his ward, and she did not take the challenge. He had not done the girl actual violence, and the island *was* his province. As the natural protector, he had the right to make certain decrees and expect them to be abided by.

Gideon stood somewhat shakily in front of the fireplace, dressed in clothing that was too large for him, since he had none of his own, and holding a small prayer book. The worn volume had been given to him by Jacoba soon after he regained consciousness, for his own had, of course, been lost at sea.

Charlotte and Patrick took their places in front of him, Charlotte feeling as shy and awkward as any virgin bride, Patrick standing tall. Out of the corner of her eye, Charlotte saw that his jaw was set in a grim, forbidding line.

Gideon looked at Patrick and then, somewhat sadly, at Charlotte. "Are you certain this is what you want to do?" he asked her, in a quiet but nonetheless forceful voice. "There are other options, you know."

"Just get on with the ceremony," Patrick snapped, catching his hands together behind his back, like a soldier at parade rest.

"Charlotte?" Gideon persisted, ignoring the captain's peremptory words.

She drew a deep breath and then let it out slowly,

imagining herself in Australia, helping to convert Aborigines. She wouldn't be very good as a missionary, she decided, since she loved luxuries like pretty clothes and scented baths.

Still, Gideon was not an unappealing man, and he would be a devoted, if not passionate, husband and a wonderful, steady father. She would have an interesting, challenging life with him.

Charlotte glanced up at Patrick. On the other hand, she loved Mr. Trevarren with her entire soul, impossible though he was. There were still so many mysteries about him that she wanted to solve, so many intimate bridges to cross and inner landscapes to explore.

"This is what I want," she said finally, and was pleased by the subtle sigh Patrick gave at her words.

"Very well, then," Gideon said gruffly. Then he cleared his throat and went on. "Dearly beloved," he proceeded, in a solemn voice, "we are gathered here, in the sight of God . . ."

The rest of the ceremony passed in a dizzying rush for Charlotte, while the storm grew in intensity. Just as Gideon pronounced Charlotte and Patrick man and wife, something huge plunged through a window *and* its protective shuttering, in some other part of the house, adding a grand crescendo to the wedding.

Charlotte had not expected Patrick to take the time to kiss her, since he'd been in such an all-fired hurry to get the marriage over with. She was therefore surprised when he lifted her completely off her bare feet and took her mouth with his own. Before letting her down, he conquered her with his tongue, telling her without words that her next pleasuring would go far beyond anything she'd known before.

She trembled with the need to give herself to this man, and with anger that things were so. How much easier it would have been to love Gideon, how much more sensible and peaceful. But no. Not Charlotte. She had to adore, even worship, a man who had already consigned her to a harem once, and openly stated that he would not be tied down to one home or one woman.

Patrick interrupted her thoughts with a crisp order. "Jacoba, take the women to the wine cellar." He paused to glower down at Charlotte, then toss a scathing look in Nora's direction. "You will stay there, all of you, until the storm passes."

Even Charlotte, intrepid as she was, would not have thought of defying Patrick after she heard the tone of those words. He meant every one of them, as a holy vow, and it would take an army of angels to save the foolish woman who disobeyed them.

Charlotte gestured for Nora and the others to come along, and obediently followed Jacoba down a rear stairway, made of stone, into a dank chamber that reminded her of the dungeons in Khalif's palace. All in all, the memories the place brought back were not ones a bride would have expected to entertain on her wedding day.

"You were beautiful," Deborah said, with admiration, when more candles had been lit and they were all settled, as comfortably as possible, in that grim cellar.

Nora sniffled, her face still mottled with humiliation and fury. The monkey she'd risked death to save came screeching out of the darkness and flung itself into her lap like a small and frightened child.

"I hope Patrick Trevarren has a toothache for the rest of his life," Nora said. "Not only did he shout at me until I thought the very roof would cave in—he said I have to copy out the whole first act of *Julius Caesar* before Tuesday! When I asked what he meant to do if I refused, he said I'd be wiser not to find out!"

Stella sighed, and practical Jayne tossed her mane of beautiful auburn hair and said, "Do stop your fussing, Nora. You deserved what you got. Great Scott, you could have been run through by a bough in this wind."

Jacoba frowned at both girls. "Jayne, I'll thank you not to swear. As for you, Nora, well, you're just lucky you have the captain to look after you. With your flighty ways, you'd surely have come to ruin by now if it weren't for him. In any case, I do daresay I've got enough on my mind, what with this house about to fall down around my ears, without the lot of you carrying on like schoolgirls."

"Do you think we'll be killed?" Deborah dared to ask, her voice small and shaky. Just then, she seemed even younger than she was. "Will the house really collapse?"

Charlotte reached out and took the girl's hand. "No, love. We won't be killed. Jacoba was exaggerating just now—the walls of this place are as sturdy as the island itself."

"I think we should sing," Stella announced.

"Oh, Lord," fussed Jayne. "Isn't it bad enough that we're sitting out a hurricane in a musty cellar with a monkey for company? Do we have to listen to you bellowing too?"

Charlotte smiled. "We might as well enjoy ourselves," she said, with a shrug of one shoulder. Moments later, they were all singing a silly song at the tops of their voices—except for Jacoba, that is—the monkey included.

Soon the men came, all except Patrick and Mr. Cochran, bringing blankets and a fresh supply of candles, along with baskets of food, and milk cans full of water.

Hours had passed when the wind died and the great house finally stopped trembling on its foundations. Charlotte was lying awake on a large crate, wrapped tightly in her blanket, when she heard the door creak open.

"It's over," she heard Patrick say. He sounded weary.

She sat up, tossed the blanket aside, and went to him. "Are you all right?"

He looked away, and she saw a muscle flex at the base of his throat. "Yes," he answered hoarsely, "but the cane crop is gone, and so is every outbuilding on the property."

Charlotte laid her hands lightly against his upper arms, which were hard under his torn and dirty wedding shirt. She told him, with her eyes, that she wanted to help him forget the lost crops and general wreckage, at least for that night.

I need you, he conceded, with nothing more than a look.

"Everyone," Mr. Cochran said in a merry voice, "back to your own soft beds! The worst is over."

Patrick stood looking down at Charlotte for a long time, then he took one of her hands into his, raised it to his lips, gently kissed the knuckles. They were alone—even the monkey had gone—when he whispered, "Oh, Mrs. Trevarren, why must you be so beautiful?"

She slipped her arms around his lean waist. "I don't have

any shoes on," she whispered, letting his question pass because she didn't know how to answer it.

He laughed as he lifted her hem and saw ten toes glowing like dust-smudged alabaster in the dying light of the candles. "Remind me to lecture you unmercifully for your disobedience," he said, whisking her up into his arms and starting toward the doorway.

"Speaking of that—" Charlotte began, frowning.

She felt his sigh as he carried her up the stone steps and into the main part of that enormous, wind-battered house. "If you're about to berate me for shouting at Nora earlier, wife, save your breath. Had I allowed her to get by with endangering herself like that, what would have kept the others from going off on tangents of their own and very likely getting themselves killed? There are times, my beloved, when expediency must take precedence over more gracious inclinations."

Charlotte could not refute his reasoning. In times of crisis the lives of everyone on the island depended on cooperation, and there could only be one leader. Undeniably that was Patrick.

She nuzzled his throat mischievously as he carried her through the dark house.

"Are you sorry you married me?" she asked, only half teasing.

"Right now," Patrick replied, mounting the main staircase with agile speed, "I'm very glad you're my wife. I need to lose myself in you, Charlotte, more than ever, and I can do that with a free heart because this time you really are Mrs. Patrick Trevarren."

She nibbled at his earlobe. "I am indeed."

"Don't tease me," he warned, pushing open the door to the master suite with a none-too-gentle motion of one foot. "I'm already hard as the mainmast on a sailing ship, and it's all I can do to get you as far as the bed before I take you."

Charlotte trembled with naughty anticipation. In this one area of their life together, she was willing to be submissive at least part of the time. "Then perhaps you should be satisfied immediately, Captain, so that you can take your proper time making love to me."

He set her on her feet, lifted her chin with one hand. "You are a sorceress," he said, his voice husky with emotion and the plain needs of a man. "Just touching you, just being close to you like this, makes my blood burn in my veins. What have you done to me, Charlotte Trevarren?"

She unfastened his breeches, button by button, slowly, slowly, pausing to cup him in her hand now and then and listen to his involuntary moans of pleasure. Finally she turned her back to him, a wordless instruction to undo her dress, and he was awkward in his obedience.

When the dress was gone, Charlotte took off her petticoats, her camisole, and then her drawers. Patrick stood staring hungrily at her breasts, still fully clad himself, as if entranced.

Gently Charlotte smoothed his breeches down over his sleek, muscular hips, then pressed him into a chair without undressing him further. His manhood rose high and hard against his belly, awaiting her.

Charlotte was wanton in her joy, and she came to stand astraddle of Patrick's lap, lowering herself onto him inch by pulsing, vibrant inch.

Patrick groaned and let his head fall back as she rode him, and when he tried to quicken the pace, she withdrew. He uttered a hoarse plea and she gave him his pleasure again, but sparingly.

"Oh, God, Charlotte," he finally gasped, when she had subjected him to an agony of pleasure. "Please—give me what I need . . ."

She deliberately misunderstood and leaned forward to brush his lips with a hard, ready nipple. He took it hungrily, greedily, and suddenly Charlotte's own instincts overtook her. She whimpered as Patrick took command, continuing to suckle even as he bent her back on his lap and invaded her silken shelter with the tips of his fingers. When he began to stroke her rhythmically, as well as move inside her, Charlotte went wild.

Patrick teased her for a while, then finally gave up her breast, grasped her hips in his powerful hands, and raised and lowered her on his shaft in earnest.

280

Charlotte could not have been silent in her surrender even if she had the wits to try, because the pleasure was so keen. It consumed her, like a fire, and made her beg hoarsely for satisfaction and then cry out, long and loud, while her body flexed repeatedly, in a graceful fury of passion. Patrick came violently as she sank against his chest in exhaustion, bucking beneath her and stirring a series of smaller releases that made her groan in surprised reluctance.

They sat, still joined and recovering, for some considerable time. Then, matter-of-factly, Patrick arranged Charlotte on his lap again, still filling her with his inescapable manhood. She arched backward, against his hands, while he kissed her breasts and flicked at their tips with his tongue.

Soon Charlotte was writhing once more, and Patrick had her again, stroking the sleek planes and curves of her body and speaking soft words of solace as she convulsed around him.

It was a long, delicious night, and when Charlotte awakened in the morning, there was bright sunlight coming through the slim spaces between the boards covering the windows. Patrick's side of the bed was empty.

Untroubled, Charlotte stretched sensuously, her flesh still humming with the singular well-being Patrick's attentions inevitably brought to it. This time their marriage was legal and binding in their own culture, and Patrick could not get rid of her on a whim. Their child was going to have an honorable birth, and for a time at least, Charlotte would be truly happy.

She didn't delude herself; Patrick had not changed his mind about leaving her in Quade's Harbor. Still, it might be months before they were even able to leave the island, let alone sail north to Washington Territory and get a house built. Charlotte consoled herself with the fact that she would have plenty of time to bring her husband around to her way of thinking.

After a luxurious interval, she rose, put on a wrapper, and went into the next room for a bath. When she was dressed, she descended the stairs and found that Mary Catch-much-fish and even the fierce Jacoba treated her with a new deference. They called her "Mrs. Trevarren" now, in quiet, respectful voices, and insisted on serving her breakfast on the veranda, so she could enjoy the sunshine.

The landscape was a scene of wreckage, littered with uprooted palm trees and sundered branches—Charlotte thought the aftermath of the Great Flood must have been much the same—and part of the veranda roof had fallen through. However, enough debris had been cleared away at the opposite end for a very gracious table to be set.

"Where is the captain this morning?" Charlotte asked. She reached for the teapot, but Mary slapped her hand away, making a good-natured *tsk-tsk* sound, and poured the brew herself.

"Him be out looking at the fields," the maid replied. "The cane will be wantin' to be replanted, I think."

Charlotte blushed, mortified at the sudden realization that she hadn't once thought of the island's natives, not even when the hurricane was at its very worst. "Mary . . . your people—what happened to them?"

Mary shrugged and favored Charlotte with a blinding smile. "They hide in caves when the big winds come, like ever and ever, since the time of dreams. It be well with them."

"Their homes—?"

The smile intensified. "They build new ones," she said, and then she bustled back into the house, as cheerful as if there had never been a storm at all.

21

THE CANE CROPS WERE LAID TO WASTE, AND THE NATIVE VIL-
lage on the other side of the island was in ruins, and yet the
sun shone as brightly as if God had set it blazing just that
morning. The sky was a fragile, soul-piercing blue, and the
breeze came in cool and fresh off the crystalline sea.

As Patrick inspected the cannon salvaged from the decks
of the *Enchantress* before she went under—it appeared that
all the weapons had withstood nature's rage—he reflected
on his situation.

The loss of that year's sugarcane would certainly tax his
resources, as would the necessary destruction of the *Enchantress,* but he knew he could recover from both disasters
with time and hard work. Eventually, too, a friendly ship
was sure to appear on the horizon, Rowling's blasted prayers
notwithstanding. He and Charlotte—Patrick paused to
smile, recalling what a tigress his wife had been the night
before—would eventually sail on to Seattle, where he could
arrange for the construction of a new vessel. He also meant
to oversee the building of a fine house in that community,
one that would shelter his wife and child during his long sea

voyages. That way, Charlotte could see her family often without being too close.

Once matters had been arranged in Seattle, they would both proceed to Quade's Harbor for a visit. Charlotte might stay as long as she wanted, though Patrick would come and go.

He leaned against the cold metal of the cannon barrel, his grin fading. Surely Charlotte had only been baiting him when she'd vowed to take a lover if he left her alone.

She wouldn't *dare* do such a thing—would she?

He thought uncomfortably of the time he'd first encountered Miss Charlotte Quade; she'd been fifty feet off the deck of his clipper, clad in skirts no less, and clinging to the rigging. On their next meeting, she'd ventured into the *souk* in Riz, a place where a sensible angel would fear to tread.

Hellfire and damnation, Patrick thought. If she'd risk those other outrageous escapades, what or who could keep Charlotte from making good on her threat to take up with another man?

Inwardly Patrick seethed. The image of Charlotte sharing her favors with anyone other than himself was too unbearable even to entertain.

Though he was not a man to be particularly concerned with the opinions of others, he dreaded the inevitable scandal. Every ship, every train and stagecoach and hay wagon, would carry the news of Charlotte Trevarren's wayward affections, until there wasn't a gossip in the western hemisphere who hadn't heard the sordid details.

Patrick swore, moved on to inspect the next cannon for storm damage. His countenance brightened all of a sudden as he considered Charlotte's father, the legendary Brigham Quade. Patrick was barely acquainted with the man, but he knew Quade well enough to be certain that Charlotte would be made to behave herself while in his charge.

Cochran scaled the ridge, scratched his head at the sight of his captain, who was by then whistling cheerfully as he prepared to defend his small but perfect kingdom.

"What are you so happy about?" the first mate demanded, sounding a little breathless from the climb. "Here you are, with a cash crop crushed to the ground and Lord only knows what kind of trouble coming in on the next tide—"

"Have you forgotten that I've taken a bride?" Patrick interrupted, glad to be diverted from the track his thoughts had taken. "And that last night was my wedding night?"

"I had indeed," Cochran admitted, wiping his brow with a sun-bronzed, sinewy forearm. His ears reddened, and he cleared his throat, then turned to gaze uneasily out to sea. "When do you suppose he'll show up—Raheem or whoever that bastard is, lurking out there?"

Patrick pulled palm fronds and other debris from the barrel of the largest cannon. "Probably after nightfall," he replied. "Trouble usually strikes when a man's just getting back on his feet after some other calamity, Cochran. You know that."

Cochran spat. "Well, the boys are as ready as they can be, Captain. I've seen to that." He paused, cleared his throat uneasily. "What about the women? Shouldn't we hide them somewhere? After all, if it's Raheem that's making my skin crawl and the hair stand out at the back of my neck this way, then he's come here to collect Charlotte."

Rage boiled up inside Patrick, but he immediately brought it under control. If ever he'd needed to keep his wits about him, it was now. He nodded in grim agreement, recalling Khalif's warning that the pirate would never rest until he'd gotten what he saw as justice. "It's Raheem," he said. He sighed, rolled his shoulders in an effort to release some of the tension that knotted his muscles. "And yes—we have to try to keep the women out of sight. God only knows whether they'll stay hidden, though."

"They won't want to risk the kind of scolding Miss Nora got," Cochran said, sounding for all the world as though he truly believed such rubbish.

"Have you been paying attention, Cochran?" Patrick snapped. "Not one of those chits would hesitate to defy my orders if it suited them. Sometimes I wish I were the sort to take a woman over my knee—that's the only really dependable method of keeping the creatures in line, you know—but the fact is, I just don't have the heart to do it."

Cochran smiled and slapped Patrick lightly on the shoulder. "Don't be too hard on yourself, Captain. Times are changing, and men of sound spirit know that women are for loving, not hurting."

Patrick set his teeth. He could be philosophical about the running of his household now. What would happen, though, if he came home from the sea someday and found that Charlotte had cradled some other man between her soft thighs, given a stranger comfort at her breast?

He feared what he might do in such circumstances even more than Charlotte's betrayal itself.

"Have you seen my wife this morning?" he asked, after a brief silence, as he left the cannon behind to start down the gentle slope toward the house.

"Aye," Cochran answered. "She and the others have gone to the village to help out."

"Well, get them back here right now," Patrick grumbled, thinking how easy it would be for Raheem or anyone else to row ashore and snatch his wife and wards from the midst of the peaceful villagers.

"Begging your pardon, sir," Cochran answered, falling into step beside Patrick, "but get them back yourself. I'd sooner tangle with a pack of she-wolves than try to give orders to that lot."

Patrick swore, but he didn't give Cochran a second order. He simply went to the stone stables, which, like the house, had stood strong against the storm, and saddled his sorrel gelding for his second visit to the village that day.

Deborah drew in her breath and then gave a horrified cry when she and Charlotte and the others arrived, with Mary Catch-much-fish, at the little community on the far side of the island.

Charlotte was astonished that the servant girl had spoken so lightly of the debacle earlier that morning, on the veranda of the big house. Where huts must have stood before, there were now only craters in the ground—holes filled with seawater.

Old ladies perched on rocks, wailing their laments, and babies squalled. The men were busy repairing fishing boats, while the younger women gathered foliage and sturdy, flexible wood and stacked it in piles on higher ground.

"Dear Lord," Charlotte breathed. "The destruction . . ."

"What shall we do?" Deborah asked, her lovely blue eyes brimming with tears of empathy.

Charlotte opened her mouth to speak, but before she got a word out, Jayne took charge.

"Stella and Nora and I will help the others find more building materials. Charlotte—er, Mrs. Trevarren—it would probably be best if you and Deborah helped with the babies. Deborah loves the little mites, and has a way with them, and, well, I don't think Patrick would want his new wife tromping around in the jungle."

"Please call me Charlotte," Mrs. Trevarren said crisply. "And Patrick's views on feminine deportment are hardly the issue here. I'll help look after the little ones, but it won't be because I'm trying to tiptoe around my husband's temper. I love children, and that's all the reason I need."

Jayne smiled, and Charlotte knew that in that moment she and the other woman had become lifelong friends. "Well, then," she said. "Let's roll up our sleeves and try to be of some assistance to these people."

Despite the din of the grandmothers, who mourned the village even though not one human life had been lost, and the crying of the many hungry babies, that was a happy time for Charlotte. She gathered the chubby infants close by the armload, delighting in their dark, beautiful faces, loving them for their innocence. She and Deborah dried their tears and gave them coconut milk in place of the nourishment their busy mothers could not offer.

In the meantime, Jayne, Stella, and Nora garnered foliage and thick vines and branches with as much industry as any of the natives. Everyone seemed to be feeling very pleased with themselves when suddenly Patrick came riding along the white beach, with an air of mission about him.

A baby wriggling in the crook of each arm, Charlotte picked her barefoot way around the muddy edges of the flooded village and went to meet him. The rich leather of his saddle creaked as he turned to look out to sea, then he met Charlotte's eyes again.

His expression, grim before, softened visibly. "You shouldn't be here," he said. "It's dangerous."

Charlotte hoisted the squirming babies higher against her shoulders and laughed softly. "Oh, Patrick, *everything* is dangerous. If you had your way, I'd just sit in the parlor, day in and day out, stitching silly samplers and waiting for you to come home from some grand adventure."

Patrick swung one leg deftly over the saddle and slid down to stand facing Charlotte. "Would that really be so terrible?" he asked, and he sounded serious.

A pang clutched at Charlotte's heart, unbearably sweet. How she loved this man, and how she wished she didn't! "Yes, Patrick," she answered, in a gentle tone. "For me, it would be like being cast into prison."

He sighed, this husband of hers, and reached out to take the heavier of the babies into his arms. "I'll never understand why being safe means so little to you," he admitted.

She extended her hand and ran her fingertip lightly over the buttons of his shirt, delighting in the almost imperceptible shiver he gave in response. "If you really want to protect me, Patrick," she teased, in a low, impish voice, "perhaps you should stop making love to me. Sometimes I truly think I'm going to die of the pleasure." Charlotte paused, leaned closer to him, well aware that her words had made him hard and that there wasn't a thing he could do about it. "I tell you, Captain, my heart starts racing and I can't get my breath and, well, my mind goes off somewhere on its own. It just isn't *safe!*"

"Stop it." He scowled. The base of his neck was reddening as he spoke.

Charlotte laughed and Patrick swore as the naked baby set a stain spreading across the front of his shirt. She was still laughing when he muttered another swear word, thrust the child back into her arms, and strode over to a tide pool to wash.

When he returned to her side, Patrick was bare-chested, having rinsed both his skin and the shirt in salt water. The garment was hanging over a nearby branch.

Charlotte looked at him, suffered a few poignant recollections of the night before, and felt a tightening sensation in her depths. She averted her eyes.

Patrick worked as tirelessly as anyone else through the morning, helping to construct the new huts on the rise above the old village. At midday, however, after yet another troubled glance toward the horizon, he suddenly ordered his wards back to the main house, telling them to keep away from the shore and hide themselves in the appointed place as soon as they arrived home. Then he collected his sun-dried shirt, hoisted Charlotte onto his horse's back, and climbed up after her.

"What is it?" she asked, alarmed, sensing a sharp, lethal alertness in him.

The horse danced restlessly beneath them as Patrick spoke not to his wife, but to the villagers. He addressed them in their own language, and his words sent them scrambling. They gathered the babies, the small children, and the noisy old ladies and vanished into the foliage.

"Visitors," Patrick said, taking a small spyglass from a leather pouch behind his saddle and training it on the distant blue-green line where the sky and sea met.

Charlotte's heart somersaulted over several beats, and she squinted, unable to see anything but a speck bobbing on the edge of the world. "That's good news, isn't it? If we're having company, I mean. Now we won't be marooned anymore, and perhaps Gideon can go on to Australia and get started on his conversions."

"Gideon?" Patrick echoed, arching one eyebrow. He handed her the costly brass telescope.

Charlotte offered no reply, but instead squinted to see through the glass. With some difficulty, she found the object of his concern—a slow, ominous-looking ship with no identifying flag flying from its mast.

"Pirates?" she breathed.

"Raheem," Patrick replied, quite matter-of-factly.

Charlotte gave an involuntary shiver. She knew only too well that when she'd been kidnapped in the *souk* that memorable day in June, she'd been meant as a sort of gift for the pirate. Instead, of course, Raheem's men had lost her in a gambling wager and she'd ended up being delivered to Patrick Trevarren's cabin in a burlap sack.

"He must be a very vindictive man," she observed, with a certain loftiness of tone, as Patrick reined the horse away from the village and back down the beach. "Just imagine coming all this way only to carry off one ordinary woman."

Patrick chuckled, and his voice was low as it passed her ear. "You are no ordinary woman, goddess. And I would travel much farther to collect you. On that score at least, I can hardly fault Raheem."

Despite the danger, and the general seriousness of their circumstances, Charlotte felt a rush of pleasure at Patrick's words. Most of the time he gave the distinct impression he couldn't wait to have her off his hands, and the knowledge that he valued her enough to sail the seas in search of her was uplifting.

It was romantic, like a scene from one of her fantasies, racing over the sands on horseback, encircled by the strong arms of the man she loved. When they arrived at the stables, however, Patrick was all business.

He swung down from the saddle, lifted Charlotte after him, and told her in a clipped tone, "Get inside and take your place with the others. Jacoba will tell you where to go."

"I'd like to suggest a few places *you* could go," Charlotte replied sweetly. "To blazes, for instance."

"Charlotte," Patrick growled, unbuckling the cinch and then pulling the saddle from the gelding's quivering back, "I have neither the time nor the patience for any of your mischief." He set the saddle on a stall railing, pointed Charlotte toward the house, and gave her a light swat on the bottom to get her moving. *"Go,"* he warned, when she, flushed and furious, started to protest.

She sighed and then, wishing she were bigger and stronger so she could challenge Patrick to a fisticuffs and bloody his nose, she gave up and obeyed his command. Jacoba was waiting for her inside, and immediately bustled her along an inner hallway leading into a part of the house Charlotte had never visited before.

Reaching the end of the passage, Jacoba moved a cabinet aside, revealing a door, which made no sound as it was opened. The hinges, Charlotte noticed, had been so well oiled that they gleamed in the dinginess.

On the other side of the threshold was a surprisingly pleasant-looking room, equipped with Roman couches, chairs, candelabras, and plenty of food and books. Nora, Deborah, Stella, and Jayne sat around a table, embroiled in a game of cards.

The whole scene rather reminded Charlotte of Khalif's harem. That place, like this one, had afforded many comforts, and both were little more than fancy prisons.

"Will you join us, Charlotte?" Deborah asked eagerly, scooting aside so that the newcomer might pull up a chair beside hers. "We're playing poker." She lowered her voice, as if confessing to a magnificent indiscretion. "We're wagering, too—I've already lost every hair ribbon I own—and you'll want to pay special attention because I do believe Nora and Jayne are cheating."

Charlotte found a chair and entered the circle. Nora and Jayne, instead of being insulted by Deborah's accusation, were only amused.

"You have always been a poor loser," Nora told the youngest girl.

Jayne sat with one foot resting on the seat of her chair, absorbed in a study of her cards. "Let's not bicker, ladies," she said reflectively. "After all, we might be shut up in this place for days."

Charlotte flushed. In many ways, it was her fault that the islanders were in danger and that she and the others had to hide out in a secret room. She'd begun it all by venturing out to the *souk* that day, when she'd been told to stay away. "I'm sorry," she said.

The other four looked at her in bewilderment and surprise.

"Sorry?" Nora echoed. "For what?"

"I've endangered all of you," Charlotte confessed miserably. "Those pirates are here because of me."

Nora's eyes rounded with interest; she slapped down her cards and leaned forward. "You're teasing, Charlotte Trevarren."

"Aren't you?" Deborah asked, uncertainly.

"They're after you?" Jayne demanded, gesturing toward the outside world to indicate approaching trouble.

Charlotte nodded, swallowed, then told her story in halting words, from the moment she'd been kidnapped in the marketplace in Riz to the arrival of the doomed *Enchantress* on the shores of the island only a short time before.

"Tarnation!" Stella cried, when the tale had unfolded. "That's just plain splendid!"

"You married Patrick *twice*," Deborah reflected. "Oh, that's just about the most *romantic* thing I've ever heard."

Jayne, ever pragmatic, snorted in an unladylike fashion and said, " 'Romantic'? Surely you jest—he divorced Charlotte in a fit of pique, simply by clapping his hands and saying a few silly words! In my opinion, our Patrick could use a lesson or two in simple courtesy."

Charlotte smiled but said nothing. She was too busy thinking.

Jayne was a firebrand, born, like Charlotte herself, to make things happen rather than sit back, watching and waiting and keeping her clothes clean. In a burst of inspired revelation, Charlotte knew that it was this energetic, opinionated redhead Gideon should marry—provided Jayne would have him for a husband, that is. She had the spirit for life in the Australian bush, the strength and determination and innate sweetness of heart required of a clergyman's mate.

"Why are you staring at me like that?" demanded the missionary-unaware.

"I was just doing a little matchmaking," Charlotte admitted.

Nora smiled dreamily and uttered a small sigh.

"She's sweet on Billy Piper," Deborah announced in an important whisper, indicating Nora with a wave of her hand. "He was her special patient when he and the others were down with the fever."

Charlotte hadn't even played a hand of cards yet and she was already feeling confined, restless. She wanted to be outside, with the men, part of the preparations to defend the island and all its inhabitants. She got up from her chair and began to pace, arms folded.

The others followed her train of thought without difficulty, which wasn't at all strange because the approach of a pirate ship would naturally be uppermost in just about anyone's mind.

"Do you think there will be bloodshed?" Deborah asked fearfully, her hands clasped together in her lap.

"Of course there will," Jayne blustered, and though her eyes flashed with excitement, her skin was even fairer than usual. Her freckles stood out because of the contrast. "They'll shoot at us and we'll shoot at them, and we women will either end up tending our own wounded or being ravished as spoils of war."

Deborah went gray and gave a soft, plaintive cry of terror, and Nora immediately leaned over to put an arm around the girl's shoulders. "Hush!" she scolded, frowning at Jayne. "You're frightening the poor child to death!"

Jayne shrugged. "Might as well face reality. If Patrick and the others can't hold off the invaders, my dears, we can all kiss our maidenly virtue a fond farewell!"

Deborah emitted a wail of despair.

"One more word," Nora warned, shaking her fist at Jayne, "and I'm going to blacken at least one of your eyes!"

"Wait," Charlotte protested quickly, holding up both hands in a bid for peace. "Please. We're all in terrible trouble. We mustn't turn on each other now." She sighed, then added, "Patrick will protect us."

After that, though they all tried to concentrate on games of cards, the room fairly throbbed with tension. The hours crawled by with all the speed of fat brown slugs traversing a broad garden.

The room became shadowy and Charlotte lit the candelabras. The company of women ate French chocolates and sandwiches and fruit, and they waited.

Just after sunset, cannon fire made the walls of the house quiver. Charlotte yearned to be in the center of things, where she could see what was happening with her own eyes instead of having to speculate and imagine. Had Raheem dropped anchor on the far side of the island and led his men through the jungle or along the beach? Or had he simply sailed around to the main harbor and opened fire on the house from there?

Long since bored with pacing, Charlotte finally went to the door and tried to open it. She was irritated, if not surprised, to find it locked. Since she had already inspected the rest of the room for a possible escape route during the long afternoon, Charlotte was forced to accept the fact that she and the others were there for the duration.

The cannon fire boomed; the war between the invaders and the defenders was proceeding in earnest.

Deborah covered her face with both hands and began to weep with a quiet hopelessness that twisted Charlotte's heart.

"Are you happy now?" Nora demanded of Jayne, and there was a distinct edge to her voice. "Look what you've done, talking about being ravished and all that rot!"

Jayne looked both chagrined and defensive, and she opened her mouth to respond, only to be silenced by a grating sound out in the passageway. Clearly the cabinet that hid the door was being moved.

Everyone held their breath, including Charlotte, but it was Gideon Rowling who joined them, not a leering pirate.

Charlotte practically flung herself on the man, gripping his vest as she looked up into his face. "What's happening? Is Patrick safe?"

Gently, briefly, Gideon covered her grasping hand with his own. "As safe as can be expected—"

Deborah cried out just then, in an agony of fear, and rose to her feet, sobbing.

Naturally, being a man of God and sworn to lend comfort, Gideon went to her. Charlotte hesitated only a moment, then took advantage of his distraction and slipped out through the doorway into the shadowy hall. The house reverberated with the impact of cannonballs, and a part of her wanted to stay in hiding. In the end, though, her concern for Patrick and the incessant curiosity that was her personal cross prevailed. She hurried away from safety and light and into darkness and peril.

Even though she moved as carefully as she could, Charlotte bumped into more than one piece of furniture as she made her way to the front of the house. She was bruised by the time she gained a window in the parlor, overlooking the harbor, still boarded up against yesterday's storm. Through a crack between the planks, she saw not one ship in the bay, but three, and flashes of crimson blazed on their decks as they fired their cannon.

Charlotte was too enraged to feel fear; that, she knew, would come later. For now, she wanted, *needed,* to be at Patrick's side. In life or in death, she belonged with her husband.

She was just turning away from the window when suddenly there was a deafening noise, a sensation of unimaginable shock, and then it seemed that she'd been absorbed by, become a part of, some massive creature made of light and fire.

Patrick was drawn back to the house from the ridge, where he had been overseeing the cannon defending the island, literally pulled by some inexplicable demand of his spirit. He was met in the rear dooryard by a half-frantic Gideon.

"Thank God you're here," the missionary cried, and Patrick had an unsettling feeling that he'd been brought down from the ridge by prayer. "It's Charlotte—"

It took only those two words to propel Patrick into motion again; he flung himself through the back door, Gideon's words droning at his ears like bees on a hot summer day. "I blame myself—Jayne's with her—slipped past me—"

Patrick did not have to be guided to Charlotte. Her soul called wordlessly to his; his strained to be joined with hers.

She was lying on the floor of the parlor, near a shattered window. Jayne knelt beside her, holding her hand and sobbing.

Patrick's heart slammed against his rib cage and stopped beating entirely for several moments, then started up again, painfully. He dropped to his knees beside Charlotte and would have gathered her up in his arms if Jayne hadn't warned that she mustn't be moved.

"Charlotte?" The name came ragged from his throat.

Her eyelids fluttered, but otherwise she didn't stir.

"Oh, God," Patrick rasped, and it was all the prayer he could manage, verbally at least. "Oh, God."

Gideon laid a hand to his shoulder. "We'll look after her for now," he said reasonably. All around the house, the sounds of combat raged, but Patrick didn't care about anything but the woman lying so still before him. "You take care of Raheem."

Patrick's spirit went corpse-cold at the mention of the name. Raheem, the man who had brought injury and perhaps death to Patrick's wife and unborn child.

Solemnly Patrick leaned over and kissed Charlotte's bloodied forehead. Then, without another word, without looking at either Jayne or Gideon, he rose slowly to his feet and strode out of the parlor.

Charlotte was surrounded alternately by a delicious light, pure joy made visible, and by crushing pain. In one moment, she knew everything, all the secrets of the universe, and in the next, she knew nothing at all. She wanted to divide herself somehow, and travel in two directions. Then she heard someone calling to her, in hoarse and anguished tones.

Slowly, like a flower unfolding to the sunlight, Charlotte came out of the inner world and followed a pathway of the heart that led straight back to Patrick.

22

Have you gone mad?" Cochran asked, wide-eyed with disbelief as he watched his captain strip away his boots and shirt and slip a knife scabbard onto his belt. The two men were hidden from the harbor by the darkness and by an outcropping of large rocks. The seaward volleys of cannon fire had ceased half an hour before, on orders from Patrick.

Trevarren raised a hand to silence his friend and listened. The island was eerily quiet, now that the explosions had stopped. However, just as he had expected, he soon made out the soft, rhythmic whisper of oars sliding into the water and then breaking the surface again.

At last Patrick answered Cochran's question. "Yes, my friend, I *have* gone mad. It happened a long time ago, in a faraway place." He felt cold, clear through to his soul, and did not allow himself to think of Charlotte lying abed in his house, broken and perhaps dying.

He started toward the water.

"Christ in His heaven, man," Cochran rasped, grabbing at Patrick's arm in a vain effort to stay him. "You can't take a chance like this. She's bound to awaken and ask for you—

do you mean to leave me with the task of telling Mrs. Trevarren you've gone to the bottom with the *Enchantress?*"

Patrick's smile felt like a grimace on his face; there was no humor or mirth in him that night. "Calm yourself, Cochran," he said. "You're beginning to sound like an old woman."

Cochran was evidently desperate. " 'Vengeance is Mine, sayeth the Lord'!" he quoted as Patrick proceeded into the sea.

The holy words had no impact on Trevarren, no meaning. A kind of madness had indeed taken him over, and he would not, could not, rest until he had done what needed doing. He listened again, heard the soft murmur of the tide, the dipping of the oars, and his own heartbeat.

Patrick knew Raheem believed he'd won the war as well as the battle, that the island forces had been defeated, and he was coming ashore to claim the spoils.

It was always foolish, Patrick reflected grimly, to be overconfident.

When he was waist-deep in the warm, quiet water, Patrick turned to look back once, lifting his eyes above Cochran's frantic form to the great storm-and-war-battered house where Charlotte rested. Because of him, Patrick, she might well die this night, and their child had almost certainly perished already. Since he could not go back in time and undo his mistakes, he would offer the only sacrifice, the only penance, he could.

Revenge.

"Patrick!" Cochran whispered, skittering up and down the shoreline now, like an anxious bird. "Damn your ass, you bullheaded sea snake, you get back here!"

Patrick's eyes stung as he thought of what he'd done to Charlotte, just by loving and wanting her. He told himself it was the salt water, and then glided forward into the deceptively gentle embrace of the sea and began to swim. His strokes were strong, silent, deliberate.

The dinghy was easy to track, even in the blackness of the night, for the soft slaps of the oars against the water reverberated in Patrick's ears like gunshots. The low, drunken talk of the men rowing rang out like shouts.

Patrick swam on, and bright, colorful images of Charlotte played in his mind, tormenting him, driving him on.

He surfaced within a few feet of the dinghy, on the starboard side, and none of the three men in the little craft so much as glanced in his direction. He kept pace with them easily, and when the oarsmen paused and the vessel bobbed on the calm surface, Patrick heard their consultation, and although it was all in Arabic, he understood it.

"I don't like it," a small, wiry man said; he was sitting on the port side, and a turban covered his head. That was all Patrick could make out for the moment. "Trevarren wouldn't surrender so easily as this. It's a trap."

The leader of the group, clearly Raheem, had been perched at the bow, and doing none of the rowing. "You overestimate him. He is an American; he can think only of his own comforts and indulgences. He is hiding from us, even now, and probably taking consolation from the woman, knowing he will soon lose her."

Patrick's throat filled with acid, but of course, he made no sound or movement.

"Americans like their pleasures," the third man remarked, "but they are like the cobra when aroused; there is no escaping them, and their strike is lethal."

Raheem made a hocking sound of contempt and spat into the water.

It was calm as a quilt on an old lady's bed, that water, but beneath it, things moved and lived that could bring sudden, painful death.

Patrick took a breath, held it, and slipped beneath the dinghy. Deftly he overturned it, and the outraged shouts and frantic splashes of his victims were like soft music on a balmy summer evening.

He tossed his head to shake the water from his hair and eyes, then looked back toward the three ships waiting farther out in the harbor. They were alight, and men stirred on their decks, but he had time to carry out his plan.

Singling Raheem out was an embarrassingly simple matter—he was the one drowning. His two henchmen were clinging to the side of the boat and shouting blindly for help, certain, probably, that they were about to be devoured by some giant creature of the deep.

Patrick pulled the knife he carried from its scabbard, moved up behind the struggling Raheem, and hooked an arm around his neck. With his other hand, Patrick pressed the blade to the pirate's throat.

In those moments, Patrick underwent the greatest struggle of all. It would have been so easy, so blessedly simple, to open Raheem's jugular vein and watch his blood drain into the sea, thus avenging Charlotte and the precious child who would never know the glorious pleasure and pain of living.

"Trevarren," the pirate said, when he'd gotten his breath. He was calmer now, even with a line of cold, sharp steel pressed against his throat. "My men will kill you for this, I swear before Allah."

"I wouldn't have pegged you for a religious man," Patrick replied, breathless from his exertions but unconcerned by the threat. Without withdrawing the knife, he began making his way back toward shore, pulling Raheem with him. He offered no reply to the pirate's threat, because nothing in the world frightened him except the prospect of living into old age without Charlotte beside him.

Reaching the beach took much of Patrick's strength; once, such an escapade would barely have strained his energies, but his powers had been undermined by the fever, and he was still recovering.

Twice more during the long swim, Patrick stopped, debating with his conscience. Raheem was a pirate, for God's sake, one of the most feared, even in that treacherous part of the world. He had done unspeakable things, things that would not even occur to an ordinary man. Why, then, Patrick wondered angrily, shouldn't he kill the son of a bitch and leave him for the fish?

Raheem slouched limply against him now, perhaps unconscious, perhaps just awaiting his chance. Judging by the way he'd carried on when the dinghy was overturned, he probably couldn't swim. Patrick could just slip away, let the pirate go under, leave him to die.

He, Patrick, would not even have to do the man violence.

He swore, released his captive, and watched without particular emotion as Raheem floated facedown in the water, making no visible effort to fight for his life.

Patrick turned and started toward shore, then stopped, swearing again. Cochran's quote echoed mercilessly in his mind. *Vengeance is Mine, sayeth the Lord.* Realizing he was still clutching the knife in his right hand, Patrick sheathed the weapon, swore again, and swam back to Raheem.

The pirate was just disappearing under the surface of the water; Patrick grasped him by the collar, with another curse, and went on toward shore.

Cochran was waiting there, sane, sensible Cochran. He waded in when he caught sight of Patrick and relieved him of his unconscious companion.

"I'll be damned," the first mate said, crouching to examine Raheem as best he could, given the darkness. "It's Raheem, isn't it? Why didn't you kill him?"

Patrick was half-sprawled on the shore, gasping for breath and ready to retch up enough salt water to surround a whale. He pushed his hair back from his face and regarded his friend for several moments before finding the strength to speak. "I wanted to prolong the pleasure," he growled.

Raheem was lying on the beach, coughing violently and swearing in his native tongue.

He spoke calmly to the pirate, in the colloquial Arabic he'd originally learned from Khalif. "You're going to die," he said. "One way or another, at my hand or at the end of a hangman's noose back in Europe, you're as good as dead."

Raheem vomited violently, then spat, "May you burn in your Christian hell, Trevarren!"

Patrick offered no reply, but simply scrambled to his feet and, with Cochran's help, hauled Raheem up after him.

"Look," Cochran said, with a laugh, gesturing toward the lighted ships that had been dominating the harbor all day. "They're leaving! Loyal souls, those pirates, just like their captain."

Raheem only grunted at Cochran's words, probably not understanding them, but he comprehended the sight of his three ships in retreat well enough. The pirate gave a bellow of protest, but it was all for naught. That night he was locked up in the wine cellar and, except for regular rations of food and water, forgotten.

Charlotte ached in every pore and cell of her body, but the glorious sunshine that filled the room felt like some intangible balm. She caught her breath, remembering the explosion —had it been the night before?—and laid both hands to her stomach.

"The baby?" she whispered. She could not see anyone near the bed, but she knew she wasn't alone.

Jacoba immediately loomed above her. "Awaken the captain," she said to someone just out of sight—probably Mary Catch-much-fish. Then she looked down at Charlotte, her face open and kindly. "The babe is still with you, Mrs. Trevarren," she said. "Of course, there's no tellin' whether the little one was harmed. We'll just have to wait and see."

There was a ruckus, and then Patrick appeared, looking as though he'd just returned from a mission in hell. He was gaunt, unbearably pale, and his hair was rumpled and oddly stiff-looking. His shirt didn't sit with its usual dashing grace on his upper body, and as he gazed at Charlotte, his throat worked visibly.

Jacoba slipped away with surprising grace for a woman of her size, and the door closed quietly behind her before Patrick spoke.

He moved to the side of the bed, dropped down on his knees beside it, and enclosed one of Charlotte's bruised hands gently in both his own. Then, to her amazement, he lowered his head to her bosom and uttered a ragged sob.

Gently, with her free hand, Charlotte touched his hair. Her heart was so full of emotion that she couldn't speak, and tears brimmed in her eyes.

Patrick wept, the sound low and broken, for several minutes. Then, finally, he raised his head and met her gaze. "I'm sorry," he said hoarsely. "I'm so sorry—"

Charlotte was puzzled. She stroked his dark hair. "Why?"

"If it hadn't been for me, none of this would have happened. I should have taken you straight to the authorities when you were dumped at my feet that night, but instead I thought up all kinds of excuses for keeping you with me. I wanted you for myself."

Charlotte managed a smile. "Was that so wrong?"

He rested his forehead lightly against hers for just a moment. "Yes. You would have been safe at home by now, with your father and stepmother to look after you—"

"Patrick," Charlotte interrupted, annoyed. "I'm not a child, in need of a keeper. Did it ever occur to you that if I didn't want to be with you, I wouldn't have stayed? There were a few times, you know, when I could have left—while we were in Spain, for instance. And after the uprising, when Khalif was in power again and offered me a house in France."

Patrick gave a great sigh, and in many ways, it was as painful for Charlotte to hear as his sobs had been earlier. She heard an uncharacteristic element of defeat in the sound. "I can't change the past," he said, speaking as much to himself, Charlotte thought, as to her. "But I don't have to go on making the same mistakes in the future."

Charlotte felt cold all of the sudden, and oddly afraid. "Patrick—"

He rose to his feet, stepped back out of her reach. She could almost see the stony barrier that dropped into place between them. "Enough. I won't see you die for loving me, Charlotte. It's decided."

"Patrick!" She tried to sit up, feeling panicked, knowing he had already withdrawn from her. "Patrick!" she cried again, desperate.

Without visible emotion, he pressed her back onto the pillows. "Rest," he said. "Just rest."

With that, he moved like a sleepwalker to the door.

"I've lost him," Charlotte murmured miserably an hour later, when Jayne was sitting at her bedside, keeping her company. "Patrick is my husband, the father of my baby, the only man I'll ever love. And he might as well be on the other side of the world."

Jayne sighed. "He's undergone a few shocks lately, our Patrick. First there was the storm, then the pirates attacked the island, and you were so badly hurt that we all thought you'd die . . ." She paused, smiled. "Except for Gideon, of course. He must have said a thousand prayers for your recovery, and I don't think he ever doubted for an instant that you would get well. Anyway, Patrick is still reeling from all that's happened. He just needs some time to assimilate everything, that's all."

"I hope you're right," Charlotte muttered, but her heart was in her throat and she had an awful feeling that, marriage or none, baby or none, her intimate association with Patrick Trevarren had truly ended this time.

In the sunny days to come, Charlotte recovered slowly, by degrees—at least, physically she recovered. All the while her body was growing strong, some vital part of her soul was shriveling up and dying.

It wasn't that Patrick avoided her, exactly. He sat with her for hours on the terrace outside her room, reading to her from Shakespeare, even acting out some of the more dramatic or comical scenes. He brought her succulent fruit, and told her stories about his youth.

Still, for all of that, he might have been a stranger, someone hired to amuse the patient. He slept in another room at night, never kissed Charlotte, or held her, or referred in any way to the incomprehensible passion that had once blazed between them.

It was, as she had feared, over.

Gideon was a faithful support during those difficult days, and though his grief for the lost Susannah showed plainly in his eyes, Charlotte correctly guessed that he was growing closer and closer to Jayne.

Stella, who had aspired to a romance with Gideon herself, accepted the situation with surprising good grace, and set her sights on one of Patrick's young crewmen, just as Nora had. Deborah, the youngest of the group, was content to love the harmless, dashing men who peopled the novels she loved to read.

After a month, Charlotte was back on her feet, but all the joy had gone from her life, with Patrick's affections. She supposed she would recover someday, and make a place in the world for herself and her child, but that time seemed far in the future.

Patrick no longer kept a vigil beside her, now that she was well and the baby was fluttering against the walls of her womb. He worked from sunrise to sunset with his men, clearing the rubble from the cane fields and preparing the ground for another planting.

One day, when Charlotte was at particularly loose ends, she wandered into the wing of the house where Gideon had his room, and paused in his open doorway.

A borrowed carpetbag sat on his bed, openmouthed, and Gideon was packing the shirts and trousers Jacoba and the others had made for him. He turned his head and smiled at Charlotte, eyes twinkling.

"Hello, Mrs. Trevarren. You're looking very well today."

Charlotte sighed and sagged against the doorframe. Her throat was thick and she had to wait a moment before speaking, in order to keep her renegade emotions under some semblance of control. She tried to smile. "Australia is quite some distance from here," she said finally. "Much too far to swim or row."

Gideon grinned, gestured toward a wing-back chair. "Come in and sit down."

Charlotte obeyed. "It isn't proper," she protested at the same time. "I shouldn't be here."

Her friend chuckled. "Since when, sweet Charlotte, have you been troubled by such mundane concepts as propriety?"

"You're leaving," she said, her gazing moving once more to the satchel.

"That ship I prayed for is about to arrive."

Charlotte had no doubt that what he said was quite true. Over the course of the past weeks, she'd had many occasions to see that Gideon was indeed on good terms with God. Once, for instance, when she'd been in such pain from her injuries that she hadn't been able to bear it, he'd taken her hand and offered a few words, and she'd felt a little better.

"Do you suppose you could pray that Patrick will love me again?" she dared to ask.

Gideon stopped moving about the room to come and sit

facing her, on the hassock. "That would be like praying for
the sky to be blue or the sea to be deep," he said gently. "No
man ever loved a woman more completely or sincerely than
Patrick loves you."

Charlotte shook her head. "He's decided not to let himself
care for me anymore, Gideon, and you know how bullheaded he can be."

The missionary touched Charlotte's cheek with a gentle
hand. "While you, of course, are sweet and pliant and
eminently reasonable," he teased.

Charlotte made a sound that was both a laugh and a sob.
"Gideon, don't be impossible. I came to you for sympathy!"

"It isn't sympathy you need, my dear," Gideon said, with
a philosophical sigh, leaning back and laying his hands on
his thighs. "It's patience. Patrick will come to terms with his
feelings for you in time."

"But I can't wait!" Charlotte cried, in a frantic whisper.

Gideon chuckled. "You remind me of my sister,
Elizabeth," he said. "Once, when we were small, our grandmother gave her some flower bulbs and a spot in the garden
that was to be all Elizabeth's own. My sister planted the
bulbs and then went out every day to glare at the dirt,
waiting for the blossoms to appear. After only a week, her
curiosity got the better of her, and she couldn't bear the
suspense any longer. She dug up those bulbs, just to see if
they'd sprouted, and after that, of course, they couldn't
grow because she'd killed them."

Before Charlotte could come up with a reply, Jayne burst
through the doorway, her lovely face flushed with excitement and no small measure of dread, her dark red hair
flying.

"It's here!" she cried. "The ship is here—Patrick's already spotted her, and she's flying the English flag!"

Gideon shrugged and then winked at Charlotte, as if to
say, *Didn't I tell you?*

"Well," Jayne went on, her personality like an explosion
in the room, "are you going to marry me and take me with
you or not, Gideon Rowling?"

The clergyman laughed. "Oh, yes," he said, and it seemed

to an embarrassed Charlotte that the lovers had forgotten her presence entirely. "If you'll have me, beautiful Jayne, I will marry you with pleasure."

They met in the middle of the room and clasped hands, and Charlotte fled, cheeks crimson, heart pounding with both envy and the profound joy of knowing that even death could not prevail over love.

Charlotte flew down the hall, wanting to see the approaching ship for herself, with no walls around her and no window glass impeding her view. Reaching the staircase, she decided the banister offered the quicker means of descent, and swung herself astraddle of it, skirts and all.

At the bottom, she was stopped not by the familiar newel-post, but by a strong, muscular arm.

She turned, breathless, and looked straight into Patrick Trevarren's indigo eyes. For a moment she saw something flicker there—passion, perhaps, or laughter. In the next instant, though, the expression disappeared, and Charlotte feared she'd only imagined it.

"I will thank you to think of my child's safety," Patrick lectured coldly, "if not your own."

Charlotte allowed him to lift her unceremoniously off the banister, but raised her chin to a defiant level when she stood on the steps, her face on a level with his. "Don't be tiresome, Mr. Trevarren. I've never obeyed your commands before, and I don't intend to start now." She moved to pass him, but he took her arms in a painless but inescapable grasp and held her in place.

"There's a ship coming in," he said. "It's English, probably headed for Australia. I want you to sail to Sydney and then book passage from there to the United States."

Charlotte stared at him. "And you? Where do you plan to be while I'm doing this?"

"Here," he said. "Mr. Cochran will travel with you, as your escort and protector."

Charlotte's knees gave way, and she dropped to a sitting position on the step, feeling desolate. Patrick crouched in front of her and, to her surprise, touched her face gently.

"I know it seems to you that I'm being unreasonable," he

said, in a hoarse voice. "But believe me, Charlotte, you and the child will both be better off this way."

Grief welled up inside her, overflowed in tears and fury. "That's just *your* opinion, Patrick Trevarren! Being sent away from you is like being told I'll never see the sun again!"

Pain moved in Patrick's face, but he clearly would not be swayed from his decision. "Is that any way for a 'new woman' to talk?" he asked gruffly. "What would your stepmother say if she heard you carrying on like this?"

Charlotte sobbed. "I don't care what anyone else says, Patrick—I was born to be with you, and you were born to be with me, and if we're separated, we'll both suffer terribly!"

He kissed her forehead, in the same mild way her father or uncle might have done. "How can you say that?" he asked. "Have you forgotten that your problems began when you met me?"

"The moon will go out, Patrick," she whispered. "The sea will dry up. Please—don't do this to me, don't do it to yourself!"

Patrick sighed, kissed her again, with no more passion than before, and then rose to his feet, towering over her. "It's for the best," he said. And then he walked away and left her sitting there, huddled against the banister, bracing herself for the end of the world.

Hours later, when the sea had long since swallowed the sun, the English ship sailed into the harbor and several small boats appeared. The vessel had been running short on fresh water, and seeing lights on the island, the captain had decided to make a visit.

Raheem was brought up from his prison in the cellar— this was the first time Charlotte had really laid eyes on the stranger who had been so obsessed with possessing her— and put under formal arrest by the officers of the *Victoriana*. Crewmen took him back to the main ship, carefully bound.

We'll be traveling together after all, the pirate and I, Charlotte thought miserably. Patrick had ordered her belongings packed for a long journey, and Mary and Jacoba had obeyed his command, though sullenly.

Captain Michael Trent was a handsome man, tall, with rugged features and hazel eyes, and he gave Charlotte an

308

openly appreciative look when they were introduced that night, at a formal dinner in Patrick's fancy dining room.

He'd be glad to see Mrs. Trevarren safely to Sydney Town, he said. Once there, he would personally arrange her passage to America, making certain to select the best ship and captain available.

She would be back in her own country, safe and sound, in a matter of weeks.

Patrick, who should have been pleased that his wishes were being carried out so smoothly, scowled throughout the meal.

Later that night, when Charlotte lay grieving in her marriage bed, Patrick came to her for the first time since before the disastrous explosion that had nearly taken her life. Saying nothing, offering no promises or excuses, he stripped off his clothes, stretched out beside her, and took her in his arms.

She felt him tremble as he held her close against his side.

"Don't send me away," she pleaded, but with quiet dignity.

"I have to," he answered. He rolled over, so that she was pinned gently beneath him, one of his muscled legs stretched across her thighs. "Say that you don't want me here, Charlotte," he said, "and I'll go."

She wondered that one relatively small person could contain the emotions she was feeling then without bursting. Charlotte was angry, and she was wildly frustrated, but she also loved this man, adored him with an intensity as mysterious and far-flung as the heavens themselves.

"Stay," she whispered, plunging her fingers into his hair, bringing his head down so that their mouths touched and then engaged, powerfully and with desperation.

Their lovemaking was different that night, though no less consuming. They hardly spoke—usually they teased and tempted each other until the need became too great and they hadn't the breath to speak—and when their bodies were joined, satisfaction became torment. They battled each other, knew pleasure so keen in its poignancy as to be nearly unbearable, then immediately needed to be fused again, as if there had been no communion, no release.

309

Eventually exhaustion overtook them. Charlotte, who had been to the stars in Patrick's arms, felt more alone and hopeless than ever before. She cried until sleep came.

In the morning, hasty farewells were said all around—there was no sign of Patrick anywhere—and Jayne and Gideon and Charlotte and Mr. Cochran were taken out to the *Victoriana* in long, graceful skiffs. Their baggage had apparently been loaded on board during the night.

Charlotte stared back at the island, unable to believe that the grand adventure was over, that Patrick had not had the charity of spirit even to bid her a proper farewell. Gideon took her hand and squeezed it.

The rest of the morning passed in a haze, for Charlotte at least. Jayne and Gideon were properly married by Captain Trent, and after much preparation, the ship moved gracefully toward the open sea.

Charlotte stood at the railing, watching as the magical island slowly vanished, along with her most cherished dreams.

April 1878
Quade's Harbor
Washington Territory

MILLICENT QUADE BRADLEY WAS NOT A FANCIFUL WOMAN, but as she watched her sister, Charlotte, now visibly pregnant, go about her daily life, she often thought she heard the distant howl of the banshee.

"Charlotte is dying," Millicent said to her husband, Lucas, one bright spring morning as the two of them sat on the screened sun porch of their house across the street from the Presbyterian church.

The pastor, a good-looking man with a square jaw, pale gold hair, and the calm gaze of someone certain of things eternal, put down his teacup and gazed out at the harbor. Millicent's look followed his; as always, the sight of the gray-blue water, rimmed in snowcapped mountains and multitudes of lush evergreens, lifted her spirits.

"You must have faith, darling," Lucas said. He took her hand and squeezed it, and she was thankful, oh, so thankful, for the steady, unshakable love of her husband.

Charlotte deserved just such a husband, Millie thought angrily. It wasn't fair that a fine woman like her sister should get her heart broken by that scalawag of a sea captain. Papa and Uncle Devon often argued as to who would have the

311

privilege of horsewhipping Patrick Trevarren in the street, if he ever dared to show his face in Quade's Harbor. Millicent, normally a peaceful person, half hoped Mr. Trevarren would get his due.

"Lydia says Charlotte weeps at night," Millie went on, heartbroken. "She eats only for the baby's sake, not her own, and constantly watches the bay for ships."

Lucas sighed, but did not speak. One of his greatest strengths was his ability to listen, unruffled, making no apparent judgment on anything that might be said.

Suddenly Millie began to cry. "I can't bear it, Lucas," she whispered. "It's too dreadful, seeing Charlotte suffer like this—she was always so strong, and so full of laughter and mischief!"

Lucas rose from his chair, came around the white iron table to crouch beside Millie. "Darling," he said, putting a strong arm around her, "Charlotte is home, safe among people who cherish her. Given time, she will be herself again."

Millie dried her eyes with the heels of her palms. No one, with the possible exception of Patrick Trevarren himself, knew Charlotte as well as she did. Sure, Charlotte was resilient, and there could be no question that her large and boisterous family loved her to distraction. Because there was a passageway of sorts, between her own soul and her sister's, however, Millie was aware of something the others could not sense.

The light of Charlotte's spirit, the essence, grew dimmer and dimmer as each day passed.

Lucas stood beside Millie's chair, one hand resting on her shoulder. "I have calls to make," he said.

Millie turned her head, kissed his hand lightly, and nodded, without looking up at him. When he was gone, she cleared the table, arranged the dishes in the kitchen sink, removed her apron, and set off for the main house.

Charlotte sat on the widow's walk on the second floor of her father and stepmother's grand house, hands resting on either side of her enormous belly. A faltering smile touched

312

her lips. "Perhaps it will be today," she told her unborn child. "Perhaps your papa will return to us today."

She heard one of the French doors creak on its hinges and resettled herself in her chair as her stepmother came out to join her.

Lydia was a strikingly beautiful woman, with her fair hair and strong spirit, a fine mother to her flock of sons and a good wife to Charlotte's father. Moreover, she was a power to be reckoned with in the operation of her husband's far-flung timber interests.

She stood at the railing of the narrow terrace, tendrils of blond hair lifting in the misty salt breeze. "If I could wish you one thing in all the world, Charlotte," she said, without looking at her stepdaughter, "it would be a love such as the one your father and I share. Ours is the sort of union that nourishes the soul and helps each of us to be our best selves."

Charlotte listened in silence. Lydia was not making an idle boast, for the glorious passion between Brigham Quade and his beloved wife was visible to anyone who took the trouble to look. Millie and Lucas had a similar bond, although theirs was quieter.

Lydia turned, looked down at Charlotte, who remained in her chair, awkward and uncomfortable because of her great bulk. "I would not normally speak this way, knowing what pain you're in, but I feel that I must. I think you and your Patrick Trevarren have the same kind of bond. If I'm right, Charlotte, then you must prepare yourself to fight for your marriage."

Charlotte swallowed. Patrick had, to all evidence, deserted her as well as their child. Oh, he'd ordered the construction of a grand house in nearby Seattle, and not one but two new clipper ships were being built for him, but he had never paid his wife a visit or even written to her.

"I thought we did," she said. Not a moment had passed, nor a heartbeat, since her parting from Patrick that afternoon on the front stairs of his island house that she hadn't yearned for him.

All during the sailing to Sydney, she had expected him to

come after her somehow—perhaps another ship would pass by the island. But Patrick had never appeared.

Reaching Australia, she and Mr. Cochran had seen Jayne and Gideon off on their missionaries' journey into the interior, and rested a few days, attending the theater together and exploring the countryside. Raheem, the pirate, was sent back to Britain to be tried.

Charlotte was soon restless, and she asked Captain Trent of the *Victoriana* to recommend a ship sailing north to San Francisco. There, she had said good-bye to Mr. Cochran and traveled on, via another vessel, to Seattle, where her father and Lydia and Millie had been waiting for her.

She'd flung herself into Brigham's strong arms that day weeks before and sobbed with bitterness and pain, but a part of her had still believed that Patrick would not be able to stay away from her forever. He would miss the grand adventure of their life together, just as she did . . .

Lydia's gaze held concern, but no pity. "You are a Quade, Charlotte, and you were raised to be strong. When I look at you now, however, I see a woman who has given up. Your father and I are desperately worried."

Charlotte stiffened in her chair before she could offer an answer, her womb clenching suddenly and violently. In the harbor the daily mail boat sounded its horn, a testament to ordinary things.

Lydia, who had served as a nurse during the Rebellion of the Southern States and helped Dr. Joe McCauley for years, assessed the situation and acted without panic.

"So the time has come, has it?" she said gently, helping Charlotte to her feet.

Charlotte groaned. Her brow and upper lip were wet with perspiration, and her hipbones felt as though they were being pried apart. *Patrick,* she cried, in the deepest part of her spirit, and she thought, for just a moment, that she heard him answer.

Alas, it was only the mail boat whistle.

Brigham Quade recognized the tall, broad-shouldered young bull the moment he opened the front door to him,

314

and if it hadn't been for the circumstances, he would have hauled off and decked him, right there on the porch.

Trevarren nodded a greeting and shouldered his way past Brigham, into the cool, shadowy entryway. "Where is she?" he demanded. "Where is Charlotte?"

At exactly that moment, a shriek of pain came from the second floor.

"Upstairs," Brigham answered coldly. "Giving birth to your child."

Trevarren went pale and dropped his fancy leather traveling bag, and Brigham thought, somewhere in the calm center of his own distraction, that there might be hope for the rogue sea captain. The man might have some shred of decency in him after all.

"Where?" he rasped.

"First door on the right," Brigham answered, though grudgingly. Another cry met their ears as Trevarren bolted up the stairs, and Brigham winced. It had been bad enough, standing by helplessly while Lydia bore each of their five strapping sons, but to hear his firstborn daughter suffer so was worse in some ways.

Still, Brigham smiled as he lifted his eyes to the ceiling, recalling Trevarren's reaction to the news of imminent fatherhood. The man had looked as though he'd swoon, then gathered himself and scrambled up those stairs as though his life depended on reaching Charlotte's side.

Yes, Brigham reflected. There was still hope.

Charlotte's back arched as the pain seized her again and she thought she was hallucinating when she saw Patrick burst through the door, sending it crashing against the wall, and collapse on his knees at her bedside.

Lydia, unflappable, did not look up from the delivery. "If you're going to be underfoot, Patrick Trevarren," she warned, "I'll have you dragged out of here."

Charlotte groped for Patrick's hand, found it. "You're here—you're really here?" she asked stupidly. Again a contraction racked her, again her body rose high off the bed.

"Yes," Patrick said gruffly, when the worst had passed. He

315

was still holding her hand in a tight grasp. "I tried to stay away, but God help me, I couldn't."

"If God's going to be of any help to you, Captain Trevarren," Lydia commented dryly, at the same time examining Charlotte, "I should think He'd have to hit you alongside the head with a shovel first, in order to get your attention."

Patrick's mouth curved slightly upward on one side at Lydia's words, and Charlotte took the familiar smile inside her, where it worked like some magical potion to ease her pain. He kissed Charlotte's knuckles and said, "Perhaps He has, Mrs. Quade. Perhaps He has."

"Don't leave me," Charlotte gasped. She was ashamed to need Patrick so much, but there it was, the stark reality.

"I'm here," he assured her, kissing her hand again, this time on the palm.

Charlotte would have been happier if he'd said, "Never again, darling" or "We'll be together forever," but she hadn't the time to quibble. The pain came again, raised to an agonizing pitch, and she had to scream.

Patrick didn't flinch at her cries, but held her hand, smoothed her hair, and whispered gentle words of encouragement and reassurance.

Finally, after several hours of hard labor, the child slipped from her body.

"A girl," Lydia said, with joyous tears in her voice, as she tended to the child. "Dear heaven, I thought we were never going to see a baby girl in this family again!"

Charlotte looked at Patrick as their small daughter was placed between them, and saw that his eyes were wet. "What shall we call her?" she asked gently.

He was staring rapt at their child, as if he'd never seen a baby before. "Is there a name fine enough for such a creature?" he whispered, tentatively touching the infant's tiny cheek.

Charlotte laughed. "Yes. Annie, I think. Annie Quade Trevarren."

Patrick was still gazing at the child, obviously marveling. "We created her, you and I together," he said. "I can't believe it—it's a miracle."

Lydia left the room, but Charlotte could hear her voice as she spoke quietly to someone in the hallway—probably Brigham. No doubt Millie was there, too.

Patrick reached carefully past Annie to smooth back a tendril of Charlotte's hair. "Why didn't you tell me you could work magic like this?" he teased, his blue eyes shining as he looked at his wife.

A sob of relief and joy rose in Charlotte's throat. Patrick was there; the sun would shine again, and the moon would spin around the earth, and the stars would take their rightful places in the night sky.

For now, she could not allow herself to believe he might leave her again.

"I love you," she said, opening her soul to him.

He kissed her—with the sort of respectful passion the situation demanded—but the old spark was there. "And I love you," he answered.

Presently Lydia returned with Millicent, and Patrick was gently shooed from the room. While Millie rocked the newborn baby, her eyes shining with delight, Lydia bathed an exhausted Charlotte, helped her into a fresh nightgown, put fresh sheets on her bed. Since Charlotte's milk hadn't come in yet, Annie was to be fed from a bottle.

"Sleep now," Lydia said when Charlotte was in bed again, bending over her stepdaughter to plant a gentle kiss on her forehead. "You've had a momentous day."

Charlotte wanted Annie beside her, and Patrick, too, but she was too weary to argue. She closed her eyes, just for a moment.

The room was dark, except for a flood of moonlight pouring in through the windows, when Charlotte awakened. Patrick was lying beside her, sheltering her with his size and strength, holding her in a loose embrace.

"How did you manage to get here just when I needed you most?" she asked, knowing he was awake even though he had given no indication of the fact.

Patrick kissed her temple. "I couldn't stay away," he said, his voice hoarse. "Have you been to see the house in Seattle?"

Charlotte recalled all the loneliness she'd endured since

their separation and bristled. "No," she said. "I knew about it, because your lawyers wrote to me, but frankly I didn't feel any desire to see the place."

"Why not?" Patrick sounded confused, and not a little injured. "That house wouldn't even be built if it weren't for you and Annie. You're supposed to *live* in it."

"Annie and I are not china figures, to be arranged in a fancy cabinet and occasionally dusted, Mr. Trevarren. We will not set foot under that roof, I promise you, unless the three of us are going to be a real family."

"How can we be anything else?" Patrick asked, clearly still at a loss. "Annie is our child. You are her mother, I am her father. That makes us a family."

"No," Charlotte argued. "This—what Lydia and Papa and the boys have, in this house—is a family. They live here *together,* loving and fighting, laughing and crying, all of it." She paused, drew in a deep breath, knowing she was about to take the greatest risk of her life but unable to avoid it. "If you are going to leave us again, Patrick, then I must ask you never to come back. Papa has powerful friends—he can arrange for a discreet divorce."

She felt Patrick stiffen beside her, and his embrace tightened, but he did not make the promise her soul hungered to hear. Perhaps it wasn't even possible for him to do that.

"Until today, I thought I couldn't go on living without you," she went on, finding strength, somehow, even in the midst of her great weakness. "When I saw you, I knew I loved you more than ever, needed you even more than before. But then, out of that terrible pain, came Annie. She's a gift from God, Patrick, a miracle, just as you said. And until I'm strong in my own self again, she can be my reason to live."

Patrick laid a hand lightly against Charlotte's face and no doubt felt her tears. She suspected, by the trembling she felt in his large frame, that her husband might have shed a few tears of his own in those moments. "God in heaven, Charlotte," he marveled brokenly, after a long time. "You are surely the most remarkable woman who ever lived."

It was no answer, but for that night, it was enough. Charlotte held her husband, and allowed him to hold her, and slept peacefully for the first time in months.

A week after Annie's birth, when he could be sure that both his wife and child were well, Patrick traveled to Seattle to inspect the enormous house he'd commissioned long before his arrival in the United States. He did not even stop to check on the project of his two new ships; that could wait.

The brick mansion stood on one of Seattle's several hills, facing the water. Every huge, gracious room seemed to brim with sunlight, and it made Patrick happy to think of Annie growing up in such a place. Being her mother's daughter, she would no doubt slide down the banisters and skim over the sleek wooden floors in her stocking feet.

Cochran's voice didn't startle Patrick, even though he'd believed himself to be alone. "Tell me, has she agreed to wait for you here, your lovely Charlotte, and receive you in her heart and her bed whenever you come home from the sea?"

Rage filled Patrick. Cochran was his oldest and best friend, and he had a way of going straight to the painful center of things. He turned to face his first mate.

"No," he replied coldly. "Charlotte told me, in effect, to go straight to hell. She claims she would never live here without me."

"And?"

Patrick sighed. "And I couldn't promise her that I would. We're at an impasse, Charlotte and I."

Cochran's usually jovial face hardened with impatience and contempt. "Dear God, man, it never ceases to confound me, what a fool you can be. You're only half-alive without Charlotte, and you know it!"

Patrick moved to one of the towering, arched windows that reached from the hardwood floors to the ornate ceilings, with their plaster moldings. The harbor was dappled with sunlight and brimming with ships. "She's safe there, near her father. So is Annie."

"You're *afraid*," Cochran muttered, as if stunned at the revelation. "All during our long association, my friend, I've

319

regarded you as a brave man, a leader, deserving of the title of captain. But I see now that I was wrong—you're nothing but a coward."

"Damn it," Patrick spat, in an explosive undertone, "I have *reason* to be afraid—on more than one occasion, Charlotte nearly died because of my love! And now there's Annie."

Cochran was plainly furious and not in the least sympathetic. "I never thought I'd say it, but they're both better off without you. A great lady like Charlotte needs a *man* to share her life, not a sniveling little whelp scared to take any risk that really counts!"

"Get out!" Patrick flared, gesturing wildly toward the great double doorway of the room that had been meant to be the front parlor. His voice echoed in the emptiness.

"Gladly," Cochran replied, wounding Patrick with the cold finality of his tone. "You'll sail those two fine new ships of yours without me, *Captain* Trevarren. I can't take orders from a gutless wonder like you."

Patrick closed his eyes against the pain, for the loss of his closest friend was a brutal blow. He wanted to ask Cochran to stay, to understand, but his pride would make no allowance for such a gesture.

He flinched when he heard the front door slam in the distance. After a while, he went outside and walked the grounds. Here, there would be a garden, there a marble fountain, there a shallow pond bright with goldfish to delight his child.

Dreams, Patrick scolded himself. Just so much smoke. Charlotte would never live in this house, their daughter would never run, laughing, through fragrant, colorful gardens. He lifted his gaze to the leaded windows on the second floor, where there was a large suite, complete with an antique French fireplace and smaller rooms for dressing and bathing.

Charlotte would never lie beneath him there, in the grand bed he had planned to install, never open his breeches, take him inside her, and ride him in that sweet, merciless way she had. He would never call out her name in the singular desolation of passion, or hear her call his.

320

Broken, Patrick turned and walked across the large yard and through the gate, where his hired horse and buggy stood. He didn't look back, not even once, but instead took himself to the shipyard, where his new mistresses, the half-finished clippers, awaited him.

That night, instead of returning to Quade's Harbor, and Charlotte, by boat, Patrick took a room at the Union Hotel.

After six weeks, Charlotte had grown strong again. She packed her things, and Annie's, and set out for Seattle, though certainly not in pursuit of Patrick. The pain of losing him throbbed within her, but she had turned a corner of some sort with her daughter's birth, and she meant to make something of her life, with or without Patrick.

She rented a small house, not far from the one Patrick was building, and engaged a young woman named Martha Landis to serve as Annie's nurse. That done, Charlotte met with her father's lawyers to arrange a divorce, then ordered furniture and art supplies and more new clothes than one woman could ever need. These last, she charged to Patrick's accounts, since he was still her husband.

She had set up an easel on the side porch and was busily painting the harbor, of which she had a limited view, when Mr. Trevarren himself deigned to appear, driving a buggy. He promptly abandoned the vehicle and bounded up the walk.

Patrick was wearing dove gray breeches and a flowing linen shirt, just as he had when Charlotte had first known him, and he'd let his hair grow long again, too. It was tied back with a narrow black ribbon.

"What the hell is this all about?" he demanded, waving a sheaf of papers as he stomped up the steps and onto the porch.

It was like having a hurricane blow in, and Charlotte promptly reached out to steady her easel. Her heart was thudding against her rib cage, but she managed a bewildered smile and raised one eyebrow in pretended puzzlement.

"You've gotten the bills for my clothes and furniture, I see," she said airily. "Well, it's the least you can do, Patrick, considering—"

"I don't give a *damn* about clothes and furniture, Charlotte," he said, and there was something of the whisper in his voice, as well as something of the shout. "These are divorce papers!"

"Oh." She smiled, smoothed her skirts, which happened to be of simple black taffeta. Her hair was arranged in a puffy cloud around her face, and her blouse was fitted to advantage, though modest. "That."

"Oh, that," Patrick echoed, obviously furious. "I never agreed to this, Charlotte! How dare you sic a lot of smarmy lawyers on me!"

She sighed and sat down on a wicker settee, hoping Patrick could not see that she was trembling. "Well, it seemed the only sensible thing to do, given your attitude. Besides, it isn't as though I didn't mention divorce to you, Mr. Trevarren. We spoke of it just after Annie was born."

"A fine thing!" he sputtered, looming over her. "Our daughter a few hours old, and we were already talking about getting ourselves unmarried!"

Charlotte bit back a grin, though she couldn't imagine what possessed her to want to smile. After all, the situation was hardly humorous. "I should think you would be anxious to be legally free of me," she said, smoothing her skirts. "It's common knowledge that your ships are nearly ready to sail, and there's even a rumor that you've been seeing a woman from San Francisco."

"Madeline is not a woman," Patrick snapped. "She's an investor. Good God, Charlotte, exactly what kind of scoundrel do you think I am?"

"The kind who needs his pleasures. It's been months since we've been together." She paused—even her heart seemed to stop its beating—and looked up at him. "You don't mean to imply that you've been faithful all that time?"

"I have," Patrick replied, with such proud gravity, such masculine resentment, that Charlotte knew he was telling the truth. "Mind you, I didn't say it was easy. There were times, my dear, when I thought I'd go insane with temptation. But I have been true to you."

She looked away to hide the tears of bittersweet relief that had brimmed in her eyes.

322

To her surprise, Patrick reached out, took her hand, pulled her to her feet. Then he drew her against him.

"Charlotte," he said, linking his fingers together at the small of her back and searching her eyes, "I'm so scared."

"Of what?" she asked, genuinely puzzled. Her heart, stopped before, was now racing dizzily, and her whole body was weak with the need of this man.

"Losing you. Losing Annie."

"Patrick, you're not making sense. You turned your back on us, and now you're telling me you're afraid of *losing* us?"

"Charlotte, look at all that's happened to you since you met me—you've been held captive in a harem, nearly ravished by pirates, blown up in an explosion—"

She laughed. "And it was glorious, all of it. The kind of grand, wonderful adventure most women only dream of having. Oh, Patrick, I wouldn't trade a minute of that time for anything, not the pleasure, and not the pain."

He gazed at her in amazement. "You are the damnedest woman, Charlotte Trevarren. And I can't live without you."

She pressed closer, letting him feel the promise of her body, well aware of his hard readiness. "Will you stay with us, then?"

Patrick stared deeply into her eyes for a long moment before countering with a question of his own. "Will you sail with me, when I can't bear the land anymore and have to go to sea?"

Charlotte stood on tiptoe and kissed the cleft in his chin. "Oh, yes."

He frowned. "What about Annie?"

"She's your daughter. My guess is, she'll be as at home on the open sea as you are."

Patrick bent slightly, lifted his wife into his arms, and kissed her with brazen abandon, right there on the side porch. "Is there someone here to look after our child?" he asked when, at last, they had disentangled their tongues. "There's a threshold I'd like to carry you across, Mrs. Trevarren, and a bed where I've dreamed of having you."

She blushed with pleasure and anticipation and the pure joy of loving this wonderful, enigmatic, impossible man.

"Martha!" she called sunnily. "I'm going out for a while. Please look after Annie while I'm gone."

"Yes, Mrs. Trevarren," answered a female voice from within the house.

Patrick set off down the porch steps and then the walk, still carrying Charlotte the way a groom carries a bride. People peered from windows, and stared from the backs of horses and from wagons, but Patrick paid them no mind.

He simply strode on, passing through the open gates of the mansion he'd built for Charlotte, moving up the driveway, over the wide veranda, and finally through the front doors.

His heels echoed on the bare floors, for most of the house was still unfurnished, apparently.

"Patrick, I'm perfectly able to walk," Charlotte said as he started up the majestic curved stairway.

"Ummm," he said, taking a right turn at the top of the stairs.

Charlotte drew in her breath when he carried her into the master bedroom. There were no chairs, no wardrobes, and certainly no flames flickering on the hearth of the elegant marble fireplace. Against one wall, however, stood a massive bed, sumptuous enough for royalty.

Patrick tossed Charlotte unceremoniously onto that bed and bent over her, one hand pressed into the mattress on either side of her head. "You'll stay with me?"

She nodded. "For always."

"Even when I'm difficult?"

Charlotte laughed. "When have you been otherwise?" She extended her arms, and he came to her eagerly, opening her blouse, baring her breasts.

He paused just when he would have taken a nipple, and frowned to see Charlotte smiling in amusement. "Is it all right? Would it hurt you?"

She stroked his cheek, gently urging him to take her breast. He tongued her until she thought she'd go mad with wanting him, then hoisted her skirts.

"Take me inside you," Patrick pleaded in a gruff voice. "Now, Charlotte—please—now."

Gently Charlotte opened his breeches, freed him, held and stroked him. Later there would be time for leisurely loving, but it had been months since they'd been together, and Charlotte wanted her husband as urgently as he wanted her.

She arched her back as he tore away her drawers, and they both groaned as Patrick sought entrance and then delved deep inside her.

In that instant of glory and fire, their future truly began.

POCKET BOOKS
PROUDLY ANNOUNCES

THE LEGACY

Linda Lael Miller

**Coming in Paperback
from Pocket Star Books
Summer 1994**

**The following is a preview of
The Legacy . . .**

Ian Yarbro was in no mood for a party.

Dingoes had brought down four of his best sheep, just since Monday.

Water holes all over the property were coming up dry.

And worst of all, Jacy Tiernan, damn her, was back from America.

The first two plights were sorry ones, all right, but a man had to expect a fair portion of grief if he undertook to raise sheep in South Australia. That last bit, though, *that* was something personal, an individualized curse from God.

With a resounding sigh, Ian leaned back against the south wall of the shearing shed, a mug of beer in one sore, lacerated hand, and scowled. Every muscle in his body throbbed, for he'd shorn more squirming woollies than any man on his crew in the days just past, and he felt as though he could sleep for a month, should the opportunity arise. That wasn't going to happen, of course, not with all he had to do around the place.

Ian took another sip from his beer, which had lost its appeal while he pondered his troubles, and surveyed the rustic festivities.

The music of the fiddles and mouth harps seemed to loop and swirl in the warm summer twilight, like invisible ribbon. Shearers and roustabouts alike clomped round and round the long wooden floor of the shed, some dancing with women, some with each other. The night air was weighted with heat, since it was January, speckled with dust and bits of wool fiber and rife with the smells of sweat and brewer's yeast, cheap cologne and cigarette smoke.

And Jacy was back.

Ian muttered a curse. It had been bad enough, this past day

or so, knowing Jacy was living right next door, at Corroboree Springs, but at least she'd had the good grace to keep her distance. Until about five minutes before, that is, when she'd walked into the celebration with her father.

Ian could have ignored her completely, and would have, if it hadn't meant slighting Jake. Jacy's father was one of the best mates Ian had ever had, and he was just out of hospital as it was. Collie Kilbride had flown the pair of them, Jake and his daughter, up from Adelaide in his vintage plane the day before yesterday. If he was going to live with himself, Ian reasoned sourly, he'd have to go over to Jake and shake his hand and tell him it was good to see him up and about again. No need for so much as a glance in Jacy's direction, as far as he could see, but if an acknowledgment was required, he'd just nod at her in the most civil fashion he could manage.

Frowning, he pushed away from the wall, tossed what remained of his beer through the open doorway of the shed, and handed the mug off to Alice Wigget as he passed her. Wending his way between the spinning couples was like moving through the gears of some enormous machine.

The colored light from the paper lanterns dangling from the rafters played in Jacy's fair hair, which just reached her shoulders and curled riotously around her face. She'd put on a bit of weight since he'd seen her last, as well. Too bad, Ian thought uncharitably, that it had all settled nicely into just the right places.

Drawing nearer still, Ian saw that Jacy's blue-green eyes were luminous with affection as she gazed up at her father's face. She was good at *looking* as if she gave a damn, but where had she been for all those years, while Jake's luck was getting worse and worse by the day? Where had she been when her dad's health had started failing?

Ian was seething by the time he reached them. He felt a muscle twitch in his cheek, set his jaw in an effort to control the response, then thrust out his hand to Jake.

"It's about time you got back and started tending your property, instead of leaving the whole place for your mates to look after," he said, half barking the words. Even though he tried hard, he couldn't force a smile to his mouth.

Jake, always good-natured and full of the devil, had no such problem. He beamed as he pumped Ian's hand, but his grasp was not the knuckle-crusher it had once been, and he was thin to the point of emaciation. There were deep shadows under Jake's pale blue eyes, and his face had a skeletal look about it.

"Well, then," Tiernan teased, "let's see what you've made of the job before you go complaining too loudly, Ian Yarbro. I've just been back for these two days, and for all I know, you've 'helped' me straight into the poorhouse."

Ian was painfully conscious of Jacy's nearness; he felt her gaze on him, caught the muted, musky scent of her perfume. And God help him, he remembered too damned much about how things had been between them, once upon a time.

"Hello, Ian," she said. He felt her voice, too—soft and smoky, evoking all kinds of sensory reactions.

She was going to force him to acknowledge her. He should have known it wouldn't be enough for her, just coming there and stirring up all those old memories again.

He forced himself to look down into her upturned face and instantly regretted the decision. Jacy was twenty-eight now, as was he, and far more beautiful than she'd been at eighteen. He saw a flicker of some tentative, hopeful emotion in her eyes.

"Hello," he replied, and the word came out sounding gravelly and rusted, as though he hadn't used it in a long time. Jake and the shearers and the roustabouts and their women seemed to fade into a pounding void, and there was only Jacy. Ian hated knowing she could still affect him that way, and he hated her, too, for ripping open all the old wounds inside him.

The dancers pounded and thumped around them, shaking the weathered floorboards, and Ian had an unsteady feeling, as though he might tumble, headlong and helpless, into the depths of Jacy Tiernan's eyes. He didn't notice that the music had stopped until it started again, louder than before and strangely shrill.

Jake put one hand on Jacy's back and one on Ian's, then pushed them toward each other with a gentle but effective thrust. "I think I'll sit this one out," he shouted, to be heard over the din, and then he stumped away through the crowd.

By no wish of his own, Ian found himself holding his first love in his arms. He swallowed hard, battling a schoolboy urge to bolt, and began to shuffle awkwardly back and forth, staring over the top of her head. Jacy moved with him, and they were both out of step with the music.

Nothing new in that.

"Is it really so terrible," she asked, in the familiar Yankee accent that had haunted his memories for a decade, "dancing with me?"

"Don't," he said. The word was part warning, part plea.

Ian felt exasperation move through Jacy's body like a current, though he was barely touching her.

"Will you just lighten up?" she hissed, standing on tiptoe to speak into his ear. "You're not the only one who's uncomfortable, you know!"

Ian's emotions were complex, and he couldn't begin to sort them out. That nettled him, for he was a logical man, and he hated chaos, especially within himself. He wanted to shake Jacy Tiernan for all she'd put him through, but he also wanted to make love to her. He was furious that she'd come back, but at one and the same time he felt like scrambling onto the roof and shouting out the news of her return.

He clasped her forearm—it was bare and smooth, since she was wearing a sleeveless cotton sundress—and half-dragged her to the door and down the wooden ramp to the ground. The farmyard was filled with cars and trucks, and the homestead was a long, low shadow some distance away.

"What are you doing here?" he demanded in an outraged whisper.

Jacy raised her chin and put her hands on her hips. Her pale yellow dress seemed to shimmer in the rich light of the moon and stars, and her eyes sparked with silver fire. "That depends on what you mean by 'here,'" she retorted just as furiously. "If you mean why am I here at this damn party, then the answer is, because my father wanted to come and see all his friends and neighbors, and I came along to make sure he didn't overdo and land himself back in the hospital. If, on the other hand, you mean why am I in Australia, well, that should be obvious. My dad had a heart attack and I'm here to look after him."

Ian was fairly choking on the tangle of things he felt; he might have turned and put a fist through the rickety wall of the shed if his hands hadn't already been swollen and cut from all the times he'd caught his own flesh in the clippers while shearing sheep. Instead, he said, "Ten years you stayed away. *Ten years.* Do you think he didn't need you in all that time?" *Do you think I didn't need you?* he thought.

Her eyes brimmed with tears, and because Ian wasn't expecting that, he was wounded by the sight.

"Damn it, Ian," she said, "there's no need to make this so difficult! I'm here, and I plan to stay for an indefinite period of time. If you can't accept the fact, fine, just stay out of my way, and I'll stay out of yours. When we have the misfortune to run into each other, though, let's try to be civil, shall we? For Jake's sake, if nothing else."

Ian couldn't speak. He was reeling from her announcement that she wouldn't be leaving the area anytime soon. Only one thing would make him crazier than her absence had, and that was her living at Corroboree Springs, day in and day out.

Naturally, she couldn't leave well enough alone and keep her mouth shut. Oh, no. That would never have done.

"Well?" she prompted, with a sort of nasty sweetness.

Ian shoved a hand through his dark hair. With all the business of mustering and shearing the sheep, then dipping them in disinfectant to prevent infection in the inevitable scrapes and cuts and to keep the blowflies away, he'd let it grow too long, and it felt shaggy between his fingers.

"You should have stayed in America," he said stubbornly. "Jake has mates here. We'd have been glad to look after him, with no help from you."

She dried her eyes with the heel of one palm, smearing the stuff she wore on her lashes, and then tossed her head. "God, Ian, you can be *such* a bastard. Would it kill you to be polite, at least?"

"Would it have killed *you* to say good-bye before you left?" he snapped, regretting the words even as they tumbled from his mouth. "Even 'go to hell' or 'drop dead' would have been better than just leaving the way you did."

"So now it was all my fault!" she flared, making little effort to keep her voice down. "Has it escaped you that Elaine Bennett came up to us in front of the movie house in Yolanda and announced that she was carrying your baby?" She threw out her hands for emphasis. "But maybe you *did* forget. After all, you certainly never got around to mentioning that you'd been sleeping with her while we were going together!"

Ian tilted his head back and glared up at the stars. He didn't know why he bothered to tell her, since she'd never believe him, but the truth was all he had to offer. There had been many occasions in Ian's life when a lie would have been convenient, but he'd never gotten the knack of it. When he tried, he stuttered and his neck turned a dull red, so he'd long since given it up.

"Elaine and I were all through before I ever touched you, Jacy." He made himself meet her eyes, and saw there the incredulity he'd feared all along. "And somewhere deep inside yourself, you know it. You knew it then. You just needed something to throw between us, some excuse to run away, because you were scared to death of what you were feeling!"

Jacy retreated a step and hugged herself as if a chill had struck her, even though it was nearly ten-thirty and still hot enough to smother a camel. "Okay, so I was scared," she murmured testily, but with less conviction than before. "I was only eighteen."

"So was I," Ian responded brusquely, giving no ground whatsoever. "And I was just as frightened as you were. But what I felt for you was real, and so was the hell I went through when you walked out on me."

It was all he could trust himself to say. He turned to walk away, toward the long, one-story cement homestead he shared with his nine-year-old son, Chris, intending to wait out the party there. Chances were, no one would miss him.

She clasped his arm, and Ian stopped cold, bracing himself, refusing to turn and face her. "I'm sorry, Ian," she said. "Please believe that."

He wrenched free. It wasn't good enough, after the way he'd suffered. "Do us both a favor," he said, still refusing to look at her. "Go back to America . . . and stay there." With that, he strode off toward the dark and empty house, where the light and music of the party wouldn't reach, and it was like walking into his own soul.

Jacy stood watching as Ian disappeared into the shadows, trembling a little, flinching when she heard a door slam in the distance. She hadn't expected their first meeting in ten years to be easy, not after the way things had ended for them, but she hadn't anticipated anything so wrenching and difficult as this, either.

She needed time to compose herself, not wanting her dad and the friends, neighbors and workers jammed into Ian's shearing shed to see how shaken she was, so she sat down on a crate in the shadows, drew a deep breath, and folded her arms. Some of the things Ian had said stuck in her spirit the way briers and nettles stuck in the sheep's wool and the callused fingers of the shearers—especially that bit about her being afraid of the love she'd felt for him. It had been as vast and deep as an ocean, that youthful adulation, full of treacherous beauty and alive with mysterious currents. She'd thought, sometimes, that the great waves would encompass her one day, and she'd drown.

Jacy sighed, looking up at the summer moon, mentally tracing its gray ridges and valleys of cold light. Another of Ian's accusations had struck its mark, too; she'd neglected her dad, keeping her distance those ten long years when she'd known how much her visits meant to him. It had been hard staying away, because she and Jake had always been kindred souls, but she simply hadn't been ready to face Ian.

She still wasn't, she supposed, though she hadn't had much choice in the matter.

"Jacy-me-girl?"

Startled by her father's voice, gentle as it was, Jacy jumped a little and turned her head quickly.

Jake was standing at the base of the ramp, leaning on the cane he'd been using since he left the hospital. His heart attack had left him weakened and gaunt, and Jacy still hadn't gotten used to the change in him. He'd been so strong as a younger man, as vital and tireless as Ian, though always more good-natured.

"It didn't go well, then?" he asked, in the lilting accent she loved.

Jacy blushed, knowing Jake had had hopes of his own for the evening. He had been a second father to Ian, since the elder Yarbros had passed on within a few years of each other, when Ian was still very young. Jake had never made a secret of his belief that Jacy and Ian belonged together.

"It couldn't have been worse," she said, with a sigh and a rueful, shaky smile. "Except if he'd drawn a gun and shot me, that is."

Jake made his way to the crate with a slow awkwardness that was painful to see, then took a seat beside his daughter. "Give him time," he counseled. "Ian's a hardheaded sort, you know."

"I hadn't noticed," Jacy mocked, but she moved a little

closer to her dad and let her head rest against his thin shoulder.

Jake patted her hand. "Once he works it all through, he'll come round."

Jacy stiffened. "I don't want him to 'come around,' Dad. Not in the way you mean, at least."

The glow of the moon only highlighted the amused skepticism in Jake's face. "Is that so? Then I'll confess to wondering why a simple shearing shed would be filled to the rafters with blue lightning from the moment the two of you spotted one another. There was so much electricity flying about in there that I'd have been afraid to step in a puddle of spilled beer."

Jacy couldn't help smiling at his description of the tension that had coiled between her and Ian earlier in the evening. She slipped her arm around Jake and said, "I've missed you a whole lot."

"Don't be changing the subject," he replied, his accent thicker than ever. It happened whenever he was being mischievous or having trouble controlling his emotions. "This is a small community, and you and Ian won't be able to avoid each other forever. You'll need to settle things."

She linked her fingers with her dad's and squeezed. Jake had a point; Ian's property bordered their own, and if that wasn't enough, they were bound to meet in nearby Yolanda, in the post office and the shops. Or in Willoughby, the slightly larger town fifty kilometers to the northeast, where homesteaders and townspeople alike went to see the doctor, purchase supplies, and attend to various other errands that couldn't be taken care of in Yolanda.

"Are you sure you wouldn't like to come back to the States with me, just until you're feeling strong again?" she ventured, though she knew as she spoke what the answer would be. Jake had nothing against America—he'd married a Yank, after all—but he'd often said he was no more suited to the place than a kangaroo was to Manhattan.

He simply arched an eyebrow.

"All right," Jacy burst out. "Then we'll go up to Cairns again, like we did when I was twelve. We could collect seashells and lie out in the sun and eat those wonderful giant avocados." She still had some of the colorful shells she'd gathered back then, displayed on a shelf in her room at the homestead. To her, the shells symbolized eternity, and the extravagant, careless continuity of life. "We could leave tomorrow. What do you say?"

"I say that you're trying to run away again." Jake paused, still gripping her hand, to study the spectacular display of stars, their majesty undimmed by the lights of any city. When he looked at her again, the expression in his eyes was sad and gentle. "You've done enough of that in your young life, Jacy. It's time to stop now and face matters head-on."

She averted her eyes, afraid of all that was in her heart, good and bad, noble and ignoble, terrified that all those mixed-up emotions would spill over and disgrace her if she let down her guard for so much as a moment. There was no point in denying her father's words anyway, because he was right. Jacy's unspoken credo had always been, She who loves and runs away, lives to love another day.

Only she had never loved again. Not before Ian, and certainly not after.

"What do I do now?" she asked in a soft voice.

"Nothing much," Jake replied easily, tenderly. "Just stand still for a time, Jacy-me-girl. That's all. Just hold your ground and see what comes toward you."

She laughed, but the sound resembled a sob. "What if it's a freight train?"

Jake chuckled, slipped an arm around her shoulders, and gave her a brief hug. "See that you don't stand on the railroad tracks, love. Now, let's take ourselves home, shall we? I'm tuckered."

Jacy was relieved to be leaving Ian's place. At the same time, she was worried about Jake's physical condition. "You're all right, aren't you?" she asked, peering at him anxiously. "We could drive over to Willoughby and see the doctor, just to be on the safe side—"

"And rouse the poor bloke from his bed?" Jake spoke amicably, as he almost always did, but Jacy knew the suggestion had annoyed him because he shook off her hand when she tried to help him stand. "Get a grip on yourself, sheila. I can't go waltzing off to the doctor every time I feel a bit worn down, now can I?"

Wisely, Jacy said nothing. She just walked along at Jake's side, and when they reached his dusty old truck, she got behind the wheel and left him to hoist himself into the vehicle on his own.

Jacy rose early the next morning, even before Jake was up. It was her third day back, but she was still greedy for the sights and sounds and smells of the place. She loved the house, with its green lawn and sheltering pepper trees and the old-fashioned roses Grandmother Matty had planted at one end of the veranda. Loved the shed, although there were no sheep there now, and the paddocks, though there were no horses. As little time as she had spent there, the homestead and the land surrounding it were dear to her in a way her mother and stepfather's luxurious townhouse in Manhattan had never been.

She lingered on the veranda for a while, watching the sunlight sparkle and dance on the surface of the spring-fed pond a little distance away, in the midst of a copse of thirsty trees. From there, the water flowed away through the paddock in a wide stream, eventually forming the border between the Tiernan land and Merimbula, the huge cattle station to the south.

Standing still, she heard her mother's voice in her mind. "You're an Aussie, through and through," Regina had often said, always adding a long sigh for effect. "It's in your blood, that hot, lonely, harsh place, and for that, my darling, I offer you my sincerest apologies."

Jacy smiled. She'd spent most of her life in America, but there was an element of truth in her mother's words. She *was* an Aussie, in so many ways.

Some of her pleasure faded. Despite her Australian heritage, Ian and not a few other people would always view her as an outsider. It would be naive to believe her former lover was the only one who thought she'd failed Jake by staying away all those years; in the bush, where everyday life was a challenge, abandoning someone was just about the worst thing a person could do. A betrayal of one was a betrayal of all, and the homesteaders around Yolanda had long, long memories where such matters were concerned.

She turned, reluctantly, and went back into the cool shelter of the house.

Jake was still sleeping, apparently, so she returned to her own room and pulled Grandmother Matty's handmade quilt off the bed. The coverlet hadn't been washed in a long time, and it had a musty smell to it.

In the homestead's primitive kitchen, Jacy heated water on the gas-powered stove, making as little noise as possible. Then she rinsed out the quilt in the kitchen sink, wrung it gently, and carried it out to the clothesline in back of the house. While it was drying in the warm morning sun, she brewed a cup of tea and sat on the back step to drink it, watching with delight as a mob of kangaroos sprang across the paddock separating her father's property from Ian's.

She was exhausted, and not just from the hasty trip across the international date line after she'd learned about Jake's heart attack and the long vigil at the hospital in Adelaide that had followed. There were troubles waiting back in the States, snarls to untangle, things that, true to form, she'd run away from.

The way she'd run away from Ian.

"Ian." She spoke the name softly, but aloud, and it hurt more than she would ever have expected. Memories overtook her like a bushfire; tears stung her eyes, a sob escaped her and, finally, she knew it was futile to try to hold back her grief any longer. She wept in earnest.

When the personal storm was over, Jacy sniffled, tilted her head back, and closed her puffy eyes. Scenes from that awful time ten years before played on the screen of her mind in Technicolor and stereo.

She made herself walk through the memories, facing them one by one. Having done that, she reasoned, she might be able to look Ian in the eye the next time they met without losing her dignity.

Jacy saw in her thoughts a smaller and wilder version of her twenty-eight-year-old sophisticated self, a sunburned waif in blue jeans. Her dark blond hair had been short then, and she'd ridden all over the property, and some parts of those adjoining it, on her aging white mare, Biscuit. She'd been free as a gypsy in those days, knowing nothing of heartache. Even her parents' divorce hadn't truly touched her, for she'd been too young to remember leaving the homestead with her mother, and she'd made the long trip Down Under often throughout her childhood, to stay with Jake.

Ian, like Jacy, had been just eighteen the year the world turned upside down, but more man than boy even then. He'd already begun taking over the responsibilities of running the property he'd inherited from his father.

Jacy had fallen in love with Ian at a spring party, much like the one the night before, after the shearing had been done and the wool baled and sent off to Adelaide in semis to be sold. Miracle of miracles, he had felt the same way about her, or said he did, at least, and in secret places on her father's property and his own he had taught her to glory in her womanhood. He had introduced her to the most excruciatingly sweet pleasures and, in fact, no man had touched her so intimately since.

They'd planned to marry, over Jacy's mother's frantic long-distance protests. Regina Tiernan Walsh was strong and smart, but she'd entered into a rash marriage in a foreign land herself once and, subsequently, her bridegroom, Australia, and her own disillusionment had combined forces to break her heart. Not surprisingly, Regina had been terrified that the same fate awaited her daughter.

In the end, though, it had been Elaine Bennett, daughter of the American manager of Merimbula Station, who had brought Jacy's dreams down with a soul-shattering crash. She'd come up to Jacy and Ian outside the theater in Yolanda, looked Ian straight in the eye, and told him she was going to have his baby.

Even after a decade, Jacy could still feel the terrible shock of that moment, and the helpless, fiery rage that had followed. Ian had not denied the accusation, neither had he troubled himself to explain or apologize. He'd simply expected Jacy to understand.

A distant bleating sound jolted Jacy from her musings, and she rose slowly from her seat on the step. Way off, she saw a sea of recently shorn sheep approaching, kicking up the dry red dust as they came.

Jacy's heart rose immediately to her throat and lodged there. The sheep were Ian's, she had no doubt of that, on their way to the springs to drink.

For a few moments, she nursed the scant hope that someone else would be driving the flock, or mob, as the locals called it—one of Ian's two or three hired men maybe. Even before Ian himself came into view, however, mounted on that enormous liver-colored stallion Jake had written her about, she knew she couldn't be so lucky.

She wasn't ready, she thought frantically.

Not so soon.

The baaing and bleating of the sheep grew until the racket filled Jacy's skull and stomach, and she watched the mob divide like water coursing around a stone. Two lean dogs kept the odd-looking beasts moving when they would have stopped to nibble the grass in the yard, and great clouds of red dust billowed in the hot, still air, covering the freshly washed quilt with grit.

Jacy just stood there on the back step, like a felon on the scaffold, waiting for the noose to tighten around her neck. Her clothes, jeans and a white T-shirt, felt all wrong, her hair probably looked like hell, and she hadn't bothered to put on makeup. She'd never felt less prepared for anything.

She figured she'd be really upset about the quilt, once her thoughts calmed down, but at the moment she was too distracted.

In the dazzling light of a summer day, it was plain that Ian's features had hardened with maturity. His violet gaze seemed to slice through her spirit, cutting cleanly, leaving no jagged edges.

Her knees went weak and she sagged onto the step. Jetlag, she insisted to herself, though it had been more than three weeks since she'd landed in Adelaide.

Ian was wearing perfectly ordinary clothes—a battered stockman's hat, a blue cambric workshirt, the front of which was stained with sweat, jeans, and boots, and yet the sight of him stole Jacy's breath away.

"How's Jake this morning?" he asked, shouting to be heard over the last of the sheep and swinging down from the saddle. There was nothing cordial in the question; she could see by his expression that things hadn't changed since the night before.

"See for yourself," she replied, amazed that the words had gotten past her constricted throat. Her heart was pounding like a ceremonial drum, and she feared she might be sick to her stomach.

Ian tethered the horse to a rusted hitching post, resettled his hat, and crossed the yard to stand facing her. "See for myself I will," he answered in that low, rumbling voice that had once urged her to passion and then consoled her afterward, when she'd feared that all the scattered pieces of her soul would never find their way back to her. "If you'll just get out of my way."

Jacy looked straight into those impossibly violet eyes, and

her heart shattered all over again. She rose and turned her back on Ian, praying he wouldn't guess how shaken she was.

"Dad was sleeping, before your sheep came tramping through here like a herd of buffalo," she said in a moderately acidic tone. She could feel him behind her, though of course they weren't touching, feel the heat and hardness of him in the small of her back, the space between her shoulder blades and her nape, the tender flesh of her thighs and the insides of her knees. "I don't suppose you noticed what those creatures did to my clean quilt."

They entered the kitchen.

"I don't suppose I did," Ian said, utterly without remorse.

"I'll tell Jake you're here."

"Thanks for that much, anyway," Ian grumbled. In an involuntary backward glance, Jacy saw him hang his hat on a peg beside the door and shove splayed fingers through his hair.

Suddenly the old anger crashed through all her carefully constructed defenses, swamping her, and it took every ounce of Jacy's self-control to keep her voice calm and even. "What did you expect, Ian? That I'd welcome you with open arms? That I'd thank you for teaching me that love has fangs?"

Ian's jawline hardened but, before he could speak, Jake appeared in the inside doorway, leaning on his cane.

"Hello, mate," he said. "I wondered when you'd get round to paying an old man a visit."

Ian's laugh was a low burst of sound, only too well remembered by Jacy and somehow excluding her. "You think I've got nothing better to do than eat biscuits and sip tea with the likes of you, Jake Tiernan?"

Jacy hurried outside before her father could suggest that she put the kettle on. She'd eat a bale of raw wool before she'd make tea and fetch cookies for Ian Yarbro. If he wanted refreshments, he could damn well serve himself.

⁓

Look for

The Legacy

Wherever Paperback Books Are Sold
Summer 1994

CPSIA information can be obtained at www.ICGtesting.com
Printed in the USA
LVOW070622130313

324052LV00001B/55/P